The
Chalice
and the
Blade

Bantam Books

New York
Toronto
London
Sydney
Auckland

The
Chalice
and the
Blade

GLENNA
MCREYNOLDS

THE CHALICE AND
THE BLADE
A Bantam Book / October 1997

All rights reserved.

BOOK DESIGN BY ELLEN CIPRIANO

MAPS BY JACKIE AHER

Library of Congress Cataloging-in-Publication Data

McReynolds, Glenna.
  The chalice and the blade / Glenna McReynolds.
    p.   cm.
  ISBN 0-553-10384-9
  1. Wales—History—1063–1284—Fiction.
  2. Borders of Wales (Wales)—History—Fiction.
  3. Llewelyn ap Iorwerth, d. 1240—Fiction.   I. Title.
  PS3563.C75C48   1997
  813'.54—dc20   96-39010
                                                      CIP

Published simultaneously in the United States and Canada

Bantam Books are published by Bantam Books, a
division of Bantam Doubleday Dell Publishing Group,
Inc. Its trademark, consisting of the words "Bantam
Books" and the portrayal of a rooster, is Registered in
U.S. Patent and Trademark Office and in other
countries. Marca Registrada. Bantam Books, 1540
Broadway, New York, New York 10036.

PRINTED IN THE UNITED STATES OF AMERICA

BVG   10 9 8 7 6 5 4 3 2 1

To my parents,
Richard and Lois Gillis—
always in my dreams,
never far from my heart.

Acknowledgments

For the generous gifts and loans of historical, astronomical, and ofttimes magical tomes, and for other various bits of whimsy, inspiration, support, and knowledge, the author would like to thank: Margaret Aunon, Sandra Betker, Debra and Tom Catlow, Victoria Erbschloe, Margaret Frohberg, Joy Hopely, Jane Ronald-Houck, Mary McReynolds, Jean Muirhead, Susan Parker, Olivia Rupprecht, Debra and Tom Throgmorton; Dean and Kerrie, for making some magic; also, Rebecca Kubler and Lance Gillis, for their enthusiastic reading of the manuscript; Cindy Gerard, lovely muse, for not only reading the manuscript with enthusiasm (over and over again), but for doing so with a pencil in her hand, which she used; and Stan, Kathleen, and Chase McReynolds, for contributions too numerous to list—all of them from the heart.

My special thanks and appreciation go to Elizabeth Barrett, for her empathy, her insights, her patience, and for taking what was and making it better. 'Twas ever thus—*namasté.*

Author's Note

Writers doing research are a sojourning breed. We spend our days wandering through other people's work, diligently searching when we know what we want, exploring for epiphany when we don't; dallying for a short time between one set of bound pages, practically setting up house in the next.

In the writing of this novel, I incurred some rent, most notably to Giraldus Cambrensis and his *Journey Through Wales 1188.* It was also with great pleasure that I discovered the work of Mircea Eliade; in particular, his book *The Forge and the Crucible: the Origins and Structures of Alchemy,* and an article he wrote for *Parabola,* "The Myth of Alchemy."

On a historical note, during the Middle Ages the frontier between England and Wales was known as the March. The March lords, originally followers of William the Conqueror, were barons whose holdings comprised the borderlands. They were laws unto themselves, subject to the king of England, but not to English Common Law. What they had, they kept by the power of their swords, building castles and warring on their neighbors—the Welsh—and ofttimes on each other. On the other side of the border, the Welsh did the same, their disunity being their greatest flaw, with the Welsh princes as inclined to war on each other as on the land-hungry barons. The March was an integral part of the history of Wales for over four hundred years, reaching its demise under the reign of Henry VIII with the act of February 1536, statute 27 Henry VIII clause 26 (in this century referred to as the Act of Union), whose purpose was to incorporate Wales into England.

One historical fact that I turned to fancy concerns the Thief of Cardiff. The story is true, though the nom de plume is not. A Welshman, Ifor Bach of Senghennydd, did steal a Norman earl from his bed one night in retaliation for the confiscation of some land. Over a hundred men-at-arms and an even greater number of archers guarded the castle keep at Cardiff while the "immensely bold" Ifor scaled the walls and made off with William of Gloucester. Ifor did not release the earl until the stolen estates were returned.

A number of Welsh names and words appear in the book, and I would offer two notes on pronunciation: c always has the "k" sound, as in candle; dd is pronounced like the English "th," as in those.

On the map of Wales, Merioneth has been resurrected to an autonomous principality from an earlier time. The River Bredd, along with Carn Merioneth/Balor Keep, and Wydehaw Castle, have been conjured from imagination, the caverns beneath Carn Merioneth even more so. As for the *tylwyth teg,* I cannot help but believe, so sure am I that I've met a few. *Amor . . . lux . . . veritas.*

GLENNA MCREYNOLDS
October 1996

The
Chalice
and the
Blade

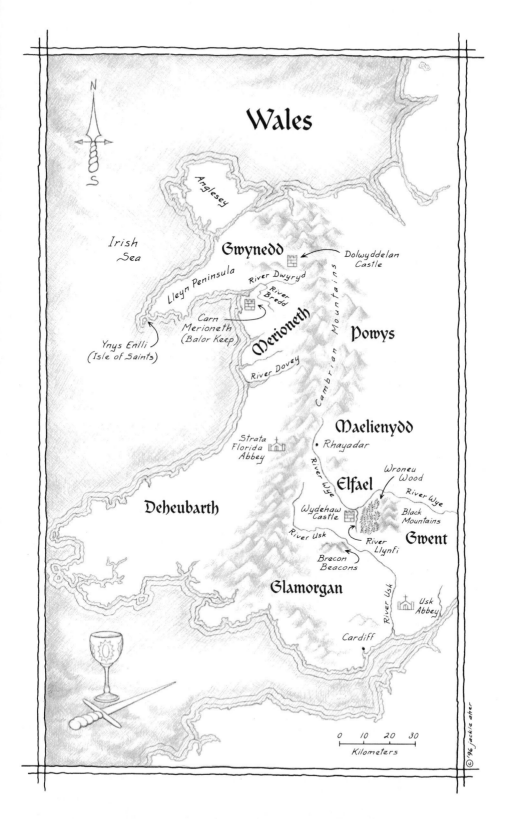

The Caverns Beneath Carn Merioneth

N

Carn Merioneth
(Balor Keep)

Irish Sea

River Bredd

Dragon's Mouth

Light caves

Cavern of the Scrying Pool

Canolbarth, the midland caves

Pryf Nest

Lanbarrdein

Damson Cliffs

Tunnels to the gates of time

Mor Sarff

(Serpent Sea)

Cast of Characters

CARN MERIONETH

RHIANNON—*Lady of Carn Merioneth from the matriarchal lineage of a Magus Druid Priestess from Anglesey*

CERIDWEN AB ARAWN—*daughter of Rhiannon*

MYCHAEL AB ARAWN—*son of Rhiannon, twin brother to Ceridwen*

ARAWN—*Lord of Carn Merioneth*

NEMETON—*famed bard of Brittany,* Beirdd Braint *of the Quicken-tree, builder of the Hart Tower*

MORIATH—*daughter of Nemeton*

ᛞᛟ

WYDEHAW CASTLE

DAIN LAVRANS—*the mage of Wydehaw*

LORD SOREN D'ARBOIS—*a March lord, Baron of Wydehaw*

LADY VIVIENNE D'ARBOIS—*wife of the baron*

ELIXIR AND NUMA—*Dain's hounds*

RAGNOR THE RED—*captain of Wydehaw's guard*

MADRON—*witch who lives in Wroneu Wood*

EDMEE—*daughter of Madron*

MORGAN AB KYNAN—*Thief of Cardiff, a Welsh Prince*

MORGAN'S BAND OF MEN:

       OWAIN—*the captain*

       RHYS

       DREW

       RHODRI

       DAFYDD

BALOR KEEP

CARADOC—*the Boar of Balor, ruler of the keep*
HELEBORE—*excommunicated priest, Balor's leech*
SNIT—*minion of Helebore*
GWRNACH—*destroyer of Carn Merioneth, father of Caradoc*
GRUFFUDD—*a guardsman at Balor*

THE QUICKEN-TREE

RHUDDLAN—*leader of the Quicken-tree*
THE QUICKEN-TREE: MOIRA
                     ELEN
                     AEDYTH
                     NAAS
                     LLYNYA
                     SHAY
                     NIA
TRIG—*captain of the Liosalfar*
THE LIOSALFAR: WEI
                  MATH
                  BEDWYR

OTHERS

LLYWELYN—*ruling Prince of Gwynedd from 1194 to 1240*
JALAL AL-KAMAM—*Saracen trader, slaver*
KALUT AD-DIN—*Saracen trader, slaver*

In the year 1190, Richard the Lionheart set forth from Europe on a divine mission, to wrest the Holy Land from the infidels. A vast host of Christian soldiers took the cross and followed, and failed. Some survived, many died, and a few—either by their own wishes or forced through the will of others—disappeared in the deserts then under the dominion of the great Saladin.

Of those that were lost, three found their way out of the wasteland and home. One, scarred beyond redemption, made his way north into the mountain fastness of his father to wreak his vengeance on strong and weak alike. Another bound himself to God, family, and country as a balm to his wounded body and heart. The last took all that he had learned of pain and mystery and bliss, of magic and medicine, of desires and acceptance and power, and set himself up as a sorcerer . . . the Blade.

Seven years before the Lionheart's crusade, England's battles had been fought closer to home, in sweet grass meadows and shallow fens, through dense stands of the king's forests and deep in the mountains of Wales. The Welsh people, Cymry in their own language and warriors in any language, took up arms against the invading English and one another with equal vigor. Palisades were burned, villages ransacked, and new lords proclaimed where others had reigned.

Only three, a woman and two children, survived the battle for Carn Merioneth, a prize on the coast of the Irish Sea. The woman, wise beyond her years in ancient ways—a fey creature—made her way south, hiding the children from the destructive force unleashed on their home. For the first, she found sanctuary in a monastery, and over the years he lost himself in a life of quiet contemplation. For the second child, the woman chose the abbey of her own youth, knowing well the secrets hidden there and trusting the girl to find them. The child did not fail, and in time she became the catalyst of her own destruction and the key to her own salvation . . . the Chalice.

Prologue

OCTOBER 1183

CARN MERIONETH

MERIONETH, WALES

For the third night in a row the harp played upon the cliffs overlooking the Irish Sea, the strings caressed to life by delicate, ring-bedecked fingers that wove secret melodies and set them free to float like feathers upon the wind. In the northern sky, a single star fell toward the water in a glittering arc of celestial dust, enchanted unto death by the sweet music.

Rhiannon, daughter of Teleri, daughter of Mair, created the enchantment. She nurtured it and cherished it, listening to her heart, and the song, and the waves crashing into the rocks hundreds of feet below, for every moment of enchantment was one less of fear in the endless night of Calan Gaef.

An errant breeze caught on the headland and curved around the natural bowl where she played, tangling through her hair and bringing the ocean mists up to the land. Flames from a fire of yew, oak, and ash lit the cavern walls behind her and flickered over the dark, sinuous lines etched into the stone by a people long lost to memory. As a child she'd traced those paintings, standing on tiptoe, touching the strange, ancient creatures, and feeling their power and beauty echo through time and her fingertips.

Dragons, her mother had called them, sea dragons, guardians of the gates of time, who lived in the deep beyond, rolling their mighty bodies to churn the tides and keep the moon coming back to the sun. Her mother had seen them and had promised Rhiannon she would see them too. *In time, in time.*

And so, in time, she had.

The wind gusted, and Rhiannon's fingertips swept across the harp strings, plucking each in turn with blinding speed, matching her song to the rhythms of the storm brewing far out to sea.

Inside the keep at the top of the cliff, Ceridwen awoke with a start. She hadn't meant to fall asleep at all this night, but her mother's music had lured her into dreams without so much as the tiniest struggle on her part.

"Damn," she whispered. 'Twas her new word, "damn," a daring choice for a child of five years.

The harp played no more outside. Its melodic tones had been replaced with the driving rhythms of a hundred bodhran drums. The ceremony in the caves had already started, and they were going to miss it, if they didn't hurry.

"Mychael, wake up." Ceridwen rolled over in the bed and shook her twin. "Wake up."

'Twas fair dark where they slept at the end of the great hall, still well before sunrise, though Ceridwen felt the difference in the air that told her the night was rising toward day. The low flames of the hearth fire helped to cut the gloom, but she still wished the maid Moriath had left them a candle. They were going to need light to get where she wanted to go, or risk a few stubbed toes.

"Come on, now," she said to Mychael. "Here's our chance, sweeting."

A muffled grumbling was all she got for her effort, and the sight of a tousled blond head burrowing deeper under the covers.

"You sleep more than a suckling babe," she said in disgust, giving up her crooning tone and flouncing back on the bed.

"Do not."

The reply was near useless without accompanying movement, but she took heart. At least he was awake. How he continued to play slug-a-bed when the very heart of the earth was pounding beneath them was a mystery to her. Most everything Mychael did was a mystery to her. He was quiet, she was not. He was thoughtful, she was not. He behaved, she most definitely did not. She had no intention of staying put all night while everyone else in the keep ate and drank and danced in the caves.

She bent her head close to the covers. "Like a suckling babe," she said.

Nothing happened, and she sighed.

The caves were the most wondrous part of Carn Merioneth—the labyrinthine tunnels, the still-water pools, the pillars of stone. These things lingered in her imagination long after each brief expedition into the caverns. She and Mychael were never allowed to go alone, and ofttimes—as on this night—they were not included when others went. Occasionally, their mother took them down into the caves open to the cliffs, to the Dragon's Mouth of the Light Caves, or to the Canolbarth, the midland caves, but occasionally wasn't enough for Ceridwen, and neither were the upper caves. She wanted to see the deeper caverns, the ones beyond the Canolbarth, the ones she was sure were filled with treasures and mayhaps dragon bones. Her mother told wonderful stories about dragons and the *tylwyth teg,* Welsh faeries who lived in the mountains and no doubt in the caves too, though her mother had not exactly said as much.

Ceridwen would dearly love to see a dragon or a faerie. She could spend days exploring the tunnels, and she would, if Mychael would just show more interest in the grand adventures she devised. Instead, he preferred to sit and dream. Going without him was unthinkable. She never went anywhere without him.

"Babe," she said, loud enough for him to hear even under all the coverlets, and at last, she got her reaction. The covers whipped up, revealing an angry face remarkably like her own.

"I am not a babe." He scowled at her.

His eyes were blue like their father's, a pale, silvery ocean blue that all the women cooed over. So were Ceridwen's, but no one cooed over her except their mother.

"Can you hear it?" she asked, too relieved that he had finally roused himself to be piqued over his scowl. "Listen!"

From deep below them, the primal rhythms of the bodhrans rose and fell. The sound in the hall was faint, barely discernible. Ceridwen hardly heard the rhythms herself, but she felt them strongly, pulsing against her skin and slipping inside to course along her veins. The rough-hewn timbers of the keep resonated with the richness of the drums; the bed trembled.

"They're finished with the dancing," Mychael said after a moment of thoughtful silence. "I'm sure of it."

"There'll still be food. Let's go see." She scrambled off the bed, pulling him with her. They wouldn't get as good an opportunity as this again for months, maybe years, with Mother and Father and everybody busy down in the caves, and no Moriath watching them like a hawk.

"Ceri, stop." Mychael balked before she could get him completely off the bed. "It'll be cold."

"I'll let you wear my cloak." She gave him another pull, but he didn't budge. "The one with the white fur and the little black spots on it." She coaxed again, still to no avail.

"I don't think we're s'posed to be in the caves tonight," he said, his face scrunched up with doubt.

"We're never s'posed to be in the caves," she said, thoroughly exasperated with his lack of vision. "I'll get you a honey-pie from the kitchen. I saw where cook hid them." The bribe was her last resort, and she had hoped not to need it so soon in their adventure.

In the end, it took two honey-pies, her ermine cloak, and her new deer-hide boots, and a close call with a roaming guard before they made it to the south side of the bailey and the entrance into the caverns. Inside the opening were two paths. One led to the Light Caves and the sea cliffs, the other snaked deep into the bowels of the earth. Ceridwen didn't hesitate. She followed the steeper tunnel, encouraged by the torches blazing in the iron sockets bolted to the rock walls and lured by the pulsing sound of the bodhran drums.

She could not.

Rhiannon held the sacred cup of dragon wine to her lips, but she could not drink. All around her, the wild folk of the mountains and meadows and caves mixed with the people from Carn Merioneth. "Quicken-tree," the wild ones called themselves, lone descendants of an ancient race. She oft thought of them as *tylwyth teg* and knew she wasn't far from the mark, though they made no such claim themselves. They gathered in groups along the ledges of stone that circled the floor where the scrying pool bubbled and steamed at her feet. Their leader, Rhuddlan, stood next to her as guide of the threefold union she and he and the Druid would make. Across from her, glimpsed through the slowly swirling mist, stood Nemeton, the grove priest himself. He waited, his hands raised in supplication, his auburn hair streaked with one stripe of gray flowing down onto his shoulders, his sky-blue robes shrouding him to the floor, and still she could not drink.

Nemeton was an imposing man, tall and gaunt, with eyes of a rich, verdant hue, a famous bard from Brittany brought by his lord to the March of Wales because of his healing powers and the high art of his divinations. Rhiannon's mother had recognized him as even more, just as he had recognized Carn Merioneth as being more than it seemed.

'Twas said he'd seduced and murdered his baron's wife and thus had been exiled to the north with a price on his head, and was still sought by Welsh princes and mountain chieftains. Up until then, he'd lived as well as his lord, in great comfort behind castle walls, a stark contrast to the cave he was said to inhabit on the island of Anglesey, or the rough summer huts of willow and thatch kept for him in the mountains by the Quicken-tree.

Four times each year Nemeton came to Carn Merioneth, welcomed by Rhiannon's mother in her time and now by Rhiannon. One of those times was always Calan Gaef, cursed night of faith when Rhiannon had no faith left to sustain her.

There had been feasting and dancing and music: harps, flutes, the bowed lyre *crwth,* and voices raised in songs sung in many parts. The bodhrans had been picked up one by one to start a new song, and slowly, the bodhran song had overcome all the others, until nothing but the sound of hands thrumming on skins remained.

It was Rhiannon's moment to drink the dragon wine, when the drums reached their crescendo and held, but she could not. The gold rim of the jewel-encrusted chalice was warm against her lips, the smell of the wine filled her nostrils and made her near swoon, but fear stayed her hand.

She slanted her gaze to Nemeton, wondering what he thought of her delay, but she detected no impatience in the Druid. He was, seemingly, more inclined to see what was than to see what he could make of things.

Had he really murdered the long-ago baron's wife? Or, as was so wont to happen, had his physick merely gone awry? 'Twas said crocus seeds had killed the noble woman. A more deadly plant could hardly be found. Even with all her own skill, Rhiannon never dealt with crocus. Did it have a taste at a deadly dose? she wondered. Did it have a color? A scent?

The wine eddied as her hand trembled, lapping at her lips, but still she did not drink. For each of the past five years, since her mother's death, she had taken her share of the dragon wine and looked into the scrying pool to mark the eternal cycle of life, death, and rebirth. Never before had she doubted the safety of Nemeton's potion. But never before had she been betrayed by one she loved as life itself.

Her gaze fell upon her husband, Arawn.

You have eyes as green as rowan leaves in high summer, she'd overheard Arawn tell Nemeton's daughter in a voice made harsh by the passion of the kisses they had shared. When had it been? Just three days past?

It seemed another lifetime. She closed her eyes against a wave of pain. Moriath was the grove priest's daughter, an unpious novice expelled from the abbey at Usk. Rhiannon had welcomed the girl, given her the charge of the children, who had grown too rambunctious for their old nurse to handle alone. She had seen no unpiety in the maid, only a shade of feyness that she could well understand would arouse suspicion and misgivings in the Christian ladies of Usk. Did not Rhiannon's own presence do the same when visiting clergy came to Merioneth? For though she was Christian, her Christianity was grounded more in the Celtic church than in the Catholic, and through her mother her religion reached back farther still, back to the heritage of a Magus Druid priestess from Anglesey.

She looked again at the wine. Would Nemeton poison her so he could put his daughter in her place? The priest had drunk first, but 'twould be as nothing for him to perform a quick sleight of hand as he lowered the cup from his mouth. Rhuddlan had drunk, but 'twas said—and she believed—that there was naught on earth that could poison a Quicken-tree.

Had Arawn thought of the dangers he might bring upon them with his dalliance, or had his thoughts not gone past his braies? 'Twasn't like him, and yet the girl was uncommonly beautiful in her own strange way.

Rhiannon lifted her gaze to the rest of the cave. There were others besides herself to consider this night. She could not delay forever. The far reaches of the great cavern were lost in darkness, beyond where the light from all the fires could reach, but Rhiannon knew the people were there, watching and waiting, and feeling the cold. The time had come.

Her gaze settled on the pool. Curling tendrils of steam floated across the top of the bubbling water, a few ethereal strands escaping to reach upward past the darkness, to drift into every tunnel, nook, and cranny, and wind their way to freedom in the night sky, leaving behind their essence, which would sink down, and down, and down into the abyss, where earth, air, fire, and water became one. 'Twas from the abyss that she drew strength.

She was Rhiannon, daughter of Teleri, daughter of Mair, back to the daughter of Heledd, and farther back to the first daughter of the Mother Goddess. She was Rhiannon, mother of Ceridwen, strongwilled child of her heart, the one who would follow to play the harp and call the dragons from the deep beyond in the years to come. She was Rhiannon, mother of Mychael, sweet, unforetold son.

Her children were very dear, and thus her decision was made.

With practiced grace, she tipped the cup—away from her lips, letting the arc continue until all the wine poured over the jewelencrusted rim into the pool. She would not drink. She would not die for the gods this night, nor for an unpious maid.

Her eye caught that of Nemeton, but if he had noticed her sacrilege, he gave no sign. There was naught else to be done, other than to wait for the scrying pool to settle, cooled by the dragon wine into a smooth, reflective surface. Words would be spoken and sights sought, but none would be seen on this night of Calan Gaef, when her task was to open the doors between the worlds and look into the depths of time. A sigh passed her lips where the wine should have gone. What was done, was done. Whatever fate befell her for cheating the gods with the wine, 'twould not be worse than what she'd already endured.

The drum sound softened, making way for the chant rising up from Nemeton. The priest's voice was joined by others, lifting and falling in a hypnotic rhythm of sameness, lulling Rhiannon's mind into a quiet place. She softened her gaze upon the pool and allowed her thoughts to wander freely over the subsiding ripples and remaining traces of steam. She expected nothing, looked for nothing, and so was surprised by the streak of ruddy light that raced across the water. Another came on the heels of the first, gray and green, bright and twisting like the flick of a fishtail. By the time she saw the third, a smile played about her mouth. The dragons were coming.

Beautiful they were, the fleet rods of lights. She had not called them, yet the connection between her and the dragons was strong. Mayhaps they'd felt her need. As she watched, the colors came together, rolled over on one another, and broke apart into twice as many pieces. They moved so fast, darting here and there, joining again and breaking apart, doubling once more, over and over, until the whole pool glowed and pulsed with their movements.

"No." The one word was spoken into the silence as if it were death itself.

She glanced up at the unexpected sound, her smile fading.

Across from her, Nemeton breathed the word again, his countenance unutterably grim as he stared into the pool. "No."

Rhiannon jerked her gaze back to where steam was again rising off the water and caught a final glimpse of what he'd seen in the seconds he'd held her attention.

The dragons themselves, coming in from the deep beyond, on a course that would take them to their nest.

One was ruby-colored, Ddrei Goch, its huge, scaly body coiling in upon itself, awash in seawater; the other was pale green, Ddrei Glas, riding the sea foam. And ahead of them on the cliffs of Carn Merioneth, an allied war band of Welsh and English soldiers advanced upon the keep in the faint light of dawn, a war chant filling the air around them.

She cried out, a cry to arms. People close to the pool reacted quickly, and none quicker than Arawn, whose shouted orders echoed off the cavern walls and sent men running for the passageways leading out of the caves.

"Yer lost."

"Am not."

"Yes, you are, Ceri. Yer lost and me too."

Ceridwen shook her head in denial even as she squeezed her lips together to keep them from trembling. It was awful. They were lost. Everything looked the same no matter which way she went. The stone walls were all dark and cold; every path was an endless tunnel into nothingness.

She had made a horrible mistake wanting to come to the Canolbarth alone. There were no dragon bones, no faeries, and no treasure. There was nobody and nothing but dark and more dark, and clammy wetness, and smells she didn't like.

"I want Mama." Mychael sniffled, and a hiccup followed.

"Hush." She wanted Mama too, probably more than he did. Why didn't anyone come? They'd been gone for a very long time. Someone must be looking for them, and they were right there, standing in the middle of the tunnel in plain sight. The drums had stopped, the festival was over. Where was everybody?

The bright torches they'd followed from the cave entrance had given way to small oil lamps. She didn't know when the change had happened, or why, or where. She'd just looked up once and noticed there wasn't as much light as there had been. When they'd tried to follow the lamps back, they'd ended up someplace different, someplace wetter and darker than the other tunnels.

Where they were now, water ran down the walls in trickling streams to puddle on the floor. Her shoes were soaked, and she was freezing. Mychael shivered at her side, a sad sight in her wet and dirty cloak and ruined deer-hide boots.

"I'm tired, Ceri, and hungry, and yer going to be in trouble when we get home. Do you have another honey-pie? Or some cheese?"

She listened to him babble on with all his hundreds of complaints and threats. They were already in trouble, but she didn't tell him. He was scared enough. So was she.

"I'm thirsty, and if'n we're not in bed when 'Riath comes to get us, we'll be in trouble with her too." Another hiccup punctuated his mournful tirade.

Ceridwen sighed, her gaze searching the walls for what she didn't know. Moriath could be a terrible scold, but she would rather be scolded to Ynys Enlli, a holy island of saints, and back again rather than spend another moment in the caves.

" 'Riath," Mychael suddenly called out, and Ceridwen whirled on him, ready to tell him to hush again, only to find him running off into a tunnel.

"Mychael!" A new wave of fear struck her as he rounded a curve and disappeared into the nothingness. "Mychael, you little bugger! Come back here!"

She chased after him, legs pumping, skirts flying. Aye, and when she caught him, she was going to wallop him a good one. Little as he was, though, he was able to stay ahead of her, splashing through the puddles, always a few steps too far away for her to catch. She got a stitch in her side and swore. She hadn't thought things could get any worse. Damn Mychael for proving her wrong.

She yelled at him, and he kept yelling for Moriath. The sounds of their voices crossed over each other in the maze of passageways and ricocheted back, then were swallowed up whole by the sheer density of the rock surrounding them. Twice more she lost sight of him, and each time spurred her on to more speed.

When next she saw him, she made one last effort, hiking up her skirts and running pell-mell. She reached out, and her fingers brushed against the cloak. She stretched them farther, grasping on to the cloth and fur before giving him a jerk.

"Mychael," she warned when he tried to squirm away, her voice no less angry for being breathless. Then he was down, and she was on top of him, making a pile of arms and legs. She would have punched him, if she'd had the strength. She did not.

They lay, still and winded, getting soaked everywhere they touched the ground.

"Ceri, look," Mychael said before she could catch her breath enough to light into him. He was pointing at a place on the wall above one of the oil lamps. Marks were etched into the stone, showing white against the rock, and an arrow pointed into the heavier darkness of a rough shaft.

Ceridwen recognized some of the white lines as letters, and she knew letters made words, but that was the extent of her knowledge. There were straight lines and curved lines, and lines that crossed each other. On either side of the letters were symbols she recognized from a ring her mother wore.

Fighting the weight of her sodden skirts, she struggled to her feet and reached up to touch the marks. *PRYF.* 'Twas a small word. She traced over it with her fingertips, wondering what it meant, wondering if the arrow pointed the way out or deeper into the caverns.

"Come on." Mychael pushed her, coming to his feet beside her. "Let's go. 'Riath is in there. I saw her, and she can take us home."

Ceridwen gave the shaft a wary look. 'Twas narrower than the others and not as smooth. It did not look like the way home.

"I didn't see her."

"I did. Come on." He pulled this time, wrapping his fingers in her cloak.

She balked, holding her ground. The smell was stronger than it had been before, emanating from the shaft, sweet, and earthy, and warm. Rich.

"No," she said. "I'm not going in there."

"Now who's acting like a suckling babe?" Mychael asked, indignant.

She would have defended herself from his accusation, given time, but time ran out. A draft of wind swirled up from the shaft with a keening sound, extinguishing the oil lamps one by one in quick succession, leaving them in total darkness.

"Damn, damn, damn, damn." Ceridwen swore for every lamp they lost, grabbing Mychael and backing into the wall. Her eyes searched in vain to see anything other than black emptiness. "Damn, damn, damn."

"Yer goin' to be in trouble. Yer goin' to be in trouble," Mychael taunted between gasping cries of fear, trying to climb on top of her and hide inside her cloak at the same time.

She pressed them closer to the wall, two small bodies huddled together as the warm breath of the earth poured over them. Then, as suddenly as the wind had come, it retreated, and the glowing light of a torch bounced and weaved an erratic path out of the darkness to her right. The sound of stumbling footsteps came with the light, and soon, hard breathing and crying.

Agony was in the voice, despair in the great gulping sobs. It was a woman. The pitch was unmistakable.

" 'Riath," Mychael whispered, and Ceridwen believed. No matter that he'd found her behind them rather than in front of them; he'd found her.

That it truly was Moriath became apparent the closer she got. Her pretty reddish hair was fallen from its crown of braids and was all mussed. Tears streaked her face, and her bloodstained clothes were half torn from her body.

When she looked up and saw them, she fell to her knees with a cry of shock, the torch rolling out of her hands. Mychael reached her first and threw himself into her arms, with Ceridwen less than a hairbreadth behind.

The maid held them so tightly they could hardly breathe, dampening the last dry places on them with her tears. Ceridwen took what comfort could be eked out of such a pitiful, but nonetheless heartily welcomed rescue, before allowing her curiosity to get the better of her.

"Did you fall?" she asked, reaching out to smooth Moriath's braid where it fell over her bared shoulder. The maid was dirty and scratched something awful, and Ceridwen thought she must have fallen all the way from the top of the cave. She gave the loose braid another gentle pat. Poor Moriath.

The maid didn't answer at first, but wiped her eyes with her torn sleeve, which did no good a'tall, because her tears kept falling. When it was obvious no progress would be made on that front, she took up the torch and rose to her feet with unnatural awkwardness.

"Come, children, hurry. We must be away."

"Away where, 'Riath?" Mychael asked, lifting his head from where he stood buried in her skirts, his arms wrapped around her legs.

"To the mountains, and when the snows come, we will go south. 'Twill be an adventure."

Something was wrong, Ceridwen thought. Moriath was not one to cling and cry. Nor was she one to fall down and get dirty and tear her clothes. Moriath always looked nice. Her eyes were the prettiest green. Ceridwen had never seen them all red and puffy before.

"You like adventures, don't you, Ceri?" the maid said, caressing her cheek with a trembling hand. A watery smile graced her mouth.

"No doubt 'tis how you came to be in the caves. Your instincts are good, little one, even when they are misguided."

"My 'stincts'?" Ceridwen repeated, confused. Nothing was making sense.

Mychael laughed and pointed his finger at her. "No, silly Ceri. 'Riath said you stink."

"Did not." She hit his hand away, then looked to Moriath for reassurance. The woman was not paying them any attention. She had the torch lifted high and was staring down into the winding shaft. She stood very still for a long time, as if unsure of what she should do next, until Ceridwen grew uneasy and Mychael pulled at her skirts.

"Aye. We must go," she said softly, then turned the torch on the white marks etched into the stone. She dragged the fire across the strange word, obscuring it with a layer of smoke and soot, making it indistinguishable from the rest of the wall.

Ceridwen watched as the letters and symbols disappeared, turning from gray to black and melting back into the stone, and she wondered what Moriath was hiding, and from whom.

From the shaft to fresh air and freedom was not overly far for one who knew the way through the maze of tunnels. Moriath had said no more in the caverns, only sometimes burst into a fit of sobbing and tears that she eventually controlled, until the next fit hit. Ceridwen thought the whole adventure one big, miserable disaster, and she didn't understand why they couldn't just go back to their bed, or at least the keep. She didn't want to go to the mountains. She was tired and hungry, and she wanted to go home. She wanted her mother.

A bramble thicket covered the cave entrance when they reached it, one more unpleasantness to add to her day. They fought their way through the thicket, getting pricked and stabbed, except for Mychael. He was safe in Moriath's arms, his cheek resting on her shoulder, his soft snores making Ceridwen's exhaustion nearly unbearable.

"Damn," she said under her breath. A bramble thorn caught in her gown, ripping the cloth, and she swore again. "Damn."

"Child," Moriath said, stopping on a small rise just past the thicket and reaching a hand back. For an instant Ceridwen thought she was going to be reprimanded for her language, maybe even boxed on the ears.

That was when she heard it, the distant clang of metal on metal and the popping and hissing of a great fire. She pushed forward and came to a sudden, horrified stop by the maid. Her heart started beating furiously. A flush of fear washed down her body.

Below them, Carn Merioneth was burning, its palisades, the keep, and all the life within being devoured by flames and war cries.

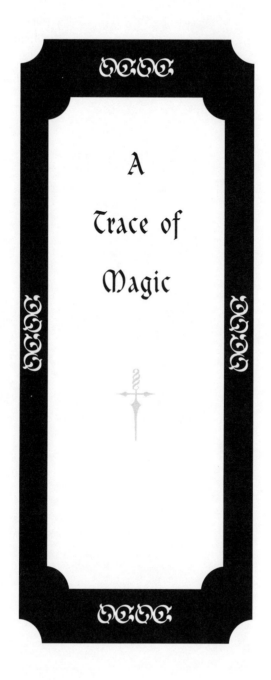

A

Trace of

Magic

Chapter 1

MARCH 1198
WYDEHAW CASTLE,
SOUTH WALES

"Jesu. Sweet Mary." The groom, Noll, crossed himself as he cowered in the darkness at the bottom of the tower stairs. He'd gotten through the bailey under the power of fear alone, but his legs would take him no farther. Rain-slickened stone supported his back. Nothing would support his knees—not muscle, nor sinew, nor bone, nor his faith in the Virgin, Holy Mother of God.

His lord had said to fetch the sorcerer, but his lord had asked for too much. Noll tilted his head back and stared up at the malevolent shadows of darkness that deepened with each curved step into the tower. Rain ran in rivulets down his hair to his face, obscuring his vision and adding to the torment of the godforsaken night.

There! Where the gray stone changed to black! Was it a trick of the light, that bare flicker of movement and scratch of life? Or was it the sorcerer, Dain

Lavrans, conjuring up demons out of the mists of fog and sending them down the stairs to greet him?

Noll's heart stopped in a moment of terror, then his blood ran cold and fast on a track of pure fear. He could take no more and turned to run, or to crawl on trembling knees, if need be, back to the great hall where only minutes before he'd had the pleasure of pinching a comely maid with sprigs of lavender tied in her hair.

He paused in mid-retreat, the light from his lantern looming and diminishing with each gust of wind that swirled through the open arch leading to the barbican.

The baron would have him beaten if he failed, and what of the comely maid then, when he lay bloody and bruised in a heap by the hearth, nothing but meat for the dogs? What man would press his face into her fragrant bosom then?

Hugh, no doubt, the cur, a stable boy with no idea of the refinements needed to lay a kitchen wench. The maid deserved better, and hadn't she smiled at Noll? A mite toothlessly, to be sure, but a smile nonetheless, and what man needed teeth in a woman when her bosom was soft and ripe like peaches in late summer?

Noll glanced again at the tower stairs running up into darkness, his fear and trembling growing to courage under the impetus of lust. His lord had said fetch, and no serf who valued his life would disobey a baron of the March, one of the land-hungry Norman freebooters who had seized territory in Wales and held it "by the power of their swords and by fortune."

With his back to the outside wall, Noll slunk up the spiraling stairs of the Hart Tower, using his feet, his knees, and the one hand not holding the lantern to guide himself. A fainter shade of gloom and wet gusts of air denoted each arrowloop he passed. Halfway up the first full turn, the chiseled steps turned from gray to black. Noll crossed himself again and thought of buxom pleasures, the scent of lavender, and the sweetness of peaches. A quarter turn farther, a step shone creamily white in the lamplight. The next was black, and the one after it white, full warning that he was entering the sorcerer's domain.

"Sweet Mary." The prayer hissed from between his chattering teeth as an oak door set into Druid stone and banded with iron came into view. A gargoyle of the most hideous countenance barred the way, leering at him from the centermost plank with a bronze knocker hanging from its fangs. Rock crystal eyes glowed in the flickering lantern light, first blue, then gold and green.

Gods! Was nothing what it seemed in this corner of the keep?

Noll lifted his hand to grasp the knocker, and as he did, the hair rose all along his body, each tiny strand standing up to tremble alone. He knew it was the sorcerer's power, and the moment his flesh touched metal, a great crack of lightning rent the air with a blaze of white fire and a concussion of thunder.

Noll sucked in a paralyzing last breath, clutched the knocker with a spastic grip, and fainted dead away.

Inside the tower, the resulting clang of bronze striking bronze reverberated like a pale echo of the lightning strike. Dain Lavrans turned at the sound, his fingers curling around the large chunk of cinnabar he held in his hand, a fortune in vermilion for scriptorium monks, and a source of mercury for those who—like himself—dabbled in a different faith.

Behind him, sleet and rain beat on a glazed window. The lightning had struck close, probably the ramparts and, if what he felt was true, one of the metal-headed minions patrolling there, sealing his helmet to his skull. The baron would call for him, as if he could unfry brains roasted in such a manner.

His upper lip curled in sullen humor. They expected too much, these Norman Marchers, from their Danish sorcerer.

He put the cinnabar on a high shelf, then crossed the chamber to answer the first summons of the evening, lifting the cowl of his cloak over his head to conceal his face with shadows. The clasp he adjusted to bring the cloak over his worn leather gambeson was his by right of plunder, a garnet-encrusted Celtic scroll with a cabochon of amber on either side. Deer-hide boots covered his feet and were laced to his knees with strips of leather.

Tonight he did not look like his Norman lord with silk hose, samite tunic, and ermine-trimmed mantle. Tonight Dain was a hunter—and he was not pleased to have his hunt delayed by some fool's folly.

He pulled on the door, and when it did not open, bared his teeth and pulled again. The night was proving to be full of more than the normal discord and dissent of Wydehaw Castle.

Slowly, the banded door swung open, dragging the wretched summoner in its wake. The man's bony fist was frozen around the knocker, while his body hung like a wet rag to the floor. His other hand still held a lantern, which threatened to spill flame into the rushes.

Cursing, Dain picked up the lantern and stomped on the cinders and the smoldering edge of the groom's tunic, an act designed more to save his chambers than the man's life. The Baron of Wydehaw valued not his servants. This man would not be missed, though it was apparent nothing short of Lord Soren D'Arbois's own command would have brought this weak-boweled knave to the sorcerer's door.

Dain ground the last ember into dust. He wouldn't be thanked, and in truth, he'd done the man no favor, for he was leaving the clod where he hung on the door, a bold warning to any others who might think to disturb Wydehaw's mage. By midnight every castle cretin would know the story of how Dain Lavrans had frozen Noll the groom to the gargoyle's fangs, and how the magician's powers had flowed through Noll's body and singed his clothes. By morn, the whole village would know. The knowledge would seep into the forest, slide through the trees, into grottoes and glens, alerting every outlaw and saint of the black heart that lived within the keep's tower.

The thought brought a wry smile to Dain's mouth. His reputation was hard-won and most decidedly well deserved, though he would be the first to admit his debt to his predecessor in the tower. The magical deeds of Nemeton, a Brittany bard, were still whispered with awe and fear in the demesne. The most tangible proof of the man's high standing in his time was the existence of the tower itself, with its parti-colored stairs, three tiers of rooms, and the near magical workings of what the castle populace called the "Druid Door."

For many years, Dain had given no more credence to one religion than another and little enough to any, especially the dead and ancient ones like Druidry. Still, he'd found much of interest behind the Druid Door and in the surrounding forest of Wroneu, enough to keep him at Wydehaw when it should have been no more than a night's stay on a journey much farther north.

"Erlend," he called to the servant hiding somewhere in the chaos of the workroom.

"Aye." A wizened old man stuck his head out from behind a heavy damask curtain drawn across a crescent of the chamber. Smoke followed him in a halo around his sparsely haired head.

Service to the sorcerer was considered a sentence akin to death by most, but old Erlend seemed to have sinned apurpose to land himself in the comforts of the Hart Tower. He'd once told Dain that at three score and two he had nothing left to fear from God, the Devil, or anyone in between.

Dain had only smiled.

"Watch the brazier and don't drink from the marked cask." Dain issued the orders in the tone of someone accustomed to being obeyed.

"Aye," Erlend answered in the manner of someone growing unaccustomed to obeying.

Dain arched a dark eyebrow, a warning better understood than ignored.

Erlend squinted through the gloom. "Poison, is it?"

Dain held the man's gaze a second longer, then turned and stepped over Noll's limp body. A hand gesture brought two sleek hounds loping out of the shadows of the chamber to join him. The old man would make of the evening what he would.

The great hall of Wydehaw Castle was filled to bursting with the feigned shrieks of maids and the roars and laughter of men-at-arms well into their cups. Chaos ruled the servants below the salt, scattering them this way and that, their hands gripping leather jacks and trenchers, their feet nimbly dodging disaster and the dogs.

Most of the assemblage had forgotten about the prisoner chained to the wall to the left of the dais, but not the red-haired knight. From beneath the veil of her lashes, Ceridwen ab Arawn watched his gaze rake her body, the intensity of his attention like that of a feral cat stalking prey, waiting for the right moment to reach out with an unsheathed claw and snag a morsel for its mouth.

She shivered, the sensation racking her from her head to her toes and awakening her pains. Never had she felt such an icy chill so deeply in her bones, yet if she could die from the cold this night, she would count herself blessed.

The knight shifted on the bench, a veritable mountain of iron-studded leather and concealed blades. A fresh infusion of panic quickened her already ragged breathing. Panting, her chest hurting, she fixed her gaze on the floor, seeing naught beyond the clay tiles flanking the hearth. Red-hot embers snapped and popped out of the fire, rolling onto the chased floor, and slowly it dawned on her that the designs etched into the squares of fired clay were of animals copulating.

Revulsion and nausea churned to life in her belly. One corpulent boar, beady-eyed and barrel-chested, leered at her in a perfect parody of the knight; and, even worse, in a frighteningly accurate depiction of the vile bridegroom she had desperately tried to escape. The abbess at Usk had oft warned her she would come to no good, but the lady could not have foreseen such a despicable end.

Ceridwen turned her face into the weak comfort of her shoulder, closing her eyes and praying the giant wouldn't rise. The sound of wood scraping on stone and the accompanying grunt of a great weight lifting dashed her last feeble hope, and a wave of despair flooded through her body. He was coming for her.

Rape was the least she expected and more than she thought she could endure, especially at the hands of the red-haired knight. He had been the one to capture her in the forest. Through the scent of her own sweat and blood, she could still detect traces of the stench he'd left upon her clothes. She remembered the hotness of his breath upon her neck, the cruelty of his mouth when he'd marked her with his teeth—leaving a double crescent of bloody, bruised wounds on the shoulder he'd bared by tearing the sleeve of her gown and part of her chemise.

Her legs had given way hours ago, leaving her to hang from the iron cresset like a sacrificial lamb, but she forced herself to regain her footing for one last fight. Pain shot through her limbs and nearly put her to the floor again. The brute had wrenched her ankle past the breaking point when she'd tried to escape him at the river. He'd near drowned her in the turgid gray waters of the Llynfi, but her damned luck hadn't held.

She grasped her chains with both hands and balanced on her good foot. Her nose was bloody from his fist. More blood ran down the side of her face from her temple. Her ribs ached from where he'd crushed her to him with his mailed arm on their mad ride to the castle.

He drew closer, and tears she'd been too frightened to let fall before now welled in her eyes and spilled onto her cheeks. She had failed to save herself, failed to reach her brother, Mychael, and the sanctuary of Strata Florida Monastery. All was lost. There was no going back, and a quick death was too much to hope for within the debauched halls she'd been brought to.

A dog snapped at the knight as he passed and received a swift, vicious kick to its flanks. Whimpering, the animal slunk away. Another cur snarled a warning over a prize bone, but stayed well out of foot range. The maneuver did him no good, for the knight side-stepped quickly and landed a blow with his boot. The meaty haunch fell to the floor and the rest of the pack descended on the bone, snapping and growling into a tumble at her feet.

With a strangled cry, Ceridwen drew back toward the wall. Jesu! If the knight didn't tear her to shreds, the hounds surely would.

An alaunt, looking more wolf than dog, rushed forward and claimed the haunch with a blood-chilling growl, standing its ground not a hand's span from her, hackles rising. Ceridwen pressed herself closer to the cold stone to no avail. The hunger-crazed mongrels circled, bringing her within the lines of battle. A raucous cheer rose from the lower tables at some fool's antics—and the red knight kept coming, plowing a way through the cordon of teeth and mange.

All was truly lost, and in her heart she surrendered. Her knees buckled, allowing her to sink to the floor and pray for death among the dogs.

"*Salvator mundi,*" she whispered, her eyes closing. "*Salva nos omnes. Kyrie, eleison; Christe, eleison; Christe, eleison—*"

A sudden hush in the hall stole the supplication from her lips. She opened her eyes and peered through the tangled length of her hair. The knight halted in the strange silence, his eyebrows drawing together in momentary confusion. An undercurrent of anticipation— or was it apprehension?—snaked through the cavernous chamber, touching servants and diners alike. Scattered laughter was quickly quelled, calls for more ale ignored. The dogs tensed and grew still, then one by one padded away with their heads lowered, their tails tucked between their legs, making for hiding places under the tables.

Ceridwen watched the red giant's confusion change to unease as he slowly turned toward the great oak doors at his back. Within the space of a breath his complexion grew waxen, and when she followed his gaze she felt the blood drain from her own face.

Two huge hounds stood on the threshold, one so black its coat glistened blue in the torchlight, the other so white it hurt her eyes to look upon its sleek hide. She shifted her attention to the space between the beasts, drawn by the merest hint of movement in the shadows, the briefest glint of eye and whisper of sound.

A new sense of dread, above and beyond the fear that had weakened her knees, filled her and brought panic in its wake. Though she trembled with the cold, sweat broke out on her brow. With a certainty that pierced her heart, she knew that whatever lurked in the gloom was the true terror of this place, a danger more lethal than the knight. Latent, primal instincts rushed to the fore, overriding her heart's surrender. She stumbled to her one good foot and jerked at the chains leashing her to the wall. They rattled and clanged with the force of her desperation, but they held. She jerked again, her hysteria mounting—until the shadows parted.

A hooded figure disengaged itself from the darkness with the ease of an eclipsed dawn rising from the night. The shape within the black folds of cowl and cloak lifted a long, graceful hand in a fluid gesture, and the hounds loped forward, clearing a path for their master.

At that moment even hysteria seemed too pallid a name to put to the strange mix of terror and fascination rising in her.

Chapter 2

From within the concealing depths of his hood, Dain surveyed the people in the crowded hall. He knew many by name, though few dared to call him by his. The baron, Lord Soren D'Arbois, was one, and also his lovely whore-wife, the lady Vivienne.

Ragnor the Red was there, looking both fierce and frightened, a combination Dain knew only he could produce in Wydehaw's most bestial knight. The man had atavistic tendencies, and Dain fully expected that one day the Norman would go berserk in the grand tradition of his Viking forefathers. For himself, Danish though he was, Dain had no such fears. The methods and mayhem of war had long since lost their hold on him.

He preferred a more academic life, if quick fingers and a vocation of turning lead into gold could be called academic. Some called it trickery. Some called it magic. He called it both decoy and dangerous, for the path led its followers far beyond riches.

His steps brought him abreast of Father Aric, and the priest near stumbled in his haste to avoid the shadows cast by the dogs and their master. Elixir and Numa continued on, aware but not offended. Dain claimed no such magnanimity. He paused and bowed, hands clasped at his breast, knowing well how many hours the young priest would spend on his knees to wash away such a black stain of acknowledgment.

Father Aric crossed himself again and again, his eyes squeezed shut, his hand a blur of devotion as it raced across the stations of the martyr's tree. The church had raised superstition to the very apex of art, and Father Aric was one of its more skilled artisans, a disciplined practitioner of religious cant and canon.

Dain debated whether to hold the pose until the priest exhausted either his piety or his arm, and prudence won. The hour was not so late as to preclude his hunt. He lowered his hands and moved on, but got no farther than the corner of the hearth.

Numa blocked his path, her milk-white body trembling, her gaze fixed across the flames and rising smoke to the far wall. Ragnor was there, and the bitch liked him no better than any maid, yet it was unlike her to disobey merely to indulge a fit of personal pique.

"Gå," he whispered, modulating his voice to make the command little more than a breath.

When she hesitated, he looked once more across the fire, trying to discern what held her so enthralled. A pile of rags had been chained to the cresset, and it undoubtably contained an urchin or, considering Ragnor's vicinage, a virgin. Still, there were urchins aplenty in Wydehaw and enough virgins if one gave the definition a broad range.

A swath of white-blond hair tangled in the small heap held his interest for a moment. Then he moved on, a flick of his cloak against Numa's hock telling her he would abide no more rebellion.

When he reached the foot of the dais, he found himself turning once again toward the hearth. For a man compelled by very little besides his own whim, that he turned at all surprised him. He blamed the deviant behavior on Numa's unprecedented interest. The face he saw lifting from the pile of rags was another surprise, and for that he had nothing to blame but an unknown facet of his own nature. He hadn't realized he harbored a conviction that jewels should be chained only when they were to be worn about the neck.

Pale blue eyes with the startling crystalline quality of gemstones peered out at him from gamine features streaked with blood and mud. Terror marked the maid's gaze, and though he took pride in his ability to frighten the innocent and the not-so-innocent alike, he was disconcerted by the girl's reaction. She would have to be made of sterner stuff if she was to survive a night of Ragnor's attentions.

Dismissing the novelty of a new conviction—which brought him up to a grand total of two, possibly three—he returned his attention to the lord and lady of the manor. He was not above preying upon their more insidious weaknesses when he had the strength, but he hunted other game this night. His friend, the Welsh rebel Morgan ab Kynan, had been sighted in the mountains on the Coit Wroneu, a month late by Dain's reckoning, but no less welcome. Dain was in need of some good company after the long winter, and Morgan and his band of men were companionship at its best.

Also, rumors had been flying for months concerning their old friend, Caradoc, whom some now called the Boar of Balor Keep—an inauspicious name to Dain's way of thinking. Most of what he had heard was either too fantastic or too atrocious to hold more than a grain of truth, yet even in the grain there was that which disturbed him. Morgan could be counted on to have winnowed the wheat from the chaff.

"Lord D'Arbois, my lady," he addressed the pretty, young pair on the dais.

"Dain, good friend." Vivienne spoke, her voice coy and silky. "I pray our request has not taken you away from more important concerns."

"I am always ready to serve, milady."

The briefest smile twisted Soren D'Arbois's mouth. "Aye, 'tis one of your more endearing traits, *sorcier,* this willingness to serve."

The lord and lady were a matched set, both high of brow and cheek, with honeyed hair and fair faces. Soren was more hawklike in the shape of his nose, but Vivienne's mouth held the stronger streak of cruelty. Rumor said the old baron had married the blood too close in the match of his eldest son. Looking upon the husband and wife, Dain was inclined to believe the story.

"Willingness can be a virtue or a vice, Baron."

"The lady assures me 'tis not one of your vices," D'Arbois answered dryly, lifting a goblet of wine in feigned salute. He drained the cup and wiped his sleeve across his mouth. "But to business, Lavrans. Ragnor has brought me a mystery."

"And I thought he hunted roe," Dain said, softly mocking.

"So he did," D'Arbois said. "The buck escaped, but not the doe." Pleased with his accidental rhyme, the baron allowed a smile and gestured toward the hearth. "Behold."

An anguished cry echoed through the hall. Dain turned to see Ragnor hauling the girl up by the scruff of her neck and gown. Numa trembled at his side, baring her teeth in a silent growl. To soothe her, Dain traced his finger along the length of her muzzle.

Ragnor shook the girl, and she cried out again. Fresh blood seeped from the long gash at her temple, making a garish stripe of red against the colorless strands of her hair. Numa lifted a paw in readiness to attack. Dain swore silently and motioned for Elixir to move to his left side and control the bitch. One forlorn maid was not worth a fight, no matter the prettiness of her eyes.

"My lord," he said casually, "the next time you require a mystery, send a lighter hand on the hunt, for Ragnor has broken the one he's brought."

"More than I would have wished," D'Arbois agreed, though without any regret in his tone. "I trust you will be able to put her back together, and when she is of apiece, return her that we may together plumb her secrets."

Dain refrained from reminding his lord that when the occasion or the need arose, he would prefer to plumb female secrets alone. The possibility of all manner of mésalliance involving at least himself and D'Arbois had already been much hinted at by the baron and refused by himself, though never openly discussed. D'Arbois's single strength was his ability to keep from being directly rejected. Still, Dain would have preferred not to physick the chit. Maids screamed when he stitched. They cried for all manner of reasons. Sometimes they pleaded, but never for the right things.

"If it pleases my lord." Dain stepped toward the hearth, because he really didn't have a choice, and was rewarded with a warning howl of outrage from the red giant. On another, the theatrics would have seemed overplayed. With Ragnor, such was to be expected. They were at check—and Dain realized that the true sport of the evening had just begun. He had been summoned to perform a part in a nasty tableau; that of being the one to take the jewellike beauty from the raging beast. No one else, not even D'Arbois, had dared. With good reason.

All around him, Dain heard trestles being pushed back or taken down to make room for the combatants. The hunting dogs and mongrels moved with the tables, careful to avoid drawing Elixir's attention. Dain, himself, was more wary of Numa. Being female, she was the less predictable of the two, as she'd so aptly proven with her response to the girl.

Servants scurried through the hall like silent wraiths, eager to empty the tables and refill the cups, making all ready for the rare entertainment to come. Dain hoped not to disappoint, though he'd thought he'd done his night's work by freezing Noll to the Druid Door.

Fresh pitch was added to the cressets. Torches were set out in iron stands to ring the hearth, enclosing the section of wall where the girl hung from her chains and Ragnor's fist. Dain entered the blazing circle alone, leaving the hounds behind with a quiet command. The odds were already in his favor, assuming the maid was on his side. He looked at her, a pale outline against the soot-covered wall, and saw her blanch.

He could be assuming too much.

Numa whined behind him, so like a woman, but to have his bitch tear out the knight's throat wouldn't leave much room for his own personal glory—and he was more than a trainer of hounds, much more.

A low hum snaked around the perimeter of the great hall, as wagering took place with lightning speed. Ragnor was near seventeen stone in weight, but Dain had no intention of letting the exhibition disintegrate into a physical ordeal, not when the knight's mind was as weak as his arm was strong, and not for a mere maid. Finesse and timing were the keys, and an invocation to turn Ragnor's guts into a churning, knotted mass of fear.

A smile flitted across his mouth. He knew just the thing.

He moved forward with slow, measured steps, giving Ragnor enough time to contemplate his immediate future and all of eternity should he be defeated by Wydehaw's mage, but not enough time to steal the opening gambit. At five paces away, he palmed a bit of miscellanea out of a pocket in his cloak. A quick glance proved it to be a black stone. He slipped it back and tried again. Draconite had its purposes, but felling giants wasn't one of them.

A chunk of petrified snake's tongue came next, but he always needed more snake's tongue than he had. Pieces of mermaid's purse, wren's teeth . . . he found naught he could use until the end, and a costly trick it would be besting Ragnor if the green bauble was broken or lost in the bargain.

Just out of striking distance, Dain stopped. His nose twitched in distaste; the knight stank more than would seem humanly possible. He turned his attention to the girl and let his gaze drift over her, noting the depth of her head wound, the glazed look in her eyes, and the circle of bloody marks on her shoulder.

The last gave him pause. A flame of anger sparked to life in his breast, irritating him no small measure. The knight didn't smell human because he wasn't, but 'twas none of Dain's concern. The urchin's fate was incidental, as nothing. He looked again at the ragged bite, and much to his disgust his anger flamed high enough to singe his reason.

"There are better ways to eat a maid, Ragnor," he chided, shifting his gaze to the knight. He took a step closer and bowed his head to whisper for Ragnor's hearing alone. "Shall I have D'Arbois chain thee to a wall in my tower so that I may teach you the tender placement of teeth and the gentler uses of thy two tongues?"

The knight stumbled in a brief retreat, hissing a name that caused Dain to laugh aloud. If he could claim buggery as his only sin and be done with it, a better man he'd be than the one he was.

He advanced a step, his laughter softening to menace in the stillness of the hall. "You rutting whoreson. I could eat thine balls to break mine fast and know nothing but the pleasure of having food in my belly."

"S-sodding bastard." Ragnor edged closer to the wall, hauling the maid and her chains with him. The metal links jingled against the iron cresset and scraped along the wall.

"You repeat yourself, lackwit," Dain said, following him. "If 'tis name-calling we come to, I will need a mightier foe . . . but, for mortal combat, we are a fair enough match. Be still, valorous knight, and I will reveal my weapon." With a wave of his hand, the green bauble appeared in fingertips that only a second before had been empty.

Ragnor flinched, pulling back as far as the girl's chains allowed. Torchlight shot through the transparent ball no bigger than a small hen's egg, setting it afire to burn hot and green in Dain's hand.

"Do you know of serpent's stones, dear fool?" Dain rolled the ball across his fingers and down the back of his hand as if it floated on his skin, a droplet of water going home to the sea, smoothly, without a ripple. He stopped the green orb on his wrist and smiled at Ragnor. "Ah, yes. I see that you do." The ball slipped into the vee between his index finger and his thumb, balanced for the space of a breath, and dropped into his open palm.

"I give you Brochan's Great Charm!" he called out, lifting the orb high and letting his voice rise to fill the hall. "Born of the froth of a thousand serpents tangled in a frenzy beneath the stones of Domhringr, laced with their venom and blood and hardened by their fiery breath!"

A gratifying gasp sounded around him. He leaned forward and extended the gift on the tips of his fingers. "Leave the maid, Ragnor, or take her and the stone. You may have both or neither. These are the terms I offer."

In answer, the knight drew a blade. A nervous tic jumped at the corner of his right eye, causing the whole side of his face to twitch and jerk. "This is my term, w-wizard. Take your cursed stone or I'll p-prick thy heart."

"Upon the peril of your soul, Sir Squint." Dain glided forward, his attention focused on the dagger, and began chanting under his breath. "With this stone, whether you take it or nay, I impose upon thee that thou mayst wander to and fro through a land of faerie dreams. That small dwarf, whose power could steep the king's host in deathlike sleep . . ."

The dark melody of the sorcerer's voice drew Ceridwen like a moth to flame, entrancing her with a promise of sweet oblivion. Death it would be, she thought, a faerie's death to escape the devil named Ragnor, a faerie's death to put her forever beyond her accursed betrothed's reach. A more fitting fate Abbess Edith herself could not have foretold. Indeed, she had foretold Ceridwen's fate as such: that a troublesome maid who delved too deeply into the mysteries and heresies found in the discards of the ecclesiastical scriptoria would no doubt, and most deservedly, come to her end by way of evil enchant-ment.

What the pious lady had not known was that evil enchantment would appear as the path of salvation compared to the damnable heresies and prophecies Ceridwen had read in those discarded manu-scripts. Written upon timeworn parchment bound in red leather had been her name, and below her name, her destiny, and below her destiny, her fate.

A shudder passed through her. She would not be led like a lamb to slaughter, not by ancient prophecy. She'd said as much, whis-pered in silence from her heart to God's ear, at every office of every day, until she'd convinced herself the damning passages referred not to her, but to the same-named goddess of the old religion. And wasn't every word of the old stories heresy anyway? And what was heresy if not the most despicable lies?

Then, not a fortnight past, the despicable lies had become truth. A princely summons had come to the abbey, betrothing her to the son of Carn Merioneth's destroyer, returning her to the very place she had sworn to avoid at all costs, for fear she was the wretched Ceridwen of the red book. She'd been torn between despair, denial, and anger ever since.

A sob rose in her throat. Death it would be before more of Ragnor's degradation, death before she accepted the eternal damna-tion of her proposed marriage.

". . . and let it be known"—the sorcerer's voice lured her back—"that whosoever tries to unbind the dire enchanting art of the spell, before the thousand years are done, shall join thee in an everlast-ing hell . . ."

A thousand years of sleep and grace? Ceridwen thought. 'Twas more than she could have dreamed for. Thus emboldened, she lunged for the deadly serpent stone and caught it. Instant warmth pulsed across her palm and up her fingers, bringing painful life to frozen limbs, until with a gasped cry, she clutched the talisman to her breast and succumbed to the promised, enchanted sleep.

Dain watched, stunned, as the maid crumpled to the floor with his ball of green glass locked in her grimy fingers. He had sorely miscalculated the sternness of her stuff. None other would have stolen his bauble from beneath his very nose.

Rapid footfalls sounded Ragnor's retreat. The coward had

dropped her the moment she had touched the stone, letting out an unmanly scream of fright.

Sighing, Dain looked around. It was done, for better or for worse. He spotted the seneschal and beckoned.

"Unchain the maid."

The man bustled forward to do as he was bid. A snap of Dain's fingers brought Elixir and Numa to his side, for a moment anyway. Numa soon deserted him for the girl receiving the seneschal's ministrations.

Strange chit, Dain mused. Who would have thought she had enough fight left in her to grab the charm and save herself from the beast of Wydehaw? Now if only she had enough fight in her to vanquish the screams sure to rise in her throat when he stitched her together.

A small smile played about Lady Vivienne's mouth as she watched Dain advance on Ragnor, watched Ragnor pale with fear. 'Twas always a pleasure to see the sorcerer, just to watch him move, such a lovely, dangerous man. Elusive. He hadn't come to the hall for weeks, and she'd long since run out of excuses for sending for him. Lying could be so tiresome, especially when it didn't get her what she wanted.

It took a true crisis to bring Lavrans forth anymore, though how one small beggar constituted a crisis was beyond Vivienne's comprehension. Yet she was grateful for the opportunity, and for the break in the drudgery of her evenings. Had she known that marriage to a March lord would amount to little more than exile in a heathen land, she would have fought her father harder on the match. Had she known that marriage to Soren would so quickly turn platonic, she would have refused altogether, no matter her initial attraction or the alternative of scandal.

As a younger maid, she had dabbled in amorous yet innocent liaisons—a whisper, a caress, a kiss, mayhaps another caress—then had delighted in tantalizing her priestly confessors with the most highly detailed and, in the beginning, embellished accounts of her sins, revealing the deeds with all the breathless fervor and subtle hesitations of a king's courtesan. More than one priest had sought her out in the dark recesses of the church after giving her absolution and penance.

All but one had found her impossible to bully and difficult to seduce, but then, the one to whom she had succumbed had been young and beautiful, and had approached her with naught but an ingenuously eager smile. For two weeks she had confessed to him night and day, so sweet had been their love. In the end, impetuosity had proven to be no friend of discretion, and they'd been caught in flagrante delicto.

The young priest's punishment had been three years' exile from Paris to be spent contemplating his sins in a Benedictine abbey. Hers had been life imprisonment in the March of Wales.

No man had pleased her since, except for Soren when they had first been wed. If he pleased his men and boys half as well as he had pleased his wife, they were lucky indeed. 'Twas not unheard of, this affliction of her husband's, but it was damned frustrating in a place as isolated as Wydehaw, where the most interesting possible replacement was a recluse living in a tower whose only entrance was a door that could not be breached.

She'd tried drugging Lavrans once, so she could have him brought to her bed, but he'd no sooner lifted the cup of wine to his mouth than he'd smiled his most charming smile and poured the drink into the rushes. She'd been told the draught was imperceptible. The damned leech who had sold it to her had paid for his mistake with a bout of her fury he had not soon forgotten, not with his simples smashed all over the floor and her refusing to pay for the damage. She'd heard he was still suffering from the setback. Fair enough. She was suffering too, suffering from love, or mayhaps lust. Sometimes it was difficult to tell the two apart.

Dain's voice rose in the hall, and Vivienne leaned forward in her chair, her smile fading in anticipation of his next move. The crowd gasped as he lifted a charm into the air. A serpent stone, rich magic indeed to save a beggar girl.

Ragnor drew a blade, holding it in a manner better suited for protection than attack, but Vivienne was reluctant to take a chance. She reached for her husband and bent her head near.

"Ragnor's prize is not worth the sorcerer's blood. Stop your beast before he goes too far."

"No." The Baron of Wydehaw's gaze did not waver from the torchlit circle.

"I would not have him marked," she insisted, staring at her

husband until he was forced to acknowledge her with a shift of his gaze.

"Have you no faith in the man?" he asked.

"Only faith that one day he will be mine, and when that day comes, I do not want him scarred with Ragnor's rage," she said through her teeth, her irritation growing with the delay. "Stop the beast."

A strange scream rent the air, jerking both their attentions back to the drama taking place by the hearth. Ragnor had dropped the dirty beggar and was beating a hasty retreat from the hall.

Soren burst into laughter, a hearty chuckle unlike what she'd heard from him in some time.

"So much for the beast, my dear," he said. "I think our *sorcier* has won the day and the girl, while Ragnor proves to have the balls of a newt."

Vivienne sank back into her chair, partially relieved and yet even more discontent. Her husband's wording did little to improve her mood, as the statement wasn't exactly correct. Out of desperation, she'd taken Ragnor to her bed once, and a more miserable experience she'd never had, coarse and brutish, like the stupid man himself, worse even than her nights with the seneschal, who had merely bored her to death. The cook, at least, had smelled like fresh bread when she'd had him. The squire didn't bear remembering at all.

'Twas Dain Lavrans she wanted.

"Aye," she murmured to herself, watching him with a narrowed gaze. 'Twas the sorcerer she wanted.

Chapter 3

Dain threw home the bolt on the Druid Door, locking out the servants who had carried the maid into the tower and then taken Noll away, and anyone else who might think to seek him out that night. Ragnor would be lying in wait for the girl throughout the keep, but braver men than the red giant had sweated out the last of their courage in the northern tower of the upper bailey. Dain knew the knight would not press so much as the toe of his boot on a black or white stair. The maid was safe from Ragnor the Red whilst she was in the Hart Tower. Mayhaps she was safe even from Wydehaw's mage. Dain hadn't decided yet.

He turned and passed her where she lay on a pallet next to the fire. She looked deathly pale, but his cursory examination had shown the bleeding to have stopped and her breath to be warm and even. The bastard had broken her ankle, but Dain had set a good share of bones. After he got the swelling down, he could do this one better than most.

Elixir and Numa settled themselves on either side of the hearth, elegant heads resting on outstretched paws, tails curling toward the heat. Erlend had been evicted from his rough bed to fetch eggs for the work ahead. A lightning-struck guard had indeed been brought into the hall shortly after Ragnor's retreat, but D'Arbois had relegated the poor sod to the village leech so that Dain could mend the urchin.

He shrugged free of his cloak and hung it up to dry and steam by the fire. The gambeson followed, unlaced by a deft hand. Rain fell in frozen sheets from the night sky, beating against the wooden shutters that sealed the two unglazed tower windows. The winter had been long and hard, a test of survival for all who resided within the castle walls. Even his resources, varied and covert as they were, would not stretch much farther without the pinch being felt. It was not a good year to be taking on extra mouths to feed.

He glanced over his shoulder at the maid. 'Twas unlikely she would survive through to Beltaine, May Eve, let alone become a burden on his larder. Ragnor had already had a taste of her and judging from his reaction, one taste would not suffice. Small comfit that she was, it wouldn't take more than another bite or two to finish her off.

An irritated grimace tightened his mouth. Hapless victims of marauding knights were not his responsibility, but were there a reason to do so, he could save her from Ragnor. The knight was easily swayed by the casting of magical spells and dark incantations. Yet in the end 'twould prove futile. If not the red beast, another with more lust than superstition would claim her. Dain only hated to see good work and physick go for naught.

He lifted his hand to the shelves of storage jars lining the curved wall of his chambers. Clay vessels held most of his desiccated *materia medica*: herbs, simples, and less pleasant concoctions. Receipts requiring days of steeping were kept in glass containers. Dried herbs, flowers, and other plants hung from the rafters. He had his own collection of relics displayed on the mantel, but to date, none of the small bones had revealed any saintly powers.

The truly powerful artifacts and fossils he had collected over the years were kept in an iron chest chained to the foot of his bed. Much of his past and most of his heritage were nestled in the folds of crimson wool contained therein. Many of his secrets and a few of his regrets shared the cloth.

He glided his fingers across the letters marked on each container and chose what he needed for the making of *pudre ruge*. By twos, he carried the vessels over to the table holding his mortar and pestles. From the highest shelf, he gathered henbane and white poppy for a sleeping draught. If the maid awoke from her faint before he started, he would render her insensible again, or at least as insensible as he deemed reasonable. Too much of the draught accomplished what his green serpent stone could not—a true death-sleep.

The chit still had the bauble clutched to her breast, which suited him fine for the moment. He had a generous tolerance for those who believed in his wily magic.

Bandages came next, set out on the table in neat piles. He filled the cauldron with water and swung it over the fire. A leather spice pouch was laid close to the brazier. Most of the castle folk went to the village leech or the witch, Madron, who lived on the forest edge of the demesne, to have their ills cured and their wounds stitched, which also suited Dain fine. He had no desire to see his days filled up with puking and mewling varlets; and in truth, he went to Madron himself when in need. He and the witch had much in common with their simples and their tricks, and with the deference given them both by the wilder folk in the forests.

A frantic clanging of the bronze knocker announced Erlend's return. No one else would choose to make such a racket with the gargoyle staring them down.

"Milord, milord." The old man's voice cracked with a hint of desperation. "Open 'er up, milord."

Milord? Dain stopped in the middle of reaching for the marked wine cask. The graybeard must have brought more than eggs and asked for none of it.

Dain strode over and opened the door, and the old man stumbled inside, his hands full of booty, his beard flecked with pastry crumbs. Below him, down in the darkness of the stairwell, a man cursed loudly.

"The devil take ye, ye swivin' bread-bandit!"

"Bread?" Dain asked, eyeing the load of foodstuffs.

"Aye." Erlend's rheumy eyes nearly twinkled. "Good wastel

and some little fig pies I ate on the way. I'm most sorry I am, jongleur, but me mouth got away from me and they're all gone, every one."

"The Devil, ye hear!" the man called up. "Aye, and methinks he's already in yer company, ye soddin' old bastard."

"And the eggs?" Dain asked, ignoring the insult echoing up the stairs.

"Enough for all." Erlend hobbled over to the table and emptied his hands of the rain-splashed bread, except for a pasty he tucked under his arm.

Dain bolted the door and walked back to his shelves. "How many is enough?"

"Seven."

"Let's have them, then." He pulled down a copper bowl and set it before the old man. Patting pouches and the roll of tunic above his belt, Erlend managed to locate and retrieve five eggs. Dain looked down at them in the bowl. "And the rest?"

"That's all of 'em. All seven of 'em." The old man beamed.

"Of course," Dain said, chiding himself for expecting a truer count.

"Will you be needin' me for anything else?" Erlend asked, doing a poor job of trying to hide the pasty with his sleeve.

"I'll call for you, if I want you."

"She's a bit o' a wee thing, ain't she," the old man said, looking down where the maid lay on the pallet. "I s'pose I could help ye with gettin' her gown off."

Dain felt a muscle tighten in his jaw. "I think not." He concealed his irritation with as little success as Erlend concealed his pasty. "Go eat your filched supper and find a bed elsewhere."

"Elsewhere? I'd not be safe elsewhere, not with me . . ." He stopped himself, his thin mouth tightening in a stubborn line.

"Pasty." Dain provided the missing word with impatience. Nothing about the night had gone according to plan.

"Aye," the servant confessed, albeit grudgingly. "It's a pasty." He pulled the loaf-sized pie from beneath his arm. "But not much of one, I'd swear it on me old mother's heart."

"No need," Dain said, ready for the man to be off. "I've eaten Renaud's pasties." What did it matter to him if Erlend wanted to peek up the maid's skirts? Nothing. Nothing was what it mattered, yet he wasn't going to allow it. "You may use the room below stairs tonight."

Erlend opened his mouth, then hesitated, his lips working silently before he spoke up.

"It stinks like the Devil's own fiery pits down below, what with all yer mixin' and fixin.' Ye know it as well as yer standin' there."

"The upstairs chamber then?" Dain asked, one dark eyebrow arched in false innocence. He could tolerate only so much insurrection in an evening. Fortunately, his words had the desired effect, saving him from the bother of a more vile threat.

"Yer a wicked, selfish man, bard-boy," the old man grumbled, heading for the stairs that led to the room below. " 'Twouldn't be no fat off yer calf for me to have a look up 'er skirts. Nothin' there I ain't seen afore. Nothin' worth spendin' the night in yer strange damned eyrie."

Dain had thought not.

Erlend disappeared below the hatch in the floor, mumbling and grouching. Dain turned back to the wine cask he'd been reaching for, a small cask of D'Arbois's best, compliments of the ever-hopeful Lady Vivienne. The seal was intact. A smile crossed his face. 'Twas good to know there were a few things the old man didn't dare.

He put some wine on the brazier to warm, adding a portion of water and spice. A mighty clap of thunder boomed and rolled across the heavens. Wind rattled the shutters. With a careful hand, he tapped measures of henbane and poppy into his mortar. The Wye and Llynfi rivers, which flowed on either side of Wydehaw Castle, would be rising higher with each hour of rain. Mayhaps the maid had saved him from a useless foray. The renegade he sought had no doubt watched the weather and the rivers and long since moved to higher ground.

When the draught was mixed, he poured a cup and knelt by the maid. Sad and bedraggled thing. Lost and alone. He dipped warm water out of the cauldron into a basin. All manner of evil and misfortune befell women who found themselves in such dire straits, and she seemed to be faring worse than most, having ended up in the Hart Tower of Wydehaw with only himself to keep her safe. He wet a cloth and carefully wiped it across her brow. Mud and blood came away, revealing skin as tender as a seraph's smile.

He drew the cloth down the center of her nose, then under each eye. She had been sorely abused. Besides the wound on her

temple—a hand's-span length of torn flesh he would have to mend—
she had dark bruises on her cheeks and a deep red mark on her neck
where Ragnor must have sucked hard on her, no doubt in preparation
for the bite on her shoulder.

Dain let his gaze drift downward. There would be the mess of
the rape to clean up. Ragnor was brutal with a maid. He should have
thought before to check her there for bleeding. He had enough irony
in his nights without the girl's life seeping out from between her legs
as he so carefully tended her head.

He reached down and pulled up the hem of her coarse woolen
gown and kirtle, modesty being beyond his means or his inclinations.
The poor quality of the gray cloth was enough to prove her lack of
worth, except that the chemise beneath the outer garments was of fine
linen trimmed with silk riband—a mystery, indeed—and below the
chemise another mystery. Her naked limbs were smooth and clean,
the hair of her mons softly curled. She had not been touched, not by
Ragnor, not by anyone within the last few hours.

Mayhaps never?

Something about her pristine mound put the question in his
mind, and once there, it demanded an answer. He straightened from
where he knelt at her side and went to his shelves again. Tucked into
a corner between the wall and a corbel he found a small vial of rose
oil, a gift to him from the maid Edmee.

It was a simple enough examination, performed with a gentle
and fragrant hand. When he was finished, he sat back on his heels and
pulled down her gown. Aye, she'd been sorely abused, but she was
virgin still.

He'd needed a reason to save her, and he'd been given two.
There could be a rich ransom for a virgin wearing a linen-and-silk
chemise, providing he could keep her out of the baron's clutches and
Ragnor's bed, and providing he could track down the one willing to
pay.

A low moan shuddered from her lips, sounding of pain and
distress. He reached for the sleeping draught.

"Mychael." She spoke the name in an agonized whisper, giving
him pause. He shifted his gaze to her face. She was bruised and
swollen, yet there was a delicacy about her features that he found
appealing. He would do his best not to scar her overly much.

Unbidden by intent, he reached out and stroked the side of her face, using much the same manner as he used to soothe Numa. It would be easy enough to arrange to keep her in the tower with him. If Soren wanted her whole, he could be convinced to wait until Dain pronounced her healed. Ragnor could be put on a short leash, or sent away to maraud farther afield in Elfael. The favor to her and her lord would cost Dain little and possibly bring him much gain. Such was life in Wydehaw.

He traced the curve of her cheek with his fingers. Aye, he would keep her . . . *and keep her virgin?* His thumb glided across her full lower lip, his skin warming with the sigh of her breath.

The night was not what it should have been. Had things gone according to plan, he would be in Morgan's camp, feasting on stolen D'Arbois cattle and digesting the latest news from the north. Wine would have been passed and stories told, and no doubt they would have gotten around to the curious tales whispered of Caradoc. Patricide was not unheard of, and there had been no love lost 'tween father and son, but 'twas the manner of the rumored murder Dain found disturbing and thus hard to believe.

On the morrow he would search out Morgan and learn how far Caradoc had wandered from the straight and narrow path that had led three boys to take the cross and follow Richard the Lionheart into hell. For they had been boys on the Crusade, he and Caradoc and Morgan, and not the men they had thought themselves to be, a fact proven on the bloody sands of Palestine; and proven for Dain again as a captive in the tents of the Saracen trader Jalal al-Kamam.

Some, though, need not go so far from home to find their virtue hanging in the balance. Dain lifted a handful of the maid's pale hair and remembered the startling light blue of her eyes. She stirred, releasing a breathy groan, and he let the white-gold strands fall back to her side.

She was pretty.

Hours later, Dain washed the last of the girl's blood from his hands. A dozen candles blazed on the floor surrounding the pallet and in the torchères he'd set at his side for more light. Never had he taken so many stitches in so small a space, both on her face and her shoulder. He'd given her a portion of the sleeping draught before he'd put the needle to her flesh, knowing he was in no mood for screaming and crying.

Now a sound or two, or a tear, would be welcome. She was too quiet, and becoming more intriguing all the time. He'd found a book in the folds of her ragged cloak, bound in red leather and marked on the cover with gold, a rare thing to be carting around the wilderness.

He finished dressing her wound with his concoction of *pudre ruge* and sealed the whole with albumen. Ragnor had cut her deliberately; the wound followed her hairline too closely for it to have been an accident. With time, the scar would barely be noticeable, but he wouldn't be complimenting the knight on the accuracy of his torture. Damascene steel was required for truly subtle blade work. Compared to what Dain could inflict, Ragnor's neat slice looked like butchery. Mayhaps one day he would give the red beast a personal lesson with his Syrian dagger.

He returned to the foot of the pallet and removed the cold compress from her ankle. The swelling was finally down. He felt carefully along the bone, probing with his fingertips to determine which way the break lay. When he knew as much as he would, he braced himself and, taking her foot in his hands, pulled.

Her pained cry brought the flicker of a smile to his lips. He had never yet killed anyone with henbane, an omission on his list of sins he had hoped not to remedy with the maid.

After splinting and wrapping her ankle, and listening to her cry and sniffle through the whole procedure, he moved to her side. He could do nothing more for her, except wipe her tears.

He leaned across her for a cloth, and the sniffling stopped with a soft inhalation. The contact he'd made was chest to breast, a position already proven to be rare in her life.

Without moving away, he looked to her face and found her eyes open, huge and glazed from the poppy, her irises milky-blue rims of luminosity around the dark abysses of her pupils. Her lashes were long and wet and tipped in gold.

He held her gaze, curious about this woman he had labored over so mightily. To his surprise, she stared at him with equal intensity.

"*Chérie,*" he murmured. The Norman term of endearment was not one he used often, but it came easily when looking at his mystery maiden.

He used his palm to smooth the hair back off her brow. She was warm, but not fevered. Her skin was soft, like a child's, but she was no child.

"Are you awake, lady?" he asked.

Awake? Ceridwen thought hazily. How did one awaken into death? And who would choose not to be awake when Death's messenger was so achingly beautiful?

She gazed up at him, taking him in piece by exquisite piece and putting him together into a dreamlike whole. She faintly remembered that she had stolen a green charm cursed with a faerie's death-sleep, stolen it from an ominous, black-cowled demon flanked by spectral hounds.

Or maybe not a demon. His charm had brought her to this new land of death, where her limbs felt heavy, but her thoughts and her heart were too light to hold; where a creature of unsurpassed comeliness beckoned to her with a gentle touch and the sweet, dark melody of his voice.

A sigh swelled in her chest. She would not have expected glittering black eyes from a faerie prince, yet his eyes were darker and brighter than a night full of the moon and stars, an onyx color to match the sleek, flowing length of hair that framed his face, streamed down his chest, and pooled on her breasts in a loose, silky confluence.

Ah, and his face. She lifted her hand and lightly traced the near perfect symmetry of his features. His was the kind of strange beauty no mortal man embodied and no mortal woman could resist. Truly, he was a magical being, for only magic could have created such an artful line from brow to chin—she caressed his cheek and let her fingers trail to the long, masculine curve of his jaw. Or create such a mouth as to make even a maid think of a kiss. Her fingertips brushed his lips.

He smiled, and she felt color suffuse her face. Amazing, that she could blush even in death. Clear as night, his eyes teased her, sparkling with an inner light like the stars sparkling around his head. Never had she seen such stars. The cosmic orbs danced both high and low in flaming shades of yellow, red, and blue, leaving trails of fire in their wakes. The sheer dazzle of him in his heavenly firmament left her breathless with awe.

"Sweet prince of the *tylwyth teg*," she whispered, thoroughly taken with him. Death had been the choice of wisdom, after all, and not the final act of a coward.

Dain's smile turned wry. Silly chit, to mistake him for something even half so pure and noble as a prince of the faerie folk. Though had he been elfin, he was sure he could have found salvation in the adoration shining in her eyes, for the old stories said elves lived in hope of gaining a human's love.

He had long since abandoned any such aspirations himself, but he knew he engendered lust with ease, and he saw that, too, in her eyes. Poor, untried virgin. He would do his best to return her untouched to her Mychael and spare her the more interesting pastimes available to those with adventurous natures.

"What's thy name, *chérie?*" he asked in his most mellifluous voice, honey sweetening his words to draw her out.

"Ceridwen," she whispered. "Ceridwen ab Arawn. And yours?"

He hesitated for only a moment. "Dain."

"Dain." She repeated his name on a soulful sigh, and Dain couldn't help himself; he grinned. Vivienne could take lessons from this one.

"Where is your Mychael, little one?"

"Strata Florida."

His grin faded. Just his luck. He'd been given the keeping of a Welsh maid with the name of a white monk rather than a rich lord on her lips. Then again, hadn't a prince of Powys, Rhys ap Gruffudd, granted the Cistercian monks large tracks of upland grazing all the way to Rhayader? Surely over the years even the most ascetic of orders had managed to accumulate some profit on such bounty.

But would they part with it for a woman?

He mulled over an answer to that for more than a minute and couldn't quite turn it to his liking. Women and holy men didn't mix nearly as well as they had before Gregory VII had cleansed the church of "fornicating priests."

"Dain." She spoke his name again in a dreamy voice, infusing it with a good deal of wonder, and wonder she might. What was he going to do with her?

"Is Mychael your uncle?" he asked, hoping for an abbot.

"Brother," she answered.

Worse and worse. The brother of one as young as she could hardly have had time to advance in the church—and yet there was the chemise. Someone coddled the girl.

"Wherever did Ragnor find you, *chérie?*" he asked, absently caressing her from her cheek to her ear and letting his fingers slide into the softness of her hair. He didn't really expect an answer to his question, and he certainly didn't expect the one she gave.

"On the Coit Wroneu." She sighed and turned her face into his hand. "Running for my veriest life."

His gaze narrowed, and his fingers stopped their aimless, sensual wanderings. "From whom?"

"Mine own cousin." Her tone became distressed and angry. She lifted her face to him. "The Thief of Cardiff, Morgan ab Kynan. May God curse his knave's soul for the hypocrisy of his sins." Her voice broke with a sob, and she closed her eyes to hold back a fresh round of tears.

Anyone with a heart or a care would not have bothered her further. Dain had neither, not when she'd spoken Morgan's name. Here was a story too rich to miss, of how a Welsh prince and thief of unsurpassed skill had lost this rare jewel, and even more intriguing, how much he'd be willing to pay to get her back.

"Aye, Morgan's a sinner." He commiserated with her, knowing his words were far from the truth. The only sin he could lay at his friend's door was that he'd never told Dain of his precious cousin, not that their meeting would have been more opportune under different circumstances. Dain had forsaken good opportunity with highborn virgins when he'd put down his sword and taken up more esoteric apparatuses.

"With no heart," she added, the tears running freely down her face.

"Aye, no heart, not a trace," he agreed, then added in an offhand tone, "What do you believe to be his most heartless deed?"

Her lips trembled, so sweetly it took an act of will not to lower his own to still their fluttering. "The deed that would leave me ground to dust between the Boar of Balor's jaws."

"Carado—"

Her eyes flashed open. "Shh," she admonished him, pressing her fingertips to his lips. "Don't speak his name. 'Tis said the sound alone is enough to call him forth."

Dain refrained from laughing aloud, even though he remembered many a morn when yelling at the top of his lungs had not been enough to call Caradoc forth from a night of drink. If the maid believed such was possible, she had heard rumors he had missed.

"Sweet Ceridwen, why would the Lord of Balor want to hurt you?" He couldn't bring himself to call his old friend "Boar."

"No bride of the Boar of Balor will survive her wedding night," she said in a hushed voice, her eyes growing even larger, if that were possible.

Dain felt his lips twitch with the makings of a grin. "Mayhaps 'tis the alliteration they cannot abide, *chérie*."

"Mayhaps," she agreed somberly.

Then it hit him, the significance of what she'd said.

"Morgan takes you to Balor as a bride?"

"Aye."

Ragnor would be dead within the month and Morgan probably soon to follow, Dain thought, after Caradoc stripped the flesh from Ragnor's bones and staked him out in the wilderness to die. One did not abuse the betrothed bride of a powerful lord without penance being paid. One did not lose a bride either—and for certes one did not go around plying rose oil between her legs.

The thought gave him pause, and he was taken with an urge to check her again, to make sure he'd done no damage.

"But no longer," she said, her hand trailing down the front of his tunic. A beatific smile played about her mouth. "Now I have died and come unto you."

Before he could assure her that she had not, he felt her fingers tangle in his hair and exert gentle pressure, pulling him down.

"A kiss of peace, sweet prince?" she asked. "To welcome me into paradise?"

She was not very strong, yet somehow was strong enough to have her way, drawing him ever closer. Her gold-tipped lashes drifted down, giving him a moment to reflect on the doubtful wisdom of his next action—but a moment wasn't nearly long enough to stop him.

Their lips met, hers sweetly, innocently closed, expecting the blessing of a saint. He couldn't have delivered that even if he were nobly pure of heart, for when his mouth touched hers, instinct usurped his reason.

Warmth was his first sensation, then softness, then something more. For all she gave, Edmee did not kiss, and there was much he'd forgotten—much he'd missed. He parted his mouth to trace the curve of Ceridwen's lips with his tongue, and was rewarded with a sigh.

The resonance of that sound set up a vibration very near where his heart had once been. Their breaths mingled and became the same, flowing from one life to the next. The luxuriance of the ether filled his senses and went straight to his head, finer than wine, more potent than his deadliest draught. She tasted like a woman, every woman, all women, a rich mélange of flavors he couldn't begin to absorb. They ran through him, rousing a wildness he had long thought broken to his will.

With that realization, he dragged his mouth away from hers, his blood racing faster than he would have admitted to anyone. In contrast, the woman below him was the picture of peace, drifting off to sleep with a smile on her face, blissfully unaware of the havoc she had created in less than a minute, with less than conscious effort.

Dain knew he was a charlatan. He also knew when he was in the presence of someone else who wasn't what he or she seemed, though in the maid's case, he couldn't put a name to what he'd felt in her kiss.

He reached out to touch her, but caught himself and drew his hand back. Her hair had dried into a cloud of haphazard curls and was spread out around her like the light of God, a halo of illumination surrounding her small, bruised face. Farther down, the remains of a thick, damp braid lay in disarray beneath one of her arms. She needed someone to tend to her, but he had done all he dared—mayhaps more than he should have dared. Nothing remained but for him to find Morgan and arrange for her return.

A smile twisted his mouth and a soft curse escaped him. She was to be the bride of Caradoc, and through the grace of God and Dain's own rough magic, nothing had transpired that would keep her from fulfilling those vows.

Chapter 4

Ceridwen heard bells ringing in the distance, ringing prime, the hour of prayer at dawn. So much time seemed to have slipped away from her, 'twas good to recognize a singular moment. She'd been drifting here and there in her memories, hither and yon in her mind to strange places she'd never seen before.

Despite her myriad pains, the soft lapping of a warm tongue on her fingers brought a faint smile to her lips. She lifted her hand and felt a dog's muzzle.

"Good Jack," she whispered, thinking of her father's old lymer, though it seemed a very long time since she'd seen the dog or her father, or home—Carn Merioneth.

With a lazy effort, she turned her head, and a scream froze in her throat. 'Twas no lymer at her side, but one of the spectral hounds, the white one.

"Awake ye are, finally," a raspy voice said close to her other side.

She jerked her head around, a mistake with instant repercussions. A searing bolt of pain made the room swim and grow hazy. She squeezed her eyes shut and fought the dizzying blackness that threatened to claim her once more.

"Yer s'posed to drink the bard-boy's potion, ye are." A warm cup was pressed to her lips.

The hound was real, not part of the wild, wondrous dreams she'd had of a dark-eyed prince of the *tylwyth teg,* and if the hound was real, so was the black-cowled demon.

She forced her lashes to lift, giving her a glimpse of the man next to her. It was not he. Relief dissipated a measure of her fear, but none of her pain. Her head throbbed and so did her bones; her body ached, feeling tight and bruised.

"Drink," the old man ordered, lifting the cup and dribbling wine into her mouth. "Dain'll skin me arse and feed it to the bitch, if ye don't."

She swallowed the sweet wine, more to keep from choking than to save the graybeard's backside.

"Ye'll notice I hain't laid a finger on ye. Not one. I'm touchin' the demned cup and not so much as one of yer fine white hairs." His voice trailed off into unintelligible mutterings of which she heard only the words "soft," and "pretty," and "what's it to 'im."

A low growl rumbled out of the hound on her left, and a wave of terror washed through her body. She did choke then, and spluttered, and near fainted when the dog lunged across her—but it was to the old man the dog went, with her head twisted down and her albino jaws closing around his throat.

"Call 'er off! Call 'er off!" he croaked, frantic.

Ceridwen watched in horrified fascination as the dog's sharp white teeth slipped through the old man's papery skin. All she could think was, *Aye, this is a trick the dog knows well.*

A gurgling sound from the man startled her into speech.

"Hound" was the only word she knew to use and "come."

Her voice, weak and scratchy, barely carried the necessary distance, but it was enough to gain the dog's attention. Pale blue eyes turned on her.

"Come," she repeated, and gestured with her hand.

The dog, a levrier, sleek and lean and powerfully built, complied, releasing the old man into a heap on the floor and returning to Ceridwen's side.

The graybeard coughed, dragging up spittle he wiped on his sleeve. He touched his throat, and his fingers came away smeared with blood. Ceridwen expected him to leave, but he reached instead for a shallow pan on the brazier and refilled the cup he'd spilled.

"The jongleur'll owe me for this." He pressed the cup back to her mouth and leveled a beady gaze on the dog. "Watch yerself, Numa, or one night ye'll find yerself skewered and hangin' o'er the flames of hell."

Numa, Ceridwen thought, wondering at the strangeness of the name. She'd heard another odd name in this place. Dain, that's what the sweet prince had called himself. Dain.

A smile flitted across her mouth. In her dream, he'd kissed her.

"Drink," the graybeard said, tipping the cup higher and pouring a few drops past her lips. "I'll not have ye dyin' on me watch."

Death had been in her dream too, but 'twas clear now she hadn't died, and if she hadn't died, she was still betrothed to the Boar of Balor. Despair found a foothold in the thought. She would be going home, but Carn Merioneth was no more. The wooden palisades of that fair place had long since been razed in fire and replaced with the stone blocks of Balor. The flames still burned in her nightmares, reaching past the skies to the heavens and the vengeful God who had unleashed Gwrnach, Caradoc's father, upon them.

Those who had escaped the flames had been butchered in the bailey, ending the beautiful dream that had been Carn Merioneth. All had died except for the two who had been lost, she and her dear sweet brother, Mychael, and the one who had found them. Moriath had been the name of the maid, and she had disappeared years ago. Except for the letters Ceridwen treasured as life itself, Mychael had also been lost to her, from the day Moriath had put him in the monastery at Strata Florida.

She swallowed the wine the old man had given her and pushed his hand away. "No more."

"All of it."

She shook her head and lifted her other hand to ward him off. She was more successful than she'd hoped. He jumped back out of reach.

"Be careful with that demned thing," he hollered, then swore a jumble of curses.

With a sense of bemused wonder, she became aware of the serpent stone still clasped in her hand. Its green depths caught the first rays of morning sunshine streaming in through the windows and reflected it back, casting prisms of light against the striped damask draped at the corners of the huge bed in which she lay.

Brochan's Great Charm. She opened her fingers and let it float in her palm, as real as day. And if the stone was real, why not the place it had taken her, the sweet oblivion of a faerie's death-sleep?

She lowered her lashes and closed her hand around the stone, drawing it to her breast. Aye, better to try the faerie death again than to find herself in Caradoc's cruel grasp. He wanted her at his mercy, not her hand in marriage. She'd read it, read it in a book that held the key to the Boar's dark, impossible desires. Only Mychael could save her. Mychael, sweet saint, was unassailable by evil. Mayhaps if she'd shown more religious fervor, she, too, would have been beyond Caradoc's reach.

She had not, however, and God had forsaken her, set her adrift in the strange world of men with little to help her find her way.

A wave of languor washed through her, muddling her thoughts. She wanted sleep, and that was where her heart led her, back to the heavenly lair of Dain, the dark-eyed prince of the Light-elves. Letting out a soft breath, she gave herself up to the welcome heaviness seeping into her limbs and showing her the way to the stars.

Erlend held the half-full cup and clucked in disapproval. She hadn't finished the draught. 'Tweren't his fault, not a bit of it, but he'd be demned if there was anyone else to step for'ard and take the demn blame.

The misty light of dawn filtered through an ancient grove of oak and hazel in the Wroneu Wood, capturing the form of a young man running through the trees. Morgan ab Kynan watched the sentry from the open flap of the tent where he'd gotten barely two hours of sleep. He could tell by the irritated expression on Rhys's face that Dain had been sighted, no doubt already breaking the boundaries of the camp with his levrier hounds running alongside.

"Lavrans?" he called out, grimacing as he pulled on his boots. His jaw tightened against the old pain in his right leg.

"Aye. Below the falls," the young man said, coming to a stop in front of the tent, breathless from his sprint up the mountainside.

"I asked to know of his coming before he reached the river."

The sentry fought to hide a grim smile. "Ye know as well as me that e'en in broad daylight he's like a shadow in the night."

Morgan nodded. "And Ceridwen?" He reached for the wine-skin he'd hung on the carved and tasseled tent pole and took a mouthful. He rinsed and spat the wine out onto the ground.

"No sign beyond the ravine. She's still on this side, and we'll find her. Dafydd is scouting west of the camp." Rhys used his sleeve to wipe the sweat from his brow. A shock of brown hair fell back over his forehead. "I've never seen a maid so skittish about marriage."

Morgan's mouth tightened. "You haven't met Caradoc." He cinched his belt around his waist and reached for his bow.

"Then why do you take her to him?"

The sentry's eyes revealed a disapproval he didn't dare voice. It was a problem Morgan remembered well from his youth, the penchant to fall in love easily and usually where one shouldn't. He understood Rhys's attraction. Ceridwen ab Arawn was reasonably fair of face and had all her teeth. It took little more to get a boy's blood running, yet Ceridwen had more—a sweet smile when she chose to use it, which wasn't often, and a voice like cool water running through a forest glade. She also hadn't used her voice often in the past sennight, except to accuse or plead.

Her pleading was not his problem this morning, finding her was, the troublesome wench. He and his band of five men had combed the hills the whole night long, but neither luck nor skill had been enough to bring her safely back to camp.

"She goes to Caradoc," Morgan said in answer to Rhys, "because the most powerful prince in all of North Wales wills it, so she can bear her sons on the land of her ancestors. 'Tis the same reason Caradoc wants her, to be doubly bound by blood to the land he's won."

"Won by treachery and betrayal, and God knows what else." Rhys shuddered. "Some say 'twas his own blade that hewed Gwrnach from gullet to cock."

"Some say," Morgan agreed. He'd heard the tales, and he

knew the hatred Caradoc had nursed for his father, but he also knew how the smallest twist of the blade and the merest shift of intent could turn a killing into a mutilation. Two thousand seven hundred Moslems had been slain by the Lionheart's Crusaders at Acre. Decapitation had been the order, but by the end of it, they'd all been hacking away at the hostages, slogging through blood and gore up to their knees. How many had he killed and how many mutilated? He would never know. Death was death, and by the sword 'twas never pretty.

He slipped his quiver over his shoulder and took off with long strides toward where the horses were tied.

Rhys followed alongside, his boy's jaw jutting out. "Methinks she would have been happier remaining with the nuns at Usk."

If Rhys would rather protect her than bed her, Morgan thought, there was hope for him yet, for it was always the bedding that caused young men to completely lose their senses.

"Have Rhodri and Drew cross the river, and send Owain to me," Morgan ordered, ignoring Rhys's summation of the situation. The boy was a good tracker, and with time he would become even better, but his feelings for the maid had clouded his judgment. Ceridwen was no nun, not yet. "She heads for Mychael and Strata Florida."

"Why?" the young sentry asked, surprised. "The monks won't take her, even if her brother is one of their order."

"She doesn't go for sanctuary, but to rouse Mychael out of his monkish ways, to put a sword in his hand."

"She thinks Mychael will fight for Balor?" Rhys's tone implied a hefty share of doubt.

Morgan shared those doubts. He'd known Ceridwen's brother since his birth, and Mychael was more likely to be sainted than knighted. The boy had taken to the monkish life with a fervor. "When her father had it," he answered, " 'twas called Carn Merioneth, and if Ceridwen could win it back, Mychael would no doubt let her have the castle and no lord a'tall, or mayhaps the lord of her choice."

"And has she chosen?" A betraying amount of hope crept into the young voice.

Morgan stopped short of his destination and flashed the sentry a reproving grin. "She asked me, cub, but I don't think her heart was in it."

Accusation glared from Rhys's eyes. "Then why did she run?"

Another knowing grin spread across Morgan's face. "I told her I had more to offer a woman than my sword arm. Should she but care to notice and make me an offer with more . . . um, heat in it, she might gain what she hoped."

Rhys, no stranger to the bawdy inclinations of camp life, was plainly shocked by his lord's brazen overture.

"You could have wed Ceridwen ab Arawn, the most beautiful, sweet, and kindly maid in all of Christendom, and you offend her with lewd and—" He stopped abruptly, his gaze shifting to a place beyond Morgan's right shoulder. A bright flush coursed over his cheeks. "I'll give Owain and Drew your orders," he said curtly, and turned on his heel, striding back to the camp.

"You are a hopeless romantic," a distinctive voice—one capable of mangling both French and Welsh with equal ease—said from behind him.

"And you are a hopeless cynic," Morgan said, slowly turning to face his friend.

"Du kommer sent." Dain pushed off the oak tree where he'd been waiting and listening. "You're late. I expected you before St. Winnal."

The Welshman winced. "Every time you speak a saint's name, I expect a bolt of lightning to strike nearby."

Dain laughed. "Lightning, Morgan? At dawn? For a mere heretic?"

"You're more than a heretic. You're pagan. Maybe worse."

"An infidel?"

"Easily, by anyone's definition, Christian or Moslem." A reluctant smile curved his mouth.

The dark-robed Dane stepped out of the shadows into a shaft of sunlight, striding into the clearing with a natural elegance that some mistook for softness—until they'd seen the grace and power of it behind a blade. Morgan had seen it as such, more times than he cared to recall.

"The forest is alive early this morn, mostly with your men," Dain said, offering the wineskin he carried. A horse, fifteen hands of dappled white and gray, stood quietly in the trees behind him. "Mayhaps my wine will be more to your liking."

Morgan accepted the skin. "None of them sighted you," he said. "It's a wonder our throats aren't slit in our sleep. Where are the hounds?"

"Numa guards my chambers, and Elixir guards the Druid Door and the tower stairs."

"Stolen yourself a rich prize, have you?" Morgan asked, part of his humor returning. His sentries had missed only Dain and his horse, not Dain, his horse, and two dogs. It was small comfort, but still comfort. The horse, he noted, had not moved, yet even now seemed to be disappearing in the shifting shadows of the forest.

"A rich prize? Mayhaps." Dain gestured at the tasseled tent. "And what of you? Welsh war bands seldom travel in Saladin's style."

Morgan ignored the reference to the desert king, the past being better forgotten, especially when the present was in such a tangle.

"The tent was a gift from Llywelyn, Prince of Gwynedd, to another, a maid I was asked to fetch, a will-o'-the-wisp who escapes me with damning regularity."

"Have your charms worn so thin?" Dain lifted one rose-red tassel and turned it into the light.

"No thinner than yours, I trow." Morgan cocked a teasing eyebrow. "How is the dear Edmee?"

"Thorough." The word sat in the air with a thousand implications while fingers skilled in the arts of enchantment sifted through the silken cords, then let them fall back against the tent. "And your maid?"

The Welshman guffawed. "Not so thorough and not even mine, despite her wishes. She goes north."

"So she told me." Dain watched as Morgan's eyes widened almost imperceptibly before he controlled his surprise. Of the three of them, only Morgan had returned from the Holy Land with so much as a trace of innocence intact, but then, only Morgan—by far the youngest of the three—had taken much innocence with him.

"You have Ceridwen ab Arawn in your tower?"

"Aye. She was there all night."

More than one maid had been seduced by Morgan's guileless manner and fair face, and his eyes as blue as a summer sky. Dain wasn't surprised that Ceridwen was yet another, but he was annoyed. However had she kept her maidenhead intact when it seemed she propositioned every man she met? Strange woman.

"Then I'm a dead man." Morgan slapped a hand over his face, and a swath of dark hair fell across his brow. Just as suddenly, he jerked his head back up. "And you . . . no." He paused, changing his mind. "Caradoc wouldn't kill you, not over a woman."

"Not even a betrothed bride?"

"Jesu, Dain," Morgan swore. "She told you and you still debauched her? Have you no honor left at all?"

The answer to that was so obvious as to make a reply redundant, yet Dain did reply.

"I make my way in the world. Nothing more."

"It's been four years since we left Jaffa, seven since Acre. Can't you forget?"

"Can you?"

Morgan held his gaze, then swore again and took a long swallow of the wine.

"It matters not," he said, handing the skin to Dain. "I still want her back."

"And I am here to bargain"—Dain smiled—"for the return of a virgin."

After a moment of dumbstruck silence, Morgan returned the smile and called him something foul. "I should have known an unskilled maid would not rouse your interest."

"Had not so much to do with her lack of skill as her lack of consciousness."

The smile disappeared in a heartbeat. "She was hurt?"

"Insensate. One of D'Arbois's knights, Ragnor, caught her on the track and brought her to Wydehaw. He was not gentle."

"Then he's the dead man in this. Owain!" Morgan turned and called out to his captain. A large, rough-looking man answered, rising immediately from his place by the fire. "Mount up the men. We go to Wydehaw."

"Wait." Dain put a restraining hand on his friend's arm. "Come alone. We'll talk after you've seen her."

Wariness in his blue eyes, Morgan hesitated before he spoke. "You ask a lot, dear friend, for a Welsh prince, even a poor one, to enter a Marcher castle without his men at his back."

"If 'tis necessary, I'll be at your back," Dain promised. "But I rather doubt anyone will know you're there, unless you make your way into the great hall and announce yourself at supper."

"What's this then, conjurer?" An imp's grin returned to Morgan's face. "Do you spirit us inside your tower with the wave of a rowan wand?"

"If I could but find the right switch, I would," Dain said, one eyebrow arched in emphasis to the sincerity of his wish.

Morgan lifted his hand to make a warding sign, then he caught himself and gave Dain a shamefaced smile.

"Sometimes you frighten me, Lavrans. I wonder that you do not frighten yourself with all your dabbling and inquiry into things better left alone," Morgan said, though he could no sooner judge what his friend had become than what his friend had once been. If not for Dain's protection, he would have been as lost to God as his friend, his faith stripped from him by the mortal transgressions and dark arts of the Saracen.

"Tell your men to keep camp," was all Dain said. "You'll be here at least until the morrow. And don't worry, Morgan. The way into the tower isn't by the casting of spells, though you may wish it were before we're there."

"What's this, then?"

"I've found another entrance through the lower chamber."

Morgan grimaced. "That's a rank place."

" 'Tis the sulfurs I use for the alchemy."

"Very rank sulfurs," Morgan grumbled, though he smiled in forgiveness. 'Twas what he always gave Dain, forgiveness, for deep in his heart he feared God never would—and deeper still, in a place he hardly dared to look himself, he feared he was to blame for the darkest of all the acts Dain had committed in the name of survival, those that had allowed the Saracen to reach deep into Dain's core and change him from the stoic warrior he had been into the dangerously sly and clever mage he had become.

No, he could not judge. He could only forgive and be grateful he hadn't seen the half of what had transpired 'tween Dain and Jalal al-Kamam, for the half he had seen haunted his nights.

*   *   *

"Christ's blood."

"Don't touch her," Dain warned, and Morgan curled his fingers away from Ceridwen's face into a fist.

She lay on Dain's bed, nestled into the pillows and quilts, the sunlight streaming down upon her slight form through the glazed window. Edmee's gentle touch was apparent in the tidy braid she'd fashioned out of the maid's thick mass of curls. Even so, separate strands floated cloudlike around the small face.

"Where is the butcher who dies for this?"

" 'Tis not as bad as it looks, Morgan. She will be scarred, but most of what you see is physick, not blood. The bruises will fade." Dain moved aside the neck of the clean chemise Edmee had put her in and checked the stitching on her shoulder. He sensed Morgan's stance grow even more rigid as the ragged bite came into view. "This, too, will look better with time," he said. His finger lightly traced the double crescent incised on the pale curve of skin. She was well and truly marked. The bite wound would heal, but would never be discreet. He dipped a cloth into a bowl of warm water.

"And the rest?" Morgan asked.

"You can assure her lord that with luck she will not be lame."

A low, guttural curse came from the man. "The Prince of Gwynedd may be appeased with so little, but I must take more than luck and assurances to Caradoc."

"More?"

"Ragnor." The name was spoken without mercy.

Would ease the maid's life too, if the beast was taken away, but Dain doubted D'Arbois would relinquish the knight. Other methods would have to be employed.

"You are not called the Thief of Cardiff for naught, Morgan. Steal him if you want him." Taking care not to awaken the maid, he drew the damp cloth across her shoulder, cleaning away the previous night's dressing. A mouth, especially one as rotten as Ragnor's, was more likely to leave a festering wound than a dagger. When the bite proved free from infection, he turned to the finer cut framing the side of her face.

A shout arose from outside, the noise accompanied by the sound of many horses.

"Better Ragnor's head than mine," Morgan said, stepping back to the window's embrasure to stare down into the bailey.

"Are you sure it needs be someone's head?"

"With Caradoc, nothing less than blood will suffice, the more the better." Angry curses and the crack of a whip mixed with the sound of a horse's scream.

"Then what I've heard from the north is true?"

"Most, if not all." Morgan gestured to the window. "Who arrives with such a clatter?"

" 'Tis your man, Ragnor." Dain didn't need to see the knight to recognize his voice or his typical homecoming. He returned his attention to the maid. In the light of day, his stitchery looked good, a fine tracery of thread down the side of her face. 'Twould be a shame to have it all ground to dust between the Boar of Balor's jaws, if such a thing were possible. "Tales have been told of Balor," he said, "of strange happenings and harsh dealings reminiscent of Gwrnach."

"Caradoc is a hard man," Morgan admitted. "Mayhaps he's grown a little wild, but he is no worse than any other."

"I heard the castle wall was a gift from the captain of Llywelyn's war band."

Morgan chuckled. "I was there the night Llywelyn's *penteulu* lost his fortune in Balor's pit, wagering on a boar. Aye, more than one has said Caradoc built his keep with pig's blood."

The ruckus outside caused the maid to stir, the barest fluttering of her lashes betraying her rise from the depths of a drugged sleep. Dain dipped his finger in a cup of weakly opiated wine and wet her lips. He was not ready for her to awaken, not with Morgan there. When her tongue licked, he lingered, letting her take the draught from his fingertip, even as he both studied and fought his desire to do the same.

"Caradoc won't thank you if you deliver him an opium-eater for a bride, Dain." The words were spoken softly with a concern that went beyond the woman.

"I am judicious," Dain said, but stopped and passed his hand down over her eyes, willing her to sleep awhile longer. 'Twas not much as magic went, but he'd never been one to underestimate the power of a sincere thought, especially when accompanied by the appropriate simple. He lowered his hand and found her lashes to have done the same. Sometimes it seemed he had a knack for such things.

"Will Ragnor hunt again on the morrow?" Morgan asked, returning his attention to the bailey.

"Aye," he said just as Ceridwen spoke his name on a sigh. Maybe not such a knack after all, he thought, touching her mouth with a thought for silence.

"What?" Morgan asked.

Ceridwen smiled beneath his caress, and Dain cleared his throat.

"Aye," he said louder, standing up and drawing the bed curtain behind him. He would see to the maid after Morgan left. " 'Tis boar he's after, and he will not rest until he slays one."

"What of his lord?"

"D'Arbois hunts tamer game."

Morgan laughed softly, keeping his attention on the man outside. "I have never thought of you as tame, Lavrans."

"Neither should he. Come." He gestured toward the worktable, where food had been set out: ale, bread, cheese, stewed fruit, and a sweet cream pudding. "Let us eat and bargain."

In the end 'twas decided to leave the maid at Wydehaw, in the Hart Tower. She was too broken to take a journey over the mountains, too nubile to be given to D'Arbois's care, and too precious by the ancestry of her blood for Caradoc to complain overly much about her health taking precedence over his immediate needs and desires to have her at Balor Keep. The Boar of Balor could have his bride at Beltaine.

Morgan laughed at that. "She has escaped me three times in less than a sennight, and you think you can hold her for a month? Could be your best trick yet."

" 'Tis not much of a trick when Numa doesn't let the maid out of her sight." Dain leaned forward and finished off the last bite of pudding with his silver spoon. "Now, have you got the list?"

"I'm not likely to forget it. Almonds, rice, saffron, spices and grains of paradise, oranges—you'll never get those, not out of a Welshman—violet sugar, for Christ's sake, and a hundred marks. It's more than Caradoc would have spent on her in a year, two, even three! And I doubt if he'd know a strand of saffron from a sheep's buttocks!"

Dain arched his eyebrow and fought a smirk as he licked his spoon.

Morgan was scandalized. "If you heard that, you heard a lie."

"I've heard worse."

"Worse!" Morgan exclaimed, as if it were impossible for anything to be worse than swiving sheep.

"Just give him my greetings, explain to him the importance of rich food to restore her health, and convince him the money is well spent for a bride of such great beauty and grace . . . and virginity." A slow grin spread across Dain's face.

Morgan scraped his chair back from the table, muttering, "Don't tell me any more. If I don't know, he can't get it out of me, and then he won't have to kill you for 'dabbling' where no man should dabble lest he be wed. What of D'Arbois? What will you tell him?"

"I'll gut a chicken before he sups and divine the importance of the maid." Still grinning, he stood up to see his guest out. "Can you find your way back through the siege tunnel?"

"Aye, and I'll meet you in the copse at the other end at dusk with her belongings, not that there's much. The only dowry she brings is her lineage." The Welshman hesitated for a moment, his gaze catching Dain's. "She had a book, a red book, some pages half written in, some pages not written in at all, and some written in no language I ever saw. Strange as it is, it could be the most valuable thing she owns. I'd hate for her to have lost it."

"Rest easy, Morgan," he said, turning toward his shelves. "The book was on the maid when she washed ashore. Here it is." He reached up and pulled down the red leather-bound volume.

"Aye, that's the one. No, I don't have to see it," he said when Dain offered him the tome. " 'Twas eerie enough at the first thumbing through. I'll not need another."

"Magic again?" Dain asked with a teasing grin.

"Mayhaps," Morgan answered. "Or mayhaps it's something else. I'd not have the book, but Ceridwen pored over it every night, and for her sake, I'm glad she'll not have to do without it."

Dain put the red book back on the shelf, more intrigued than ever. If Morgan feared to tread its pages, the chit's missive must be rare indeed.

Chapter 5

Dain stood in front of the tower room's hearth, holding the bundle Morgan had given him that evening. His friend had been right. There was not much.

He moved closer to the fire, running his thumb over the tiny braids of leather tying Ceridwen's clothes and personal items together. Snow melted in the dark folds of his hooded cloak and dripped onto the hearth to hiss and steam. Winter was upon them again, lingering past its time. The soft, frozen flakes had begun to float down while he'd waited for the Welsh prince and his men in the small wood surrounding the tunnel entrance. More of a thicket it was than a wood, necessitating an approach by foot, but the forest took up again near the rivers, making a safe place to conceal a horse.

The Cypriot had waited there for him all day, with a patience no destrier could claim. Dain had left the mare that morn, when he and Morgan had made their first trip through the tunnel. As he'd expected, Morgan had not been able to find her when he'd gone back through alone, and he'd looked for her, long and hard. Nothing would do, the Welshman had said, except for Dain to give him a foal capable of disappearing in the wink of an eye.

Dain smiled. 'Twould take more than the Cypriot's blood to enable another horse to fade into the mists. A curse echoing up from below stairs broadened his smile. He'd banished Erlend to the alchemy chamber again, and the old man was not happy about spending another night amongst the crucibles, flasks, and vials, and what he called the "demned smelly" scorifying pans.

Shivering, Dain tossed an extra fagot on the fire with a liberality few others in Wydehaw could afford. The flames crackled with new life. Rare it was that he missed the heat of the desert, but those years had weakened his resistance to the cold and exposed him to certain comforts and luxuries he enjoyed more than was good for him.

But if to be accused of decadence was the price of his pleasure this eventide, he was prepared to pay. He'd sent for Edmee and had Erlend heating water on all the hearths for a bath.

He reached for the clasp on his shoulder to remove his damp cloak—and stopped, warned by the frisson of energy sliding down his spine.

Instincts honed by a thousand nights of captivity stilled his body and slowed his breath. Numa lay on the bed with her head poking out from between an opening in the curtains, a low sound rumbling up from her chest. 'Twouldn't be Erlend setting her off, he thought, though he had been surprised at the marks on the old man's throat. Fortunately, the dog hadn't bitten as deeply as was her wont.

He looked to the Druid Door, but heard no footsteps, felt no skulking presence sneaking up the tower stairs. Next, he glanced over his shoulder at the hatch in the floor, then at the door leading to the eyrie. Nothing disturbed either opening. There was only Elixir sitting by the hearth, staring at him with a near innocent expression on his black-as-the-hounds-of-hell face.

The look, so at odds with the animal's usual aloofness, aroused Dain's suspicions. He slowly turned back to face Numa and had his wildest conjecture confirmed: The bitch was growling at him.

"*Kom.*" His command was harsh, demanding. The situation with the maid had gotten completely out of hand.

Looking thoroughly chastised, the albino began to slink off the bed. Another voice coming from deep within the quilts and coverlets stopped her.

"Numa, stay."

And the bitch did.

Anarchy was a novelty within the curved walls of the Hart Tower. As a diversion, it was not welcome.

Dain set the bundle on the table and walked toward the bed, tilting his head to see past the partially drawn curtains. He didn't call the dog again. The battle lines being drawn were beyond her ken.

Ceridwen clutched the sheets and quilts to her chest, her fingers digging into the thick sable fur lining the topmost coverlet. Fear pounded through her heart on every breath, telling her to flee, but flight was no option. Her head ached to near blindness, and her senses were not sharp. Her ankle was broken and weighted down with splint and bandages too heavy to lift.

She had no choice but to face the demon. She had naught but her wits and Numa to save her.

Damn the dog for drawing his attention.

"She eats the throats of men who come too near," she warned, and was dismayed by the tremulousness of the words. She needed better from herself to save this day, but like flight, better appeared out of her reach.

"In the manner her master taught her," the shrouded figure replied, and continued his soundless approach. Backlit by the flames from the fire, he cast his shadow across the end of the bed.

Ceridwen strained her eyes to follow his movements through the slitted opening of the curtains. "Numa has a mistress now," she said, willing strength into a voice that in sad truth still had none.

The figure disappeared at the corner of the bed, melting behind the lengths of cloth swagged from the canopy posts, and her heart began to race. Seconds slowed into small eternities, flowing from one to the next with painful silence. He was out there, she knew it, stalking her with evil intent, but she couldn't detect his position—until the curtains at the side of the bed were swept open.

"And now the mistress also has a master," he said, looming over her, darkness and death personified. A cry strangled in her throat. "Take care, *chérie,* and do not put your trust where in the end it must be betrayed. The bitch is mine." The voice came from deep within the cowl, frightful in its conviction, yet also faintly—surprisingly—familiar, reminiscent of a pleasanter interlude, of gentleness.

Gentleness? From such as he? Had her instincts, always so true in the past, verily her greatest strength, also deserted her in her hour of need? Confused by the fleeting sensation, she dropped her gaze from the dreadful, featureless chasm of the hood and looked instead at the clasp on his shoulder that held his cloak. 'Twas large and rich in gold, a noble piece.

Candlelight danced across it, bringing garnets and amber to warm, pulsing life and licking through the intricate knots of a dragon's tail. No invincible specter this, no all-powerful demon, she thought, for beneath the cloak he wore a gambeson of thick boiled bullhide, dyed green. The color ran darker around the iron studs that fanned out across his chest in a series of arcane symbols, proving him in need of much protection, both in heavy leather and charms.

She gave him a discreet, measuring look, wondering what manner of man she now dealt with for her life. He was tall, though not nearly as tall as the devil-beast from the forest. More to the point, he hadn't struck her dead, which meant he must have use of her.

Aye. She lowered her lashes, giving in to a fresh round of pain in her head. That was always the way of it, a man had use of a woman whether she had a use for him or not. She took a deep breath and tried to let it out carefully. A ragged sigh was what she got for her trouble, and a throbbing ache she felt clear through her brain.

What a God-cursed sennight it had been since Llywelyn's summons. She had thought herself long forgotten, which she would have preferred over being remembered by one such as Caradoc. Twice she'd slipped through Morgan's guard, only to be caught. The third attempt at freedom had been her undoing, leaving her physically wrecked, helpless in the hands of the dark-cloaked man who had saved her for ends of which she knew naught.

Eyes closed, she bent her head down and made the best of a shallow breath. She felt so many different agonies, none of them too much to bear alone, but the sheer number of wounds she'd suffered overwhelmed her. The pain would be the death of her. She needed weapons and the spirit to wield them, not weakness.

A hand touched her face, light and strangely soothing, surprising her by proving her memory of gentleness.

"Do you need more of the poppy?"

"Nay," she whispered, suddenly disconsolate. Kindness from an enemy was a sure sign of his impending victory. "I have taken too much as it is. I cannot think when—"

"Shh." He stopped her with the soft sound and stroked a single tear off her cheek. " 'Tis no sin, *cariad,* to ease your pain. I will make a weak draught."

He didn't know, she thought as he walked back across the chamber. What she wished was a sin, to give up the fight, to be returned not to Usk, but to the Otherworld she'd glimpsed through the stone. Another man awaited her there, a man of dark, brilliant light, a man who would keep her forever free. She had been a prisoner for too long, fifteen years in a nunnery and seven days in the world of mortal men. It seemed a woman could not escape the politics and prophesy of a profane marriage with any more ease than a child could escape convent walls.

She looked up, watching her captor, and wondered if he could send her to the heavens again; and if he could, did she dare go?

He stopped between the table and the hearth, and in a single sweeping motion removed his cloak. He had a way about him of moving, so fluid. She remembered how he'd made the serpent stone appear in his fingers. She'd seen others with the skill, but none as fine as his. He dropped the cloak onto a carved oak chair and turned to a row of shelves. For less than the space of a heartbeat his face was revealed by the firelight, and her breath caught in her throat.

'Twas Dain, sweet prince of the *tylwyth teg.*

His hair was not black, as she'd thought, but a deep chestnut-brown and even silkier than it had looked in the night, a long mane swept off his forehead and falling to the middle of his back. The line from his brow to his chin was long and angular, but still artful enough to rival a more conventional beauty. And his mouth, it was as she remembered, full in the lower lip and expressive in the upper, with a mocking sensuality hovering in the deep crease bracketing one side.

He glanced over and caught her staring. Brown his eyes were, and bright with intensity, his eyebrows angling up like unfurled wings. One arched in a knowing gesture, and a hundred realizations washed through her, leaving her with nothing but humiliation and regrets.

" 'Twas you all along." She didn't even attempt to keep the dismay out of her voice, and she couldn't hold back the tears welling in her eyes. There was no help for them when life grew bleaker at every turn.

"*Ja,* it was I," he admitted, slipping deeper into the strange melody of speech she now remembered clearly. He was not Welsh, nor Norman, but neither was he what she had dreamed.

"There was no prince of paradise." A tear spilled over, and she wiped at her cheek with the back of her hand. An intolerable weariness took the last of her strength. She had told him everything, of Morgan and the Boar, of Mychael, her one hope, and God only knew what else. 'Twas all too much, so much failure at once.

Dain watched as she looked down at the bed, searching for something and coming up with his serpent stone.

"And this?" she asked, her voice taking on a nervous edge he didn't think boded well for either of them. "Brochan's Great Charm?"

"Italian glass."

He could have lied, but he didn't, and he wasn't sure why. Like the recent bout of anarchy and insurrection, he hoped the thoughtless telling of truth wasn't the way of things to come.

She made a small sound of distress at his answer.

Mayhaps a tonic of betony and vervain would suit her better, he mused. She was becoming overwrought, something he had hoped to avoid for her sake, but the condition was predictable. She had been beaten and tortured, captured, chained, and had awakened in a strange place with only him for company. Stronger hearts than hers would have trembled at the thought.

"The kiss?" she asked.

Ah, she would have done better not to have asked him of kisses, but the maid obviously did not know when to leave something alone.

"Real enough," he said, telling the truth when again a lie would have served them both better.

A much larger sound of distress reached him upon that announcement. She slipped down into the pillows, crying—nay, sobbing—about being doomed to be cheated and ruled by men and kissed by demons, lumping him together, by name no less, with Ragnor and the Boar of Balor Keep. Normally he wouldn't have thought anything of such a misassociation, especially when made by one so naive, but his more refined sensibilities insisted on taking offense.

"Ragnor is far too much of an idiot to make a worthy demon," he said, pitching his voice to carry above the sound of her weeping, "and what he did to you was not kissing. As for Caradoc, as I recall, he knows his way around a maid well enough to make any contact a pleasant one." Betony and vervain, and honey for taste, he told himself, taking the jars off the shelf. She was beside herself with nervous affliction.

"What of you?" Though still full of tears, her tone took on a sudden intensity.

Him? He stopped halfway to the table and turned his gaze upon her. What of him? She had a rare talent for surprising him, he knew that much.

"More than bright enough to be a demon," he said, hoping to God she wasn't asking him about knowing his way around a maid, as he'd been rather free with finding his way around her, "and quicker and more learned than most I've met."

"You've met many?" A sniffle accompanied the question, and she used one of the bandages by the bedside to wipe her nose. Even with her hair braided, she was a mess, bruised and swollen, her skin discolored by his red powder. Had he really thought her pretty?

"A few," he corrected her, continuing on to the table where he set down the ceramic jars.

"The Boar of Balor? You know him?"

"Aye." He looked up to the hundreds of dried and drying plants hanging from racks suspended from the rafters. A few steps brought him to the one he sought, and he broke off a portion of stem.

"Then help me," she begged, the intensity in her voice turning to pure desperation. "Or let me go that I may help myself."

"You cannot walk," he pointed out with no pleasure. Ragnor would begin paying for his violent manners upon the morn.

"Do you keep me for yourself, then?"

"No." The vervain went into the mortar to be ground into powder. "When you are healed, Caradoc will come. Your cousin, Morgan, goes to him on the morrow to carry the news of your delay."

"Better to kill me now." Her desperation slipped into despair, then into anger. "And Ragnor too, for the Boar will not go light with him."

He gave her a brief, discerning glance, then added another piece of vervain to the mortar, a short piece to help lift her spirits an extra notch.

"Ragnor will meet his just fate, while 'tis only marriage you face, little one," he said, trying to improve her perspective. "Most women like it well enough."

"I am not most women."

He tended to agree, but kept the opinion to himself and dipped a measure of water into the pan on the brazier.

"And if you believe all I face is marriage, you are a fool, the more so for speaking of what you know naught."

Some of the water splashed into the brazier. He'd never heard sarcasm and despondency blended together so neatly, in such a tight package of condemnation. She'd called him a fool.

He struck flint to tinder and started the water heating for the infusion.

"You cannot hold me," she continued, adding a good portion of resolve to her despair, proving herself to be a rare, multifaceted chit. Even so, the novelty of her presence was wearing thin. He would send a courier to Morgan, letting him know the price had gone to two hundred marks.

She'd called him a fool.

"I will hold you, *chérie*." He arched an eyebrow in her direction. "I will hold you until I have a mind to let you go."

Only silence greeted his pronouncement, which was as it should have been. Or so he thought.

"Beast." The word came at him from the depths of the bed.

His jaw tightened, but he didn't deign to give her another look. "If needs be, I can play the beast."

Her answer, for he was sure she had one, no doubt tart, was arrested by the clomping sound of Erlend climbing the stairs, cursing on every step. The hatch was pushed open, followed by the old man.

"Yer goin' ta make yerself sick, what with all yer bathin'." He hauled a pot of water up after him, holding the hot handle with a folded rag.

"Fill the tub and bother me no more," Dain ordered impatiently, pouring the ground herbs into the brazier pan.

Erlend stomped around the room, emptying the pot he'd brought as well as the cauldron of boiling water on the hearth into the wooden tub, grumbling beneath his breath about some people's ideas. Dain busied himself with putting honey into a cup and fighting the temptation to silence Ceridwen's tongue with a stronger sleeping draught. She was the foolish one, provoking him with her misplaced rebelliousness.

A soft, rhythmic tapping at the door stopped both men. Erlend looked up at Dain with a wicked, toothless grin.

"That one, eh?"

Dain ignored him and went to the door. Edmee, at least, could be counted on as a calming, noncombative addition to the evening.

He opened the door and greeted the maid with a touch of his hand on her cheek, which made her smile. Then he took the tray she carried and gestured for her to come inside, an offer hampered by Erlend scuttling to the fore, bobbing and bowing like a child's toy in front of the maid, cap in hand.

"Good e'en, Edmee. Aye and ye did a fine job with the gel, a demned fine job gettin' 'er to drink the physick and all. I was wonderin', tho, if ye might have a minute here or there." He laughed, a dry, cackling sound. "I got me an ache ye see, and I was—"

Dain was in no mood for the servant's lecherous wooing and with a gesture, he set his black hound on the man. Erlend yelped and jumped away from the dog's bared teeth with a spryness Dain would have thought beyond him.

"Be gone with you," he said, then called the dog off with a hushed command, despite the appeal of letting Elixir eat the old bastard for supper and being done with him.

"I'm goin', jongleur. I'm goin', I am." Erlend's voice trailed off into mutterings of "demned dogs" and "demned ungrateful masters."

Dain followed him to the hatch and shoved home the bolt after the man was down. That all his problems could be dealt with so easily.

Turning back to Edmee, he asked, "Did she eat well today?"

The maid nodded and spoke to him in her way, with her hands and expressions, using a graceful pantomine to clarify when needed.

"The lord and the lady? Together?" He repeated her words aloud with an inflection designed to make her smile. Edmee had a beautiful smile. He walked back to her side. "Mayhaps 'twas better I wasn't here when they came. I've never yet had to fight them both off at once. Could be too much for me."

A merry light came into her eyes, and her shoulders shook. He'd made her laugh. The night wasn't a complete loss.

Her fingers flew in a series of quick gestures and signs, and it was his turn to laugh.

"No, Edmee. I can't cast an un-love spell, and you know as well as I 'tis not exactly love that brings them to the Hart Tower." 'Twasn't exactly lust that had brought them this time either. As he'd told Morgan he would, he'd gutted a chicken before them and had seen them both pale with the mention of Caradoc's name. He was sure they'd come to see for themselves whether or not the maid fared well.

From her vantage point propped up in the bed, Ceridwen watched the pair with growing interest. The mute maid had come before, earlier in the day. Something was familiar about her, the smooth oval of her face, her auburn hair, and soft green eyes, yet Ceridwen knew they had not met. There had never been a mute at Usk.

The maid and Dain were strikingly beautiful together, a fair match. He had warned her against putting her trust where it would be betrayed, but he'd warned her too late. She knew it made no sense to feel betrayed by a mythical being who had never existed, but her heart was not paying heed to sense. From the moment Caradoc had found her at Usk, she'd needed a savior, and in the night, under the influence of Dain's potion and dazzled by the dark fire of his gaze, she'd thought she'd found one in him.

She'd been wrong.

Sinking into the bed, she pulled the coverlets up to her face. She was alone, again, the more so because of the easy friendship she witnessed between the other two on the far side of the chamber. All friendship and family had been stolen from her. Even if she wished, she could not return to the nuns and novices at the convent, not with the Prince of Gwynedd wanting her married and at Balor. There were no other people to whom she belonged, except a thieving cousin doing the prince's bidding.

An unwanted tear ran down her face. She wiped it with a corner of sable fur. Her tears must stop soon. Maybe they would leave with the pain. She had never thought she would miss the convent, but she did—the quiet bustling of the nuns, the serenity of long hours spent in silence, the comfort of combined prayers. Living with Morgan and his men, even for just a few days, had made her wonder if she was more suited to the religious life than she had thought. She missed her friend Bronwyn, and Sister Judith, and Sister Isobel.

Fighting a sob, she squeezed her eyes shut and began a silent round of prayers. The familiarity brought a measure of comfort, as did the faith. She dare not forsake her God.

An easy touch on her arm brought her head around. It was the quiet maid, bringing her supper. With a sure and knowing touch, Edmee helped her sit up and offered her Dain's draught in a silver goblet. Ceridwen took a sip and found it sweet. The thought to refuse the drink or the meal did not enter her mind. She needed to heal, and she needed strength either to fight or to run to the ends of the earth to escape Caradoc.

Chapter 6

The maid had helped her to the chamber pot before settling her back in the bed and closing the curtains, but Ceridwen didn't think the girl had left the tower. She hadn't heard the great door creak open, and there were too many sounds of movement in the room.

Laughter reached her ears, rich and full. 'Twas Dain, she knew, recognizing the edge of his cynic's heart in the sound. She snuggled deeper into the bed and willed herself to ignore her pain and go to sleep. She had no use for his laughter or his company, and she would not ask for his simples, but sleep evaded her with the same dogged nimbleness as freedom.

Water was poured somewhere in the room, a great rushing stream of it splashing down into more water. The laughter stopped and was replaced by a rumbling groan of pleasure coming from deep within a man's throat.

Inside the safe confines of the curtained bed,

Ceridwen felt the vibrations of that great sigh roll across the chamber to touch her. She shivered, but not with cold. Numa whimpered and scooted to the end of the bed to push her head out between the lengths of green and yellow damask. Candlelight poured in through the opening along with the murmurings of a one-sided conversation.

"Are you sure you want to do that?" Dain asked, his voice as mellow and satisfied as a cat's purr.

The silence that followed confirmed Ceridwen's suspicion that it was the mute maid and not the old man who remained in the tower room.

"If you're going to play dangerously," Dain went on, "mayhaps I'll increase my wager."

His laughter came after a short break of silence.

Curious, Ceridwen angled her head to see him—and saw more of his backside than she could ever have imagined, given all her years in a nunnery. Her first thought was to look away, but her second thought waylaid the first with surprising alacrity. He was beautiful and naked, lean and muscular and wet, with a warrior's body from the breadth of his shoulders to the curves of his buttocks and the length of his flanks.

Her gaze drifted over him, lingering in the shadows between his legs, following the lines of muscle across his back and farther to where he was marked with the sign of an ancient religion: A dark torc circled one of his upper arms in the slinky, graceful lines of a woad tattoo, and above the torc was a repetition of the arcane symbols on his gambeson. The man was bound by charms even down to his skin.

As she watched, he reached up into the drying racks hanging over the tub and chose a few flowers, some with the bloom of freshness still about them, picked—no doubt—from the pots of plants set beneath the window. He sank back down into the water, smiling at the maid sitting on a stool close by. Between them was a table set up with a gaming board and playing pieces.

Edmee was fully clothed and already had sweet violets in her hair, to which he added blue iris buds and pink roses, gently slipping each stem into the crown of braids circling her head. The effect was that of a riotous spring garland. The maid didn't move once during his ministrations. Her attention was focused on the board.

"Take care, Edmee," he warned, tucking in the last flower. "If you check me now, I'll have you mated in two moves."

The maid glanced up with sloe-eyed impertinence, then went back to concentrating on the board.

He laughed again and removed one of the roses he'd just put in her hair. Steam wafted up around him, dampening and straightening his chestnut mane into lank strands and adding a silvery sheen to his skin. He brought the flower to his nose and lazily twirled it, waiting for Edmee to make her move.

Ceridwen watched everything, fascinated and oddly disturbed by the scene, by the sensuality of it, the hint of unknown dangers. What she saw was laced with the forbidden, the more so for being observed by herself, yet the two of them appeared so casual, Dain most natural in his nakedness. Women oft bathed men. 'Twas not that which brought a blush to her cheeks, but rather the play between them. The air was ripe for something more.

Her gaze touched upon the studious maid and the chess game, then was drawn back to Dain. Candlelight marked him with shifting shadows; they slid around the sinuous blue-black torc and the curves of muscle in his arms, and down the bared length of his back. They hovered in the darkness of his eyes and dwelt in the crease at the corner of his smile.

The rose brushed against his mouth, and he blew into it, separating the pink petals and setting them aflutter, his gaze never leaving Edmee—except when he brought the flower back to his nose to inhale its scent, and he gave the bed a discerning glance.

Ceridwen blanched. The look was personal, focused on her with an impossible intensity. There was no way for him to see her in the depths of the great bed, to know she was awake and watching— unless he truly was the sorcerer Ragnor thought him to be.

She lowered her lashes in defense, not knowing if the invasion she felt was real or her own imagining. She had believed in his magic in the great hall, when he'd swept in with his cloak billowing about him and his dogs on either side. Now that vision seemed more of a fancy, a glamorous trick to snare weak minds.

She did not suffer from that affliction. The strength of her mind, Abbess Edith had assured her, would be the end of her one day. He would not snare her. If he had power, most likely 'twas only the power to deceive . . . and the power to fascinate, she admitted, her head coming up at the sound of his laughter. He was unlike any other, playing both the spectral demon and the Light-elf with equal ease; and the beast also, she was sure, when the mood was upon him.

Edmee made her move to check. The game ended quickly, just as he'd predicted, in two moves, but 'twas Edmee who took his king, not the other way around.

"You witch's daughter," he said, laughing again. "You have beaten me. Be off with you, then." He made a dismissive gesture. "Take your winnings and leave me in peace."

He rolled over onto his back in the tub and rested his head on the rim, seeming to ignore the maid as she walked up and down his rows of shelves with a pleased sashay to her hips, picking and choosing what she would take.

"Not that one," he called out, "unless 'tis for your mother. She knows well enough the use of crocus seeds."

Ceridwen saw the girl take one seed capsule and return the jar to the shelf before moving on. When she was finished, she went back to Dain and spread out her bounty on the gaming table for him to see.

"You play well and choose wisely, Edmee. Madron will be proud of you."

In reply, the girl made a gesture Ceridwen couldn't see, but Dain grew still.

" 'Tis never part of the bargains we make." And then, "Aye, you know well how to please me, but . . ." His voice trailed off as the maid dipped her hand beneath the water.

"Jesus," he cursed softly. "Your mother would put a hex on me to shrivel my balls if she but knew what we did."

For herself, Ceridwen wasn't sure what they were doing, or rather what the maid was doing to him, but she knew enough to understand that the hushed noises he made bespoke pleasure, not pain. There was no mistaking the encouragement lacing his whispered words, just as there was no mistaking the effect those words had on Ceridwen herself. A flush of excitement coursed over her skin, making her painfully aware of her body while at the same time overriding the pains she felt.

All the rules of God and men told her to look away, but she could do naught but watch the whole of it: the intent tenderness in the maid's gaze and the smooth rhythm of her touch; the small waves of water lapping upon the taut shore of his abdomen; the arch of his throat as he bent his head back over the rim of the tub, sending a damp slide of hair to the floor.

She could do naught but watch and wonder and feel the strange heat of what she saw.

Dain let his eyes drift closed as he sank into the spell Edmee wove with her hand. He released a breathy groan at one of the particularly enticing moves he'd taught her, but the sound was only half pleasure, the other half being frustration. Whenever Edmee visited, he always hoped 'twould come to this or more, but he never asked, had never asked, not even the first time when she'd so innocently seduced him with her mouth.

Her mouth was not so innocent now as it had been at the Yule. She'd proven adept at everything he'd taught her—from chess, to receipts her mother had sent her to learn, to the art of driving a man over the edge.

Aye, the witch's daughter knew her way around a man's shaft with her tongue, as she'd prove again soon enough, but tonight he wanted more. Tonight he wanted a kiss.

'Twas the chit's fault, for sighing in his mouth with a sweetness he still could taste.

A kiss. Was it so much to ask? He lifted his head and, silent and fluid, moved through the water to reach for Edmee. The maid eluded him with a quick step. Cursing and laughing, he sank back into the tub.

"You are unreasonable," he exclaimed. "Could we not once do this thing face-to-face? With all the parts where they fit best?" And there was the truth of it, he thought. 'Twas more than a kiss he would have taken if he'd caught her. After four years of chastity, he had succumbed to Edmee's mouth, and now he wanted to be buried deep inside a woman.

Edmee shook her head, and he cursed again, this time without the laughter.

"I know what you think, Edmee, and for the thousandth time, you are wrong. I can give you much without getting you with child." He watched her answer and grew more grim. It wasn't only the possibility of a child that stayed her. She was virgin, and though he'd promised to leave her as such—at least the first time—she was adamant about saving herself for marriage.

No matter to her that what she did with him was considered by many to be the ultimate intimacy, she would not take him any other way; and in Wydehaw, he would have no other. In truth, other than Vivienne, no other would have him. Some of the women were too pious to consort with a wizard, and all of them were too frightened. Piety and fear, the same pair of reasonings that kept him out of Lady Vivienne's much-used bed.

As for Edmee's kiss, he chose to ignore why she would not kiss for the same reason he chose to ignore what had brought her to him in the first place. Magician's milk, she'd called it in her way of things. He'd never heard the like, not even in the tents of Jalal al-Kamam, and as a cure for muteness, he ranked it no higher than the most ridiculous concoctions he'd seen for sale in marketplaces from Akabah to London.

Smart maid, she hadn't told him what she really wanted until she'd had him three or four times. By then he'd been well on the path of a momentary addiction. Three months later he was still on the path, and no amount of talking had been able to convince her that while he couldn't cure her, he also couldn't harm her with his kiss. Actually, that idea did have merit, of sorts, for a few years earlier she'd kissed a boy who had soon after died of fever. Within a week of his death, she'd had the fever, and 'twas the sickness that had taken her voice.

He'd had the story from her mother, who was under the mistaken impression that a maid who wouldn't kiss wouldn't do anything else. Madron didn't make many mistakes, as either a healer, trickster, mage, or mother. Dain could only hope the one involving him lasted throughout his lifetime; and he could only hope Edmee would return to his side now and finish him off. 'Twould ease him greatly, both in mind and body, if not in spirit. His spirit needed the succor of a kiss.

Edmee circled the tub, teasing and wary, giving him no more than he deserved for trying to push the boundaries she'd set, but he was not overly worried. A finer art he'd never mastered than the tricks to tease and entice, to turn sex into a sensually charged battle-ground of wills and willpower. For all she'd learned, Edmee was no master of the art of seduction. He'd been easy prey. He still was, but in this game, so was she.

"Come," he said, sweetening his voice and lifting his hand to her. She hesitated, so he added a guileless smile. "Please, Edmee. Come have your way with me."

At that she took his hand, the babe, and he slowly drew her near. With each of her steps, he rose higher out of the wooden tub, until he stood before her, water running down his body and excitement pooling in his groin.

Murmuring a soft sound, she sank to her knees in front of him. He reached down to cup her head in his hands. The first touch was always a gentle one, to prime a lover for what was to come. He'd taught her that, and she had not forgotten. She never forgot about the first touch, nor about anything else. She played him like a bard's harp, and there was a mindlessness in the act that he adored: the short and long glides of a tongue, the feel of a wet mouth closing around him, the delicately calibrated scrape of teeth, and him with nothing to do but receive the rain of pleasure it all created.

She pressed her tongue into the slit at the tip of his glans, and his thighs tightened. God, she was good, so very good, but tonight that would not be enough. The thought hit him even as the fires of release kindled in his loins and he made his first thrust.

Damn the chit. He wanted a kiss to go with the rest of it. He thrust again, easing his shaft deeper, and Edmee clasped him about the hips, so that together they could forge an ancient rhythm out of heat and friction. A dark thrill coursed down his spine—and was made even darker and more thrilling by a new awareness he felt slipping through him.

She watches.

He lifted his heavy-lidded gaze from Edmee to the bed and searched the shadows there, wanting and needing to feel Ceridwen's caress upon his body, even if 'twas only the luminous caress of her eyes.

The delights of voyeurism were well within his repertoire, but this was different. It went deeper, his need to make contact on an elemental plane. Ceridwen had kissed him and been enchanted, and enchanting.

A candle on the end of the table guttered out its life in a sudden blaze, throwing a flash of light past the damask curtains to the pillows and proving what his instincts had told him. She did await him there, watching, pale blue eyes glittering with shock and the pure undefiled heat of desire.

It was enough.

His head fell back as he groaned, and a surge of pleasure coursed through him, releasing the potion Edmee coveted.

Chapter 7

Busy, busy, busy. So busy. Snit scuttled through the murky dark along the inside of the curtain wall, clutching his leather bag of hard-won booty: eyes of newts, and legs and tails too, and worm spore for his master, Helebore, plus a little something for his master's master, Caradoc.

Caradoc the Ingrate, Snit thought, for nothing seemed to please the Boar. Why, only two days past Snit had brought the lord a rare wee beasty he'd found trapped in a spider's web, and the Boar hadn't deigned to give it a glance. But this eve's prize was sure to bring a boon. A beautiful mottled gray rock it was, studded with fallen stars. Most of the stars that fell above Balor landed in the sea. Even if they started well inland, by the time they reached the earth, their course had shifted them over water where they fizzled and sank. Why, Snit conjectured, there must be a veritable mountain of fallen stars off the coast of Balor.

But one— A wide grin split his face as he fondled the stone through his pouch. One had crashed into the land, and he, Snit, had found the shards of it embedded in a smooth gray rock.

"Rich, rich, rich," he hummed to himself. "Aye, I'll be rich."

He came to a corner and stopped, his gaze darting this way and that. 'Twas safer to stay close to a good stone wall, but 'twasn't always possible.

"Ofttimes the bailey needs be crossed," he told himself in no uncertain terms, girding himself for the mad dash that would take him to the keep and his master's chambers.

The wide-open space loomed in front of him, flooded with a full moon's light and all its accompanying shadows, each one a sure hiding place for robbers and cutthroats, and him with his precious rock to get home.

He swore, a tangled garble of words. More robbers and cutthroats than usual since Morgan ab Kynan had returned from the south with his war band and the prisoner Ragnor. Caradoc was going to rend the red giant from limb to limb for his crime. Balor was to have had a lady, a real lady, and now they all must wait. Snit felt a particular affront at the delay. He'd been hoarding gifts for Balor's bride for over a fortnight and was most eager to shower them upon the maid.

Morgan's band wouldn't stay long. They never did. Never long enough to learn anything, or see anything, or hear anything. Even those who lived in Balor never saw the things Snit did, or heard the sounds of the deep dark.

The Thief of Cardiff was a strange friend for someone of the Boar's great importance. Morgan was light and clear—odd for a thief—barely a smudge of darkness about him, a man of no depth when compared to Snit's lord. War had made them friends. Snit knew all about it from hearsay and rumor, as the Boar never spoke to him directly. 'Twould be unseemly.

A cloud passed over the moon, and Snit took it as an omen. He dashed across the bailey, hunching his shoulders around his leather bag, hiding himself in the cloud's shadow. With a loud gasp, he came up against the wall of stone that was the south side of the hall. Nary a robber or a cutthroat had laid a hand upon him.

"Fie!" he called out into the bailey, crowing his victory.

A guardsman on duty at the bottom of the keep's covered stairwell crossed himself and muttered a prayer. Snit caught the gesture out of the corner of his eye and spat toward the man's feet. Fool.

He turned and felt his way along the wall until he came to the place he sought, a door no bigger than the lid on a wooden chest. Indeed, 'twas what the door had been, which accounted for its shape. Snit fumbled on his belt for his key and undid the lock on the hasp. Then he let himself in and barred the door behind him with an oak plank.

Inside the great hall of Balor Keep, Morgan watched as Caradoc raised a flagon of ale and quaffed the whole of it. When the earthenware vessel was dry, the Boar crashed it onto the floor with a mighty heave and called for another. Thick golden hair fell on either side of his face in cascading layers, but did naught to soften the harshness of his visage or the dark fury in his eyes. He was a striking figure, large and powerfully built, dressed in fine black camlet and samite in preparation for the bride that had not come. His surcoat was quilted and embossed with a rich gold thread, the damask tunic he wore underneath was pure white and embroidered with the same gold thread, a veritable fortune in clothes, and all for naught.

No talk or laughter rose from the tables spread down either side of the hearth, though all were full. Men ate in silence, the pall of their lord's anger infecting every bite they took. The only one who dared speak was a small child, no more than three, by Morgan's guess, and Caradoc's daughter, by the look of her. A serious thing she was for one so little, and imperious, scolding the servants and making demands of a dark-haired woman Morgan guessed was her mother. Both would have to go when Ceridwen became Balor's lady.

Morgan sat far to the left of the pair and his friend, though the term "friend" seemed to apply no longer. When Morgan had delivered his news of Ceridwen, Caradoc had nearly struck him down, indeed, would have, if Morgan had not blocked the blow. Of his own men, Rhodri and Dafydd had been closest, and both had drawn their daggers to protect him. Though no blood had been shed, such actions between men-of-arms left an irreparable breach. The next messenger sent to Balor by the ruling Prince of Gwynedd would be one other than Morgan ab Kynan. He would not return, and he would warn

Dain to take extra care with the maid, for old ties were being forgotten.

Thwarted in his first attack, Caradoc had taken his mood out upon anyone not quick enough to elude him. Half a dozen servants had been cuffed with the back of his hand, one so badly he had not gotten back up but still lay bleeding into the rushes behind the dais.

Morgan's band didn't often dare to travel by night, even when the moon was full, but the risks of facing the night were far less than the risks of remaining within the reach of Caradoc's rage. Another slip like the thwarted blow and 'twould be warfare. So they ate as if on tenterhooks, biding their meal and their manners until 'twas seemly to leave.

Sitting at the table below Morgan, the youngest of his band, Drew and Rhys, could not manage even that little bit. Their trenchers were hardly touched, nor their cups. Morgan doubted if 'twas the thought of fighting their way out of the keep that twisted their guts. Something more than a belated bride was amiss in Balor.

The castle was abuzz with the discovery of two men that morn, one dead, the other said to be gasping his last breaths in the leech's chambers below the hall. Crushed he was, the dead man, Caradoc's guards muttered, his bones ground to dust within his skin. The second man was said to be only half-crushed and raving of demons in the dark, of ungodly heat, and unbearable pressure. The two had been washed up on a shingle beach half a league south of Balor, after having been missing for a sennight.

Drew and Rhys had argued for staying inside the castle walls rather than face whatever had done the deadly deed. Morgan had prevailed, but it had taken Owain to convince the two younger men of the wisdom of leaving.

"Balor's misery is its own and naught to do with us," he'd said. "We'll be far safer in the mountains of Eryri."

Aye, and Morgan could hardly wait to get there. He had known Balor Keep when it was called Carn Merioneth and was related to both the former and the present occupants. He and Ceridwen were cousins, though not close ones, and the cousinry of him and Caradoc, although traceable, was even less close, but all were of the ancient ruling line of Merioneth.

'Twas an old story of blood and love. Gwrnach had vowed to

marry Rhiannon—they'd been first cousins, as Morgan remembered—pledging to her both his love and the strength of his sword, but he'd lost the maid to Arawn and lost Carn Merioneth with her, until he'd taken it all by force and murdered his fair cousin in the bargain, or so the story went.

Thus by dint of his relations, Morgan had seen many changes in the holdings. Yet the place had changed more in the last year than it had with the destruction of the wooden palisades and the building of the wall and castle keep. He liked not what he felt when he came to Merioneth nowadays.

Much of his aversion was due to Helebore, Caradoc's leech. The man's name meant death, and truly he looked the part with his cadaverous pallor and sunken cheeks. Helebore had nary a hair on his head, neither on pate nor eyebrow. Burned off by the devil himself, Rhys had murmured several times since their arrival. Morgan wouldn't go that far, but the lack did give Helebore a strange, eerie look about him, stranger even than his twisted little consort, Snit.

Aye, Caradoc had taken to keeping strange company of late. So 'twas well enough they were away after the meal.

Owain came up beside him and bent his head close. He was a heavy man, large and rough-looking. " 'Tis time, Morgan," he said. "To tarry longer can do us no good this night."

"The horses?"

"All is ready in the bailey. You have only to bid adieu to our most congenial host. Try not to lose your head in the doing of it." The last was said with what passed for Owain's smile, a tight curve of his lips and no more than a twig's worth of warmth in his eyes.

"My head is safe," Morgan said, lifting his cup. "I saved his life at Acre. For tonight that memory will suffice, but no more, I fear." He drained the cup of ale and wiped his sleeve across his mouth, then gave Owain a wry grin. "See if Drew's and Rhys's knees have stopped trembling enough that they may walk out of the hall without disgracing the lot of us."

Their escape, for 'twas nothing less, went smoothly enough, mayhaps too smoothly. Caradoc seemed only too glad to be rid of them, all but shoving them out the gatehouse doors and dropping the portcullis behind them. Owain feared a trap, but none was sprung. Morgan's fears were of a much less tangible nature. He'd brought a bound and gagged Ragnor to Balor, and that was as it should have been, and yet, because of Ragnor, he hadn't brought Ceridwen ab Arawn—and mayhaps that was as it should have been also. Mayhaps the maid knew more of what wasn't aright with Balor Keep than Morgan had allowed.

Caradoc sat sprawled in a chair by the hearth in Helebore's chambers, watching the leech perform the ritual of extreme unction on the injured man they'd found that morn, Simon, one of Balor's guardsmen. The other man had been named Cobb. Failures both, to have gotten themselves killed in the maze of caves underlying the keep and then spat out upon a cold shore.

Damn Morgan. He'd failed in his quest also. A simple enough matter, Caradoc had thought, to fetch one sniveling virgin and bring her back where she belonged. She had a brother, though, and Helebore thought that mayhaps the boy would suffice as neatly as the girl for his needs. Strata Florida was not so far. He would send someone in the morn.

Helebore's thin, colorless lips moved as he spoke the last rites, his voice nearly drowned out by his patient's mutterings, ravings, and occasional screams. Every now and then, much to his distaste, Caradoc caught one of the ritual Latin phrases. Each one darkened his mood. He had been keeping himself on a tight tether, letting his anger steep, and sizzle, and burn, and fill him with the power of rage. Now he was close to breaking. His skin couldn't hold the pulsing, white-hot thing that his fury had become much longer.

He had wanted her, only her, and she was being denied him.

He clenched his hand into a fist and forced a deep breath into his lungs, holding himself in check. 'Twasn't time yet to give in. The man who awaited him on the ramparts deserved his undiluted wrath, the one who had taken her from him—Ragnor.

"Two hundred swiving marks and oranges." The words soughed through his lips, soft and hissing.

None other than his old friend would have dared to ask for so much, yet 'twas as nothing compared to what the girl was worth. He knew Lavrans, too well, and he knew no woman would escape the jongleur. Lavrans would put her in chains if needs be to collect his two hundred swiving marks.

The thought brought a ghost of a smile to Caradoc's lips.

'Twould be good practice for the maid to live with Dain Lavrans as her keeper, for no one had less of a heart, excepting possibly himself. They'd both had those fickle organs cut out of them piece by bloody piece in Saladin's prisons and by their desert masters. 'Twas only Morgan who had come through unscathed.

Dain must have been good, very good, Caradoc thought, his mood growing darker, for Jalal al-Kamam did not have a reputation for sparing his slaves. Yet Morgan had been spared much. Not so himself. Kalut ad-Din had spared him nothing.

"Libera nos, quaesumus, Domine," Helebore murmured. Deliver us, we beseech Thee, O Lord.

"Old habits die hard, eh, priest?" Caradoc called out, his lips tilting into a sneer. He had no use for the Church's drivel, and he liked it not when Helebore regressed into his former ways. The man had come to Balor from Ynys Enlli, the isle of saints off the far west coast of the Lleyn Peninsula in North Wales. The Culdee monks on that sea-girt rock had tossed him off a cliff one fine spring morning, expecting he would be drowned by the weight of his grievous sins.

They had been wrong.

Helebore rolled his black eyes in Caradoc's direction, implying both disdain and chastening without missing a syllable of the rites. Caradoc paid no mind, his attention having strayed to the scuffling sound and the flash of movement behind the brown-robed leech. He bared his teeth and slowly leaned forward in his chair, growling, until the little weasel, Snit, yelped and scrambled to safety inside the dusty cupboard he called home.

Helebore ignored both of them, making the sign of the cross on the soles of the dying man's feet.

"Perducat te ad vitum aeternam." And bring thee unto life everlasting.

"Enough!" Caradoc roared, his limit for piety suddenly and violently reached. He thrust himself to his feet and brought his fist down hard on the table holding the dying Simon. The table rattled with the force of his blow, and the half-crushed guardsman let out a pitiful, whimpering moan. "If you *must* pray, pray my *bride* is come to Balor," Caradoc hissed at the gaunt leech, and hit the table again. "If you *must* pray, pray Ragnor is strong enough to endure my attention that my pleasure may last." Once more his fist came down, rattling the boards as he leaned in close. "If you *must* pray, dear Helebore, pray all you have told me of the *pryf* is true, for if 'tis not, Ragnor's fate will seem as a *blessing* compared to yours."

A moment of tremulous silence followed the tirade, then another moment into which Helebore injected a most pious "Amen."

Finished with his service, the leech cocked a hairless eyebrow in his lord's direction. Caradoc glared, and between them Simon—jiggled to the edge by all the pounding—slipped off the table, fully expired.

"Milord," Helebore said, after a brief glance at the dead man. He gestured toward the spiral stone staircase that led to the ramparts. "Shall we attend to the next dying man?"

"Aye," Caradoc muttered, reaching for his cloak and swinging it over his shoulders. "Attend and rend."

Morgan and his men rode north and east, fording the River Dwyryd, leaving Merioneth and heading deeper into the wild mountains, into the heart of Gwynedd. Morgan would report to Llywelyn, who was rumored to be at Dolwyddelan Castle, before turning south again to warn Dain. Caradoc bore watching, by both his neighbors and his friends.

The wind picked up toward midnight, swirling down the precipitous mountain track and bringing the last stubborn flakes of winter snow. Spring was coming to the valleys and lower forests, but not to the mountains. The high, rocky crags would be dusted white afore morn. Morgan called a halt at the next small clearing. The men quickly set up camp and huddled down close to the fire.

Owain took the first watch, with Morgan to follow, but Morgan had hardly closed his eyes, when the captain was back at his side. Owain said nothing, only knelt down and gestured to the south. Morgan looked in that direction, wondering what he was to see, but then he heard it, a low keening sound, a death wail coming from a far-off distance.

He shuddered and crossed himself, and wondered if the half-crushed man had died, or if there was even more mischief afoot at Balor Keep.

Chapter 8

Lavender streams of clouds coursed across a darkening sky, bringing with them a sunset breeze laden with the fresh smell of spring. The scent drifted into the Hart Tower and mingled with the savory essence of dried herbs, before winding a path around the thousand flowers hanging from the racks and ceiling. Of all the rooms in the tower, Dain had made his bedchamber the most pleasant. The northern solar always smelled rich and soft and sweet, a combination to soothe even a troubled mind to dreams and sleep.

For all his regrets over what he had allowed—nay, encouraged—to happen at his bath a fortnight past, Dain had not lost any sleep. And he did have regrets, one anyway, possibly two. He wasn't dwelling on them, but he was aware of their existence and their cause—Ceridwen ab Arawn, the innocent one who had seen too much.

She had spoken hardly a word to him since the

bath and remained far too mortified to meet his gaze. She averted her eyes and a blush blossomed on her cheeks whenever he neared, a necessity he had avoided whenever possible, hoping not to upset her delicate sensibilities any more than he already had.

His consideration was paying off. She was healing, her bruises fading, her spirits lifting. She was able to limp around on her own and use the chamber pot unaided. He'd fed her only the best food and insured her rest with a bit of sleeping draught in the evenings, and was well pleased with her progress. The only complaint he might lodge would be against her incessant praying. All that soft muttering coming from his bed unnerved him.

He walked to the end of his worktable and searched through the vessels on the worn planks for one containing *aqua ardens*. For all the good that it had done, he was finished with coddling her. Edmee had seen to her needs for the last two weeks, but he did not care to have Edmee constantly underfoot. If the chit would eat this night, 'twould be from his hand.

He understood her wariness. He'd once felt so himself, under somewhat similar though less benign circumstances, and it was time she learned not to be cowed by the unexpected, even the shockingly unexpected. Though had he the chance to do it all over, he would not have shocked her as he had. She was already overly skittish about marriage. What he and Edmee had done could not have reassured her in any way. Quite the contrary, she was probably more determined than ever to escape, and that he would not allow.

So it was time to woo and conjure.

He found the jar he was looking for and returned to the middle of the table, to the stage he'd set for her entertainment. He had decided on a very special trick, tricks being so much more reliable than magic, a trick so sublime even he believed in it. Two bowls sat in front of him, both empty, and beside them a pair of linen strips. In between lay his rowan wand, and scattered here and there were a few jars and pots containing nothing more than water. A tallow candle flamed nearby.

He began with a wave of the wand, always a good place for a magician to begin. Then, with a flourish, he used the tip of the wand to lift a linen strip and float it down into the first empty bowl. A brief incantation followed, delivered with authority. His confidence was high, the more so for knowing he had succeeded in capturing her attention from where she lay in his great bed. A rustling of damask and a near soundless slide of furs announced her piqued interest.

He tried the trick the first time with only water, soaking the linen and passing it over the candle. A doused flame was what he got for his effort. He had expected no more, but he should have known she wouldn't let his failure pass without a disparaging remark. "Fool man," the chit muttered, just loud enough for him to hear.

A grin tugged at his lips, but he managed to control it.

The remaining linen strip received only *aqua ardens* with the incantation, and when he passed that cloth over the newly lit candle, a gasp came from the bed, followed by a snort of laughter.

He had expected no less. The linen had disappeared in a whoosh of flames, burned to a cinder. He was not discouraged. He was playing to an audience of one, and a little calculated failure did much to soften the mark.

He had no more linen, so he looked around the room, seeking an alternative. Luckily, a miracle occurred. From out of thin air, a soft and dark blue ball appeared in the palm of his hand. He looked appropriately startled and amazed, but did nothing beyond lifting his hand in front of him. Slowly, the indigo orb blossomed in an untwisting spiral, folds of cloth slipping through his fingers, a length of it rippling down his forearm.

Silk, Ceridwen thought. Nothing else moved like silk, and nothing moved like silk in the hands of a master, though she would have done well to call him thief as well as fool. Her red book was missing. Worse yet, with the book gone, she'd lost Mychael's letters.

She gingerly tested her jaw, but did not move her arm. The bite there ached clear through to her bone. Thief Dain might be, but on the whole, her lot had improved since her night with Ragnor, albeit temporarily. Unless she could free herself and reach Strata Florida, she still had Caradoc to face.

A series of Dain's fluid moves had the gold-and-silver shot cloth floating in the air, swooping and soaring with barely the tip of his wand used for direction. She watched the graceful flight of silk and hoped he had the sense not to try his magic on such a costly piece of cloth.

He did not, for his next move sent the scarf sliding through the air into one of the bowls. She cringed, and almost dared not to watch. Nothing had happened with his first spell, and that was the best she hoped would happen again, for his second spell had obviously gone awry.

Dain chose a jar, but in the deepening gloom, Ceridwen couldn't tell if it was one he'd already tried. She soon realized it didn't matter, for he poured into the bowl the contents of that jar as well as most of the other jars and pots on the table. The incantations began in earnest then, his voice rising and falling with the rhythms of bewitchment. During a particularly potent-sounding phrase, he transferred the silk to the other bowl and poured one last bottle of liquid over it, preparing it for certain ruination, she was sure. When he lifted the sodden mass on his wand and passed it over the candle, her heart sank in expectation of the worst.

Fire sizzled and caught on the edge of the silk and, faster than she could follow with her eyes, encased the whole length of cloth with flame. She gave it up for lost . . . but the cloth did not burn.

Her eyes widened in disbelief. Fire encircled the silk like a sheath, flames and heat swirling around, spiraling up, sparks of light flashing off the gold and silver threads, but the silk itself remained untouched. When the flames died, Dain floated the scarf again, in the air and up and about, an indigo swallow soaring through the aftermath of his magic.

She watched him, her heart beating faster. He was as Ragnor had said after all, a sorcerer, a practitioner of the dark arts she'd read about in the parchments hidden in the convent's manuscript room, the place where she'd found her red book.

Heresies for sure, and pagan magic too, the cleric who had shown the parchments to Ceridwen had said, translated and transcribed by an eleventh-century monk who had thought he had an eye for ancient history. The church had disagreed with bell, book, and candle. Ceridwen hadn't known that day what to believe of the cleric's disjointed and breathless ramblings, except when he'd loosed his braies, she'd known enough to run.

Curious, she'd gone back when the lustful cleric was well and truly away, and she'd found wonders within the heresies, story upon story woven into a fantastical whole, along with faded illuminations showing a time of not one God, but of many gods and goddesses and the mighty wars of enchantment they'd fought.

In the beginning, she'd found great comfort within those worn pages, for they recounted the stories of her childhood, stories about the

Children of Don, the Mother Goddess; about Ceraunnos, the "Horned One"; about Ceridwen, her namesake and the mother of the great Druid Taliesin. Those tales had been told over and again by a beautiful mother to her children, her gentle fingers combing through their fair hair, her voice falling like an angel's sigh upon their ears. Rhiannon had been her name, and Ceridwen missed her still, her loss having left an emptiness nothing had ever filled.

The years had passed slowly, and Ceridwen had spent many days eluding the prioress so she could explore the nooks and crannies of the scriptoria, but the deeper she'd delved into the century-old parchments, the less comfort she'd found. Obscure references to Carn Merioneth had been written in the margins of one of the manuscripts, leading her to another one written in the same hand and bound in red leather. The finding of that book had set her upon her present doomed course, for what that scribe had reported as myth, Ceridwen had known to be fact: Carn Merioneth had been a land of golden apple trees, its orchards praised far and wide for the sweetness of their fruit; a land of amber honey and forests rich in game, home to hart and hind, fallow deer, roe, and boar. All this and more had been protected by a palisade of beauty and grace built on the cliffs above the wild Irish Sea—and it had all been destroyed by a giant who rose up out of the dark night wielding a flaming sword.

With such truth from the past facing her, how could she not believe what the book had gone on to foretell of dragons and blood and evil men and her own grim future? And if perchance the history of Carn Merioneth had simply been told by one who had been there, and the prophesy was no more than an imaginative tale, how had that person known of *pryf*? For the dark mystery of the deepest caves below Carn Merioneth had been written upon the pages of the red book as surely as it was written in her memory and on the walls of that long-ago tunnel.

Damned book. No power on earth could make her call dragons, and the only blood she would deal in was the blood of Christ her Savior in Holy Communion. As for evil men, who could it be besides Gwrnach and Caradoc, and as she loathed the father for his murderous destruction of her home and family, she loathed the son.

Yet her fate had arrived, in the guise of a handsome rogue whose smile had brought a blush to even Abbess Edith's sour face, and she had not eluded it. Since the night the good woman had put Ceridwen into Morgan ab Kynan's hands, betrayal had become the watch-word of her life. The betrayal of all she'd learned in childhood, the betrayal of the convent's teachings, and the most painful betrayal of all, that of a mother who had filled her head with dreams that had become nightmares, and then left her to face them alone.

Her gaze followed Dain as he moved around the table. If she couldn't escape the nightmare, she would have to fight, and within the depths of such a master's knowledge could lie the seeds of her salva-tion, if she had the strength and the means to use them against Cara-doc.

The Boar was reputed not to fear any living man or beast, but if the red book was true—and she dare not doubt it any longer—he would have need of magic, and she would rather give him magic than her blood.

Dain had such magic. He had just proven as much, despite his earlier denials. He may not be Light-elf or *tylwyth teg,* but neither was he a mere leech. A man did not mark himself with strange symbols he did not believe in, and she'd felt the heat of Brochan's Great Charm herself. Italian glass, indeed. The old man, Erlend, had not thought so. He'd nearly jumped clean out of his skin when she'd brandished it. As an ally, one like Dain could lend strength to her fight. As an enemy, though, he would do nothing to help her, least of all let her go.

She closed her eyes, dismayed that she had fallen so quickly into the depths of degradation, needing an ally such as him to save herself from eternal damnation. Not even the abbess had foreseen such an early demise of her moral fiber.

Wicked man. She'd recognized his seduction two weeks earlier for exactly what it was, an act of utter depravity, and she could not imagine what had induced the maid Edmee to rouse him in such a manner. For herself, she heartily wished she had never been a part of what she'd seen.

But she had been. She'd felt his slumberous gaze upon her, and she'd felt his deep groan of pleasure vibrate through her after their eyes had met. That lush, primal sound had changed her somehow, touched her in places she had never been touched, and every time she looked at him now, she felt those vibrations stir anew. Nothing in the nunnery had prepared her for him, not even the lustful cleric.

There were men connected with the abbey, to be sure, the chaplain mostly. At least three times a year the archdeacon came, more rarely the Bishop of St. David's. Men from the village purveyed with the order or labored in the fields, but none of them had been like Dain, neither the holy men nor the villagers. The son of a Welsh prince had come once, requesting food and lodging for his men; and as his father had endowed the abbey in the name of his mother, the laws of claustration had been eased enough to allow them to camp close to the convent walls. Ceridwen remembered looking upon the tall and handsome young man, and she'd felt a longing, not for him particularly, but for what Gwrnach had stolen from her, the chance to love and the birthright to marry well. She had not known then how foolish her longing had been.

That long-ago prince and Dain shared a similar arrogance in their bearing, but the younger man had not had Dain's seductive grace, nor the intensity of his gaze. Over the last fortnight, she'd often felt the touch of the mage's dark eyes upon her. It was more than instinct that warned her when he was watching; there was a tactile quality in the attention he was able to level across a room. No other person she'd known—man, woman, or child—had possessed such a talent. Nor had anyone else been able to set a dancing flame to silk and leave the cloth untouched. Neither had she ever seen stitchery as fine as that which graced her face and shoulder. That alone was enough to convince her Dain worked in concert with powers she did not yet understand.

He was rare, this Dain, and he held a good portion of her fate in the palms of his hands and in the tips of his skillful fingers. She knew no better reason to enlist his aid through whatever means necessary, or almost any means. She would not do what Edmee had done. She would not barter sexual favors for his trinkets or his help. Not that she could imagine him wanting such from her. In traveling with Morgan and his men, she had not noticed anyone reacting to her with so much as a raised eyebrow. Morgan himself had certainly wasted no time in turning down her offer of marriage in return for his fighting arm at her side.

No, she would not entice a man with her body or her favors, least of all a sorcerer accustomed to sinful pleasures. As for her friendship, it had no value beyond the gift itself, and she had no gold with which to buy his services or his teachings. In truth, she had nothing to offer him except the chance to save her life, and he'd already done that once and done it very well.

She lifted a tentative hand to the side of her face. She would bear scars. Whatever beauty she might have had, Ragnor had stolen from her, but 'twould make no difference to Caradoc. He did not want her for the fairness of her face and form. He only wanted her.

He only wanted her at any cost.

The realization slowly registered, bringing with it the first hint of advantage she'd had in many long weeks. She had no need of gold to gain Dain's support. Her leverage lay in herself. She had worth to Caradoc, therefore she had worth to Dain. No doubt he had made that clear to her cousin before he'd sent Morgan north. She wondered if he'd dared to ask outright for ransom.

More than likely, she decided. She was betrothed to a Welsh lord, and she was being held in a Marcher castle. The seeds of conflict were well sown in those simple facts. Should she escape, the wizard would get nothing for his trouble, except a war.

Her bargain would be clear: in return for his teachings of magic, she would not escape him as she had Morgan, for despite its poor outcome, she had escaped Morgan.

Ceridwen almost smiled. Should the chance to escape arise, she would take it without a backward glance or an ounce of guilt, no matter what she promised Dain, but it would have to be better than a fair chance. She could not afford any more failures, neither physically nor emotionally.

She looked up to where Dain was again working at the table. In the fading light he looked more than a match for the Boar. Mayhaps not in bodily strength, but no one could deny the sheer presence of the man.

It might be enough.

She knew from Mychael's letters that Caradoc was said to resemble his father, and Gwrnach had been a golden giant, a sun god gone berserk. His enraged stance in the blood-soaked bailey of Carn Merioneth would forever be engraved in her memory. Her mother's maid, Moriath, had held her close as they stood on the hill above the keep, drawing her to her side and warning her not to cry out at the horror of what they saw. Mychael had been spared the final sight of their home in flames, for he had not awakened in Moriath's arms until they were well and away.

Mychael, dear sweet brother, was her only real hope of salvation. 'Twas folly to believe in another, especially a dark sinner like

Dain, yet Mychael might have been lost to her. She'd received no letter bearing his mark for nearly six months, and two of her own had gone unanswered.

Dain would have to do. Her gaze swept over him in a measuring glance. Yes, the black-cowled sorcerer would have to do.

From his vantage point in the middle of the room, Dain pretended indifference to Ceridwen's perusal, continuing with the intricate work of refolding the silk. He had more than accomplished his goal. She was near bursting with awareness of him, and unless he was mistaken, was actually considering speaking to him, something she had not done since she'd called him beast—an appellation he had wasted no time in proving.

Ah well, he thought, giving the silk ball an eighth of a turn and tucking in a fold, what was one more mortal sin in a life so rich in transgressions? 'Twas as naught, because it had to be. Otherwise he would have been buried by sin many long years past, if not in his first weeks with Jalal, then certainly by the end of the first month, when death had looked to be his only hope for redemption.

He pressed a completed fold with his thumb while turning the silk and tucking a new edge. Turn, tuck, press. With each movement, light from the tallow candle flashed against the inside of his right wrist where a thin white scar would always be visible proof of what a young man could no longer bear.

"Are you hungry, *chérie?*" he asked without looking up. Turn, tuck, press. "I have quail roasting."

He waited a long moment to hear her say, "Aye."

"Good." He finished with the costly cloth ball and wrapped gauze around it to help the silk hold its shape. When the gauze was in place, he set the ball in a box and closed the lid. He deliberately did not look her way, because of her disconcerting habit of lowering her lashes whenever he so much as glanced in her direction.

He didn't blame her, not really.

"Now then," he said, carrying the box over to put on the shelf with his simples and receipts, mixing magic and medicine in his way of things, "would you like to eat in bed again? Or do you feel well enough to attempt the table?"

"The table, if you please."

If he pleased? The night was going better than he had dared to hope.

"No, Ceridwen, 'tis only as you please." He paused to give the spitted birds a turn over the fire. "I have been charged with your care."

"By whom?" she asked, the hesitation in her voice betraying her wariness.

"Soren D'Arbois," he answered, "the lord of this castle."

"And of you?"

At that, he looked up, unable to resist the subtle challenge in her tone.

"Not quite," he said, suppressing a smile. "I live within the walls of his keep, 'tis true, but at his request, not his orders. In truth, my presence is sanctioned through the grace of others who were here long before the baron."

"Others?" she repeated. "With authority over a March lord? Do you speak of the English king, Lionheart?"

Damn the chit. She was forever tripping him up.

"Only under duress," he muttered, his voice dry as he lowered his gaze and gave the birds another turn.

"My lord?"

The smile won out, teasing a corner of his mouth, until he lifted his head, by which time his face showed nothing. " 'Tis not King Richard I speak of, and I am no one's lord, mistress. I hold no titles you would recognize. I have no lands other than the few feet of dirt holding up this tower. You may call me Dain, or Lavrans as you wish, and I will answer."

"I have never heard of anyone owning a tower who did not also own the castle, Lavrans," she said with the barest hint of sarcasm. He would not have dreamed it possible for such a sharp tongue to have survived convent life.

"Wydehaw has no less than ten towers, of which the Hart is the least strategically important, both in size and placement," he explained, hiding his disappointment at what she'd chosen to call him. No one had blended the name Dain with such an innocent sigh of appreciation since . . . since too long ago to remember. "The peace and services D'Arbois gains by my tenancy is well worth the sacrifice of a bit of ground."

"Peace with whom, if not Richard?" she asked. "For I cannot believe your Norman lord would allow a Welsh spy to reside in his keep to appease his neighbors."

"The peace of his mind, and I am hardly Welsh," he said, wondering if she was capable of making merely polite conversation.

"Neither are you Norman," came her quick reply.

"I am no spy, lady. It matters not to me which way the winds of fortune blow between the English and the Cymry."

"I am no lady."

He arched an eyebrow in silent but profound agreement and walked to the bed to remove the coverlet of sable pelts. When he had it arranged to his liking, padding one of the pair of massive oak chairs by the table, he returned for her.

She flinched when he slid his arms beneath her. He noticed, but continued with his task, lifting her close to his chest. She was, as he'd expected, awkward within his embrace, not knowing where to put her hands, or where to direct her gaze, or what to do with her body besides stiffen it into unmanageable angles.

"Can you relax, mistress? I would prefer not to drop you," he said, adding a false note of strain to his voice to give her something to worry about besides the places where they touched. He was doing enough thinking about that for both of them, much to his bewilderment.

Her looks had improved with the fading of the bruises, yet 'twas more than the pretty delicacy of her face affecting him. His breath had changed when he'd picked her up, altering ever so subtly to her scent. The curve of her thigh filling his hand made his fingers want to feel her skin; her breast was a seductively discernible softness against his chest. She felt very much a woman in his arms.

Her only concession to his request was to tighten her muscles even further and to draw her lower lip between her teeth. With a concession of his own, he refrained from telling her that if she needed to suck on somebody's lip for courage, or any other reason, she was more than welcome to suck on his.

"That's better," he lied, and did his best to get her to the chair without doing more damage or making her any more uncomfortable.

As he stepped down off the dais holding his bed, she shifted against him, relaxing a little, her hand hesitantly sliding up his shoulder, retreating, then reaching fully around his neck to balance herself. He glanced at her and caught the beginnings of a blush as she quickly looked away.

Poor chit. He understood her dilemma. She was half horrified by him and half fascinated, neither of which suited his purpose of wanting to heal her and send her on her way with the fewest possible complications and the most possible gain.

He tilted his head to one side to avoid a lengthy bouquet of drying rue, bringing their heads close together for the space of a heartbeat. Trailing wisps of her thick hair brushed up against his, her curls of white-gold winding around his own dark brown strands like pale ivy. It was an undirected act of intimacy, an act of innocence, yet the effect on him lacked all innocence, reminding him well of the methods of entanglement between a man and a woman. Reminding him also of the rewards.

The thought crossed his mind to stop and tease her into blushing some more, to force her to meet his eyes and to play a game he had long ago forsaken, until Edmee had lured him back.

But this thing with the chit, this was not Edmee's fault. It had an appeal all its own, the more so for being forbidden, even if 'twas forbidden only by the needs of his purse and old ties of friendship.

"There is a tale told of the tower hereabouts," he said without missing a step, continuing on toward the chair by the hearth. "They say 'tis on this very spot that Arthur slayed the Boar Trwyth."

"I am all for slaying boars," she said, quiet fervor overcoming her shyness, "but Monmouth says no such thing."

"You've read the *Historia Regum Britanniae*?" he asked in a manner to reveal his doubt.

"Aye," she said, casting him a glance. "I can read . . . and write."

He did not miss her inference, nor the fact that she had forgotten she was in his arms.

"Your book is safe from harm." He set her down in the draped chair, resting her broken ankle on a bench and folding her within the sable coverlet. He started to rise and leave, but her hand grasped his wrist.

"The red book is mine." Her fingers tightened, underscoring the tension in her voice.

His gaze lifted slowly from where she held him to her eyes. "And a merry chase through the old stories it is in places, mistress, half of one thing, half of another, leaping over the eons, mixing prophesy and heresy with myth. 'Dragons living lounge with poyson so stronge'?" he quoted, allowing a smile. "Poison made, no doubt, from the maiden's blood which the book says will call the dragons home should all else fail—an original bit of whimsy, that. Dragons in the north prefer gold to blood."

"I care not for the preferences of dragons beyond Carn Merioneth," she told him.

His smile broadened that she should speak of dragons with such seriousness. "Ah, yes. Carn Merioneth of the golden apples, fruit of heroes and goddesses, of mortal men's joy and . . . love." He turned his hand over beneath hers, bringing them palm to palm. " '. . . comfort me with apples: for I am sick of love.' "

She snatched her hand away, her face warming with the blush he'd expected. Sweet novice. There was naught like the *Song of Solomon* to discomfit the piously celibate.

"Your Mychael, it seems, hasn't written for some time," he said, relenting from embarrassing her, "whereas you have been very busy scratching away with ink and quill. Though I daresay you don't know much about the scribbles you make, or about the odd script filling some of the other pages."

"I daresay you know even less," she replied, her voice surprisingly steady. She had steel in her somewhere.

He gave her a gently sardonic smile. "A word of advice, chit. If I were you, I wouldn't admit to knowing much either. 'Tis a wonder they didn't burn you at Usk for all the pagan trifles expounded on in your little red treasure."

"I am no grove priestess."

"Despite the book, that much is painfully obvious, *cariad*. You pray more than a saint." His smile softened as he touched her face and slowly traced the line of diminutive stitchery starting at her brow. Her lashes lowered and another wash of pink came into her cheeks. She made as if to move away, but he fanned his fingers and slid them down to her jaw, trapping her chin.

She was a woman, not a girl, however virginal. There were signs of age upon her face he had not seen that first night. Her skin was smooth, but not taut. A hint of the lines to come feathered the corners of her eyes. More telling, those pale, luminous eyes were shaded with a hardness that had nothing to do with color and everything to do with the will to endure.

His thumb skimmed her lower lip, and her blush deepened and spread to her throat. Aye, and probably to her breasts too, he thought.

He lowered his gaze, but could see no farther than the hemmed edge of her chemise. Without looking up, he caressed her lips again, letting the pad of his thumb discover the curve and softness of her mouth. The gentle swell of her breasts rose into his touch on a sudden breath; then she stopped breathing altogether, growing utterly still. 'Twas all he'd wished. Within the depths of such a telling response lay the promise of much more, yet the game was no good.

Sighing, he let his hand drop.

"Breathe, *chérie*," he suggested, smiling at her. "No matter what a man does to you, always breathe."

Chapter 9

"Dear Numa," Ceridwen crooned, sliding her fingers up the dog's muzzle as the hound lapped water from her bath. "Your breath will be as sweet as spring flowers."

The sky had been overcast at dawn, but midmorning had brought faint rays of sunshine streaming through the window, along with the unexpected delights of bathing in Dain's bowered tub.

Aye, the fates had shifted and were smiling on her now. Her gaze drifted to the bed. Dain had left his knife unattended after their supper, and she'd wasted not a second in the stealing of it. 'Twas hidden in the ropes that held the feather mattress, a lovely gold-and-silver-hilted blade, waiting for the time for her to escape.

Breathe, the fool man had said, as if such was possible when he was looming over her, filling the very air with subtle menace. In truth, a menace so subtle she had trouble defining from whence came the danger, whether from him or from within herself. He stole her breath, that she knew. He was a master at it, catching her gaze with his own and robbing her lungs of air; curving a corner of his mouth in an amused smile and stopping her breath. Breathe, he'd said, and she'd blushed like a girl.

Damn him. The night had been awkward and insufferable, and she'd done naught but dread the morning. Strangely enough, her salvation had arrived in the form of Edmee, for the maid had banished Lavrans from the solar.

Numa licked her under her arm, and Ceridwen laughed, tickled by the dog's rough tongue. She splashed the animal away, sending a small wave of water and a few rose petals over the tub's side, then settled down into the luxurious warmth, her head resting on a pillow on the rim of the tub, her splinted ankle lying on a board Edmee had rigged to keep her bandages dry. She'd never known such pleasure. Bathing in the convent had been quick and cold, and done out of necessity.

This, though. This soaking in bucket after bucket of hot water scented with roses and lavender, this was decadence, if not outright sin. A person with a future as uncertain as her own should no doubt be more careful, but 'twas difficult to think of sin when heat was melting her body all the way down to her bones and steam was softening her skin with its fragrant mist.

Dain Lavrans lived well for a man who was lord of no one. The previous night's quail had been succulent with a hint of something sweet she hadn't recognized. Oranges, he'd said when she'd asked, too entranced by the taste to feign indifference.

Oranges. His wealth appeared boundless within the confines of the tower he called his. He had rose oil and almond milk, a glazed window, and heavy tapestries on the walls. His clothes were of fine linen and the most skillfully spun wool. The bed was rich with silk coverlets and rare furs, the sable robe being her favorite. The dark pelts were lush and thick and were the ones she wrapped around herself for sleep. Everything in his chamber seemed to wrap around her—the scents of his herbals and flowers, the bed with its heavy green-and-yellow-striped curtains, the lovely sable, the curves of his wooden tub. His magic. His presence.

She trailed her fingers across the top of the water, sending ripples through the flower petals. Her intense awareness of him bordered on both the frightful and the ridiculous. He wore his hair long, like a barbarian from the north, which he'd all but told her he was, having confessed to being from Denmark. Yet his manner of movement, the way he spoke, and ate, and dressed, belied any trace of barbarism.

Breathe, he'd said, and she hadn't been able to until he'd moved away.

Edmee came up behind the tub with a comb in hand, and Ceridwen gave herself over to the maid's ministrations. With each draw of the fine-toothed ivory, a fresh infusion of lavender rose from the soap the maid had used on her hair. Utter decadence, Ceridwen admitted, to be cosseted and fussed over. She cupped her palm and lifted a handful of water to her breast. Utter, delightful decadence.

Copper of Calais, two parts: soak in alum and vinegar for two days. Realgar, ruddle, one part each, native sulfur, one part, lead, two parts. Boil in divine water for three days.

Dain stopped reading and looked around for something to hold the book open. A skull on the shelf behind the worktable came easily to hand, a human skull. He set it on the page, eye sockets facing out. Off to his right, an anthanor heated a still and two scorifying pans.

Nemeton's tower was full of the exotica used by men of learning in their quests for knowledge about Nature and truth—and mayhaps about dark arts, if such a man was so inclined. The very walls of the alchemy chamber were marked and incised with formulas in Latin, Norman, and Cymraeg, along with mysterious incantations Dain had yet to decipher, but which were written in characters similar to runes. Murder as well as magic was attached to Nemeton's name, and talk of banishment and of a violent death much deserved, according to rumor. Yet Dain had sensed nothing of violence in the Hart. There was power within its curved walls—aye, power to be sure— and enough arcana to daunt a less determined man, but no violence. Would that he could have spent an hour in Nemeton's presence and saved himself years of searching for the unifying truth of all the Brittany bard had left in his tower.

"Divine water," Dain murmured, holding a lamp high and

moving its light down a row of jars. He'd just made some divine water and would swear he'd put it on the shelves of the tunnel door.

Laughter drifted down to the alchemy chamber from above, and was followed by a stream of water running through the floor-boards. Ceridwen's bathwater. Dain reached out, letting the warm liquid run over his fingers until it stopped. The scent of roses and lavender survived for no more than a moment in the harsh atmo-sphere of burning sulfur and distilling wine, but a moment was enough to disconcert him.

Edmee must be in good form to get laughter out of the chit, he mused. With luck, if the mute maid did all aright, she would soon have his guest sighing in pleasure.

He had taken the stitches out the previous night after filling Ceridwen with roast quail and leeks and sops. She'd squirmed a bit and sucked in her breath a few times, but no actual yelling had taken place. She was healing well, except for the stiffness that had set in. That was why he'd sent again for Edmee. He doubted Ceridwen would have allowed him to bathe her and oil her body, no matter that he was skilled at kneading stiff joints and tight muscles, having learned the trade from a eunuch trained in a caliph's harem.

Ceridwen wanted her book back. She'd made that very clear. He had promised to return it soon, and had warned her that mayhaps she should not share it with anyone else after he did, especially with the name Ceridwen written here and there among the pages—which, he'd gone on to explain, could refer to any number of Welsh maidens, and most likely referred to someone legendary or long dead. Her only reply, of course, was that she hadn't shared the book with him. He'd stolen it.

He'd read it too, most of it, and a strange thing it was, a tome in many languages worthy of Madron's perusal. Pagan philosophy and prophesy were not usually found in Christian abbeys, nor tales of sea dragons and maiden's blood, stories to rival anything he'd heard in the deserts of Arabia.

There were all manner of dragon tales about these days, the stories having become popular since the Christians had sainted a Cap-padocian martyr and dragon slayer, George, and made him the patron saint of England. Nowadays the creatures were a metaphor for every-thing from demons and devils, to snakes and mercury. Even alchemy had its share of dragons, as allusions to matter, body, and metal; with the dragon's sister representing spirit, soul, and the elusive quicksilver. The two in opposition created a whole, and the pair were oft depicted as a waxing moon in opposition with its waning counterpart.

As to the red book's references to "evil men," well, he'd never had to look very hard to find an evil man, though he'd never met one determined to take a woman's blood for the sole purpose of luring sea serpents up from the ocean. The most curious Latin snippet he'd read—the one language in the book he'd recognized—had been about something called *pryf*. They had been referenced to the bowels of the earth and universal salts—whatever those might be—and to secret essences, all of which had sounded alchemical to him and therefore worthy of further study. The book said there were places, mostly caves and such, where one could hear the *pryf*'s keening cries, and that at those same places one might smell a certain rich earth scent, redolent with a sweetness oft associated with *pryf*. Unfortunately, there had been no physical description of *pryf,* but he would keep an eye out, having no aversion to a little dissection if it would provide him with some untried substance for his still.

Ceridwen's brother's letters, which she kept in the book, were no less intriguing. Mychael's mind had a delightfully mystical bend to it. So much so, Dain wondered if he practiced alchemy and the red book was actually his. 'Twasn't unknown in the monasteries. As to her brother's lack of current correspondence, mayhaps he'd accidentally killed himself. It happened with alchemy, a thought that brought Dain back to the job at hand, purifying metals for transmutation.

Divine water, he reminded himself, lifting the lamp again.

Taking care of the maid had cut into his work, putting him days behind schedule, yet he felt closer to success than he had in a long time. Purity was the key, utter, absolute purity, and he was achieving it with his new apparatus and the long-awaited eastern cinnabar, the substance used for making mercury, "the dragon's sister." The purest metals could be changed into gold by the purest sublimations, the end goal of many, but the least important to Dain's mind, what with every charlatan in the realm able to double gold. By the same process, the purest gold could be changed into the Philosopher's Stone, a rare feat for even the most skilled alchemists. And then, by taking the purest Stone and bringing it again through the elements of earth, water, fire, and air in their purest states, the alchemist could extract the elixir and the pneuma, those few precious drops of liquid with the breath of spirit about them, which could transform not just mere metal, but man himself.

Transformation. That was what Dain searched for in his lowest chamber, true magic.

Edmee came for him much later, slipping down the wooden stairs in her quiet way. Ceridwen slept, she said with her hands.

"Did she eat the chicken pottage?"

Aye, and a good portion of bread too.

"And you, dear Edmee? Did you also sup?"

When she answered, he understood that he no longer had any nut and honey sweetmeats in his cupboard, for she and Ceridwen had enjoyed every last sticky piece.

He grinned at the audacity of the maid. The sweets had come dear. "Mayhaps you'll come another day, after I have replenished my supply of comfits."

A teasing light lit Edmee's eyes, and his smile broadened. She laughed then, the silence of the sound in no way diminishing her enjoyment. Edmee loved nothing better than getting the best of him, and God knew, she had a rare talent for that.

He was tempted to reach for her, but it wasn't to be. One of his pots bubbled over, sending a pale golden liquid hissing into the brazier. By the time he'd saved the pan of egg distillate, she was gone. He caught the last flash of her skirt as she disappeared up the stairs and dropped something behind her. A rolled bit of parchment it was, floating to the floor with uncommon grace.

He wiped his hands on a rag before picking up the message and bringing it to his nose. Madron. There was no wax seal, which in no way meant the letter was not important or private. Madron never lowered herself to flagrant measures when the subtle sufficed. The scent of smoke and the herb *selago* was enough to warn any local ruffian of whose wrath he would engender should he violate either the messenger or the message. A thief from outside the demesne would not fare so well.

The witch had shown Dain the magic of it one night, taking a letter written to another and passing it over a brazier of coals holding a sprig of the herb. Smoke had curled up and around the folds of parchment while she'd chanted the person's name. When she'd given it to him, the letter had been warm but unchanged. He'd felt it all around and found nothing, then he'd opened it and damn near burned his fingers on the flame that burst forth and consumed the message. Much to his annoyance Madron had not shared the secret of the trick, and he'd been too full of wine that night to discern it for himself.

Not so this afternoon. The only wine he'd had was what he'd put into his still.

The letter opened without mishap, but not without effect. 'Twas an invitation to dine in the witch's own lair, always an interesting evening, and this one promised to be even more so. He had never been encouraged to bring a guest, let alone commanded to bring one. Ceridwen, it seemed, was the exception. Madron wanted to meet the maid.

The Cypriot picked her way through the moonlit forest, her warm breath clouding the night air, her delicate hooves snapping twigs and crushing dry leaves. Ceridwen flinched at each sound, sure they were announcing their folly to wolves and any number of beasts and brigands.

"These woods are safe, else I would not have brought you," Dain said at her back, shifting his hold on the reins to better cover her with his cloak.

His assurance helped but little when combined with his nearness and her unshakable conviction that they were being watched.

" 'Tis not far," he added—as if that helped. She saw no reason to meet the woman named Madron, especially when it meant riding through the Wroneu Wood at night. She'd told him as much and had made not a dent in his course of action.

He had not won all, though. One good thing had come from the night's journey. She now knew there was another way out of the tower besides the door in the middle chamber, which, unlike any other she'd ever encountered, did not open when the latch was lifted. There were no locks on the damn thing. It looked ordinary enough, but it did not open. The first time she'd struggled with it, she'd thought mayhaps it was the weight that kept it from moving—'twas a huge door set into bluestone. But she was stronger now, and when she'd found herself alone for a few moments that morning, she'd tried it again. Nothing had moved. Escape, if it was to come, she'd realized, would have to come by another route, and tonight Dain had shown her the way. True, she'd been blindfolded, but she had other senses. There was a door in the lower chamber, a vile, sulfurous-smelling room, and beyond the door was a tunnel leading to freedom.

A shiver coursed down her spine. She had not liked the tunnel, the closeness and the cool damp of it, the echoes of sound bouncing from wall to wall. It had reminded her of another long-ago place that was reaching out for her again, calling for her to return—the caves beneath Merioneth and the passage marked *pryf*.

"Are you cold?" he asked.

"Nay, 'tis only—Ahh." She let out a gasped cry as the mare snorted and reared up.

Dain swore and lunged forward, flattening Ceridwen against his chest as he grabbed a fistful of the Cypriot's mane.

"*Nej!*" he commanded, pulling the horse's head down by the reins. She obeyed immediately and stood trembling beneath them, her flanks heaving. "Llynya, damn your hide, show yourself before the mare's heart bursts from fright." He called the words out into the trees, but was answered with naught but silence.

Her pulse racing, Ceridwen searched the overhanging branches and reached for the gold-and-silver dagger she'd hidden in her boot. Her instincts had been right. They were being watched.

"Llynya," the sorcerer warned in a tone that set the hairs on Ceridwen's nape on edge. He'd used much the same voice the night she'd tried to sic Numa on him. Llynya would do well to run while she had the chance, though what a woman was doing in the forest alone at night was beyond Ceridwen's imagining.

"O Great One," a female voice boomed out, coming from on high.

The Cypriot shied to the left, into a patch of gorse, and was startled all over again by the prick of a spine. Ceridwen pulled her knife, prepared to fight.

"What's this?" Dain grabbed her wrist and turned it to throw light on the blade, letting the horse prance between shafts of moonlight and the shadows.

"Mayhaps my life," she said through gritted teeth, trying to jerk free and failing. "Or yours."

"I think not." He disarmed her with one hand and hollered again, "Llynya!"

A faint rustling was heard from above, followed by a branch falling to the ground and a soft curse.

"Aye, you're losing your touch, sprite." Dain laughed and pulled Ceridwen even closer, much to her dismay. "Come hither and state your case."

" 'Tis not my case, O Great One, but Rhuddlan who bids you welcome in his camp." Another curse followed the pronouncement, then a dark-haired angel fell out of the sky and landed in a thicket of elderberry bushes.

"Jesu." Dain was off the horse and racing for the woman even before she hit. "Llynya." He pushed his way into the bushes and bent over the slight form.

Ceridwen didn't wait to discover if the foolhardy Llynya had died. She leaned close over the Cypriot's neck and kicked the horse hard. The mare broke into a run, only to be brought up short.

"*Bliv!*" Dain barked out the command, and Ceridwen's escape came to a hoof-sliding halt.

She kicked the horse again and was rewarded with a nip to her leg. She would have given it another try, but suddenly she was surrounded. Half a dozen men dropped from their hiding places in the trees, each one landing with a lightness that belied the height from which they'd jumped. Like nighthawks they were, with their hair streaming down behind them and their cloaks spread out like wings.

Four instantly nocked arrows into their bows and stood facing out from the circle they made around the edge of the clearing. The fifth sprinted toward Ceridwen and took the Cypriot's reins. The sixth, their leader by his bearing, strode directly to Llynya and Dain. All the newcomers were tall and slender, with broad shoulders, long legs, and all but one had pale hair that shimmered in the moonlight. Their cloaks were multicolored in shades of gray and green, their leggings and tunics the same, all belted with braided strips of a tawny hue. More strange than the commonness of their dress were the marks upon their faces, broad swaths of darkness painted on in lines both horizontal and diagonal. Ceridwen near swooned, sure she and Dain had brought wood demons down upon themselves.

"How fares she, Lavrans?" The leader spoke, his voice soft and deep, and clear like the winds of spring, not at all like any demon she'd imagined.

"She is of the Quicken-tree clan, Rhuddlan," Dain said. "It will take more than an elderberry bush and a fall from an oak to kill her. See, already she comes back to us."

Assured somewhat by Dain's familiarity, but heartily wishing he had not taken her knife, Ceridwen strained to see around him and the man called Rhuddlan to where the woman was beginning to stir.

" 'Twas Shay I sent to find you, not Llynya," Rhuddlan said, "but she is always overeager to prove herself. We caught up with her just as she fell."

"I didn't fall." Still splayed across the elderberry, the woman spoke in a weak voice. "Shay pushed me."

"Did not," the young man holding the Cypriot's reins said, his shoulders squaring and his chin jutting out. His paint was diagonal, as were all the bowmen's, leading from his right temple to the left side of his jaw, and his hair was dark, near black. "Ye slipped."

"Slipped with your hand pressin' on my back," Llynya retorted with surprising strength.

"I was trying to keep you from breakin' your neck."

"And you knocked me clean off my perch with all your care."

No woman, this, Ceridwen thought, listening to them bicker. Llynya sounded no more than a girl. A tousled head lifted up from the bushes between Dain and Rhuddlan. Twigs and leaves were stuck this way and that in the tangled and plaited hair surrounding the imp's dirty, but otherwise unmarked face. She stuck her tongue out at the stoic Shay, confirming Ceridwen's guess.

" 'Twould be safer to let them resolve the shoving match in camp," Dain suggested, helping Rhuddlan free the trapped Llynya.

"Aye." Rhuddlan laughed and dusted the girl's bottom before setting her loose. She disappeared in a twinkling, melting into the forest with nary a sound to mark her passing.

The unnatural feat brought a frown to Ceridwen's face, tugging as it did at a memory she could not quite bring to the fore.

"Come," Rhuddlan said, clapping his hand on Dain's shoulder. "Share our meal and let us fill you with drink."

"The air fair reeks with hospitality this e'en, Rhuddlan," Dain said, smiling at his friend. "Madron has also invited me to sup."

"That one will do naught but work you over," Rhuddlan warned with a knowing grin. "Let her wait until morn."

"She takes to waiting like an unmilked cow," Dain said dryly.

"Aye," the Quicken-tree leader agreed, "but we travel north before dawn, and I would talk with you."

"North?" Dain repeated, not bothering to hide his surprise. "You could have hardly more than arrived, and are weeks early, at that." The people of Quicken-tree did not often come to Wroneu Wood before Beltaine. "What awaits you so urgently in the north?"

"Trouble at the least," Rhuddlan said, his expression growing somber. "Mayhaps more."

The Quicken-tree camp was set deep in the heart of the woods, approachable only by a trail that wound a narrow path behind the cascade of a thundering waterfall. Ice crystals glazed the water-worn track, glinting in the torchlight and adding treachery to each step. Dain led the way, the river sheeting in a liquid arc over his head.

He had not been to the secluded grove of oak and rowan since the Yule, when the river had been frozen and the trees had been deep in snow. He'd spent the night alone, nursing a strange melancholy and tending a fire in the remains of one of the previous summer's willow shelters. 'Twas the first time he'd been in the grove alone; Rhuddlan and his people had long since left. They were always gone before the first snow and never returned until after the last one. Summer folk they were, with the freshness of spring always about them, new and green like tender young shoots. Except for the bowmen. "Liosalfar" they were called, and they had the demeanor of an elite guard.

Madron knew them well, though she'd said little beyond the advice she'd given him when he'd first come to Wydehaw, that any service he could provide the Quicken-tree would be repaid tenfold.

Dain smiled. Madron was a witch. He had no doubt that she had known exactly what service Rhuddlan and his people would need of him and exactly how much it would cost him to provide it. They wanted nothing less than on one night a year, May Eve, that he who believed in nothing should believe enough for all of them. Beltaine, they called the night in an older tongue, and Galan Mai in an even more ancient language, but by any name the night was filled with the heavy magic of a fecund, blossoming earth.

His smile faded as he pulled his cloak tighter around himself. It had been a lot to ask of a cynic, yet time and again he returned to the Quicken-tree. Their demands were not so great that he could not comply, and they paid him well enough: this year in cinnabar, the year before in gold. Their first gift had been the Cypriot, freshly foaled from Rhuddlan's mare.

The Quicken-tree leader was generous with his knowledge of the planets and the stars too, and was especially learned when it came to the elements of the earth. He had also known Nemeton, builder of the Hart Tower.

In truth, Dain had come to look forward to his time with the strange, landless folk who wandered at will, bound up in a religion that no longer existed except in their own hearts. Wales was full of pauper princes, men with a noble lineage and little else, men like Morgan. Rhuddlan and his band fared better than most, carrying with them no more than the poorest desert tribes did, but never going hungry, and never reduced to wearing rags to keep out the cold.

The midway point of the water track was marked by a rock jutting out of the overhanging ceiling. The massive stone sliced an opening in the falls, leaving a space for the river fog to gather into a misty, earthbound cloud. Farther back, a cave entrance loomed darkly, sucking little wisps of vapor toward its mouth. Dain looked over his shoulder to check Ceridwen's location before stepping into the mists.

Rhuddlan brought up the rear of the small band, his gaze straying often to Rhiannon's daughter, searching in vain for signs of the mother. For all the fairness of Ceridwen's face, a softness was missing, a softness of spirit that had enabled Rhiannon to stand in the gateway of time and see the present clearly. He had been in the caves the last time she had done so, the night men had brought war to Carn Merioneth, the night she had died.

He would have saved her life if he could have, but all the fighters of Quicken-tree and Carn Merioneth together hadn't been able to hold the keep against Gwrnach and his war band. All of Quicken-tree had been unable to save Nemeton. There had been only one victory for Rhuddlan that night. Deep in the caves, much deeper than the place where a maid had used fire to protect the ancient ones, he and another had drawn the ether up from the earth and the tides and had sealed the doorway to the *pryf*'s dark maze; and by so doing, had sealed their own fate.

They had not had a choice, not with Rhiannon dead and Nemeton dying and all of Carn Merioneth in flames and overrun by men. The union of the two, forged in the crucible of the dragon wine, was of the Sun and the Moon, was the weir of balance, and it had been torn asunder. The sanctity of Carn Merioneth had been breached. With chaos ruling above and all of Quicken-tree on the run, the gateway could not be left open and vulnerable.

For fifteen years they had been exiled from the land beyond the labyrinth, unable by themselves to break the seal. Nemeton, their Beirdd Braint, a privileged bard, had been lost to them, but Rhuddlan knew another always came. *In time, in time.*

And so, in time, another had come. Dain Lavrans, a mage who, Rhuddlan knew, didn't fully understand his own adeptness and skills. There were subtle levels of power within himself that Lavrans had yet to discover, and others he had yet to control. The paths to such discovery and control were wound throughout the Hart Tower, hidden within the structure and yet blatantly exhibited for those who could see. Certainly Lavrans had found enough of interest to keep him in residence.

The Dane had been the one to open the Druid Door, closed tight and unbreachable for all the years since Nemeton's banishment. The feat had been beyond the skills of the hundreds who had tried, hoping to gain Baron D'Arbois's favor and his prize of gold. Lavran's success where so many others had failed had brought him the double-edged blessings of Rhuddlan's patronage and Madron's scrutiny. So far, the sorcerer had survived both.

Now the north was again in turmoil, and they had need not only of Lavrans, but of another like Rhiannon. Rhuddlan doubted if the woman riding the Cypriot would suffice. There was strength in her, to be sure—he felt it even from a distance—but no softness. She would break before she would bend, doing none of them any good.

The mists ahead of him swirled with a gust of warm air, earthy and rich, startling the woman. He followed her wary gaze to the mouth of the cave, and a surge of excitement laced with unease pulsed into his veins.

Someone was trying to break the seal, someone with an unsure touch. He'd sensed the stirrings of Ddrei Goch and Ddrei Glas in the deep beyond, and he'd felt the crude power of the one calling them ripple through the earth and rouse the *pryf*. 'Twould be good to go home again, but not at the cost of having strangers invade the dragon nest.

Chapter 10

Lanterns were tied to tree branches throughout the grove, glowing like low-hung stars and warming a night wind filled with the scent of budding flowers and the soft nickering of horses. People were here and there amongst the rowans. Ceridwen had glimpsed Edmee in one of the groups, seeming quite at home. The maid had lifted a hand in greeting and smiled before going about her business. A few people were making camp under the huge, graying oak that rose up at the base of a densely wooded limestone cliff, the western defense of the hidden place the Quicken-tree called "Deri." To the east and north of the grove the trees and thickets gradually grew into an impassable tangle of vegetation called The Bramble. The river guarded the south.

Ceridwen learned all this during the meal, surrounded as she was by women pleased to talk about their home. There were apple trees in the wood, they told her, and hazelnuts grew close by, along with dewberries and mulberries. Grain they harvested from the wild grass.

'Twasn't wheat, Ceridwen thought, taking another bite of the small cakes they'd served. Nor barley, oats, or rye. The cakes weren't spiced, yet were nonetheless flavorful. The flavor of what, she couldn't guess.

"You've been hurt," a woman named Moira said, her fingers stroking the scar along Ceridwen's temple. Moira had a cherub's face composed of soft curves, rose-blushed cheeks, and grass-green eyes. Her hair was a honey brown and plaited into a crown around her head. Like all the others, her tunic was made from a cloth with patchwork shades of gray and green, though in better light Ceridwen noticed the gray shimmered more like silver and the green shifted hues with every movement of the cloth, not that there was much cloth to move. The women's tunics were far shorter than anything Ceridwen had ever seen, falling to just past their knees. Startling enough, but nothing like the shock she'd felt when an inadvertent glance had shown them to be wearing braies with their hose *en coulisse*.

Convents were not courts of fashion, yet Ceridwen couldn't fathom that women's clothing could have changed so drastically in fourteen years. The dresses she'd seen at Wydehaw had seemed normal enough.

"Is this Dain's healing work?" Moira asked, her fingers again stroking down the side of Ceridwen's face.

"Aye," she said, and wondered at the lightness of the woman's touch. 'Twas as if the tips of Moira's fingers were warmed by an inner fire.

" 'Tis good work," Llynya said, her hands busy as she combed and plaited Ceridwen's hair into the little braids she'd promised to make. A thousand at least, she'd sworn, mayhaps more. The sprite had claimed Ceridwen for her own, staying close to her where they all sat on thick rugs in a lean-to of woven willow wands. The rugs were of exceptional quality, uncommonly soft and heavy and woven in the most intricate sinuous patterns. Ceridwen could scarce keep her hands from rubbing along them.

"Aye," another young woman said, "but he should have

brought her to us." She clicked her tongue and reached out to touch the scar. Her fingers, too, felt warm and soothing.

"We weren't here yet, Elen," Llynya said, her voice like birdsong in Ceridwen's ear.

"Then Madron should have sent for me, at least," Moira said. "Elen, bring me the *rasca* salve."

The younger woman excused herself and went to do as she was bid.

"Madron could not have known," Ceridwen said. "My own traveling companions didn't know what had happened to me until well after Lavrans had locked me in his tower."

Moira dismissed the explanation with a wave of her hand. "Madron knows everything."

"Locked?" Llynya asked, her confusion showing in the tilt of her head. The tumbled mess of her coal-black braids and twigs shifted with the gesture. For all the care and attention she was lavishing upon Ceridwen's unruly curls, she'd given no notice to her own. "The Druid Door has not been locked for years."

"I've brought Aedyth's salve," Elen said, returning from the neighboring lean-to. " 'Tis her newest batch."

"This will set you right." Moira smoothed a dab of the stuff onto Ceridwen's skin, but the patient's interest was focused on Llynya, who obviously knew something about the damn door.

"It won't open," Ceridwen said. "I've tried. The latch lifts, but the door won't open."

"Did you speak the magic words?" Llynya asked, her nimble fingers making quick work of one plait after another, each bound with the tiniest strip of silver-gray cloth.

"I know no magic words."

"Ah, there's your problem." The girl laughed and leaned forward, placing a kiss upon Ceridwen's cheek. "You must get Dain to teach you the magic words."

Ceridwen lifted her hand to where the kiss warmed her skin. Sweet green-eyed child. There was much she wanted to learn from Dain Lavrans, especially in magic words, though she had yet to approach him on the subject. She looked around the grove, searching until she found him near the oak.

He and Rhuddlan sat on the leaf-covered ground, apart from the others making camp in the maze of the giant tree's roots. The gnarled curves swept as high as a man's waist close to the trunk, providing shelter and privacy. The boy Shay was acting as their cup-bearer, taking the two men murrey, small cakes, and flagons of warm honeymead dipped out of a cauldron set amidst a circle of banked coals in the middle of the grove. Dain and Rhuddlan appeared deep in conversation over the small fire burning in the brazier set between them.

"He has one very special word he uses," Llynya said, her voice growing thoughtful. " 'Tis a strange one, it is, 'sezhamey.' 'Twas what he said the first time he opened the door and won the tower and the gold."

He had not mentioned gold to Ceridwen, nor anything of winning his richly appointed tower. Would that she could have such luck and be left alone the way he was, with rooms to spare and no overlord. The night wind came up, lifting a portion of his hair and carrying it like a veil across his face. He smoothed the loose strands back and brought the whole length of his hair over one shoulder, securing it with a smoothly twisted knot.

Her gaze danced over him, following the lines of his cloak from where it broke at his shoulder and draped his torso before pooling on the ground. One of his legs was bent to support his elbow in a casual pose. Tawny leather boots, cross gartered with more of the same, reached to his knees. His tunic was black, his chausses forest-green like his gambeson, and his every move was fluid, full of the sorcerer's grace.

Llynya liked him well enough, calling him O Great One. For herself, Ceridwen didn't need to like him. Neither did she have to stare at him every waking moment he was in her presence, surreptitiously watching him from beneath her lashes, always on guard to shift her gaze should he glance her way—but she did.

"Sezz-hamm-ey." She tried the word out on her tongue. She would use it the next time she faced the door alone.

"Oh, aye, that's good. He's a great magician, he is," the sprite continued. "Why, I've seen him bring up roiling clouds of smoke from the bare ground. He can turn fire into rainbow colors and make the stars fall from the sky." She bound the loose ends of another tiny braid and parted off another section of hair. "I saw him dance with lightning once. 'Twas amazing."

Ceridwen stared at the girl in astonishment. Dance with lightning?

"Now hold still," Llynya gently chided, pushing Ceridwen's chin around to keep her braidwork even.

Ceridwen's gaze immediately returned to Dain. Dancing with lightning. She could well imagine how amazing such a sight must have been: Lavrans calling down a deadly bolt of sky fire and taming it to his will, his dark robe billowing in the wind, his face alight with the force of nature's blazing radiance—and the lightning, twisting and turning a path across the earth, the air sizzling in its wake as it fought the reins of his magic.

By the grace of God, that was the trick she needed, whatever the cost.

Dain let his last sentence trail off into silence, noting that his friend was not listening. Rhuddlan's attention and his eyes, whose irises were so clear a gray as to be almost colorless, the hue saved only by the verdant rim reflecting into the middle, were fixed across the grove on Ceridwen ab Arawn. Flames from the campfire cast a tracery of shadows across Rhuddlan's profile, alternately concealing and revealing his high brow, finely chiseled cheekbones, and narrow jaw. Blue paint covered a strip of his face from just above his eyebrows to the bridge of his thin, slightly upturned nose, running from temple to temple and into his pale hair. 'Twas a badge of his high standing, the same badge Dain wore on the night when he became Quicken-tree.

He looked past Rhuddlan to where Ceridwen sat among the women, and he knew what held the other man's gaze. She was lovely, ethereal with her hair reflecting the moonlight. The feeling of contentment in the camp had softened her eyes and brought a liveliness to her features he had not seen before. He'd felt the same his first time in the hidden forest where Nemeton had once held sway, as if he'd come home. The Quicken-tree had generous spirits and a rare talent for bringing strangers into their midst and making them part of the fold or, more precisely, part of the warp and weft.

Llynya was braiding her hair. Madron would give him hell for that, but he wasn't going to stop the sprite. A woman alone needed all the protection she could get from whatever quarter. He was glad they'd come, though it seemed Rhuddlan had nothing more urgent to speak of than the growing of trees and how far to extend The Bramble this coming year, the careful work the Quicken-tree did of weaving each bush and shrub into the next. He had spoken no more of the trouble in the north, but Dain was acutely aware that Ceridwen's future lay in the same direction.

"How fares Elixir and Numa?" Rhuddlan asked, returning his attention from across the grove.

"Well, as always."

A smile curved one corner of the Quicken-tree's mouth. "If I'd known you would call them so strangely, Dain, I would have given you their true names and insisted you use them."

"Numa has taken a fancy to the maid," Dain said, grinning himself.

"Aye, she's always been a smart one."

Dain made a noncommittal sound, his gaze having drifted back to the women.

Moira finished with the salve on Ceridwen's face and reached to unwrap the bandages he'd used to splint her ankle. 'Twas too soon. He made a move to rise, but Rhuddlan's hand on his arm stopped him.

"Moira will do her no harm," the Quicken-tree leader said. "The lady needs to be tended."

Dain hesitated but a moment before sitting again.

"By her own admission," he said, "she is no lady."

"She has gentle manners and a fair face," Rhuddlan observed. "What more needs a lady?"

Dain laughed. For all that his friend had been staring at the maid, there was much he had not seen. "A less sharp tongue is counted a necessary virtue by many, and yon maid's tongue is sharper than a well-honed blade."

Rhuddlan turned aside to pick up the flagon of honeymead Shay had propped against the roots. "Her mother's was the same, when 'twas needed," he said, refilling his cup.

The statement fell into a pool of silence . . . and sudden understanding. Dain should have known.

Thoroughly bemused, he drained his own cup in one swallow. He gave his friend a measuring look, and as he did, he realized it was much the same look Rhuddlan had been giving Ceridwen all night, apparently with good reason.

"Wasn't me you wanted at all this e'en, was it, Rhuddlan?"

"You're good enough company." The reply was typically oblique.

"How did you know I had her?" Dain asked, refusing to be dissuaded.

"Moriath," he said, calling Madron by a name only he used for the witch.

"Ah," Dain murmured. "So the witch arranged our meeting in the wood."

"No." Rhuddlan took a long draw off his cup, then wiped his sleeve across his mouth. His was a face that hid the years, retaining the freshness of a youth Dain knew to be long past by the streaks of gray blended into Rhuddlan's silverish-gold hair. "She is still expecting you, probably none too charitably by now, but I wanted to see the woman taken from Usk Abbey."

Dain didn't like the sound of that. He thought the chit's life was complicated enough without drawing the interest of yet another, especially another man.

"I have not known you to bother yourself with lost brides of Christ, Rhuddlan. What is she to you?"

Rhuddlan's answer was a long time coming and arrived in a voice full of ill fortune. "Not enough of her mother's daughter, for my needs. Nor enough of her mother's daughter for what lies in her path."

The words were no sooner spoken, the breath of them still on the wind, than a frisson of prescience skittered upward from the base of Dain's skull and rolled over into a fleeting vision: serpentine coils moving through dark obscurity at unfathomable depths, their power great and ponderous.

The sight held him for an instant, no more, creating a strange pulling tension in his limbs before he shook free. Disconcerted, he reached for the flagon.

"And what have you seen in her path?" he asked, easing the question into a semblance of calm. His damned gift of sight never gave him a clear vision. Aye, he could have told Ceridwen that he had magic, just not enough. 'Twas the first time he'd felt tangible force with one of the murky pictures, though. That unusual turn he attributed to being in Nemeton's grove. The bard had left traces of magic everywhere for the unwary to trip upon, a subtle insight Jalal had

despaired of him ever discerning. He never had in the desert, not even
with Jalal there to guide him, but Dain had no other explanation for
some of the happenings in Deri, including those on Beltaine that drew
him back year after year to a wildness he was never sure he would
survive.

Rhuddlan gave him an inquisitive look. "More important, I
think, is what you have seen."

Dain didn't answer the implied question. The Quicken-tree
leader's intuition unnerved him at times, reminding him too much of
his desert master.

Rhuddlan relented and lowered his gaze to the small fire they
shared. "I have seen danger in her path," he said. "Danger, hardship,
and trouble."

The trouble part Dain understood. The maid was the very
essence of trouble. He himself could distill it no finer. Nor was hardship difficult to accept. Everyone's life was full of hardship.

But danger was altogether different, implying a threat.

"Danger from what, or whom?" he asked.

Rhuddlan shrugged. "Mayhaps herself."

"She is not foolhardy," Dain assured his friend, "only desperate." And more keenly intriguing than he ever would have imagined
when he'd first seen her hanging from D'Arbois's chains. Everyone in
Wroneu Wood and half the people out of it wanted the maid. No
wonder she was skittish, being tracked as she was, and being caught
all too often. Numa had known her worth, sensed it immediately with
her female intuition.

"Then mayhaps the danger comes from her desperation,"
Rhuddlan said.

There was truth in that. Desperation made a dangerous companion, but the maid didn't strike him as the type to do herself
harm.

"Or mayhaps from her betrothed?" he suggested, despite his
still strong doubts on that score.

"She is to be wed?" Rhuddlan's head came up, his quickened
interest somehow more disturbing than his prophesy of doom.

"Aye, to the lord of Balor Keep."

Disgust crossed Rhuddlan's features. "Gwrnach is too old to
breed her, though 'twould seal his fate to get a son on Rhiannon's
daughter."

Dain felt his own disgust rise at Rhuddlan's words, disgust edged with an unwanted anger.

" 'Tis not Gwrnach," he said, hiding his irritation by feeding a few stray twigs into the flames. "Gwrnach is dead. His son is lord now." The breeding of Ceridwen ab Arawn was none of his concern.

"Balor has a new lord?"

"Aye, the old one was gutted and left to rot on the ramparts."

"By the son?" Rhuddlan questioned, his eyes piercing in the flickering light of shadow and flame.

"Caradoc," Dain confirmed.

An unholy smile spread across Rhuddlan's face. "Then his fate was met as Nemeton foretold, that the destroyer would be devoured by his own spawn."

Well versed though he was in unsavory deeds, Dain felt a chill at the satisfaction in Rhuddlan's voice. 'Twasn't like the Quicken-tree to rejoice in another's demise.

As if sensing his uncertainty, Rhuddlan turned and met his friend's gaze, the smile fading into a grim line. "No one will mourn Gwrnach."

Dain knew the words to be true. " 'Tis said the corpse hung from Martinmas through St. Winnals before someone buried what was left of him."

"From mid-November to March?" Rhuddlan repeated, surprise evident in his tone. Dain understood. 'Twas an ungodly long time to let a family member hang.

"Aye."

Rhuddlan's gaze shifted past him to the river track. "From Ngetal to Nuin," he said in a distracted voice, using the ancient time of trees. "Just over a month past."

The sound of women's laughter, and of one woman in particular, came from across the grove, drawing Dain's attention away from the unpleasant conversation. Shay and Llynya were performing acrobatic feats for an appreciative audience, with none more appreciative than Ceridwen.

The forest at night suited her in a way that disturbed him, bringing mystery and depth to a face already too alluring by half. Llynya had woven a garland of oak leaves and set it upon her brow like a wondrous, disheveled crown. Freshly budded leaves in soft and bright shades of green dangled and curled around her gamine face;

they circled her head in a living fillet and trailed down her back in a
swallow's tail of entwined petioles. She was transformed, sitting in a
nimbus of silvered lantern light, looking very much the grove priestess
he had told her she was not. Her skin glowed, her hair flowed down
across her breasts to her waist in a river of white-gold braids, and her
mouth . . . Her mouth beckoned.

Shay was out to impress, walking backward on his hands, then
lofting himself into a back flip. Ceridwen let out a sound somewhere
between a gasp and a squeal as he landed within inches of her. The
boy was handsome enough and obviously taken with the fair-haired
maiden. The wide grin on his face proved as much. As for Ceridwen,
all Dain saw was delight, which was more than she had allowed him
when he'd performed for her. It had not occurred to him that she
would prefer acrobatics to magic.

She'd called him a fool, while she laughed for Shay.

Dain could walk on his hands. Not that he would, of course.
But he could. Ridiculous.

He thought of Rhuddlan's words, and of Ceridwen's red book,
which was in his saddlebags. Damnable thing, it had spooked the
maid into the rash act that had landed her in her current tangle of
affairs. Madron would know how much of it to believe and guard
against, and how much to discard. The witch would also know about
things Rhuddlan had not clearly said, and she was not as given to
riddles.

Moira finished rewrapping Ceridwen's ankle and looked up at
the maid, saying something. Ceridwen replied with a smile, turning
her foot ever so slightly into the light and giving her toes a little
wiggle. Dain had to stop himself from jumping up and protesting,
though it was clear the movement had not brought her any pain.

Llynya caught his eye and winked, then leaned over and whispered in Ceridwen's ear. They were a sight, the sprite's dark mélange
of braids and not-so-decorative leafy twigs, and the pale fire of Ceridwen's hair topped with a lush green crown. She lifted her gaze as
Llynya spoke, a slow rise of gold-tipped lashes. He waited, watching
their upward sweep and the gradual revealing of ocean blue, until her
eyes met his through the trees.

'Twas all the excuse he needed.

Startled to find Lavrans looking at her, Ceridwen quickly lowered her gaze, but not quickly enough. He had already risen. She

should have believed the sprite and not given in to the urge to find out for herself if what Llynya had whispered was true: that he had not taken his eyes off her.

His boots came into her line of vision before he knelt down at her side, speaking to Moira.

"May I see the salve?"

"Aye, 'tis *rasca,*" the cherub-faced woman said, giving him the small clay cup. A leaf was pressed partway over its top. "From the rowans."

He dipped his fingers in and rubbed the salve between the tips as he brought them to his nose. From beneath her lashes, Ceridwen saw the barest smile curve his lips.

"The rowans, Moira?" His smile broadened as he tilted his head, and his hair came undone, sliding in a slow fall down the front of his gambeson.

"Mayhaps a few other things are in the mix," Moira admitted, and a giggle escaped her. "You may keep it for the maid." She clapped her hands, rising, and in moments she and the others were gone, dispersed into lean-tos and huts or disappeared into the trees.

Even Llynya had deserted her, Ceridwen noticed, not seeing the sprite anywhere.

"Moira has a lot of secrets she won't divulge," the sorcerer said, relaxing to sit cross-legged on the rug, far too close to her. His knee actually touched her. Ceridwen would have moved, but before the thought could form into an action, she was paralyzed by his hand lifting her foot into his lap. "I see she used some of her own cloth in your bandage."

"Aye," she said, a mite breathless from the shock of having her heel pressed against his thigh and her calf laid along the length of his. She cleared her throat and tried again. "Aye."

His legs cradled her ankle, which felt far better than when they'd left Wydehaw. He idly checked Moira's work, his hands no less gentle than the woman's, but 'twas strength she felt coming from his fingertips, not warmth.

The warmth came from inside herself. He'd done naught but press and probe and dose her for a fortnight, but like last evening when he'd caressed her mouth with his thumb, this touch was different, gratuitous, done purely for the deed itself. No one had touched her for the mere sake of touching in a long, long while, and no man ever.

" 'Tis uncommonly strong cloth and especially suited to the binding of broken bones," he said, his fingers smoothing a fold across her instep. "Did you notice?"

"Aye." She'd noticed the give and take of it, the way it clung, the silky flow of it when the Quicken-tree moved.

She noticed, too, the slow gliding pressure of Dain's thumb and fingers down the sole of her foot, and had to stifle a sigh. The sensation was wonderful and unsettling. Normally, she was sure she would have pulled her foot away, but she'd been sated with decadence all day and her body would have more. He worked his way up to her toes, the skilled intimacy of his touch putting Edmee's efforts to shame. 'Twas as if he knew every muscle and fiber in her foot and how to make each of them melt into his hand, a magic all in its own.

"They make the cloth themselves," he said, "like everything else they use. They are not traders, you see, except in religious matters."

"Hmm," was all she could manage, despite her aroused curiosity. If she opened her mouth, she'd release the sigh lodged in her throat.

He glanced up at the muffled noise she made, and a wide grin split his face. "Breathe, Ceri," he said. *Kaurry,* her name sounded in his far north accent.

Damn, she swore on a soft expulsion. He'd caught her again, being addle-brained.

"I would bargain with you, Lavrans," she said, retrieving her dignity and her foot with an alacrity fueled by embarrassment.

He let her go easily, though his smile was still broad. "Unlike Rhuddlan, I trade in all manner of things," he assured her, reaching for another leaf to lay across the salve. "What do you want, and what do you have to offer?"

"What I have is a promise," she began, and was surprised to see him wince and shake his head.

"A not so auspicious start, *chérie.*" He slipped the small clay pot into a pouch hanging from his belt.

" 'Tis a good promise," she exclaimed, put off by his quickness to doubt.

"Oh, aye," he said, but his smile was calling her a liar before he'd even heard her out.

"Could make you rich."

"Rich?" His interest changed, becoming less skeptical. "How rich?"

"How much ransom did you ask of Caradoc for my return?"

He hesitated a moment before answering. " 'Tis not exactly a ransom, Ceri. Caradoc knows I won't hurt you. I think of it more as recompense for care."

"How much?" she repeated.

His reply was not so quick this time, as if he debated whether to tell her the truth.

"Two hundred marks," he finally said, much to her astonishment.

She didn't believe him, not for an instant. 'Twas an outrageous sum, absurd. He'd proven so clever thus far, she would have expected better of him.

"Caradoc is no fool," she told him, though it would take less than a fool to pay that dearly for a bride, even one of her supposed uniqueness.

"Neither am I." His answer was accompanied by an arrogant rise in his right eyebrow.

"If you are no fool, then what will you do with me when he doesn't pay? For he won't, you know."

His smile came back. "Why, keep you for myself, *chérie*. What else?"

"Now there's a fool's bargain," she said with a small snort, piqued that he found humor in her situation, and that he was so sure of himself. "Unlike Caradoc, you could have no possible use for me."

Dain had to keep himself from laughing out loud. Ah, sweet innocence. Sweet sweet innocence. 'Twas only great effort that kept the satyr's expression from his face, for he had use of her, a carnal, needy use. Riding with her through the forest had been both heaven and hell, the gentle back-and-forth rocking of her firm buttocks against his groin. He wouldn't have missed a one of the Cypriot's delicate steps, and if Llynya had not fallen from the sky, they would have gotten little farther than the glade where the sprite had found them.

He knew of a place in Wroneu where the grass was softer than goosedown, where water bubbled warm from the ground, and the trees made a bower dappled by sunlight during the day and graced by slivers of the moon at night. He had reached the point of deciding to take her there, and to take her there, easing himself upon her. A challenge to be sure, one requiring any innocence he had left, artlessness working so much better with virgins than any amount of cunning.

Seduction would have taken time. Surrender would have needed kisses, slow, sucking kisses on her mouth, the kind that made breathing labored and blood rush. He wondered if she had any idea how sensitive her lips were, how much of a touch they could feel, so much more than fingertips. He wanted to teach her about kissing and her mouth, if she didn't already know.

Some nun or novice may have kissed her. Such things were wont to happen within cloistered environs, and even without. But he doubted if the unavoidable furtiveness, not to mention the guilt inevitably associated with such unions, could have allowed for the kind of kissing he had in mind.

Sweet thing, he had use of her, all right, to a pleasurable end and beyond and back again.

"And if I did have a use for you?" he asked, utterly guileless, his eyes clear and his smile straight on his face. "What would your bargain be then?"

"Not to escape you in return for your teachings of magic."

"Magic?" As he recalled, he had disclaimed any knowledge of magic. But if the maid wanted to learn how to make water burn, he was willing enough.

"Aye. One trick in particular has come to my attention."

A trick, good, he thought. He had a hundred tricks and could conjure a hundred more, whereas magic—what he knew of true magic, anyway—took more patience and skill than he could have conjured in a lifetime. And therein lay the key, according to Jalal. Immortality. True magicians didn't merely control objects or natural acts. They controlled time. Otherwise, like him, they ended up dead long before they'd figured out the secrets of true magic.

Nemeton must have had the knowledge, but Caradoc was unlikely to have mastered time in the four years since they'd last met—a brief reunion in Cardiff organized by Morgan—which accounted for much of Dain's discounting of the maid's fear. She might have to struggle with superstition, and Caradoc might turn out to be cruel, but 'twas unlikely she was in danger from the dragons and magic written in her red book—the one being nonexistent and the other being rarer than snow in Egypt.

"What trick would that be?" he asked.

"To dance with lightning."

"Ah," he murmured for lack of anything more pertinent coming to mind.

"Well? What say you?"

He waited a moment, as if there were really some conditions to be weighed, some restrictions mulled over, some cautions revealed, when in actuality there were none. He didn't have a clue as to what she was talking about.

"Well?"

He looked her over carefully, very carefully, letting his gaze wander and linger at his leisure, especially noting the curve of her breasts and how the folds of her gown creased at the juncture of her thighs. Those were magical places, and if Caradoc had turned cruel, Dain would think more than twice about granting him access there. Tender maids needed tender care.

"Aye," he said, dragging his gaze up to meet hers. "After you've regained your strength, and your ankle is healed, I think you could do it without frying yourself to a crisp. 'Tis not an easy thing, you know."

"I didn't expect it would be," she said in an affronted tone.

"So you understand the risks?"

"The risks matter not. My life is forfeit if I cannot protect myself." Her voice was calm, her gaze steady. She was so utterly sure of herself and her fate.

God, but he was a black heart to be thinking of seduction while she dealt with death, whether her fears were imagined or not.

There was only one way to know for sure.

"Come," he said, rising to his feet and reaching down a hand to help her. "Let us go to Madron."

Unbidden by intent, he looked toward Rhuddlan as she took his hand. The Quicken-tree leader slowly nodded, giving permission when Dain had not realized it was needed. He had always come and gone in Deri depending on his own wishes. Then the truth struck him, sending an odd unease down his spine: Rhuddlan didn't care whether he left or not, the permission was for taking Ceridwen back out with him.

A softly voiced command brought the Cypriot to his side. He lifted Ceridwen onto the mare and took the reins to lead them through the water track. At the edge of the falls, he glanced over his shoulder to where Rhuddlan sat by the giant oak. The Quicken-tree leader was still watching them, his eyes gleaming brightly within the broad stripe of paint.

Another nod was not forthcoming, and Dain felt the lack was more of a warning than an oversight, a strange caution from a friend. The Cypriot nudged him, and he stepped into the mist, letting the silver-sheened cascade arc over their heads before Rhuddlan could change his mind and decide to keep the maid despite her shortcomings. By all accounts, the Quicken-tree had more claim to her than Dain did, to take her north or to wherever it was they kept their winter camp. But claim or no claim, he would not have left her.

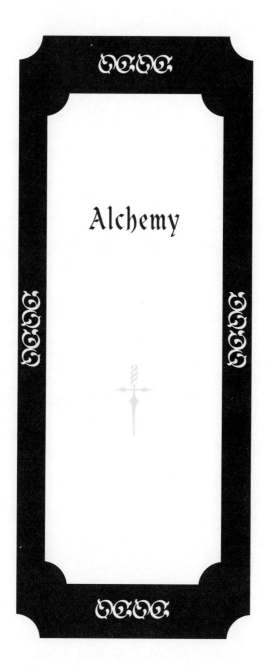

Alchemy

Chapter 11

As soon as they were free of the river, Dain swung up on the Cypriot and kicked her into a canter, heading them across a grassy stretch of meadow to the safety of the trees. He needed permission from no man to do what he wished—except, it seemed, when it came to the maid.

Look at him now, taking her to Madron, after being waylaid by Rhuddlan, while he was holding her for Caradoc. No wonder she thought of nothing beyond escape. Every move she made was met with checkmate and capture. She was as well trapped as he had been in the desert.

A quick jerk of the reins stopped the mare dead in her tracks.

"Sweet Jesus," he swore, his arm tightening around the maid like a vise, his anger at Rhuddlan flowing over into anger at her.

She squirmed within his grasp, but he would have none of it and pulled her even tighter.

"Who are you?" he growled in her ear.

Her answer was a jab of her elbow to his ribs.

"Tell me," he demanded.

"Loose me, you fool!" She tried to jab him again, but he'd lifted her off the horse and into his arms before she could connect, his feet hitting the ground as her elbow skimmed his shoulder.

He swung her around to face him, keeping her arms pinned behind her back, the reins still gripped in his fist. "There will be no more talk of fools, Ceri," he said through gritted teeth. "Now tell me who you are."

She seethed in his embrace, knee-deep in sweet woodruff with her face tilted into the moonlight. "You know who I am. Ceridwen ab Arawn, cousin to Morgan, sister to Mychael, daughter of Rhiannon, betrothed of Caradoc, and a damned prisoner to you! And each time I try to be more, someone is there to stop me!" She tried to kick him in the shins, but he hooked her ankle with his foot, his instincts faster than his common sense.

All would still have been aright, if the Cypriot hadn't chosen that moment to shy away. The struggling woman and the lunging horse proved too much for him, sending him tumbling with the maid in his arms. They fell together, with him twisting his body to take the brunt of it, another brilliant flash of instinct he couldn't have controlled for naught. He lay on the ground, the breath knocked out of him, hardly believing what he'd done.

"Are you hurt?" he asked when he could. Stupid bugger, he called himself, a thousand times worse than any fool if he'd caused her harm. He lightened his grip only a bare fraction, so if he had hurt her she wouldn't lose his support all at once.

"Are you hurt?" he asked again when she failed to respond. On the ground, in the dark, with the mare prancing around them, 'twas impossible to see her face, though it was mere inches from his. Her braids lay across his gambeson like faerie ropes, each bound end glinting with its strip of Quicken-tree cloth. "Ceri?" he said more softly, listening beyond his own rough breath for the sound of hers.

"I live." The words were mumbled against his chest.

She lives. Damn the chit for making him smile when he should be drawn and quartered.

"Are you hurt?"

"My shoulder. Where Ragnor bit me."

He swore silently and prayed Caradoc had not forgotten all they'd seen and endured in Saladin's dungeons. The red beast deserved no better.

He deserved little better himself. He'd despaired of her tears ever stopping the first sennight he'd had her. She'd wakened him before dawn at least once each morn with her crying. Her bruises had spread and grown more colorful, her eyes had been continually puffy, her nose runny. It had been only the last few days that he'd thought she would come around at all. Last night he'd been sure of it, with her show of fight over the book. True, he'd completely subjugated her again with his brief foray across her mouth, but the relapse had been minor and short-lived.

Moira had been the miracle worker, though. Her touch had healed the maid in ways far beyond his skills, bringing strength and wholeness into a broken bone, paleness into an angry red scar, and spirit back into a sorely set-upon heart. The woman he'd spoken with in Deri would have indeed been a handful for Morgan, or any man, to control; the way she'd sat there, holding court under woven willow wands, bargaining with nothing as if she held the world in her hands.

He hoped he hadn't undone Moira's work, for he couldn't recreate what the Quicken-tree woman had done, not even with the salve she'd given him, and he wasn't about to take Ceridwen back to the camp, not when Rhuddlan watched her like a hungry hawk circling prey.

Gently, so as not to disturb her more, he unwound the reins from his fist, releasing the Cypriot with a command to stay. More carefully still, he rolled Ceridwen off him and onto her side.

"Ahhh."

Her small gasp sent a wave of self-recrimination washing through him. How could he have been so careless, or so clumsy as to fall, for that matter, and how in the hell had he gotten so angry so quickly? He'd learned to curb his temper years ago—the night Jalal had so kindly offered to slit his other wrist for him with a newly tempered Damascene blade, the very one he'd taken from her earlier—and naught had made him lose his temper since, except the maid.

He looked down at her and found her looking up at him, her

eyes narrowed in wariness, her face drawn against the pain he'd caused.

"I'm sorry, *cariad*." He brushed the hair back from her brow. "I did not mean for you to fall." He never stumbled. He never got mad. Disgust had been the limit of his emotional tether for years.

"Then you should not have dragged me from the mare," she said, her tone no less cautious for the sarcasm she put into her admonition.

"Aye. I should not have." He fought another smile.

"The next time you decide to lose your wits, leave me well enough out of it."

" 'Twas not witlessness, but anger."

"At me?" Her sarcasm gave way to astonishment.

"Aye," he admitted sheepishly. Another dusty emotion dragged out of his youth, he thought with appropriate pessimism.

"And what could be more witless than that?" she demanded. "I have spoken not one word since leaving your friend's camp."

"Wasn't you, but what I was thinking."

"Then you think too much."

"So it's been said." He let out a heavy sigh and levered himself up. When she would have followed suit, he restrained her with a light touch. "Let me see what damage I have done first, and fix it as best I may."

A short time later he wondered exactly how much control over himself he'd lost. More than he'd thought, for he would swear on anything sacred that he had not meant to arrange things so according to his wishes.

Yet there she was, sitting amidst the greenery of gentian, woodruff, and celandine in the unbloomed meadow, her gown and chemise loosened and slipped from her shoulders.

Folds of the poor gray cloth and fine linen were gathered in her hands at the middle of her chest, revealing the soft upper curves of her breasts. He was on his knees, facing her, sitting back on his heels with his thighs on either side of her legs. A thousand more sins upon his head for the natural contrivance of such a provocative position.

He smoothed the *rasca* salve over the ruddy wounds, probing the muscles underneath, grateful nothing had broken open. She flinched, but he continued.

"Try to relax your shoulder, Ceri." He pressed a little harder, helping her rotate the joint in the direction he asked. The scar tissue went deeper than he would have imagined.

"You're hurting me," she groused.

"Not too much, and in the end it will do you good." He released his hold, sliding his hand down to her wrist and lifting her arm. Delightful.

"Your touch is not as warm as Moira's."

"My pardon." He released her arm and took another dab of salve. Her skin was cool where he worked the *rasca* in with his thumb and fingers, but soft, so soft. He widened the area of his massage, sliding his palm across her collarbone and up and around her throat and neck, then coming back down to her shoulder and upper arm. His gaze followed the course of his hand with a look more hungry than any Rhuddlan had cast in her direction.

'Twas the softness, he was sure, that made his mouth long to press itself against her skin. 'Twas pure desire for the erotic that made his tongue want to do the same, to taste and feel her, to trace a path to her breast.

"Does feel better when you do that," she said with a sigh, tilting her head farther to one side to give him greater access. A great fall of braids slipped over her opposite shoulder and cascaded into her lap.

Did him no good to call her innocent in his mind this time. However naively, she had opened herself to him.

"Aye, for me too." He didn't bother to disguise the huskiness in his voice. Let her hear what she did to him, he thought.

Hear she did, her breath stopping oh-so-predictably, her eyes flashing upward to meet his, the irises purple with the night, the golden lashes fading into shadows.

Beauty had never known such grace as the curves of her face and body in the moonlight. The crown of oak leaves had not been torn asunder by their fall, but still lay as a garland upon her brow, turning her evermore into the wood nymph of his dreams.

Shah mat. The phrase crossed his mind as he looked at her. The king is dead. He would have her for his own.

His hand rose from her shoulder, his palm cupping around her neck, his thumb stroking up the center of her throat. With nothing but the very best of intentions, he lifted her chin, angling her mouth to meet his slow descent.

He kissed her while she was still mesmerized with shock, the sweet, complying wench. Yet he was careful, using only his lips, partly open, and not his tongue, whose wily, plundering ways would do naught to win her until she was ready for such. And he used his breath—to warm her, to infuse and tease, letting it play across her mouth, dip into corners, and be sucked inside by her own gentle inhalation. He used his breath to tell her she would be his.

He did not lay his other hand upon her breast to feel the weight and softness of her, though he had to close his fingers into his palm to keep himself from it. He did not press her down into the grass and the budding flowers. He did not lay himself upon her, though the picture of it was clear in his mind and the feel of it was ripe in his loins. He kissed her only in the most chaste way he knew how, and still it was heaven.

Heaven, dear God, Ceridwen thought, her every sense awash with pleasure, but a heaven rife with danger. What she felt with Dain's mouth on hers was so wicked and sweet, she feared she could die of it. Her body ached and pulsed with a need to draw him closer even as her mind warned her to beware of the sorcerer's seduction. He would steal her will. Aye, he was doing it now, softening her resistance, making her yearn.

She reached for him, and in the same moment, he pulled away, leaving her hand raised in the shadows between them. His downward glance brought a chagrined smile to his face.

"I see I have moved too quickly."

"Nay," she said, snatching her hand back to the crumpled material at her breasts. "It was I."

For no good reason other than to mortify her more, tears welled in her eyes. She wiped at one with the back of her hand, but to no avail. Another took its place, and then another. Her single consolation was that the damn things had the decency to fall in silence.

" 'Twas only a kiss, *cariad*," he said, and she could have hit him. Instead, she agreed.

"Aye." She pulled her gown up, shrugging it over her shoulders, barely aware of the ease of the movement, she trembled so inside. God save her. She was damned more surely than Abbess Edith could have imagined. For if that was only a kiss, then she was wanton clear to the bone, and the object of her lust was no less than a depraved magician.

*   *   *

Evergreen woodlands grew thick all around Madron's cottage, littering the ground with seed cones and needles, and hiding the wattle and daub building from view until they were nearly upon it. 'Twas on a rocky track through the pine trees that Dain and Ceridwen had approached, with him leading the mare on foot, having decided against the hardships of riding with the maid. The cruck-built cottage boasted a storage loft and a stable in its third bay, and he left the Cypriot there, next to Madron's dappled gray mare and with a portion of hay to keep her content.

The cobbled path leading to the door was bordered by a variety of plants coming into their own with the warmer weather: enchanter's nightshade, monkshood, white hellebore, herb of grace, arnica, foxglove. All were beautiful. All were deadly. 'Twas Madron's little joke, and a true enough warning for those with any knowledge of herbs and poison.

Smoke curled from a hole in the thatched roof, putting a savory scent upon the air and making Dain wonder what it was the witch burned in her fire. The frames and shutters of the unglazed windows were carved with pictures of beasts and flowers, mountains and valleys, and the moon and the stars. He reached for the latch on the door.

"Should we not announce ourselves?" Ceridwen asked.

A catch in her voice made him pause with the door still closed.

"She knows we're here, Ceri," he said. "She's known of our coming since we passed the rise." He spoke of the hill to the north of the cottage.

"Then 'tis too late to return to the tower, or to Llynya's grove?"

"Aye." He started to pull on the latch, but once again she stopped him, this time with her hand clutching his sleeve.

" 'Tis not good, my being here," she said. "Mayhaps I should wait with the mare."

"Madron wants to meet you, not harm you, and should she change her mind, I will intercede."

"You have not proven to be particularly trustworthy." She was blunt to the point of insult.

Pleased as he was that her tears had stopped, and that she was speaking to him again, he would have wished for less honesty and more diplomacy. They had kissed, had they not? Her sweetly divine mouth had touched his. And if his plans held true, they would soon kiss again in a manner much more to his liking.

"Come," he said, opening the door. "If needs be, I will prove myself here." He slipped an arm around her waist, and thus Ceridwen found herself passing over the threshold of Madron's home—against her will and with Lavrans's hand at her back pushing her forward.

A fire blazed in a stone hearth in the middle of an earthen floor. Above it, a cauldron hung by chains on an iron tripod. Ceridwen had been in villagers' cottages before, and she had expected things to be arranged in such a manner. What she could not have expected was for all the area around the earthen circle to be planked with oak floor beams instead of strewn with common rushes.

Her eyes narrowed first in confusion, then in uneasy suspicion. If Madron was not a misplaced Norman lady—and with a name like Madron, how could she be—then there was a fortune in the king's wood at her feet, enough to send the thief, and anyone in the thief's cottage, to the gallows. The furniture upon the costly floor was no less fine and treasonous, a table, chairs, and cupboard in hand-carved maple rubbed to a warm shine. Animal skins of every type covered the plastered walls. Beaver and badger mixed with roe buck and red deer, the very sight of which made her stomach roll, for they could only have been poached from the king's forest. Any one of them was reason enough to lose an ear or a hand on the chopping block. Beautiful coverlets of ermine, weasel, and lynx lay upon the arms of the chairs, waiting to warm a guest, or hang him. She retreated a step, despite Lavrans's presence behind her, not caring that she'd backed herself against him.

"We must leave this place," she said. "God forbid one of the king's foresters or, dear Christ, the verderer should find we have been here."

"Fear not, little one." A woman's voice, dry and crackly with age, came out of the shadows at the far end of the room, near causing Ceridwen's heart to stop. "Me mistress, Madron, hast bargained well for all ye see. The Sheriff of Hay-on-Wye hi'self gave her Ursus."

A knobby-jointed hand lifted from the darkness, the only part of the woman's body Ceridwen could see, and gestured to a huge bearskin stretched between the cruck frame supporting the end wall. The head and claws of the animal had been left intact, giving the illusion that the bear had risen on its hind legs and was on the attack. A shiver raced up Ceridwen's spine. 'Twould be the gallows for sure.

"Fear not, little one," the voice came again, and after the voice, the hag herself, her bowed body supported by a staff of yew. "Ursus hast been tame fer quite some time." A cackling laugh followed the statement. "Quite some time."

The old woman used the staff with every step, her slight bulk rolling and hitching as she walked. Her clothing draped her body in hodgepodge layers of brown and muddy yellow homespun, looking more like grain sacks than a gown. The broad leather belt at her waist was hung clear 'round with various sized pouches made of skins, fur, and cloth worked with feathers. A flyaway mass of graying hair was coiled at the nape of her neck, most of it escaping from her coif. A dozen copper and silver bracelets jangled on her wrist.

She was much older than even her voice had allowed, with deep creases running from the sides of her nose to her mouth, and spidery lines fanning out from the outer corners of her eyes and down her cheeks.

But her eyes, ah, Lord, her eyes, Ceridwen thought, stepping back again. They were green like the Quicken-tree's, yet full of mystery, and deeper and darker, so much darker, as if all of Rhuddlan's people could have been born in their verdant depths and still left green behind.

"Or is it me who makes ye tremble?" the hag rasped, hobbling closer.

Partly, Ceridwen thought, but she would never admit it. She pushed back against Lavrans, expecting he would help in her retreat. He did not. He held her firm where they stood.

"Good mother," he said, greeting the old woman. "We regret the lateness of our coming, but—"

"As well ye should," the old woman interrupted, shaking her staff at him.

"But we're pleased to be in your company now," he continued, dry amusement in his voice. "Though I must say you're looking rather ancient this e'en, aren't you?"

"I thought it best," was the hag's curt reply. " 'Tis not safe fer women in the deep woods at night, as the maid well knows." She jabbed her staff toward Ceridwen, who flinched.

"If there is danger in Wroneu this night, we did not see it," Lavrans said.

"*Auch,*" the old woman swore. "And to think me mistress worried ye had been set upon by sackpurses and robbers ta ha' missed her supper, and that she would ha' to send this good mother abroad ta bring ye safely back where ye should ha' been in the first place."

Throughout the admonishing speech she directed at Lavrans, the woman's eyes did not leave Ceridwen, which added much to her discomfort as she tried to hold the hag's gaze and watch the staff at the same time. The intensity of those old, searching eyes made the skin on the back of her neck tingle. Something in the steely green perusal was familiar, familiar and unsettling, for Ceridwen believed she had endured that gaze before, at a different time, in a different place, and mayhaps when she'd had something to hide; though such a strong and detailed feeling made no more sense than Madron sending the old woman out into the woods to find them.

"But now I see what kept ye from Madron's table." The servant reached out to touch one of Ceridwen's tiny braids. "Quicken-tree cake is filling despite its taste, but mayhaps ye have room fer a posset while we wait fer the lady?"

"Aye, old mother," Lavrans said, answering for both of them. He took Ceridwen's hand and drew her deeper into the cottage.

She did not resist. The fire was warm, the cottage uncommonly comfortable—for the very same reasons that made it threatening— and posset a rare luxury. He led her to the chair closest to the stone hearth, one draped and softened with pelts of ermine. She balked ever so slightly, belatedly wondering if the king and his foresters knew of the shire reeve's generosity.

"Ye should not ha' let 'em bind her hair," the old woman said, limping back to the table. " 'Twill do her no good to have Rhuddlan's mark upon her, unless . . . unless . . . *Auch.*" She shook her head and dismissed the whole of it with a wave of her hand, sending the bracelets jangling.

" 'Tis their way," Lavrans said, taking the chair next to Ceridwen and dropping his saddlebag on the floor.

"Aye. They'd plait the trees, if I but let 'em."

"I think 'tis pretty," Ceridwen said, and the old woman slanted her a narrow look over her shoulder. For a servant of a supposed lady, she was remarkably unkempt, all ragged and loose, as if she would crumble into dust at the first good wind.

"So, the little one has a tongue?" she asked.

"Aye." Lavrans laughed, and Ceridwen shot him an offended glance.

"And she likes Moira's handiwork?"

" 'Twas not Moira, but Llynya who braided my hair," Ceridwen said, absurdly pleased to know at least one thing the hag did not.

A loud guffaw greeted her news, taking much of her satisfaction.

"Llynya? That wretched little sprite?" The old woman cackled. "Then Rhuddlan does not know your true worth. If he had, he would have dragged the white-haired ones out of their huts and made them work their fingers to the bone twisting and knotting your curls."

"Rhuddlan said he found her lacking, though he did not say in what," Lavrans confirmed, arranging himself with a knee over one chair arm and an elbow resting on the other, lounging with the air of one accustomed to both the company and the place. His ease helped assure Ceridwen of the safety of the cottage, though his words were yet another offense.

"Lacking?" The hag bridled, drawing herself up to a surprising height. "She is Ceridwen, a true-born daughter of Carn Merioneth. The only lack is in his wits." She turned to the table and began pouring milk pottage out of a pitcher and into silver goblets, hunching back down and muttering all the while. "Lacking, *auch,* we'll see who's lacking soon enough."

One by one, she took the goblets to the cauldron and dipped hot, sweet wine into each. The first she gave to Ceridwen, setting it on a small round table at the side of her chair.

"Here's yer posset, dearie. Ye might let it cool a bit."

As the old woman shuffled back and forth between the pitcher and the cauldron, Ceridwen sipped on her posset and examined the trinkets scattered across the table: two green-glass bottles, one stoppered and empty, the other half full; an iron saucer holding a pinch of salt; a family of little squirrels made of pewter. A scrap of tapestry woven in the same sinuous lines as the Quicken-tree rugs caught her eye, though it looked much older than the rugs. The color was dark and it was worn about the edges. Next to the tapestry was a candle burning bright in a brass holder marked with spiraling blue swirls. Beyond the candle, closer to Lavrans, was a plain pottery dish decorated with nothing more than zigzags, but in the dish were rocks, pretty, shiny rocks, and amongst the rocks was something she'd never dreamed of seeing.

"Elf shot," she murmured, leaning closer and reaching for the stone arrowhead.

"Hmmm?" The hag gave Lavrans his drink and peered over to see what Ceridwen held in her hand. "Oh, that. Hmmm. Int'resting choice ye made, dear."

"Is it really elf shot?"

"Oh, aye. Fashioned by the *tylwyth teg* and used in the Wars of Enchantment. Ye can ha' it, if ye like."

"What of your mistress? Is it not hers?" Ceridwen looked up, her hand closing around the precious piece of chipped stone even as she asked the question. Her mother had told her about elf shot, how the stone to make them was found only to the north of Carn Merioneth, mined by the *tylwyth teg* beneath the mountain dragon-back of Tryfan, and how the arrows would pierce only an untrue heart and nary leave a scratch on a true one.

"Ye can rest easy, little one," the old woman said. "That bit is mine to give. Here. Ye can ha' one o' me bags to hold it in." She untied a pouch from her belt and began emptying it onto the table. Two shillings and three pence shook out, clinking against the iron saucer. A fluttering of oriole feathers, soft and golden, followed the coins. The last item, she had to reach in after, her knobby fingers struggling to pull it through the leather opening. "*Auch,*" she swore, giving up with her fingers and turning the pouch upside down to give it a good shake. Nothing happened.

Ceridwen leaned closer, an offer of help on the tip of her tongue, when the first loop of gold chain slipped out. Others followed, delicate and finely wrought.

The old woman gave a grunt of satisfaction and looped the chain through her fingers. Slowly, she began to pull.

Dain sipped on his hot drink and watched the byplay. The chit was entranced already, and Madron had barely begun. Whatever was at the end of the chain was bound to be interesting. Madron never disappointed, nor did she usually wear her guise of the crone except when traveling farther than the boundaries of Wroneu Wood. She must know something about the forest this e'en that he did not. She had never searched him out before when he'd been late or gone missing—unless 'twas the maid she had prepared to search for and not him.

More likely than not, he thought with a twinge of unease at one more sign of Ceridwen's importance to someone for reasons he did not know. He'd brought the red book with him. Mayhaps was time to show it to the witch.

He swung his leg off the arm of the chair and was about to reach down, when the pouch released its prize, and the sight stopped him halfway to his saddlebag. The piece was interesting, aright, too damned interesting in the hands of one such as Madron. He did not doubt the witch's skills, be they begot by magic or tricks. He settled back into the chair to see what his friend would do with the thing.

"Is it a serpent stone?" the maid asked in a voice hushed by awe.

Her reaction was not unwarranted, for the crystal ball was cut into a thousand faces, each of them glinting in the firelight and casting a rainbow into the cottage. The orb twirled on its chain where the gold links hung from Madron's fingers. The colored lights danced about the room, swirling around and around in a dazzling, dizzying display.

"Serpent stone?" Madron asked, an eyebrow raised in his direction.

He shrugged.

"Aye," Ceri said, her gaze fixed on the glass rock. "Born of the froth of the frenzied serpents beneath Domh-ringr and hardened by their fiery breath."

The quote was good and, he admitted, somewhat gratifying. He hadn't realized she'd been listening so intently or that he'd made such a lasting impression.

"Ah, one of those serpent stones," Madron said, redirecting her attention to the maid. "No, little one, 'tis not from the Doom Rings of Judgment. This is a dreamstone."

Dain's unease increased. He had not heard of dreamstones, but there were stones enough and names enough for a good trickster to make of them what he or she wanted, and Madron was a very good trickster. Ceridwen had been quick to fall to his Brochan charm, but that night she had been pushed beyond her physical and emotional limits, and had no doubt been ready to faint dead away before he'd opened his mouth. She was strong this night with the Quicken-tree touch upon her, and she had proven to be a woman of uncommon will. Still, he could not take the chance. He had promised her protection, and he would not fail, even if it meant protecting her from her own overactive imagination rather than any physical threat.

Thus, with a lift and reach of his arm and a most fluid twist of his wrist, he passed his hand over and beneath Madron's, palming the crystal. It disappeared in a twinkling, and with it, all the rainbow lights dancing wildly around the cottage.

If Madron was surprised, she did not show it.

"Your instincts are good, if misplaced," she said, gracefully lowering her arm, all trace of the crone gone from her movement and speech. "Edmee told me you were protective of the maid, and yet, dear Dain, in this instance, you are too late. Remember that the next time Ceridwen ab Arawn needs you." The green eyes were leveled at him with the good humor of a victor and the warning of a friend.

He shot a glance at the maid and at first saw nothing amiss. "Ceridwen?"

There was no answer, and as he watched, her lashes fluttered, then lowered over the pale ocean-blue of her eyes, and she fell into a deep sleep.

"A fair trick, indeed," he said, careful to keep the anger he felt out of his voice. Anger had come to him all too easily this night, and had done him no good.

" 'Tis called a Druid sleep. The knack has been in my family for generations beyond recall."

"Nemeton," he said, knowing well the family history. Madron had been the first to come to him, as the crone, when he'd won the prize from D'Arbois by opening Nemeton's tower door. A great trick that had been, and the first time that he'd ever sincerely thanked Jalal for anything, including the saving of his life. He'd had so many reasons to hate his desert master, and not one to be grateful to him, until he'd been faced with the mechanical wonder that was the Druid Door. Not even Madron knew the secret of it, or if she did, she had not used it to secure the tower for herself.

"My father did not need a stone," she said. "His voice alone was enough to lure people into sleep and dreams."

"And what does Ceri dream?" he asked, feigning a calm he did not feel. Too much emotion was loose in the woods this e'en, that much was for damn sure, and he felt like a magnet for all of it. The maid was doing him no good. He would be better off rid of her, better off to take his marks and not look back when Caradoc came to fetch her.

"Ceri?" Madron repeated, giving him a heedful look. "Her brother called her such."

"Mychael."

"She told you?" Madron began unlacing her gown. There was nothing provocative about the action, and Dain did not react as if there was. He had seen the transformation before.

"As much as she knows," he answered. "Mychael is a monk at Strata Florida and he has not written for some time. She has a book she keeps his letters in. A red book," he added.

"Ah," Madron said, sounding well pleased. The mud-colored rags dropped to a pile on the floor, revealing a fine, shimmering lavender gown stitched and gathered with silver thread. Matching kid boots showed beneath the hem, stitched with the same silver thread. The coif came off next, and with it the gray wig. Madron shook out her own auburn hair and ran her fingers along her scalp.

"I brought it for you to look at." He reached for the saddlebag and pulled out the book. 'Twas the reason he'd come, to find whatever truth there was, as much for his own benefit as the maid's.

"That won't be necessary," Madron said, twisting her hair up into a tidy knot. "I have seen the book before, and in truth, the Latin passages are mine."

He didn't think so, not the book in his hand. " 'Tis one she brought with her out of Usk," he explained, which meant to him that it must be a very different red book than any Madron might have written in. Good friend that she was, no nunnery would have had her.

"Aye, that's the one. The one from Usk." The already much younger-looking woman walked over to the cupboard and poured scented water out of an ewer onto a piece of white linen. To that she added a few drops of oil from a vial. "I put my father's prophesies to page while I was exiled in the abbey. He gave me the book, thinking a Catholic scriptoria was the safest place to keep older truths from being forgotten, and a convent the best place to keep his daughter from being condemned for his own misdeeds." The cloth prepared, she wiped the age and lines from her brow. "Little did he understand the pious ladies of Usk."

"A convent, Madron?" Dain couldn't keep the doubt from his voice. If Madron was the kind of woman coming out of Usk, no wonder Ceridwen was unlike any novice he had known.

"Only until no amount of my father's gold could induce the nuns to keep me." She laughed softly, folding the cloth into clean quarters to wash her cheeks and chin.

No one could have that much gold, he thought, and she laughed again, casting a glance in his direction. The witch was disconcerting.

He turned his gaze back to Ceridwen. She was slumped in her chair, her chin tilted up, her mouth partway open like a child's.

"Is she virgin?" Madron asked.

Damned disconcerting.

"Aye," he said, not wanting to wonder what made Madron think he knew. Ceridwen was not the first maid he'd checked, but she was the first he'd checked strictly for his own knowledge.

"You would do well to keep her that way. 'Twill only go hard with her if Caradoc finds her virtue breached."

Ceridwen stirred, nestling her cheek deeper into the ermine. The scar down the side of her face showed silver in the candlelight, her lashes gold, her mouth soft pink.

"Mayhaps she won't go to Caradoc," he said, watching the chit and debating once more whether to keep her. Caradoc could find another bride.

"Nay, Dain," Madron said quietly, turning to face him. "She is not for you. She will go north, and she will marry Caradoc."

"Why? I see no reason for it. The Boar can find a different bride." He didn't attempt to hide the belligerent edge creeping into his voice. He was getting damned tired of people telling him what to do with the maid. He was the one who had saved her from Ragnor, wasn't he? Without him, she would have been long since dead, and the rest of them could have traveled to hell and back without finding a trace of her.

"No," Madron said, the conviction in her voice irritating him further. "The true keepers of Balor must be returned. Ceridwen was born there."

The maid had been born in Balor?

"What is this land to you?" he asked. Madron had some stake in the maid's future, and he would know what it was.

" 'Tis a sacred place, rightfully known as Carn Merioneth, the place where my father died," she answered, and he thought the stew was getting thick indeed. Carn Merioneth and Balor were one and the same. All Caradoc—and Madron and mayhaps Rhuddlan too—wanted was for Balor's chicken to come home to roost. "He held a position of great power there once," Madron continued, "and I would have it back."

"Why not Wydehaw? The tower was Nemeton's." And was now his. If she wanted to bargain with the maid for her father's legacy, let her bargain with him.

"Wydehaw is the map, Dain," she said. "Merioneth marks the treasure itself. There are not enough of us left to win a man's war of axe and bow. That much was proven fifteen years ago. Marriage is our best recourse now and the maid is the key."

"No one wins at war," he said, ill-tempered. "And damn few win at marriage, especially political marriage. In both, 'tis merely a matter of who loses less."

"This time, it shall be us." Madron moved back toward the fire and the chairs, using the cloth on her hands. Her fingers were long and slender. The bracelets were gone. She wore no rings. "With Ceridwen ab Arawn residing in the mountain of stone called Balor Keep, we can once again take up the reins of duty that have been left slack too long."

"We? Madron?" He dared to mock her with a smile and an arch of one eyebrow. "No one comes to your door. No one waits outside. In truth, I have never seen anyone other than the good Sheriff of Hay-on-Wye try to ally himself with you, and the alliance he wants would not take much of your time and little more than a lift of your skirts. No doubt he is the reason 'tis not safe for you in the woods at night."

"He hunts me, true," she admitted, drawing a footstool near and sitting close to Ceridwen. She took the maid's hand in hers, turning it over and tracing the lines crisscrossing the younger woman's palm. "But the sheriff is easy enough to elude. I speak of the Quicken-tree."

"Rhuddlan wanted to keep her, lack or no lack," he told her, as if her choice of allies might need reconsideration.

"Rhuddlan and I often disagree on the best way to proceed, but never doubt that we have the same goal in our hearts." Finished with Ceridwen's right hand, she took up the maid's left and performed the same gentle investigation.

"Often disagree?" Dain begged to differ. "I have yet to see the two of you agree on anything."

"There is Edmee," Madron said, her gaze intent on the maid's palm.

Of course.

Dain swore silently, lowering his chin toward his chest. He began rubbing his temples with an absent, massaging gesture, a poor attempt to combat the sudden pain he felt. Edmee was Rhuddlan's daughter. Good God.

The maid had been in Deri that e'en, which was not unusual. He should have guessed her parentage long ago.

"If Ceridwen is so important, where were you when Ragnor abducted her?" A change of subject was the best he could manage.

"The maid is like quicksilver to hold," Madron said. "Twice she escaped her cousin, and I managed to shoo her back. 'Twas my preferred plan, for Morgan to take her north under the protection of the Gwynedd prince, for my own involvement to be imperceptible until she was safely wed. Then she escaped once more, and the beast got hold of her before I could intervene. Fortunately, she was quickly given to you, and there is no safer place in all the world for Rhiannon's daughter than Nemeton's tower."

"My tower," he corrected her, looking up from beneath his hand. Damnable aching head. Madron must have some valerian for an infusion.

"Only for as long as Rhuddlan and I allow." She inclined her own head to see him clearly.

"You never opened the door, and neither did Rhuddlan. 'Twas I who managed to pierce its secrets and free its lock." *Coup,* he thought, and the end of it. "Do you have any valerian, Madron?"

"Aye," she said, looking at him more closely. "Poor thing. What is it? Your head?"

"Aye."

"Drink your posset, 'twill help. There is more water than wine in it, and milk always soothes. I'll fix you an infusion shortly." She went back to searching Ceridwen's palm, her fingers light upon the maid's pale skin.

He began to relax, thinking he'd won. Then she spoke.

"Neither of us opened the Druid Door, because neither of us can live comfortably among men. Rest assured we can open it if necessary, and believe me when I tell you we can close it, Dain, seal it for a thousand years, and not even your best tricks could gain you entrance."

The pain came back doubled. Madron and Rhuddlan could lock him out of his tower.

Paying him no mind with a deliberation he found exceedingly aggravating, Madron smoothed her hand over the sleeping maid's brow. "She has her father's eyes, you know, so blue they look silver." Her fingertips trailed down a soft cheek, her thumb caressing the tips of the golden eyelashes. "So pretty," she murmured, then sighed and drew her hand away. "Do not challenge me in this, Dain. She will go to Caradoc, and she will go untouched by you or any other man."

As he'd thought, Madron knew much, and none of it to his liking.

"You wrote much about death and destruction," he said, "and blood and dragons. This is what she fears so much, this bit of Nemeton's fancy."

" 'Tis no fancy, but neither does she have reason to fear."

"So you say there are dragons?" he asked skeptically.

She gave a graceful shrug. "In a manner of speaking."

And he'd thought Madron not given to riddles. "What matter of speaking is this thing called '*pryf*'?" he asked, pressing for a less vague answer.

"The word translates as worm or worm animal," she said with a glance more candid than her reply.

A fair enough metaphor for a dragon, he thought, reminiscent of lindorms and serpents and snakes and God knew what else, some real, some not. The witch seemed disinclined to differentiate.

"Time, by its very passing, changes itself," she continued. "What my father thought would be, has not all come to pass. As long as she is pure, Caradoc will not harm her. Like all men, he knows his future lies with his children. He wants those children to be of Rhiannon's blood and for there to be no doubt that they are also of his."

"Aye," Dain said, scoffing. "The book speaks much of a maiden's blood."

"The red book goes its own way, like time itself, story upon story, unheedful of man. You have done well by her, Dain. Do not concern yourself with her fate once she is gone from the Hart Tower. Where Ceridwen is concerned, there will be no blood spilled. Tonight I will give her knowledge, and naught keeps a woman safer than the power granted by knowledge."

Safe from what, he wanted to ask, but he only looked at Madron, struggling with his anger and her advice. Ceri had been right. 'Twas a bad night to be out in the woods.

"May I have my dreamstone?" she asked, holding out her hand.

He did not answer, his jaw was too tight, but pulled the stone from his sleeve and let it fall and the chain ripple into her open palm.

She threaded the chain through her fingers and held the stone up to the firelight. Again the rainbows danced and spun.

" 'Tis a pretty thing, is it not?" she asked.

"Aye," he said, and as quickly as that felt its power, a rippling awareness that flowed into his body, warm and soothing and pleasantly seductive. That was Madron's mistake, for he was wary of nothing more than seduction. "Damn you, Madron," he swore, tearing his gaze away from the crystalline rock. "Don't ply your trade on me, witch."

"Mayhaps I will be damned for other things, good friend. But not for this."

The lights were suddenly everywhere, glittering on Madron, in her hair and across her face, glittering on every cottage wall, flashing around him in rainbow hues, inescapable, creating a confusion of color and leaving but one island of serenity in the chaos, one sanctuary—the dreamstone. He looked back for no more than a moment's respite, and a pulsing brightness flickered to life at the very center of the crystal, a white flame with an ebb and flow, and it came upon him with the sound of thundering waves breaking on a far shore, filling his vision with a white, frothing sea.

"Ceri?" He called the maid's name, blindly reaching for her. Something crashed to the floor. Coins clattered. He felt his throat tighten.

"Don't fight it, Dain. Let go, let go." He heard Madron's voice drifting to him over the tops of the waves. "Sleep and dream of naught."

"Bloody damn witch," he gasped.

Madron smiled and reached forward to close his eyes. "Aye," she crooned.

Chapter 12

Madron sat on the footstool and looked at the pair of them slumbering side by side in the carved honey-maple chairs. There was much work to be done before the dawn, but their beauty held her for the moment. Dain, with his long chestnut-colored hair loose and flowing across his charm-marked gambeson, was from the earth, the hot center of it. His color was a deep dark brown—eyebrows, eyelashes, eyes, all the same rich shade as his hair, his skin lighter but having a tawny hue, his mouth like his skin but kissed to a silken texture with an underlying hint of rose. Ceridwen was ice and snow, river and sea, all things made of blue-white water and more so when mixed with air. She was the mist coming over the land, the fog-shrouded mystery of the open ocean, the dew-drops left by night upon the earth. Ephemeral, yet ever-returning. He was iron forged into steel; she was the cool temper needed to bring out its strength.

Thank the gods she was still virgin. Madron hadn't realized
how tempting the little one would turn out to be, or how strangely
vulnerable Dain had become. He had never had his head turned before by a maid; though, in truth, not many tried to woo D'Arbois's
sorcier. Those with any intelligence about them reckoned him too
dangerous, and women without intelligence failed to appreciate him.
Then there was the Lady D'Arbois. That one had a conniving sort of
cleverness to spare, and no good use to put it to other than making
trouble. Dain avoided her neatly enough. Yet it seemed he had fallen
to Rhiannon's innocent daughter without so much as a sidestep.

The Hart Tower was the safest place for Ceridwen, but under
the circumstances, the quicker she was away the better. Madron could
do much to speed her on her journey north, much she hadn't deemed
necessary until she'd seen the look in Dain's eyes as he'd watched the
maid.

She would start with checking the damage Ragnor had done.
Dain was truly skilled, and Edmee had kept her informed of Ceridwen's progress, but she would do well to look for herself, as she was
sure Moira or another of the Quicken-tree women had done.

The broken ankle was potentially the most damaging. If the
bone did not heal, or the setting of it had not been good, Ceridwen
would be crippled and always have pain. Madron had watched the
maid walk across the cottage and had been surprised at the slightness
of her limp. The injury should have been much worse, considering the
mere fortnight of time that had passed since the beast had attacked
her.

When Madron knelt and lifted Ceri's skirt, she realized why
the maid's gait was so easy—Quicken-tree cloth. Wide strips of it
wrapped her foot, ankle, and the lower part of her leg. Rhuddlan's
generosity surprised her. The cloth had strong healing properties and
was near indestructible, but the source of it had been lost the night the
Quicken-tree leader had sealed the maze. That he should give so
much to Ceridwen did not set well with her. She preferred the maid
to have as little importance to him as Dain had suggested, until her
own goals had been fulfilled.

She felt through the cloth to the ankle beneath and pressed
carefully. Her fingers detected no cause for dismay and adequate justi-
fication for relief. She'd been right to let Dain keep the maid thus far.
His skills were unsurpassed even by Moira, an amazing feat for such a

purely mortal being. The Quicken-tree woman had added speed to the healing, but 'twas Dain who had set the bone to perfection. The maid would not limp for long.

The scar down the side of Ceri's face was worse than she'd thought it would be, just as the stitchery was better. She gently touched the bright red line, her fingers pausing on each tiny set of marks left by Dain's stitching. He'd worked long on the girl. Both the cut and the sewing of it followed the curve of her hairline, though Madron detected places where he'd pulled the skin and taken extra stitches to better close the wound and lessen the scarring. 'Twas a skillful courtesy.

She left the strangest injury until last. Bones were oft broken in a fight, and knives were the weapon of choice in close combat, but biting an overpowered, much smaller opponent harkened back to a vice beyond brutality. Ragnor had tasted the maid's blood, and Madron liked that not. She'd been in the forest the day Morgan had lured the red knight into his trap. In truth, she'd helped distract D'Arbois's other men, and she'd wished the thief godspeed in taking his prize to Caradoc.

She loosened the girl's gown and kirtle and skimmed her fingers along the edge of the chemise to reveal the wound. The smell of *rasca* filled the air and brought a smile to her mouth. No remedy had been spared the maid.

A crescent-shaped scar came into view on Ceridwen's shoulder, followed by its replica in opposition. Madron's brow furrowed. The marks were oddly celestial, a waxing moon and an offset curve of a waning moon. Ragnor had a crooked jaw and an overbite, she deduced, the waxing moon being so much clearer than its waning counterpart. She liked not the look of it, but there was naught she could do. It was not festered, and for that she was grateful.

Behind her, the door of the cottage opened with a click of the latch, the accompanying breeze setting the candle aflicker. Edmee was due from Deri, and Madron turned with a welcoming smile. She'd sensed no danger, but her smile quickly faded when she saw all who entered.

She rose to her feet with regal grace, relying on a calm visage to hide her discomposure.

"Come, love," she said to Edmee, meeting her daughter partway and enfolding her in a warm embrace. "How fared you at

Wydehaw?" She tilted her head down to rub her cheek against the girl's forehead.

Edmee's answer brought back her smile.

"If all you do is eat Dain's comfits, 'tis a wonder he lets you come a'tall."

Edmee's eyelashes lowered as pink stole over the tops of the girl's cheeks, rousing Madron's curiosity. If they'd been alone, she would have inquired further into the matter, but they were not alone.

"I hope Moira fed you something more substantial," she said, gently lifting her daughter's chin to better see her eyes.

Aye, Edmee gestured, a small grin teasing her mouth. She'd had a wonderful time in Deri. Dain had come, surprising everyone by bringing Ceridwen with him, and Edmee had been able to tell them about the maid, but she was tired now and could she please be excused to go to bed?

Madron rolled her eyes at the rush of silent words and gave her daughter a kiss on the cheek before letting the girl slip away to the loft. In winter they slept close to the fire, but the nights had gotten warmer of late. She noticed Edmee stop and touch first Dain and then Ceridwen, lightly smoothing her palm over their brows, bringing her hand down the sides of their necks, and pressing her fingers against their skin. The girl would someday have Moira's touch.

Edmee glanced over her shoulder with a question in her eyes. Madron answered with a quick sign for sleep, nothing more than a Druid sleep, the easiest of spells to cast and the first she'd taught her daughter.

When the girl was gone, she looked up at the man standing by the door. He was tall and blond, with gray streaks running through his hair and a broad blue stripe painted across his face. She knew that if she ran her fingers through those silky strands along the left side of his head, as she had done once so long ago, she would find a *fif* braid, one woven out of five pieces, underneath the rest of his hair.

"So you actually thought to keep Ceridwen ab Arawn from me?" she asked.

"I wanted to see Rhiannon's daughter," Rhuddlan said, "and I wanted her to see me. She remembers nothing of the Quicken-tree."

"She remembers elf shot," Madron told him with a hint of smugness. The maid lacked nothing. " 'Twas the first thing she chose off my table."

"Then it is well she is here for you to remind her of the rest." His gaze shifted to the sleeping pair. "Though I doubt if Lavrans appreciates your methods. I would not have thought him susceptible to bewitchment."

"I'm not the one who has him bewitched." It was a partial truth, but still truth. He had been an easy mark this night. She had tested him a few times over the years with a little of this, a little of that, and had always found him unassailable. He'd caught her once trying a bit of glamour and voice on him, and had given her a smile that had chilled her to the bone. She'd been much more careful from then on.

Something or someone had softened his cynic's heart, though, and made him vulnerable. Her coin would be on someone named Ceridwen ab Arawn. A shame, really. Madron had always found his lack of faith in humanity one of his most endearing qualities, for it kept her on the edge, wondering if he would ever be proven wrong, if his heart would ever open with even the narrowest of cracks. Now it had happened. There had been no fanfare, no beating of drums, no falling stars—only a woman accidentally crossing his path.

"He does seem taken with the maid," Rhuddlan said, echoing her thoughts with far too much presumption in his voice for her peace of mind.

"Why are you here?" she asked. "Moira usually brings Edmee home." It had never done her any good to be subtle with Rhuddlan, or to be patient. 'Twas far better to know his game from the start.

"You will need my help before morning, to get them back to Wydehaw," was all he said, but she felt his reasoning fell short of the mark.

"And?" she prompted.

He looked at her from across the width of the cottage, his eyes alight with a mischief it seemed the Quicken-tree never outgrew. "I would trust you with my life, Moriath, but no further than that."

Aye, she would trust him with her life too, but no further. So she was to be watched. Well, she thought, let him watch.

"Bring more wood in for the fire," she said, disguising her acquiescence with a command, and her unease with an imperious manner. 'Twas never easy for her to be with him, especially alone. No one called her Moriath anymore, except for Rhuddlan. Her own daughter knew her as Madron. She'd changed her name to sever any ties between her and the twins after she'd left them in the religious houses, and so that she could live near Wydehaw without her father's past marking her or people connecting her with Merioneth. But through Rhuddlan she was connected, to Merioneth, to the Quicken-tree, to the past and to the future and to love.

When all was ready and her uninvited guest situated where he could observe without interfering, she crossed over to the cupboard and reached up to its topmost shelf. From there she withdrew an earthenware jar.

"*Hadyn draig,*" Rhuddlan murmured. Dragon seed. She knew he had a similar jar himself, one crosshatched with ochre and woad and sealed with beeswax.

"The scent will remind her of her last night at Carn Merioneth, of the place where I found her and Mychael in the caves."

"Will also remind her of the water track," Rhuddlan said.

She turned to face him, her brows furrowed. "You smelt *pryf* this evening beneath the falls? As far south as this?"

He nodded and leaned forward in the chair, his elbows resting on the intricately carved arms, his fingers laced together. The Quicken-tree cloth moved with the sheen and fluidity of water over his broad shoulders and across his chest. "The fragrance was rich on the track, though it lasted but a moment. 'Twas what brought me to Deri so soon in the year, the scent of *pryf.*"

She'd wondered why he'd been so early into Wroneu and able to waylay Dain and Ceridwen. Moira had been in the oak grove since the end of Nuin, but the others hadn't been expected until Beltaine. She kept her musings to herself as she picked up a small ritual blade, an athame, from one of the cupboard's shelves and incised the beeswax.

"You, too, must have been feeling the turmoil in the north this last year," he said, "especially since Ngetal."

"Aye." She had felt the stirrings deep in the earth, and she'd felt the crude power of the one calling to the children of Ddrei Goch and Ddrei Glas—too crude to be of Rhuddlan's making, she'd decided after much deliberation—and had wondered if 'twas just the *pryf* themselves rousing into action that had made the timing of Caradoc's summons auspicious. Now she was unsure. "But there can be no caller we do not know. Gwrnach knew naught of *pryf,* the fool, and I cannot believe it is his son, the one they call the Boar of Balor. I remember him as a youth, loud and boisterous, and lacking in any subtlety that would have hinted at influence in these matters."

"When first it happened, I thought it was you." Rhuddlan looked at her through eyes made evermore bright by the dark woad across his face. "Would have gone hard with you, Moriath, if I'd found that to be true."

"No less hard than on you, if what I had first thought was true," she warned him. "Now and again a stranger has stumbled onto a thread of mystery and attempted to follow it to Merioneth. You know yourself they cannot fully understand on their own, and without understanding, naught but danger and death awaits them beyond the Canolbarth." She brought the jar to her nose and sniffed. A smile curved her mouth. "This should do the trick."

"No tricks," Rhuddlan said, pinning her with his gaze. "We have waited for Rhiannon's daughter to become a woman and free the dragon spawn, because Nemeton's daughter told us 'twas the best way to reclaim what we lost when Carn Merioneth fell. But Ceridwen ab Arawn is not as her mother was, even Moira will tell you this, and now someone else summons the *pryf* from their sleep. There are those who feel we made a fool's bargain."

"Her lineage goes all the way to Anglesey, to a Magus Druid Priestess." She dismissed his concern with a wave of her hand, crossing in front of him on her way to the hearth. "None other than one such as she can bring the *pryf* up from the deep, no matter how they may make the serpents squirm."

Rhuddlan was not so easily dissuaded. "We head north this night. Let us take her with us and soon enough I can tell you if she can hold her place in the gates of time. I will even put Lavrans by her side to better her chances."

"Dain is not Nemeton," she said coldly, liking not the turn of the conversation. She would countenance no union between Dain and the maid, least of all as part of the sacred trinity of man and woman— who truly were one—*tylwyth teg,* and the cosmos.

"Neither are you Nemeton," Rhuddlan replied. "We need a key, and many of the Quicken-tree think Lavrans is the key to breaking the seal on the maze, especially if he has the maid's help."

"Then you have made him into something he is not." Anger sharpened her voice, an anger born of fear. She and the Quicken-tree needed each other. They could not win if they were at cross purposes. "Dain is a charlatan. He plays at being a sorcerer. He plays at knowing magic. The villagers and castle folk of Wydehaw take great pleasure in believing in his charms, but his conjuring is no more than masterful trickery. He knows this and would be the first to tell you it is so."

"And I tell you he has the gift of deep sight that the maid lacks. I would end this exile, Moriath, and see Yr Is-ddwfn once more."

Madron bit back a rejoinder. She and Rhuddlan always argued. They had been arguing for fifteen years, ever since she'd left him for the last time. "There is more at stake here than the opening of the maze," she said with forced calm. "What good is opening it if you can't hold it? And you can't hold it without also holding Carn Merioneth, a matter easily accomplished by a marriage the Prince of Gwynedd himself has sanctioned, and near impossible to accomplish any other way. Or would you go to the west and abandon all who are here?"

"I would not abandon man. 'Tis the duty of the *tylwyth teg* to be the bridge 'tween men and their gods. But with the maze open, we would have the *pryf* on our side."

"To what end?" she asked, finally shocked out of her feigned calm. "They are not battering rams or warhorses." Whatever in the world was he thinking? "You cannot do battle with *pryf,* nor with Ddrei Goch and Ddrei Glas. They are not there to serve us. We are here to protect and serve them."

"And we are none of us here to serve Welsh princes and English lords. Yet you would do both before you would serve me." His face grew harsh in the firelight, reminding her of all that was unfinished between them.

"I owe you much, Rhuddlan—"

"As much as you owe the damned Sheriff of Hay-on-Wye?" he demanded, pointing at the toothed and clawed bearskin.

"He gets naught from me but potions."

"And I get naught but cold gratitude."

She turned away in frustration and set about her business. In truth, her gratitude was not cold, at least not nearly cold enough. He had been her first man, her only man. Though others had tried to win her favors—or steal them, as had been the case with the lord of Carn

Merioneth—none but Rhuddlan had ever held her heart. He tempted her so, but within that temptation lay her destruction. To be Rhuddlan's woman was to not be her own, a price she would not pay.

"After Ceridwen is married," she said, keeping her voice steady, "we will have a ceremony in the caves and all will be set aright. You will be a keeper of dragons once more."

"And you?"

"I?" Using the tip of the athame blade, she withdrew a small amount of fine black powder from the jar and cast it over the flames. Blue-and-white smoke roiled up and turned in upon itself. "I will become what my father was, a watcher of the doorway of time."

Ceridwen smelled sweet, rich earth and felt warmth rolling over her body in waves. Her world had turned into one of blue-and-white mists, but it seemed not to matter. Moisture in the air beaded on her skin and tasted of salt.

"She rouses," a man said, and his voice was clear like spring winds.

A woman's voice came to her next. "Welcome, daughter of Rhiannon. Daughter of Teleri, daughter of Mair . . ."

She turned toward the warmth of the fair sounds and let the lilting music caress her skin, let the melodies of the names slip into her veins.

"Daughter of Nessa, daughter of Esyllt . . ."

A face formed in the mist, one of soft curves, green eyes, and long, flowing auburn hair. White arms trailing diaphanous wisps of violet cloth reached for her through the fog, beckoning. Moriath. Ceridwen smiled. She was safe with Moriath.

"Daughter of Heledd, daughter of Celemon . . ."

The face grew old, the eyes became wise, and all disappeared. Another face took its place, a face formed in fire with devouring flames for hair and a terrifying fury upon its features. Ceridwen felt the heat grow unbearable, felt her heart beat faster. The fire-woman loomed larger, her hair burning holes in the fog and licking at the sky.

"Daughter of Arianrod . . ."

Then it began to rain. The fury was washed away and the fire-woman's own tears extinguished her flames. Out of the tears a water-woman was born, her hair like a cool running river, her eyes like the ocean below the waves, calm and untouched by the storms passing through time.

Time.

"Daughter of Don, Mother Goddess of us all, called Danu, Dana of the light, Domnu of darkness, she who has the earth as her womb and the sun as her heart. She whose tides pull with the moon, whose limbs spread wide to hold the stars. We are all children of the one who came before. Listen, child, to your mother."

Earth.

Deeper than she'd ever been, and lost. The hushed sounds of continuous movement drew her onward, down and down, through tunnels bored smooth. Ahead of her, a cavern entrance glowed with a grayish-green light. She approached the opening with a sense of wonder in her heart and an elusive word playing upon her lips. She tried to speak the word, to make a sound . . . a soft sound from inside, and though her mouth formed the word, she couldn't hear the soft sound. Yet a veil was pulled aside, and she looked into the cavern. All was well in the pryf *nest, and she knew that as butterflies gave birth to caterpillars, dragons first gave birth to* pryf. *There were always more* pryf *than dragons, for they were the makers and keepers of the tunnels. Farther along the tunnel, much farther, another cavern appeared, and with the shape of the word in and upon her mouth, she looked inside to find the dragon nest empty.*

'Twas time to call them home.

Deeper still, the smell of brine cut through the rich pryf *scent. With the sea smell came the sound of thundering waves, of water ebbing and flowing, ever on the move in the sweeping curves of currents, and upon the shore of Mor Sarff, the subterranean ocean, were the bones of her childhood, dragon bones.*

"Thrice they come upon the land, to be born, to spawn, and to die."

The words were her mother's and clear in her mind. The knowledge was hers. This was what Rhiannon's child had been born to do: to call the dragons home to spawn and later to die, and to send the young dragons out to the deep beyond, where the rolling of their mighty bodies would churn the tides and keep the Moon coming back to the Sun, and the seasons of the Earth turning one upon the other.

She made to leave, to return to the blue-white mists, when the sound of a voice raised in full battle cry drew her head around. She looked to the caves carved deep into the cliffs lining the shore. A man stood there, the wind blowing long strands of his hair across his face like a mask. A bright sword with a hilt of braided silver and gold flashed in his hand. He

*glanced once in her direction, meeting her gaze across the shingle beach,
and she saw the warrior's promise in his eyes, equal parts of courage and
despair. She tried to go to him, but the fog rolled in from the open sea and
swirled around him, until he was gone.*

*The loss tore at her heart. Tears coursed down her cheek and pooled
in the corner of her mouth. Salt water.*

"Moriath, stop," Rhuddlan ordered.

"She but cries, elf-man."

"I do not speak for Ceridwen's sake. Look to Dain." He liked
not what he saw in Lavrans's face. Beneath the younger man's eyelids,
his eyes were twitching in a dream state too wild to be naught but a
nightmare. His color had grown pale, his breathing ragged.

*Dain had long since passed the subterranean ocean and was now so
deep into the earth he felt its molten core, the hot center of it. Sweat ran
down his face, under his arms, down his legs and the center of his back,
salty sweat. Everything was darkness in the abyss, yet he could discern
shapes.*

Concern drew Madron's eyebrows together as she leaned forward and rested her palm on Dain's forehead. His dream flowed into
her through the pores of her skin, silent and intense, a dark place with
unbearable heat and danger circling all around.

Sweet gods, she knew where he was, just as she knew he should
not be there. She started to remove her hand and bring him back, but
as the tips of her fingers grazed his brow, another image came to her,
a fleeting, tortured image of the mage's past: a full moon night on an
unsettled sea and a black tent hidden among mountains of sand; a
candle; a brazier of coals, the heavy, cloying scent of a dangerous
distillation. Three men, a bargain made, a deed done.

She jerked her hand away.

"Get water," she said to Rhuddlan, scooting her footstool
around to better face Dain. With methodical efficiency, and despite
trembling fingers, she unlaced his gambeson. She would save him
from the abyss, and then she would try to forget what else she'd seen
just as surely as he tried to forget what he'd done—and what had been
done to him.

*The walls of the tunnels were curved, bulging, and moving with a
soft hissing sound. They were alive. How long had he been there? Eternity,
a time beyond memory. There had been a woman once upon an ocean's
shore, but he had lost her long ago.*

"He should have only slept, nothing more," Madron muttered, working quickly to strip him down to his braies. "Nothing more." The gambeson came off, followed by his tunic.

When she removed his shirt, she stopped short, able to do naught but stare.

A blue-black tattoo encircled his upper arm with the interlocking curves of an ancient Celtic design. Other signs adorned him above the torc.

"Who marked him thus?" she asked Rhuddlan.

"I did. Two years back," Rhuddlan said, lowering a bucket by her feet. " 'Twas what he wanted."

"To what purpose?"

"He did not say."

He wouldn't, she thought. With her gaze, she followed the sinuous lines coloring Dain's skin. He had chosen a most painful way to remember the mysteries of her father's tower, by use of woad worked with a needle. A Druid symbol for the Sun was there above the torc, and waxing and waning moons—disconcertingly similar to the scars on Ceridwen's shoulder—and between the moons was a sign she did not recognize. More of a map it was than a symbol, being made of many parts strung together with lines. She reached out and traced the strange icon with her fingertip.

A gust of hot wind—ah, sweet breath—traveled up from the opening at Dain's feet, the wormhole. The scent was a lure, meant to entice him closer to the edge. The living wall behind him heaved and groaned, adding its own persuasion.

"Damned, swiving place," he swore. Why was he there?

He'd thought to save a woman, the answer came, and to do it with a sword. He looked down at the weapon in his hand. All was darkness, yet he could see the keen, gleaming edge of the blade. He'd thought to save her with his courage, his love, and his steel.

'Twould not be enough. Her salvation would cost his life.

Madron removed her fingers from Dain's tattoo and took the damp cloth Rhuddlan offered for cooling the mage's fevered brow. She would do what she could to protect him from the dark place, which meant protecting him from Rhuddlan. When his temperature had dropped, she wrung out the cloth again and handed it to the Quicken-tree man. "Wipe him down once more. I will bring them out of their sleep, and you may take them back to Wydehaw. Ceridwen now has the knowledge she needs. When the time comes, she'll know what she must do."

"And Lavrans?" he asked.

She got up from the footstool, making room for Rhuddlan to take her place. "I know naught what the sorcerer dreams," she lied. "I intended nothing for him."

"Yet he dreams."

"I did not say he wasn't adept. Like all of his kind, his intuition exceeds his intellect, and in his case that is a considerable achievement, as you would know if you've ever played chess with him." She bent and chose two fresh evergreen boughs out of a basket on the floor, and set them into the fire. The scent would wash the *pryf* smell from the air, creating a path for her two sleepers to follow. When Rhuddlan took them to Wydehaw, the night wind would do the rest, chasing the last of their dreams from their minds.

" 'Tis not uncommon," she went on, "for a person to be drawn into the sleep of another, though usually only when there is a strong bond between them."

Rhuddlan smiled to himself. Lavrans and the maid were bound, whether Moriath recognized the ties or not, bound by the magic that had always pulled a man and a woman together. For himself, he would see those ties wrapped ever more securely around the pair, until where one began and the other left off would be no more than a matter of pure conjecture. Ceridwen's bloodlines ran true enough for his needs, even if her art did not.

He shifted his gaze to the warrior by the maid's side. As for Lavrans, Moriath was right to fear him, for the Dane would be the one to take her father's place at the gates of time.

Chapter 13

Wine, Dain thought, groaning. He would never drink Madron's again, posset or not. His head pounded. Pain flashed in sporadic bursts behind his eyes. He felt like he'd been wrung out to his very soul, and his face was cold. The rest of him was warm, though, pleasantly warm, surprisingly warm.

He moved his fingers, lifting the tips up so he could better feel what was granting him his one level of grace. 'Twas soft, with a silky feel but a nubby weave. He dared to open one eye.

Quicken-tree cloth, a great swath of it, enfolded him like a cocoon. Another cocoon lay next to him, or more truly a chrysalis, for despite the softness of the shell, the contents showed every indication of emerging with all the beauty and delicacy of a butterfly.

He opened his other eye and swore to himself as he took stock of their surroundings. By means he found difficult to surmise, Madron had brought him and Ceridwen to the edge of Wroneu Wood. His presence this near to Wydehaw must have alerted Elixir and Numa. They could not be far, nor could the Cypriot.

"*Kom.*" The command came out a weak croak, barely audible, yet a distant nickering answered him. The dogs might belong to Rhuddlan in their hearts, but the mare was his. A moment later a far-off barking, coming from the same direction as the Cypriot's neigh, brought half a smile to his mouth. Mayhaps Rhuddlan should look to the loyalty of his hounds, especially Numa. The maid had enchanted the albino bitch as surely as she'd enchanted him.

The thought gave him pause, sparking a memory, a noticeably unpleasant memory. There had been enchantment in the night. A vague sense of it haunted him, fleeting images slipping across the surface of his mind, then diving deep where he could not follow. Damn Madron. He hoped what she'd gained had been worth the price of their friendship, for he would not forget nor forgive her trespass. Jalal, too, had been skilled at mesmerizing, but Dain had learned how to shift his awareness to a place his master could not reach. Madron and her dreamstone had slipped by his defenses, reminding him that even here, in this place, a moment's incaution could quickly turn a predator into prey—or a warrior into a whore.

Damn her. He was not without talent himself in the art of casting sleep. The witch would not do the same to him again, and she would not do it to Ceridwen.

He reached a hand out and touched the fringe of hair at the end of one of Ceridwen's braids. So soft. He'd learned much of her in Deri and even more in Madron's cottage. The red book was not to be heeded. By the author's own admission, she'd done naught but write down her father's prophesies, a term Dain was ever leery of, even from one such as Nemeton must have been. As Madron had said, time changed itself by its own passing. Prophesy often took on the trappings of myth, and myth, more likely than not, meant metaphor, a thing to be studied, but not to be feared.

Caradoc was another matter.

He tangled his fingers through the pale braids of Ceridwen's hair, letting them slip across his skin along with the shimmering threads of Quicken-tree riband. Pretty maid. Unbidden by more than his heartfelt desire, she sighed in her sleep and turned toward him. His gaze fell immediately to her mouth.

He remembered love, what it had been like to want a girl with all his body and soul, to wait and watch and suffer and need, to lie awake at night with his loins on fire despite the relief he gave himself, because his hand was not what he wanted, but the girl, the woman part of her, the feel of her beneath him, all satiny skin and heavenly mouth. He remembered the smell of a woman giving herself in love and the taste of a woman in heat. No food nurtured so deeply or with such oneness.

He remembered love, the making of love with a whisper and a caress, and he remembered lust, the edge of it cutting deep, exacting satisfaction with a fierceness that would not be denied.

And he remembered something else, something that had no part of Ceridwen, something he wished had no part of him, except he had been part of it, those dark games in desert tents, when a man wanted only what another man, or a boy, could give. He had heard of such in his youth, had even eluded a few amorous advances. But in the desert—ah, in the desert, 'twas so much different from the hasty couplings he'd imagined he would have to endure if his knife hand had not been quick and his feet even quicker.

In the desert there was heat, languorous heat, and incense filling the air and teasing the senses; and there was *kif* to inhale, to fill up your lungs and numb your mind. And there was wine, to ease the lies into truth; and the seduction of opium to put a blessed haze over your perceptions and mask the most unbearable loathing, leaving only your disgust to be dealt with later. And disgust, he'd learned, was no deterrent to survival, not after the first few times.

"Shit," he muttered, and rolled onto his back, dropping a hand over his eyes. He did not want to remember those things, not when he lay next to a woman he wanted. Edmee was so perfect in her muteness, unable to ask questions, unable to ask her teacher the name of his. *Jalal. Jalal al-Kamam.* In every nuance. "Shit."

Madron had skewed the whole of it out of kilter with her talk of locking the tower. He was too close to making his Philosopher's Stone to risk exile, and even then he needed the tower. Though he could take the Stone with him, little good it would do him without the upper chamber to guide him through the cosmos in the final steps of drawing down the elixir and the pneuma.

Transformation.

Transformation was the key to putting his past behind him, to forgetting.

His chest tightened painfully. Bloody, sodding Madron. How much of his mind had she seen? Another spasm wracked him. He pulled his legs up and eased back over onto his side, facing Ceridwen. The witch had ruined him with her damned Druid sleep.

Behind him, the sun broke the horizon, sending the morn's first true shafts of light streaming across the land, skimming treetops and pouring into meadows. The brightness touched Ceri's eyelids first, then spread down across her cheeks, and farther still to her mouth. He reached for her again, unable to resist. They'd kissed in the grass across the river from Deri.

Some people believed in the transforming power of love. Looking upon the maid, he wished he dared to believe. She was so exquisite. Her skin absorbed the dawn and reflected it back with the radiance of her soul.

He feared he was in love, and in lust. The utter, godforsaken irony of it should have killed him on the spot. But no, there would be no instant annihilation. He was a survivor, praying every day to a god he'd foresworn that he would find the redemption he no longer believed existed—except, mayhaps, in nature herself, in the shape of the sky and the substance of the earth, in the metals and minerals and stones, if he was clever enough to find the key.

But then, cleverness and keys were his strong points. Hadn't he opened the Druid Door, and hadn't he unlocked the secret of Nemeton's rotating spheres, that most strange contraption he'd found in the upper chamber, the source of Erlend's worst nightmares?

All he needed awaited him in his tower, the planets above and Earth's treasures below. He was too far down the road to chance a change in course, even for such a rare creature as lay by his side. He would give Madron no reason to lock him out of the Hart Tower.

Resigned, and somewhat steadied by reaching the only logical decision, he withdrew his fingers from Ceridwen's hair. She wanted magic? He would give her what magic he knew. To ease some of the days of her life, he would teach her of women's herbs, of yarrow and lady's mantle, vervain, rue, and water pepper. And to assuage her fears of marriage, he would teach her how to use a knife. He would give her an advantage, the edge of a blade, for few things stopped a rutting man quicker than a dagger at his throat or his balls.

He would give her the Damascene, since she was already taken with it. The hilt fit her hand well enough. 'Twould be his wedding gift to her and let Caradoc make of it what he would. His old friend was in for a number of surprises with his bride.

A loud rustling in the brush announced the dogs, yet 'twas the Cypriot who reached him first. She nudged the back of his head with her soft muzzle, warming his skin with her breath. The dogs tumbled out of the woods after the horse.

"Aye," he muttered as they bounded around and stuck their cold noses into his ear and licked his cheek. "I'm glad to see you too."

With a gesture, he directed them both to sit. Numa disobeyed with typical predictability, trotting over to be next to the maid. She gave him a quizzical glance from across the rise of Ceridwen's hip, as if asking permission for the done deed.

"Fie, bitch," he grumbled, pushing himself to a sitting position.

The albino stretched her head down to lick Ceridwen on the cheek and nose, and Dain found himself sunk to another new low: being jealous of a damn dog.

"Ceri?" He shook her arm. "Ceridwen." 'Twas time for them to be up and gone. He preferred not to be caught dallying in the woods in the light of day.

She mumbled a few words of protest, and he shook her again, then rose with an arm wrapped tightly around his ribs. Pale blue eyes squinted up at him through gold-tipped lashes.

"Come, *chérie,*" he said, forcing a smile and a lightness he did not feel. "Our adventure has lasted through to the morn, and we must find our beds."

Adventure, aye, Ceridwen thought through the haze of sleep. They'd had an adventure, she and the sorcerer, a marvelous adventure full of strange people and stranger places.

There had been a wood with wild folk gathered around a mother oak of enormous girth. A waterfall had shimmered over their heads, revealing a secret trail. They'd found a cottage hidden in a pine forest, and inside the cottage she'd found a marvel. Her hand went to the pouch hanging from her girdle, and she smiled. The elf shot was safe. 'Twas a wondrous thing to have, but there had been something else in the cottage, something less tangible and far more strange than her prized elf shot. Her smile faded. Memories had been in the cottage, her own and those belonging to others, memories of a green-eyed maid from long ago, and dreams. They had come to her in a fog and must have slipped back into the selfsame cloud, for most of them were not clear in her mind now. Yet she remembered love, strong and pulsing with the heart of the earth, luring her into a dark abyss. She remembered the anguish and the fierceness of it, and she remembered the man, a warrior.

"Come. 'Tis not far," Lavrans said, and when she looked up, 'twas him, with his flowing dark hair and broad shoulders silhouetted against the sky.

Denial quickly followed. Lavrans had kissed her, and the kissing had created confusion. He was no warrior; he was a beguiler. The man in her dream had wielded a sword, not a rowan wand.

But even the quickest of denials could not change what she'd seen, or what she'd felt. 'Twas him.

"Come, Ceri. We can be home before mid-morn."

She followed the sweep of his hand as he gestured to the west and the last shadows of night. The stone walls of Wydehaw rose into a gray sky from a distant, rocky crag, its towers wreathed in garlands of dawn mist.

The great hall of the castle was in an uproar. Servants scurried this way and that, kicking sleeping dogs and snoring guardsmen out of their way with equal vigor. Wasn't often they had the chance to get a swift foot on one of the mesnie without facing even swifter retaliation, but the overseeing black scowl of their lord, Soren D'Arbois, approved all means to his end. He wanted the hall cleared. He wanted hyssop strewn on the rushes. He wanted clean linen on the dais tables, and he wanted fresh bread and ale. The Boar of Balor was less than a league north of the Wye, bearing down on Wydehaw with a column of thirty men.

"Boar," Soren muttered.

"Milord?" A fresh-faced squire stopped in his tracks, his arms full of bee balm, and looked up expectantly.

Soren eyed the boy, momentarily distracted from his grim musings. He liked dark boys, and this one was darker than most, with coal-black hair curling across his brow and ebony eyes shining bright and innocent.

Too innocent, he decided, and sent the squire off with a cuff to the ear. "Hyssop, boy. Hyssop, I said."

Damn Vivienne. Where was she? Strewing herbs was her bailiwick, not his.

"Boar," he muttered again. The man would want his bride and Ragnor, and Soren could lay claim to only one. Damn the red beast for bringing such as Caradoc down on his head and then disappearing without so much as a by-your-leave. Having Ragnor brought to the Boar in chains would have ameliorated some of the northern lord's wrath at the treatment his betrothed had received in Soren's demesne.

What was he to do?

He grabbed a passing kitchen maid by her arm and drew her up short. "Pies," he said, sticking his face close to hers. "Meat pies."

"Aye, milord," she said, her head bobbing, her eyes round and wide.

He released her with a shove that sent her stumbling. A guardsman caught her with a hearty guffaw and "Ho, wench," but Soren would have none of that. He glared at the man until he released the maid. Ragnor's lust for the swiving of women was what had caused the calamity about to be unleashed upon them all.

And Caradoc's own carelessness, Soren thought uncharitably, and mayhaps the Prince of Gwynedd's and his man's, whoever that had been. One maid should not be so hard to hold that a fool could lose her in the woods and leave her easy prey for a hunting party. Lavrans kept her easily enough.

Of course, Ragnor had broken her ankle, an act that was bound to slow down even the quickest girl, which was certainly what the red knight had intended.

"Bah." Soren made a dismissive gesture with his hand, and three servants ran into one another, trying to decipher the cryptic command. "Bah," he growled again, giving them his evilest eye. "Bah!"

With much bumbling and mumbling, the three sorted themselves out and scattered. Fools. He was surrounded by fools, sans one, the captain of his guard, the beast Ragnor. Where had the man gone?

And why? Humiliation was nothing new in Wydehaw's hall. 'Twas almost guaranteed when Lavrans was a man's opponent. Ragnor had lost to the sorcerer before without fleeing.

There was mischief in the man's disappearance. Soren felt it. He knew it, but there was no proof, no clue that the man had done other than run off. But to where? No word had come back of him. The men who had been hunting with Ragnor that morn had reported finding boar sign and tracking the pig to its lair. There the party had split up, each circling within sight of the others, ready to cut off the swine should it try to escape, hounds yapping at their heels and the hole in anticipation of the bloodshed to come. But there had been no boar, only the scent of one to drive the dogs mad, and then there had been no Ragnor. Everyone had seen him, no one had seen him disappear, but neither he nor his destrier were to be found.

Mischief, to be sure, but by whom, Soren wondered, and to what end? There were those in the woods who were wild and particularly fond of mischief, the Quicken-tree, but they ever avoided the world of men, and they would find the rancid Ragnor particularly offensive.

Soren looked through the gloom of the hall to the iron cresset where the demoiselle had hung from her chains. Had it been magic? Mayhaps Lavrans's spell had taken hold and even now Ragnor lay fast asleep in some secret grove. And mayhaps the spell did hold time at bay, and his captain would not awaken for a thousand years.

Now there was a thought worthy of his father's great bard, Nemeton, who had dealt much with the wild ones. Nemeton, Soren thought. *The Sanctuary* in the bard's own language, a strange name for a murdering bastard.

Spells, bah. His father had believed in the power of the unseen, and what had it gotten him besides a dead wife? Lavrans was no sorcerer except by design. 'Twas the reason Soren enjoyed him so, watching the man beguile everyone from the king's sheriff to the lowliest scullery maid with no more than his wits. All except Soren himself trembled in the black-cowled demon's presence. Vivienne trembled out of lust, true, but still she trembled.

Soren would have trembled for the wizard, on his knees if need be—or actually, preferably on his knees—if it would have gotten him into Lavrans's bed, but all of his efforts had been futile. Yet he still held out hope, for there was something in Dain's dark gaze, a near unconscious sensibility inherent in his demeanor that beckoned and incited Soren in a way no other man's gaze ever had. Dain Lavrans was not innocent of any pleasure. Soren knew that truth down to his bones.

"Food or a man?" a woman asked.

"What?" He snapped out of his reverie and found his wife standing next to him by the hearth.

"Food or a man?" Lady Vivienne repeated with a bland smile. "Nothing else brings that sappy, glazed look to your eyes, Soren."

Bitch.

"I've ordered meat pies made for the evening meal," he said.

"If 'twas Ragnor's meat 'twould be better for us. I'm afraid the Boar of Balor is going to be sorely disappointed not to have anybody to torture."

Soren gave his wife a cool look. "Mayhaps I'll find someone to sacrifice before he leaves."

Vivienne did naught but return the threat with a smile. "Let us take his measure first, my love. Then we shall see who shall torture whom."

"Milord." A man came running up, breathless and pale, but moving under his own power and—a quick glance downward confirmed it—still dry in the front of his tunic. Noll had gained instant notoriety for surviving his mission to fetch the sorcerer on the night of the storm, returning singed and unconscious, struck down by a sizzling bolt of undiluted magic, a mighty bulwark overcome by the ungodly powers of bewitchment (this last being his own interpretation of events). He had become the hero of the scullery, with all its attendant benefits with the kitchen maids, and now insisted on his duty as messenger to the Hart Tower.

"Milord, I looked ev'rywhere, both up and down, right into the thick of the place, and she's not to be found."

"Who?" Vivienne asked, before Soren could fully absorb what the man had said.

"The demoiselle, lady. Neither she nor Lavrans is in the tower, or anywhere in the castle." Noll paled even further under Lady Vivienne's darkening gaze. His speech grew fainter, fading into a bare whisper of breath. "There is only old Erlend in the Hart. Not even the hell hounds are about."

He'd lost the maid. Soren felt ill, a condition only worsened by his wife turning her fury on him.

"I think mayhaps you are right after all, my love. There can be no doubt of a sacrifice being made this day."

With a bemused smile, Caradoc accepted another sugar-encrusted apple tartlet from the proffered tray. The Lady D'Arbois was putting him off, delaying him with charm, procrastinating with small talk, and treading the razor edge of his anger with a light step. She was nonetheless doomed. If Ceridwen ab Arawn was not soon brought before him, he would gut every living soul within the castle walls and burn Wydehaw to the ground.

He had asked for Lavrans with no more success. That the two of them should be missing at the same time did not bode well for his old friend. Yet Dain was no boy to be led about by his cock. The two hundred marks were with Caradoc's captain, Dyfn, along with saffron and violet sugar, enough to reimburse Lavrans for his trouble. There were no oranges, in part because there were no oranges to be had, and in part because he would allow himself to be pushed only so far by either friendship or necessity. Past that point, he would simply take what was his.

"Did you have much rain on your journey?" Lady Vivienne asked, touching her fingers to his forearm in a gesture so coyly seductive that Caradoc wondered if there might be reason to keep her alive longer than the others. The green wool of her gown was embroidered round the neck and sleeves, which were short to reveal the yellow kirtle beneath. The girdle hanging about her hips repeated both colors edged in gold.

He let his gaze rise to her face. She was pretty enough in an insipid way others might find appealing. For himself, he preferred drama to prettiness in a face, though the cruel little twist that passed as her smile held promise.

"No rain that I noticed," he said.

She laughed and touched him again, this time letting her fingers slide down his sleeve and over the bronze points on his arm guard, until they caressed the bare skin of his hand.

D'Arbois was married to a whore. How intriguing.

"How long until your husband returns, lady?" he asked.

"Oh, not long," she assured him, then, as if realizing a missed opportunity, she lowered her lashes. "Or should I say, not nearly long enough."

'Twas his turn to laugh, and he did heartily. After he gutted her husband and burned her home, he'd take this one north with him.

Vivienne blushed on cue, a well-practiced art, and wondered how much longer she could hold her guest's attention without having to take her clothes off. Soren had put her in an impossible situation. Stave off the Boar, he'd said, as if she were a soldier wielding a sword and buckler.

The shame of it was, if they were unable to produce the chit, the Boar was likely to leave in a rage without giving Vivienne a chance to properly seduce him, and she so wanted to seduce him. The sorcerer paled in comparison to this man.

Caradoc was tall, broad, and muscular, without the gross excess of flesh that marred Ragnor. His hair was not the beast's wiry red, or Lavrans's silky chestnut, but was gold upon gold, thick and heavy like a royal lion's mane. The similarity to the king's heraldry made him seem even more the warrior, as did the studded leather guards on his forearms. He was no slave to fashion, but to battle.

Yet he was beautifully fashionable. His tunic was of the softest, warmest brown wool, the shirt beneath of the finest cream-colored linen. His chausses were dark brown, his boots fit him to mid-calf. No jewelry adorned him besides a simple brooch that held his cloak, but he needed none. His eyes were finery enough. A mysterious hazel they were, with flashes of green and gold—and even white, she would swear—within the blue-toned depths.

The only unsavory thing about him was the man he'd brought with him, a leech dressed in monk's clothes with the odd name of Helebore. Fortunately, the man was not given to company. Shortly after their arrival, he had disappeared into the chambers assigned to Caradoc and had not been seen since.

"Mayhaps you would like to see the rosary," she suggested to the Boar. "There are few blooms as of yet, but 'tis enclosed with a high wall."

Caradoc leaned in close, and she saw that indeed, there were flecks of white in the irises of his eyes. "I have spent many a pleasant hour in ladies' gardens," he said, "and am sure that even without the sweetness of spring's first blossoms, yours would prove to be as fragrant as any I have dallied in."

There was no pretense in the blush that flamed in Vivienne's cheeks. The color was caused by true emotion, excitement strummed to life by the dark timbre of his voice.

"Shall we meet this afternoon?" She would have wine brought up from the cellar, and more of Renaud's apple tartlets baked. There should be a coverlet or two discreetly arranged on one of the benches. No sense in dirtying a gown.

"Aye," he answered. "Let us meet this afternoon." He smiled, and Vivienne near swooned with the thrill of it.

"Then excuse me, milord, and I shall go see what keeps my husband." And if needs be, Vivienne would shake the chit Ceridwen free of whatever hidey-hole she'd found so she could present the pale, scarred thing to her betrothed. With his mind thus eased, there would be no distractions in their tryst, and certainly no competition for his favors.

"Have you found her?" Caradoc no sooner shut the door to his chambers than he asked the question of Helebore.

"Aye, she's here now." The leech did not look up to answer, but continued staring into his silver-rimmed mazer, a maple scrying bowl he filled with water and other less pleasant things when he wanted to see what could not be seen.

"What do you mean *now*?" Caradoc asked.

Helebore glanced over his shoulder. "She was not in Wydehaw when we arrived, but she is here now," he explained. "They will find her soon enough, and then they will call for us."

Caradoc was both irritated and relieved. "Where was she?"

"I do not know."

"And her health? Is it good?"

"I do not—"

"Damn you, man! Do not tell me that you do not know." His anger slipped the bounds of irritation and became rage. He raised his hand to strike, but was stopped by Helebore's warning gaze.

" 'Tis a fascinatingly difficult thing to see inside the Hart Tower," the leech said, his voice calm, though his eyes reflected an ominous caution. "I have never encountered such a maze of veils, one after the other, like the layers of an onion. I know she's in there, and Lavrans too, but I cannot see clearly beyond the Druid Door. Will be interesting, indeed, to study it up close."

"We are not here to study doors," the Boar said tightly, and Helebore noted the effort it took for the man to lower his hand. Cretinous brute. He cared naught what Caradoc thought. The opportunity was too ripe to miss. Helebore planned on studying and touching the door, and smoothing his hands over its wood, if wood it was. Study it and learn it, feel it and devour it, for the door had been made by Nemeton, he whose name had been whispered even in Ynys Enlli. The Brittany bard had been well known among men for whom arcane mysteries and secret knowledge were the breath of life. Blasphemy, the Culdees had said, and had thrown Helebore into the sea— only him, though, when there should have been another to drown at his side, for it took two to whisper.

His lips twisted at the memory. Blasphemy to search for the source of God's power, a God Helebore believed in unequivocally, but not blasphemy to murder a brother monk? And for unjust causes? Saints, indeed. Frightened fools was more the truth, satisfied to glut themselves on piety and allegories of the abstract, when the abstract was waiting to be seized by a strong hand. Life everlasting was exactly that. Immortality was within a man's grasp. Life here and now, and then and forever. If God had not wanted man to search, He would not have made some men into searchers.

Helebore was a searcher.

Nemeton was a finder. He had not died, Helebore's fellow whisperer had said, and neither need they, if they could discover the Druid's path and the source of the *pryf,* the very key itself. Through *pryf* a man could be transformed. A past could be forgotten, a new future could be forged. The bard had known the way of it, the soft-spoken Culdee had said, and had merely slipped free of the bonds of time. Beneath Balor Helebore had seen for himself marks of the Druid's path. How much more would the Hart Tower reveal?

"I've heard the door's magic is strong," he said to the Boar, "put there by a Brittany bard and well worth close examination."

"Magic." Caradoc dismissed the word with a wave of his hand and wished he could dismiss the whole of it as easily. He would rather take what he wanted with his sword as he'd always done; and he would have, if Helebore had not washed up on the shores of Balor and shown him how much more he could win with magic. Unfathomable mysteries were hidden deep in the earth beneath his keep, mysteries of wealth guarded by strange and wondrous creatures: gold, jewels, and riches beyond most men's imagination. His father had been a fool, risking all to take Carn Merioneth for vengeance and the bounty of its land, and then allowing—nay, encouraging—the murder of the lady Rhiannon, who'd been the key to finding the even greater fortune below. Gwrnach had died as much for his lack of vision as he had for the twisted cruelty he had honed upon his son.

Helebore arched a brow. "What is it you think you keep me for, if not for my magic, milord?"

The leech's "milord" had the ring of sarcasm about it, but Caradoc could live with sarcasm. What he could not live with was failure. Helebore had promised him the power to take all of Wales, which was nothing compared to what the leech planned on keeping for himself. He'd heard the medicus mumbling and muttering to himself of a treasure untold, but if Helebore thought he could outwit the Boar of Balor, he would soon learn the feel of a blade in his gullet.

"I keep you for your wisdom, priest, and your wiles."

The leech had known the importance of Rhiannon's children, how their blood could call the beasts forth, and even more importantly, he had known they lived. Rumors of a fair-haired novice at the monastery of Strata Florida who bore a striking resemblance to a fair-haired novice at Usk Abbey had been brought to Ynys Enlli by a wandering Carmelite friar who had seen them both. It had been a stroke of Caradoc's own brilliance and a good portion of his meager fortune that had convinced the Prince of Gwynedd to sanction his marriage to Ceridwen ab Arawn, the first of the twins to be found.

His visit to Strata Florida had not gone as well. Mychael had left his monastery, and his whereabouts remained a mystery, but not for long. Caradoc had stepped up the search for Rhiannon's son. The latest news to reach the north had placed him near Cardiff, and thus Caradoc had set out to capture them both. One way or another, the Boar of Balor would have a child of Rhiannon's blood.

"Is she virgin?" he asked Helebore. *One way or another.*

"Virgin, yea, virgin, nay, it matters not," the leech answered. "Blood is blood. We will use whatever we get from her and distill it on my athanor into a potion strong enough to lure the *pryf* up from their lair. If it's the boy's we get, we will do the same. All that matters is that the blood comes from the line of the Magus Druid Priestess. It must have a familiar taste to the creatures, or they will not obey."

Caradoc knew the taste of blood, and he knew the smell of it and the feel of it running over the hilt of his blade onto his hand, but he liked not Helebore's easy dismissal of virginity. He would not be cheated out of that small spill of blood. He would mix his line with that of the Magus Druid Priestess and create a dynasty the likes of which no monk dared to imagine for fear of burning in eternal damnation.

"You will have enough of her blood to call the *pryf,* but no more," he said, returning the leech's warning look in full measure. "Remember this, priest. Before she becomes your sacrifice, she will be my bride."

Chapter 14

Putting his arm and his back into it, Dain opened the trapdoor leading from the alchemy chamber to his solar. Erlend had let the fire go out in the athanor, ruining a batch of distillations he'd been working on for seven days, and his mood was poor. The hinges creaked, the dogs pushed out from underneath his raised arm, and a gratifying but short scream of fear escaped Erlend, only to deteriorate quickly into a bout of coughing and swearing.

"Demn dogs, demn dogs." The old man cussed and flailed at the hounds. "Get yerself off me. Demn ye, Numa. Swivin' bitch."

A fine homecoming, indeed, Dain thought, continuing up the stairs until he was far enough to push the trapdoor over onto the floor. It landed with a loud bang, kicking up a cloud of dust and chaff.

The albino had Erlend by the chausses and was tugging at them, while growling deep in her throat.

The old man's soiled and tattered braies were coming down along with the drooping hose, a sight Dain could have gone three or four lifetimes without having to endure.

"Numa." Averting his gaze, he called the dog off and pointed to the hearth. A giggle came from behind him. He glanced back over at Erlend and saw him struggling to rearrange his undergarments over his bony buttocks. The old man had backed himself into the wooden shelves lining the curved stone wall, and his every move caused the pots and jars to jiggle and shake. Ceridwen let out another laugh, more of a snort this time than a giggle. He was glad she was in such good humor after their long night in Wroneu. For himself, he felt like hell.

"Be gone, Erlend," he commanded, thoroughly disgusted with the old man's filth, Ceridwen's good cheer, and the course his life had taken.

"I'd be gone," Erlend groused. "I'd ha' been long gone, if 'tweren't fer the demned castle guards layin' siege to me."

"Siege?" The word was no sooner out of Dain's mouth than he heard the commotion on the other side of the Druid Door. Voices were rumbling. The sound of feet could be heard going up and down the tower stairs. "What is this?" he demanded.

"They want the maid," Erlend said. "I let the first one in, that Noll, but he left in such a fuss when he din't find the girl that I daren't let another pass. They been out there since sunup. Yellin' and threatenin' and raisin' a ruckus on the door, but I locked 'er down tight and I hain't lettin' another one in. If'n I was ye, I'd be demn careful."

"Locked her down?" Dain questioned.

Erlend nodded. "Tighter'n a drum."

Dain swore and strode over to the door, tossing the folded Quicken-tree cloth on the bed as he passed. Fool man. D'Arbois would not hesitate long in taking a battering ram to the door, for all the good it would do him. He would do naught but seal the door even tighter by trying to breach it. The plates activated by the levers of the lock were embedded six feet into the curving tower walls on either side. The only way through the Druid Door was by destroying the tower itself.

The old baron had thought the tower sacred. He had allowed no one to disturb his bard's chambers, despite the man's falling from grace. Soren had no such constraints. Superstition had held him at bay for a few months after his father's death, until his curiosity could no longer be denied. The Hart Tower had been said to hold a treasure trove, to be a repository of man's greatest riches. It had also been said to be cursed, and thus Soren had devised his reward to induce another to do the actual opening, if they could but find the way. A hundred marks had seemed a small price to pay for the ill fortune to fall on someone else's head.

That someone had been Dain, and if there was a curse, he had not felt it until a fortnight ago, when Ceridwen ab Arawn, most cherished and sought after jewel in all the land, had inadvertently fallen into his keeping.

Damn the chit, and damn the old man.

He ran his hand over the planks of the door, feeling the pattern of iron rods pushed into the wood. After a minute, he breathed a sigh of relief and looked over his shoulder at Erlend. The man knew nothing. He'd meant no more than the securing of the crossbar. If the door had been truly locked down "tighter'n a drum," it would have taken Dain himself a sennight to open it back up. That was how long it had taken him to open it the first time. Since then, he'd not locked the door past the second minor level, and that only once. The first minor level was adequate for most circumstances. It had kept Ceridwen in.

"It's him, ye know," Erlend said, making not much sense as usual.

"Who?" Dain asked, only half listening. The third minor level of iron rods was flush with the oak planks, their exposed ends making the symbol for Venus and copper within the circular pattern of the lock.

"The pig whose troth was't plighted."

Dain's eyebrows drew together in a deep furrow. The pig whose troth was't plighted? Erlend's blubbering would soon give him another headache. A quick visual survey assured him the first and second minor levels, being the Sun and gold, and Mercury and mercury, respectively, had not been tampered with. The fourth minor level, the heretical placement of Earth, was . . . *Pig*.

His hand stilled on the oak planks. Caradoc had come for the maid. His breath grew short as he turned his head to look back over his shoulder. Ceridwen had understood. Her face had paled beyond white to ghostly.

"I—I am not ready," she stammered.

His heart beat too quickly in his chest. His thoughts were a tangle. Caradoc had come for the maid. He opened his mouth to speak, but no words would form.

"You promised me magic," she told him, blending accusation with her plea.

Magic? He had no magic. He had nothing. Had she not seen through him yet?

A great pounding started on the door, sending hard and heavy vibrations up his arms. 'Twas the ram he'd expected, a ridiculously short one, given the available maneuvering room in the stairwell, but one sturdy enough to do damage.

"Cretins," he hissed, his anger rising out of the morass of his mind and taking hold of his thoughts. He whirled on Ceridwen with a command. "Take your clothes off and hide yourself in the bed."

Erlend immediately brightened, a toothless grin forming upon his face.

"Get below, old man," Dain warned, shifting his attention to the lecherous servant, "or your next breath will be your last."

The ram hit the door again. Hollow echoes sounded through the chamber, curving around the tower walls and leaving a tinny resonance hanging in the air.

Bastards.

"Move!" he barked. Erlend jumped, but Ceridwen held her ground.

"Let me go," she said.

"No."

"My ankle is near healed. Let me return back through the tunnel and make my escape."

"To where?" he demanded. "Strata Florida? Caradoc would have you run down before you could clear the river."

"Then through the woods to Deri. Rhuddlan would keep me."

"For his own purposes, not yours." Foolish girl. Did she trust everyone more than she did him?

The ram struck home a mighty blow.

"What about your friend, Madron?" Her voice took on a desperate edge. "Her serving woman liked me well enough. Mayhaps they would hide me until I can get word to my brother."

"Madron is no friend of mine, or of yours," he snapped. "She was disguised as the crone, and while you slept, she looked upon you long enough to pronounce you the perfect bride for the Boar of Balor."

She stared at him, her hands growing limp at her sides, his words taking the fight out of her.

"The crone? But I remember a woman coming, a special woman. I felt her presence in the cottage." Her voice was unsure again. "I . . . I thought 'twas someone else."

"There is no one to help you except me." They did not have time for this debate. "Get yourself into the bed, or I will be done with you."

His threat had the desired effect, and she began stripping off her gown.

He threw off his cloak and reached for the lacings on his gambeson. They were already half undone, giving him a moment's pause and making him wonder what else Madron had seen in the night besides his mind. The witch had better beware.

He finished freeing the laces and removed the gambeson. He needed physick and a simple to make Ceri sleep, and elderberry, chamomile, and some of his precious lime to make her sweat. Blood would be good for visual effect, but he had none at hand.

Except for Erlend's.

He looked at the old man shuffling toward the trapdoor and started forward. Some of what he thought must have shown on his face, for the servant quickened his steps, making it a close race as to who would reach the stairs first. Erlend won with a sprightly jump that no doubt left a little of the needed blood on the floor of the alchemy chamber. Dain grimaced at the waste of it, then shut the trapdoor and kicked the bolt home with his foot. *Pudre ruge* would have to do.

He dipped a cup of water out of the cauldron steaming on the hearth and began pulling pots and bottles off the shelf, this and that, all the herbs he needed and half of what he didn't. The battering ram hit again, a resounding, percussive thud. A bottle slipped from his fingers and crashed to the floor, splintering glass and spilling a vile-smelling concoction. The castle guards were putting their hearts into it. Mayhaps D'Arbois had gotten out his whip. Dain bent to pick up the pieces of glass and swore when he cut himself. Now he had the damn blood. It ran down his finger and pooled in his palm. He grabbed a pile of bandages, making sure to spread the blood as far as possible, and turned to Ceridwen.

To his dismay, she was still standing in the middle of the chamber. Her gown was gone, but not so her kirtle and chemise.

"Why aren't you in the bed?"

"What are you doing?" was her reply, no answer a'tall.

He lifted his eyebrows in surprise. Her resolve had rehardened in his few moments of inattention. Though still obviously frightened, she had that sharp-tongued look about her. Would serve Caradoc well to give him the maid in such a mood.

Then why not do it? he asked himself. Why not be done with her? Her betrothed waited, if not in the stairwell, then in the great hall. He could not have her for himself—Madron had made sure of that—so why not give her to the man who could?

Because she is too ill to travel. He lied to himself with amazing ease, knowing that if 'twas not yet the truth, it would be soon enough, after she drank his potion.

"I am mixing an infusion to make you sweat and vomit," he explained patiently, working hard to keep himself from going over and shaking her. "Mayhaps I'll also give you the runs and make you delirious. I am going to wrap your head with bloody bandages, smear your scars with *pudre ruge,* and rub ashes into your teeth and gums."

He saw the light of understanding and hope flicker in her eyes. With all due haste, she worked her way out of her kirtle, pulling it up over her head and leaving him to stare at the soft curves of her body as revealed through the fine linen chemise.

"And if that does not sway your betrothed," he continued, "I will make you tremble and jerk upon the bed like a woman possessed, all the while assuring the Boar that I nearly have your demons banished and will soon have you aright."

The billowing of her clothes filled the air with her scent. He inhaled the fragrant, feminine redolence, all thoughts of shaking her vanishing like so much ether in the wind, and replaced with imaginings of a much gentler ilk. His gaze caressed each flowing curve, from her throat to the arch of her foot, up the length of her arms bared by her chemise, and down again to linger in the shadows between her breasts and lower still to the beckoning mystery between her thighs.

And if that does not sway your betrothed, I will possess you myself. I will slip into your mind, into your breath, into your body. I will give myself to you in a way you cannot resist, sweetly, so sweetly, with trickery and wiles, and if needs be, with the truth.

He was mad. His mind had finally broken. He had lost all reason in his yearning. What Jalal had failed to accomplish with his exquisite tortures and opiated *kif*, with his subtle games and degradations, one small maid had managed by the mere taking off of her kirtle. A battering ram was at his door. His hand was bleeding onto the floor. And he could do naught but stand and stare at the cause of it all and think of her kiss.

"No potion," she said, as if she were in charge. "I can make my own delirium and will have no trouble trembling in fear with the Boar in the room. No vomiting, but I will gag and spit if you wish."

Aye, he thought, befuddled and bemused. 'Twas his fondest desire to have her gagging and spitting while in his bed.

"I cannot abide the runs."

Neither could he, but desperate situations required desperate measures.

"Wet me down, if you must. Water will do for sweat. All I ask is that you do not let him touch me." She threw the kirtle onto the bed and turned to face him. "I cannot bear for the Boar to touch me."

Neither could he. " 'Tis his right."

The delicate lines of her jaw tightened and an angry glint sparked in her eyes, both good signs. "If the time comes, let it be one he will die for."

"You cannot kill him with magic, Ceri."

"Then mayhaps I'll use a knife."

Her audacity was a worthy, foolish, frustrating thing. If a man died every time a woman said *no*, the kingdom would be knee-deep in dead men before the month was out. 'Twas not how the world worked.

"Mayhaps I'll teach you how," he said for the sake of convenience, "but only if we live through the day." He lifted his hand toward the bed, trying to hurry her along. The ram hit again, making him wince and convincing her to comply.

With his pots and cup of water, he dabbed and smeared her face and neck, putting most of what he'd wanted inside her on her instead. She bound her hair up and used the bloody bandages to best advantage around her forehead. 'Twas a slapdash job at best, finished off with a rotting salve to give her a putrid air.

Were he Caradoc, he would not touch her with that smell upon her. He doused her again for good measure, then put his finger to her lips and leaned very close over the bed.

He stared at her long and hard, very hard, keeping all expression from his face, watching her eyes widen in expectation and then narrow in unease, then finally make the transition into confusion with a hint of fear. That was where he wanted her, cowed and vulnerable. The battering ram kept up its pounding, and still he continued his silent staring. He knew her, knew her stubborn courage could be the end of their game, and so he waited. When he felt a tremor run through her, when her eyes slowly widened again in greater fear, he leaned even closer.

"Not one word will you speak," he whispered, putting menace in his gaze and solemn threat in his voice. "Not one move will you make, or I will give you to him myself and be done with it. Do you understand?"

She made the slightest motion with her head, acquiescence from a woman of her word, yet he would rather have had time to get a sturdy sleeping draught into her, whether she said yea or nay.

As long as she was awake, though, he planned on putting her to good use. Reaching above her, he unwound the end of a rope and placed it in her hand.

"When I light the candle on the table, pull this and do not stop until it is done, then hide it back behind the curtain."

With her final nod, he pulled a swath of bandage down to cover her eyes and left the bed, drawing the damask drapes behind him.

"Out of my way. Out of my way, man," Vivienne shouted from down in the bailey, sending a ripple of anxiety up the tower stairs.

On the landing in front of the Druid Door, Soren blanched at the sound of his wife's voice.

" 'Twill be your head on a pike, you lice-ridden lout," she threatened one of his men.

With Vivienne bullying her way into the Hart Tower, could the Boar of Balor be far behind? Soren worried. How dare she leave her assigned post.

He looked to his newly elevated captain of the guard, Vachel, but the man refused to meet his gaze, let alone seize the moment and do something about Vivienne.

"Back, you cur. Get back." She drew nearer, causing confusion in the lower ranks.

A general milling about and breaking of the line announced her arrival on the landing. Men jostled one another, trying to make a path that would lead her straight to their lord. Soren would have them all whipped and beaten.

"Milord," she said testily, when she drew abreast of him. "What goes on here? Where is the maid?"

"The question, milady," he said under his breath, glaring at her through the shadowy gloom, "is, where is the Boar?"

"In the hall, where I left him."

"To wander at his will? To poke and pry, or mayhaps rally his men to pillage and plunder?"

She gave him a look both disgusted and priggish. "I left him in no condition to walk, let alone wander at will, and the only thing he is likely to plunder is me."

With some surprise, Soren felt the spark of his anger flicker and die. He'd thought he'd long lost his last speck of husbandly pride. Yet there he was, about to be cuckolded again and feeling the loss of it.

He could do naught but make light of the impending infidelity. "So you left him straining at his braies, did you?"

"Straining mightily," she assured him, her eyes alight with satisfaction and anticipation.

He had loved her once. She was still the most beautiful woman he had ever seen, but her heart had grown cold over the years. He had done that to her, with his strange needs, with the desires that coursed through him for what no bride could give, and for that he had regrets. She had been young and willing to please, if not quite innocent, when her father had given her to him. She had been ardent and loving, if somewhat naively confused by her husband, up until she'd found him with a boy.

So he lived with his regrets and a wife who strayed.

"But I cannot appease him indefinitely," she went on. "He will have the chit or he will have us and all of Wydehaw, Soren. I guarantee there is no compromise in the man."

He knew that much for himself.

Soren turned to his captain. "Vachel, begin again." He jerked his head toward the door.

"No," Vivienne ordered, pushing the captain aside before he could start his count for the men to swing the ram in unison. "Have you not a thought in your head? We may need Lavrans before this day is done, and the breaking of his door is unlikely to further our cause."

She strode straight to the gargoyle and stared the beast down, glowing eyes and all, for the span of a dozen heartbeats before sharply rapping on the door. Soren had to admire her courage. He'd avoided looking at the frightful thing with its bronze fangs and wicked, leering countenance.

"Lavrans," she called out, her voice ringing with authority. "Lord and Lady D'Arbois seek an audience. Allow us entry."

With no more fuss than that, the door opened, swinging wide and slow, granting entrance into the hallowed chamber where Soren had found some gold and little more than a few baubles of dubious worth for all his trouble and hundred marks.

Vivienne tossed him an exasperated, superior glance over her shoulder.

There was scarce more light in the solar than there was in the stairwell. A candle flickered on the table. The fire smoldered in the hearth. Tapestries had been drawn across all the embrasures, adding to the darkness.

Soren felt a general retreat taking place around him as his men backed away. He wanted to do the same, but did not. 'Twas the damn door that affected them so. It opened on its own in a manner he had not witnessed in many years, with nary a living soul on the other side. A bad start to the business at hand.

Lavrans could be seen—thank God—a shadow within the darkness, standing next to the table. Noll had probably not gotten any farther than the skirts of the nearest serving wench on his morning mission. He'd be beaten for that. The old man, Erlend, could be somewhere about, but he was not about the door. Damn thing. Soren remembered coming to the Hart as a child, trembling by his father's side and praying he did not wet himself in front of Nemeton, watching the door open of its own accord and praying the door to his sleeping chamber would not learn the trick and start an eerie, unpredictable life of its own.

Vivienne revealed no such superstitions. She crossed the threshold of the sorcerer's chambers without giving the door a glance.

"Dain," she cooed, sounding much her old self. "We have waited all the long morning to see you."

"My apologies for the delay, lady." Lavrans's voice came out of the darkness. "I was administering a delicate physick and dared not stop halfway."

"Of course." Vivienne forgave him with a smile. "It has been days since you came into our hall, and— Ah!" She gasped and drew back as the logs in the grate burst into green-and-blue flame and threw Lavrans's shadow across the floor and up the wall.

The men around Soren forsook all subtleness in their rush down the stairs. Vachel tried the same, but Soren grabbed his captain's arm and jerked him to a stop.

"Let the others spread tales to Caradoc's men," he said. "Your place is by my side." The day's unfolding didn't suit him, and if the sorcerer was going to go berserk, charlatan or not, Soren preferred the company of even a coward to none.

"Aye, milord," Vachel answered, sounding none too happy.

Vivienne's tittering laugh added to the tension.

"Where is the maid, Lavrans?" Soren asked. The quicker his business was over, the better.

A desultory gesture from the mage directed him to the bed. Soren wished the man would move from in front of the hearth. His face could scarce be seen with the fire at his back, and without seeing Lavrans more clearly, Soren could not discern his thoughts. Lavrans gave away little under the best of circumstances, but what little he did give came from the subtle movements of the muscles in his face, a lovely, dangerous landscape Soren studied at every opportunity.

"Vivienne." He waved his wife toward the bed. He preferred not to look upon sick women, especially if they were promised to lords with reputations for brutality. The Boar of Balor had at least that and was ofttimes said to be a bit mad in the bargain.

With the regalness of a queen, Vivienne glided over to the bed and threw back the drapes. Another gasp followed. She stumbled back with her hand clasped over her mouth and nose and turned a wild eye on her husband.

Soren wasted no time in hurrying to the bed. What he saw there made the blood drain out of his face. What he smelled there made it curdle.

"Jesu!" he exclaimed. "What has happened to her?" He looked to Lavrans for an explanation. "She was on the mend not five days past."

"Evil vapors have entered her body, drawn by the festering wound she received from Ragnor's rotten teeth."

"Evil?" Soren repeated, backing away from the bed.

"Vapors?" Vivienne followed his retreat, waving her hand in front of her face.

"Can she be cured?" Soren asked from a safe distance.

"Yes. Cured," Vivienne parroted.

"I have not lost hope," Lavrans said. The blue-and-green flames died down behind him, dropping the room back into colorless shadow. "Yet I put a warning upon the wind for her betrothed, telling him he should not delay, but come quickly if he wishes to see his bride alive."

"And he is here. Now," Soren said, startled. Mayhaps he'd underestimated Lavrans's abilities. God knew his father had underestimated Nemeton's, who had cast the baroness into a sleeping death and weeks later poisoned her from halfway across Wales.

"Good," the sorcerer said. "Bring him to the tower."

Here was danger, Dain thought. Deadly danger in the guise of a man named Helebore with his sunken eyes and hairless head. His brown robes were held to him with a soft rope tied in the knot of a Culdee monk, but Caradoc's leech was no saint.

"Evil vapors, yes, yes." The emaciated man sniffed the air above Ceridwen, moving his head from one spot to the next as if there were a difference in how she smelled from her cheek to her shoulder, from her breasts to her waist. "Women draw evil vapors to them from the very ground they walk upon, from the air they breathe. 'Tis not necessarily from a wound, though I have known it to happen thus."

Caradoc sat in a chair pulled a discreet distance away, taking in all that Helebore said. Dain had seen the dagger sheathed in his old friend's right boot and the blades concealed in his arm guards, and told himself that all men armed themselves for travel. He had noted the sallowness of Caradoc's face where once there had been a robust ruddiness and decided it was naught but the lingering touch of winter. He had watched Caradoc's gaze skitter and shift from bed to door, from hearth to Helebore, and back all over again in a haphazard fashion, searching, searching, and finding no respite or rest except for those moments when he looked upon Ceridwen's face—and Dain had told himself to take heed, for 'twas not a look of love or even mortal lust the Boar leveled upon the maid, but something of a more treacherous nature.

"The *medicus*," he said to Caradoc. "I do not remember him from our last meeting. Was he one of your father's retainers?"

"No," Caradoc replied, accepting a goblet of warmed wine from Vivienne's serving maid. A smile graced his mouth. "He is my man."

"A Culdee?"

"Excommunicated a year past, another victim of the vagaries of religion, not so unlike ourselves."

The maid blushed, returning the smile, and would have dallied, if not for Vivienne snapping at her to get back to work.

"He is learned in a variety of disciplines," Caradoc continued to Dain, though his gaze followed the girl. "But he lacks your far-reaching reputation."

"We have all come by reputations in the last few years," Dain said.

"Ah, but yours is the most mysterious, Lavrans." Caradoc turned his attention full upon Dain. "I am the Boar, he who can slay a man with a single stroke." He made a mock demonstration, his arm slashing down as if he held a sword, then shrugged. "There is no mystery in strength. Morgan steals, our Thief of Cardiff. Be it the heart of a maid or an earl from his bed, the mystery is in the how of it, not in the deed. But you . . ." His look became speculative. "No one knows exactly what it is you do, good friend, if 'tis skill or sorcery. Why even Helebore, cloistered all those years on Ynys Enlli, has heard of Wydehaw's mage and the opening of the Druid Door."

"A rare trick, nothing more." Dain downplayed the compliment. No one other than Jalal could have appreciated the complexity or, paradoxically, the simplicity of the achievement, and the Saracen was unlikely to ever know.

"Helebore would give much to learn such a trick. 'Tis the reason he made this journey."

"Then his trouble has been for naught." Dain gave the blond man a wry grin. "Though I'm glad to know his journey wasn't made solely out of your concern for the maid, for I fear he likes her not."

"Vile, horrid," the leech was muttering. He had carefully raised the coverlet with the tips of his fingers and was examining Ceridwen where she lay stretched between the sheets. He did not touch her with his hands, but used a notched silver key that hung from a chain on his belt. His voice was low and sibilant. "Sad, pitiful creatures." He laid the key on her wrist, and Dain saw her flinch. "She lives, hmmm."

Caradoc made a dismissive gesture with his hand. "Helebore but harbors a cleric's disdain for the fairer sex."

A mild summation of the disgust Dain saw on the leech's face. Helebore didn't disdain women; he hated them, a not uncommon phenomenon among men denied their sexual pleasures.

Dain saw him take note of the Quicken-tree cloth where it had come out of its folds and spread across the end of the bed. A look of curiosity lent the bald man a near comical countenance, then he reached for the cloth. Curiosity was quickly replaced with horror. The medicus let out a short screech followed by a gasp as he dropped the cloth. With all the commotion already in the tower, no one seemed to notice the incident, but Dain would swear to smelling burned flesh, and the leech had stuck his fingers in his mouth.

Behind him, Dain could hear Vivienne giving orders to the army of servants she'd had sent up: sweep this, tidy that, fresh rushes here, new candles there. Soren stood with his back to the room, staring through the green glass of the glazed window, ignoring as much of what was going on as he could. A guard was posted on either side of the Druid Door.

The Hart had been invaded, and Dain felt held at bay. He also stood, but unlike Soren he wasn't about to turn his back on either Helebore or Caradoc, friend or nay.

"Truly, I expected better for two hundred marks," Caradoc said. "She is such a small, pale thing. Even in full health, the rigors of the north may be too much for her."

Dain acknowledged the complaint with a tilt of his head. "She is normally not so pale and will recover. This is but a relapse, a not unheard of occurrence in cases of this sort."

"Rotten teeth caused the vapors?"

"Aye."

Caradoc made a noncommittal sound. "I suppose I owe you for the man."

"Morgan kidnapped him. I but made the suggestion."

"He spoke of you while under my knife."

"Ragnor?"

"Aye. He thinks 'tis you who tortures him." Caradoc looked up with a vague smile. "He'll no doubt go to hell with your name on his lips."

"He is still alive?" Dain thought back to Gwrnach's fate.

Caradoc shrugged. "Alive? Who is to say? He breathes and sweats and shivers. If he had eyes, mayhaps he'd cry, and if that is alive, so be it."

The callous sentiment brought back in force the memories of another time and place. "You learned much in the desert prisons."

"Too much," Caradoc agreed, and fell silent. The savagery of Kalut ad-Din had been well known on the caravan routes.

Ceridwen stirred on the bed. Helebore murmured something, and she stilled.

"And you?" Caradoc asked. "I oft wondered how you fared after our capture."

"We all survived, you, and Morgan, and me, and that is more than most who were taken at Jaffa."

"Ah, yes, survival." A soft, low chuckle came from the Boar's throat. "The things we do in the name of survival, eh . . . *bedźhaa*?"

The last word was spoken so quietly, with such gentleness, that 'twas more air than a word, a mere continuation of a breath exhaled at length. Yet Dain heard it. He heard it as he'd always heard it, as a whisper in the dark, as the name of a slave. *Bedźhaa.* Swan.

He suffered a momentary loss of the present, an instant when the walls around him were not the cool, damp stone of a tower, but the hot, dry wool of a tent in the sands; when the voices he heard were of the caravan, not of the March. Then, as quickly as it had happened, it was over, and the chamber he saw was his own, far from any master. He looked down at Caradoc, prepared to meet a condemning gaze, but found his old friend intent on his betrothed, his eyebrows drawn together in a thoughtful scowl.

Morgan knew, Dain thought. Even with all his innocence, he could not have been blind to the merchandise of Jalal's trade.

"I am going south to Cardiff," Caradoc said without glancing up, "and will return in a fortnight for the maid. If you value this place, she will be fully healed when I come."

"A threat?" Dain looked down with an arched brow. Caradoc also knew, the bastard, and he'd called him swan.

"A warning for D'Arbois." The Boar took a great swallow of wine and wiped the back of his hand across his mouth. A belch followed. "I will not take the Hart Tower, but if the maid dies, the rest of Wydehaw will be forfeit."

"Milord," Helebore said, turning to Caradoc. "Come quickly."

Dain tensed. The urgency in the medicus's voice was an ill-omened thing at this stage of their game. He stepped forward, ready to intercede for Ceridwen, but Caradoc stopped him with a restraining hand.

"A moment alone with my bride."

'Twas what Dain had feared, and Ceridwen. He stood by, an unfamiliar helplessness taking the place of his surety as the Boar and his leech bent over her. The damnable helplessness was what came from caring.

Their voices were low, with Helebore doing most of the talking. Dain could see a part of Caradoc's face, and his expression did not change, until the leech slipped his key under the shoulder edge of Ceridwen's chemise and lifted the cloth.

"Dragon," Dain heard him whisper, "and the dragon's sister, here and here."

A slow smile spread across the Boar's face. An unholy light flickered to life in his eyes. "Without doubt then, she is the one," he said.

"Aye, milord." Helebore laughed, a grim, rasping noise. "The marks of magic prove it."

If by "marks of magic" he meant the bite wound Ragnor had inflicted on her shoulder, then Helebore was even more of a charlatan than himself, Dain thought. Yet the definition disturbed him. Why would Caradoc concern himself with marks of magic on a bride?

The answer he came up with did not set well: Caradoc had been taken in by the vile ex-monk. Dain used all manner of soothsaying and conjuring to live at the expense of other people's money and peace of mind. He didn't like to think of Ceridwen going to a man with no more sense than to fall to someone like himself. It showed the excess of superstition she feared. Equally disturbing was Helebore's use of the alchemical allusion of the dragon and the dragon's sister to describe the scars. Morgan and Madron had both said the match was meant to return Ceridwen to her family home. There had been no talk of dragons or magic, except in the red book.

"Aye, aye, milord," Helebore continued, nodding at something Caradoc had said. "But I brought my best bleeders, and if I could but set them on the maid for a moment"—he pulled a pair of shiny, wet leeches from a stoppered gourd hanging from his belt—"we could have a small measure of her bl—"

Caradoc's hand went around the man's throat with lightning-like speed, cutting off the medicus's words and breath. When Helebore began to twitch and pale, the Boar released him.

"No," Caradoc said, then, looking very pleased with himself, he finished off his wine and set the goblet on a bedside table. "A fortnight at most," he said to Dain, walking over and clapping his old friend on the shoulder. "I would trust no one else with her keeping. Mayhaps you should come with us when we return to Balor, to celebrate the wedding."

"Mayhaps," Dain agreed, and truly thought he might, to ease his mind on the situation, and mayhaps dissuade Caradoc from dwelling so much in the past.

"Priest," Caradoc called back to the medicus. "Let us be gone, that we may more quickly return."

"B-but . . ." Vivienne stammered. They all turned to look at her. "But you have just arrived." She lifted her hand in a small gesture. "Surely you need a day, if not two, to refresh yourselves before continuing your journey."

Soren looked over his shoulder at his wife, not believing his ears. Here was salvation being thrown at their feet, and Vivienne was throwing it back. He quickly strode to her side. "The man has business in Cardiff, lady. Upon his return, we will be better prepared to entertain him in an appropriate style."

"Yes, of course, milord," she said, her voice strained, "but—"

He silenced her by pinching her arm. Her face reddened with outrage, but the ploy worked in distracting her from her doomed course of action and letting everyone else get back to their original plans.

Dain felt Helebore move up behind him and instinctively turned to face the man.

"The stitching, sir, on the maid, 'tis most fine," the medicus said. "The finest I have ever seen. Where did you come by such skill?"

Up close, Dain detected a gray cast to the man's skin and brown stains in the corners of his mouth. He smelled near as bad as Ceridwen. "In the East, from a Saracen physician."

"You were a Crusader?" The leech's dark eyes rolled up at him. "A defender of the faith?"

"For a time." Dain fought the urge to move away and wondered how Ceridwen had borne having the man hover over her.

"Side by side at Acre, we were," Caradoc added. "Knee-deep in the infidels' blood."

"A memory best left in the past," Dain suggested, though his attention was on Helebore. The man was drifting away, meandering toward the Druid Door, apparently uninterested in the conversation he had started.

"Aye, *bedžhaa*." The Boar's voice grew soft and gentle again as he spoke the hated name close to Dain's ear. "I would leave it all in the past, if the past would but leave me."

There was no mistake this time. Dain turned and met Caradoc's gaze straight on, admitting to nothing either in a look or words, but he saw much revealed in the other man's visage. Pain lurked in the variegated depths of Caradoc's eyes, along with disgust and a fascination Dain wished he had not seen. Above and below and beyond it all, wildness reigned, a strange, restless wildness he'd once felt himself.

Before he could back away, the leech cackled, a quietly deranged sound that echoed in waves throughout the chamber and caused all within the curved walls to turn and stare.

The man was running his hands over Nemeton's ruse of the Ptolemic cosmos, a series of planetary symbols burned into the wood of the Druid Door. He touched the metal-studded planks below the gargoyle, and unintelligible words poured from his lips. His fingers slid into every nook and cranny and skimmed over the top of each iron rod, tracing the patterns of the symbols, feeling his way through the mystery. When he finished Saturn, Helebore rolled his eyes back at Dain. Malevolence burned bright in the dark orbs, and a knowing Dain had never expected to see.

But the leech did not see all. With a silent gesture, Dain sicced the dogs on the defrocked priest and had him chased from the tower. The next time Helebore crossed the Hart's threshold, Dain would kill him.

Chapter 15

"Queen on color," Dain reminded Ceridwen, unnecessarily, as she set up the chessboard. He sat across from her, slumped down in his chair, his legs splayed out toward the hearth with one knee slightly bent. His chin rested in his right hand, while he juggled a knife with his left.

Was what had made her misplace her Queen in the first place, she thought peevishly, the damn knife. Up and down, the blade rose and fell with one graceful flip at the apex of its rise, the differing metals of gold, silver, and steel catching the sunlight streaming through the window and scattering it in bright rays. He called the dagger "Damascene." It was the one she'd stolen the night before he'd taken her into Wroneu, the one with which he'd been teaching her a bit of knife play. Strange enough that the blade even had a name, let alone one so exotic.

'Twas her new word, "exotic," and a highly

practical one it was for someone living with Dain Lavrans. He defined the term with his strange concoctions and mysterious ways, with his enigmatic gaze and the fluid grace of his movements. Everything about him seemed of another world.

The night in Wroneu had changed the way they dealt with each other, brought them to an uneasy alliance she appreciated, but did not truly understand. He would not speak of that evening, except to tell her there was naught to fear, but she had not forgotten that he'd said Madron was no longer his friend.

"You have beaten me twice a day for the last three days," she complained. "I see no reason to continue playing games. 'Tis the teaching of magic you bargained with, not chess."

"I only beat you once yesterday."

"Because we only played once," she informed him with a long-suffering sigh.

"Chess is magic," he argued. "It teaches you how to see the future."

Her interest piqued for a moment, then dissipated with understanding. "The future of a battlefield, nothing more."

"Life is a battlefield."

He had become boorish beyond measure since Caradoc's leaving, hardly speaking, and when he did speak, his words were cryptic or worse. The playing of chess was the only thing that kept him from pacing the chamber or staring for hours on end out the window to the forest and hills beyond. Something must await him there to hold his attention so dearly, though she knew not what. At night, 'twas the waxing moon he gazed upon, the forest being lost in shadows. Strange man. Naught could await him on the moon. She didn't know what to make of his brooding or his increasing restlessness, but she'd reached her fill of his game and of being ignored.

"You are trite in victory," she accused him. "I will play no more."

"No more chess?"

"No." She crossed her arms over her chest. The action had been unconscious, but once she'd done it, it felt right. She was making a stand, reinforcing her defenses.

To her surprise, he smiled, the first sign of life beyond moroseness she'd seen in days. She was immediately suspicious, with good reason as his next words proved.

"Then catch the knife, Ceri." The smile turned sly. "If you dare."

She looked at the dagger, and he tossed it higher than before, making it spin in the air. Sunlight burst upon the blade and blazed along the sharp edge from hilt to point, but only for an instant. Quicker than not, the whole of it fell into shadow, then completed its next arc and caught the light once more.

He had dared her to put her hand into that dangerous whirl and snatch the blade before it could fall back into his hand. She wished she did dare.

He had lied to her. The leech had touched her all over with his damned key, and someone—the Boar, she was sure, though she hadn't dared look for fear of screaming—had squeezed her thigh. Dain hadn't liked hearing that any more than she'd liked enduring it, voicing a word so crude she'd added him to her prayers, though she knew he would like that even less.

He had cheated her too. Not while playing his damned game of chess, but that they played it at all when there was so much else for them to do. She had less than a fortnight to glean what knowledge she could from him. They should be in his lower chamber, concocting magic potions for her to use.

He had kissed her, and then he'd not kissed her again, and that was the most unforgivable misdeed of all.

She watched the knife flip hilt over point and wondered when a person should make her move, if she was going to try for the Damascene.

"If I catch it, can I keep it?" she asked, her gaze not leaving the dagger. His movements were so smooth, should make it easy for someone to reach in and grab the damn thing. Every flight of the blade was like the last, the rise, the hilt over point flip, the instant of stillness at the top, then the descent.

"Yes," he promised, "but only if you do not cut yourself in the catching of it."

Aye, there was always a trick with him.

She watched and waited, biding her time and calculating her chances. 'Twas a good knife, and she needed a good knife. The thought of escape had been growing ever stronger in her mind. With the return of her health, she had no reason to stay unless he taught her something besides chess, and she had many reasons to leave.

To look upon him the way she did was a sin, remembering the feel of his mouth on hers, the taste of his kiss. Her mind strayed too often to the night of his bath, to the water streaming down his body and the soft, guttural sounds of pleasure he'd made. He had given the carnality of her nature a face, and she was ashamed. To remain with him was a weakness of both the flesh and mind, and could come to naught but damnation, no matter that her heart yearned along with her body.

The Damascene rose and flipped and fell, over and over. He never missed. The ivory grip ended in a hilt worked in both gold and silver, the metals chased and crosshatched to look woven, or braided. The design was familiar, strangely so, and not because she knew the dagger.

Then she remembered where and when she'd seen the hilt before.

"I had a dream about you," she said, and the knife clattered to the floor. He jerked his hand back and swore, but 'twas too late. He'd been nicked by the blade. "At least I thought it was you, but maybe it wasn't," she mused. "The knife was in it for sure, except it wasn't a knife, but a sword." He bent over to pick up the Damascene, still muttering obscenities. "It had the same ivory hilt, though, the same gold-and-silver pattern, and we were on a beach by the ocean, except it wasn't the sky above us, but the earth. There was more that is harder to remember, and all of it feels more like a memory than a dream, which I know sounds odd, but that's exactly what it's like."

He had stopped swearing and was looking at her, his gaze far too serious for what she had in mind next.

"You had this dream?" he asked.

"Yes. When I fell asleep in Madron's cottage." If he wasn't going to get on with teaching her magic, then she needed to get on with her own preparations. To that end, she gave him what she hoped was a wistfully charming smile. "Since you cut yourself, does that mean I get the knife?"

Without a word, he handed her the blade. His lack of hesitation surprised her, but neither did she hesitate in the taking of it.

She fit the dagger to her hand, liking the weight and the balance of it, as always. A smile came to her mouth. There had been a helper in the abbey garden, a boy who had liked knives. He would

have loved this one, except she doubted if anyone used such a fancy
piece for playing mumblety-peg. Childhood games were long past her,
but a woman still had need of a knife. She was glad to have this one as
a gift instead of having to steal it again. Her sins were mounting at an
alarming rate as it was.

"A sword as fine as this dagger could cost a man's whole fortune," she said, rubbing her thumb along the haft.

"Or a man's life."

She glanced up from beneath her lashes, distracted from her
new treasure by the sudden weariness in his voice. "You've seen one?"

He nodded, swearing softly and bringing his hand up to rub his
temples. Was a move he'd made often in the last few days, one indicative of a throbbing head. He was prone to the malady, and she felt
remiss.

"Lavrans?" She leaned forward and put her hand on his cheek,
giving in to a wayward impulse she immediately regretted. To touch
him was to remember him not as the cynic he played so well, but as
the Prince of the Light-elves, he who enchanted demons and saved
maidens. 'Twas that part of him that made her yearn for love.

He looked up, over the top of his hand, but not at her. She
followed his gaze across the room to the oak-and-iron chest chained at
the foot of his bed, then brought her attention back to him. He swore
again, closing his eyes and lowering his head, and the tips of her
fingers slid into his hair. She caressed his temple with her thumb,
another impulse she could not resist.

"Are you well?" Concern made her voice gentler than she
liked. At least she told herself it was concern and not the slow ache
she felt building inside.

"Aye," he answered, not sounding at all truthful. With the
slightest of movements, he turned his mouth into her palm, flooding
her senses with awareness. His lips were soft, his breath warm against
her skin.

Heat poured through her. She wanted to lean closer and take
him in her arms, cradle his head next to her breast; to glide her fingers
through his hair, dragging the long, dark strands away from his face,
then bend low to kiss his brow. When he'd kissed her across the river
from Deri, he had kissed her as a man as well as a sorcerer, and after
her dream of him as the savior with a sword, she'd had no more fear

of him. She had only the want of him, a need unlike any she'd felt before, undeniable. Thus compelled, she did lean closer, bringing her face ever so much nearer to his.

His breath grew shallow, and slowly his eyes opened, the gradual lift of his lashes mesmerizing her with hope and promise. Her heart pounded. Surely he would kiss her again.

Yet when their eyes met, it wasn't longing she saw in his gaze, nor weariness, but a regard so cool, she felt the icy chill of it.

She quickly pulled away, embarrassed beyond measure, and growing even more so when he lounged back in his chair. 'Twas what came from being raised in a nunnery, she thought with disgust, this inability of hers to understand or predict him, or to keep herself from her own awful foolishness.

"Forget this dream you had," he said. "It can do neither of us any good."

"Dreams cannot harm you, magician." Damn him. He had felt nothing, and she could scarce see straight for still wanting him. He was more changeable than the weather. She should have more sense than to think of him the way she did. She should have more sense than to think of him at all.

"Mayhaps," he agreed. "But for some, the whole world is a dream, and who can deny that there is harm in the world?"

"Do not speak in riddles to me." She would not cry. She'd had enough of tears. He was the one who had kissed her, was he not? She had not gone out of her way to kiss him. But then it never stopped at kisses for a man. A sister at Usk who had been widowed twice before taking her vows had told her so. With Dain, the kisses she longed for would no doubt turn into something beastly that she dared not desire.

"You do not want riddles?" He reached for his cup of wine. "Then hear the truth, Ceridwen. I also dreamed in Madron's cottage."

She stopped her silent railing and glanced up at him. "A dream like mine?"

"Enough so to make me wary." He drank and set the cup back on the table.

"Is this why you are no longer friends?"

"Aye."

'Twasn't much as explanations went, but it was something. "The thing with Caradoc. What does it matter to Madron if we wed?" She asked her most pressing question, trying to take advantage of his willingness to speak, if not exactly discourse on the matter.

"She was Nemeton's daughter, and believes if Caradoc is wed, then she can be returned to Carn Merioneth."

"Nemeton's daughter?" she said, taken aback by his answer. "I think not. Nemeton's daughter was named Moriath."

" 'Tis another name the witch has, Moriath, though only Rhuddlan calls her thus. They have known each other for many years—" He rubbed his head again, as if the pain had suddenly increased. "At least fifteen, for certes. But what do you know of Nemeton?"

"He was the greatest bard in all of Wales and often came to Carn Merioneth," she said, excitement spilling over into her voice. She'd been right. It was Moriath she'd seen in the cottage. "Everyone knew of him, and for a short time Moriath stayed with us. She was the one who brought Mychael and me south and put us in the religious houses."

"Aye, she was at Usk," Dain said, and swore silently. He'd fallen into a hornet's nest of intrigue with the maid at the center of it all.

"Did you say anything to her about the red book? Did she know of it?" the chit asked, leaning close, her face alight. Then just as quickly she moved away, a pink stain upon her cheeks.

"She wrote it," he said. "At least the Latin parts." Another unfortunate telling of truth he surmised from the startled widening of her eyes. " 'Tis not what you think, Ceri. She but put her father's stories to the page, which may have naught to do with you. I have heard stories of a Ceridwen as the mother of Taliesin, a mythical being who some say is also the Merlin of Arthur's court. There is a Ceridwen as keeper of a magic cauldron and another as—"

"They are the same," she interrupted him. "Taliesin's mother and the cauldron keeper are the same woman."

"And neither one of them is you," he said, making his point. He saw no reason to frighten her with Madron's unconvincing reassurance that if Ceridwen married Caradoc, her blood would remain her own.

Christ, but he hated the whole of it.

"You must take me to Moriath," she said. "I have to talk with her."

"No." He dared not take her back into Wroneu. In truth, he didn't know what to do with her. "There were dangers beyond the ocean in my dream, Ceri, and I know not why Madron showed them to me, or what they mean, or if 'twas really a dream."

"If not a dream, then what?"

"Mayhaps a threat. Or it could have been a vision. I have a small gift of sight."

"Small?" Obviously, Ceridwen didn't like the sound of that. "Erlend told me you were a great diviner, feared throughout the March of Wales; famed throughout the borderlands and the shires beyond."

His lips twitched with the beginnings of a grin he barely held in check.

"I would not put too much store by what Erlend says," he opined drolly. "Or spend too much of my time listening to his prattle."

"His prattle is better company than your silence. As for visions, I have no gift at all, so how do you explain what I saw?"

"Madron."

"She has magic then?"

Dain grimaced. "All with you is magic."

"It would be, if you would uphold your end of our bargain."

He made a dismissive gesture with his hand. "Magic is mostly damned hard work and nothing to be bargained with."

"Magic was your half of the bargain, sorcerer, not mine. You promised the lightning dance."

Their eyes held across the chessboard for no more than a moment before he relented. 'Twas Ceridwen's easiest victory yet over him.

He pushed himself out of his chair and stood. "Aye, then, before we jump into the thick of it, why don't we begin with something no less volatile, but much less likely to immolate you."

"Immolate?"

"Burn to a cinder," he elaborated, gesturing toward the trapdoor with a broad sweep of his hand.

'Twas about time, she thought.

*   *   *

What was Madron's game, Dain wondered, to have warned him off, and then to have given him and the maid the same dream? It had all come back to him as Ceri had spoken of his sword, come back far too clearly for his peace of mind: the smell of the dark place, the danger of it, the way the walls had moved, the utter surety of his own death. With the clarity of the dream, he'd also remembered the moment in Deri when he'd felt and seen the same dark place.

Too much darkness, he thought, filling another lamp with oil. When he lit the crystal globe, the lamp cast a shattered glow of fractured beams around the walls of the lower chamber. They danced over Ceridwen's body and wove themselves through her hair where she stood across from him at the table. He'd started her off with the making of *rihadin,* one of Jalal's most closely guarded concoctions, compact packages of mineral powders, fire oil, and resin used to change and deepen the colors of flames. Bits of charcoal, sulfur, or wax were sometimes used, depending on the desired effect. Saltpeter could be added, though he'd been strongly advised against it, and his own experiments had proven the admonition to be based on sound reasoning and in favor of self-preservation, unless one was intent on a certain amount of destruction.

A number of candles were already flaming, adding their meager light to the work at hand. He hung the lamp from a chain above them and set about filling his alchemy still with wine. 'Twould be *aqua ardens* he made for her.

He had never doubted Jalal's magic, or Madron's, only his own, and yet he'd underestimated the witch. Her dream had awakened something in him. He'd felt it hovering on the edge of his consciousness these past few days, a mystery, mayhaps magic, but a magic more dangerous than any he had imagined. Not so for Rhuddlan. More than the Quicken-tree leader's intuition had been at work in the grove that night. Rhuddlan had known the contents of Dain's fleeting moment of sight. Dain's own intuition, jogged into awareness by Ceri's dream, told him it was so.

Madron. Rhuddlan. Ceridwen. And Madron as Moriath, the one who had taken Ceridwen to Usk. The three were part of some whole, their lives knotted together for some purpose beyond a simple marriage. But what? And where was the dark place that bespoke of his death?

Rhuddlan had gone north, not to return until Beltaine, Dain remembered, and Caradoc had come from the north.

He glanced up from his still to where Ceridwen worked on the other side of the table. The maid had brought strange forces to bear on his life. She mocked him with her need for the powers of salvation he could not give himself, yet he'd be parting with her against his will.

Nimble fingers, nimble mind, she'd grasped the concept of *rihadin* immediately. She had smirked and called him "charlatan" when he'd shown her the how of it, yet she still believed his tricks were magic and asked him how he conjured his exotic powders. She had enough faith in him and the God she prayed to for the both of them, and mayhaps that was why he was loath to let her go. In Arabic, she was *alkemelych,* "small magical one."

Mayhaps he would go north with the wedding party.

"Christ's blood," he muttered, surprising himself with the idiocy of his thoughts. The maid had turned his mind to lust and his powers of reasoning to pottage. He had long since stopped yearning for death, and there was no reason to court it now, especially for a woman he could not have, let alone keep.

He forced his attention back to his work, luting the stillhead with a paste made of flour and water. His hand shook, and paste dropped into the cold brazier beneath the still. He swore beneath his breath, but let it lie. He should not have kissed her palm. He'd known that even as he'd pressed his lips against her skin, drawn by her scent and her closeness. She made him weak. A woman less easily dissuaded would have had him on his knees in minutes, but a woman less easily dissuaded would not have been Ceridwen ab Arawn.

She was visceral, slipping into his veins to wreak her havoc and bring him damn little peace.

May Eve would be upon them soon, before the week was out, and she would be gone shortly thereafter. He felt the heavy ripeness of the earth building with each passing day, and he wondered if Rhuddlan also trembled with the coming of Beltaine. Each year his own awareness heightened ever more intensely, entwining him deeper with mysteries that always lurked just beyond his ken. Yet this year they were drawing close. More of Madron's doing, and Rhuddlan's, and the maid's, and the Druid force brought to bear on the coming of spring.

Nemeton's grove and Nemeton's tower held the same secret,

albeit in different forms. Dain had realized that much the first time Rhuddlan had taken him to Deri for Beltaine. He'd behaved the perfect dissembler on the occasion, calling the Quicken-tree's goddesses and gods for them with much pomp and legerdemain, employing every trick he knew, turning the flames of their fires into rainbow hues—aye, and they'd liked that well enough to request it year after year—roiling up great clouds of smoke and using his voice to make the trees talk, which the whole of Quicken-tree had found exceedingly humorous, much to his irritation. 'Twas only later he'd realized that to them, the trees had their own voices and his had been sorely out of tune.

Yet for all that he'd made a mummery of their ceremony, he had not left the grove unchanged. The bodhran drums had done it to him. Their pounding, driving beat had slipped beyond his defenses and found an answering rhythm in what had been left of his soul. He couldn't remember now what had surprised him more: that he'd responded to the Quicken-tree's pagan rites, or that Jalal had left a part of him intact.

Pagan. The word barely sufficed to describe what happened in the grove. Edmee would not be there on Beltaine. Madron never allowed it. Mayhaps he would turn to Llynya. That one's sweet wildness had tempted him once. Or Moira. The Earth-Mother would take him in and give him comfort, bring him peace. There were others who would be willing, aye, even eager to lay down on the forest floor with the Horned One he would become—and none would be Ceridwen.

He would continue to teach her how to use her new knife, and he would show her how to distill wine into water that burned. If he dared, he could tell her somewhat of the things between a man and a woman. Though Caradoc had brought the ransom and shown concern for her well-being, he did not think the Boar of Balor would bother to ease his way into a maid's affections before easing his way into her bed, and Dain did not want her hurt, no matter the trouble she had brought to his life.

He looked up again, watching as she worked the resin with her fingers. Her brows were drawn together in concentration, but her mouth was soft, free from worry. She was convent-bred and unused to the ways of men. After shocking her the night of his bath, he felt a certain responsibility to atone. Fear did not make a good bedmate, and it could make it especially hard for a woman. He could teach her somewhat, he supposed, teach her what he dared, but not nearly all she would allow.

A wry smile curved his mouth. She wanted too much from him. He saw it in her eyes, felt it in her touch, and she didn't know the safe limits of such things. If naught else, though, he would open her mouth and give her a kiss. Much could be learned from a kiss, and the maid was quicker than most.

She would need to be, if she found herself often matching wits with Helebore. Before she left, he would give her the trick of using stone snake tongue to detect poison in food and wine. He had an extra mermaid's purse or two he could part with, though he'd never actually figured out what to do with them besides intone grim-sounding chants while waving them about.

He could teach her how to do that. Truly, the chanting was his most effective "magic," that and divining the future from chicken guts. If there were many like Erlend in Balor, the chicken trick could make her reputation, and God knew there was safety in having a reputation as a mage. His had served him well for many years, until the maid had come into his life and begun tearing it asunder from the inside out.

Chapter 16

Rhuddlan and Trig knelt by the steaming, bubbling pool deep in the heart of the caves beneath Balor. The Liosalfar touched his fingers to the stone rim, the Quicken-tree leader reached for the water itself, and what Trig smelled on his fingers when he lifted them to his nose, Rhuddlan felt in the pool.

"Desecration," the Liosalfar said, looking up.

Green eyes met green, and Rhuddlan nodded. "Whoever rouses the *pryf* dabbles in mysteries beyond his ken. Find the paths he uses and close them off." The foul being whose presence they sensed could not be left to run free.

Men from above had ventured into the caves many times since the fall of Carn Merioneth, some by accident, some apurpose to explore, and some to meet unexpected death. The caverns of the Quicken-tree did not readily reveal their secrets, and for that reason Rhuddlan had never bothered to challenge the presence of those whose thoughts did not go beyond tangible riches. 'Twas better for them to find nothing and return to tell the tale.

This one, though—the Quicken-tree leader skimmed his fingers across the scrying pool once more—this one did not think of gold and gemstones, but of a treasure beyond price, and he must be checked. The searcher would know someone had locked him out the next time he tried to descend into the caves, and mayhaps he had enough wits about him to devise a new way in, but that would take time and Beltaine was nearly upon them. After that good night, Rhuddlan would return with those he needed to break the seal on the weir gate, and once again he would be the ruler of the kingdom beneath the mountains, a dragon keeper.

Then let this foul being come below, and Rhuddlan would feed him to the mother ocean.

Travelers from the far north, from beyond even Denmark, arrived near Wydehaw midweek. The messenger who had sighted the peddler band in the forest and brought the news to the Hart had been scarce more than a boy. He had disappeared back into the night with his four pence clutched in his fist, leaving less trace of his passing than a shadow. For such an outrageous sum, Ceridwen had told Dain, she would be happy to run free in the woods all day and report back to him everything she saw. His reply had been that she had not done so well by herself running free in the woods, and that mayhaps she should just stay put. She did, while he left at the next dawn to go in search of the barbarian traders.

Glad she was to be alone. The tower was too small to hold a caged animal of Dain's size, and he acted the part no less than any wild thing she'd seen caught in a trap. He no longer spoke, he growled and snapped. He no longer slept, but prowled the whole night long. Every sound brought his head up, alert and wary. Every shift in the wind had become cause for another hour spent staring out the window upon the forested hills. He had not eaten yesterday, nor broken his fast this morn.

Worst of all, his restless pacing had infected her with the same agitated excitement, the same sense of anticipation, though she knew not what to anticipate other than the escape she must contrive before

Caradoc's return. She had put it off long enough. Less than a sennight remained.

Her plan was still to make for Strata Florida, but she was sorely tempted to go back into Wroneu and find Moriath before heading north. Despite what Dain had said about the witch, Ceridwen had felt no harm coming from her, and whether she was called Moriath or Madron, she was a touchstone to the past. Mayhaps she would have tidings of Mychael.

Before he'd left, Dain had set her to work dusting the shelves in his solar. There were hundreds of earthenware vessels to be cleaned, containers made out of boiled leather, small wool pouches, open dishes and baskets holding whole herbs, glass cruets and more jugs and pots than she'd ever seen in one place. He wanted them all tidied, though she guessed his true motive was to keep her occupied and out of trouble while he was gone.

There had been a slight accident, which in no way had been her fault, that had nearly set them afire the previous day. By the time Dain had gotten them both down to smolders sans sparks, he'd been in no mood to continue her studies. The damned distilled wine was what had caused all the commotion. She might have set it too close to the brazier, but she was not the one who had spilled it into the coals, sending an inferno of flame whooshing toward the ceiling. Numa's wagging tail had done the deed. Still, 'twas an interesting thing, *aqua ardens,* water that burned, and she was taking plenty with her when she left.

Her cleaning eventually brought her to the door that led to the tower's upper chamber. Carved in stone above the door, nearly obscured by years of soot and grime, were Latin words. "*Amor . . . lux . . . veritas . . . sic itur ad astra,*" she murmured.

"Love . . . light . . . truth . . . such is the way to the stars." The translation took her a moment and still left her wondering what the words meant.

If the answer lay on the other side of the door, she would have to do without it, for unlike the Druid Door, the door to the upper chamber was never opened. Never. Erlend was frightened of the place, though she didn't know why. As much as he prattled, he wouldn't say anything beyond "strange, demn things" when asked what it was Dain kept in the eyrie. If she probed further, he became incoherent in his mutterings. Whatever was beyond the door defied either the old man's comprehension or his power of description, or both, and was no doubt the most interesting thing in the tower. She was sure, too, that it had something to do with Dain's alchemical dabblings, with the Philosopher's Stone he was never able to successfully conjure in the lower chamber—the very key to the machinations of nature, time, and transformation, he'd told her. Few of his concoctions and containers made it past the thirtieth distillation on his still, let alone the seventieth some of his receipts required.

She bent down from where she stood on a stool and tried the latch, giving it a little wiggle, then a stronger one. She put her shoulder to it, but nothing happened. It never did.

Yet the door had a lock like any other lock, and where there was a lock, there was a key. Somewhere.

Expecting nothing, she ran her hand across the stones jutting out above the door, doubting that the mage would be so predictable. She got exactly what she expected, with the addition of a bit of cobweb. She'd had the same problem at Usk, trying to get into the library. Her solution then had been a cannily wielded kitchen knife and a sturdy oak twig.

Time was running short, she told herself, looking around for a knife other than her precious Damascene. She could not afford to respect Dain's privacy when any piece of knowledge she gained could be the one to save her.

The lock turned out to be a simple affair, yielding easily to her prodding and poking. Dain must not have thought it necessary to protect the eyrie beyond the Druid Door, for she had no doubts that he could have made it impossible to enter the upper chamber, if he had chosen to do so. Llynya had been wrong about the magic word, "sezhamey." Ceridwen had tried it time and again to no avail.

With her strong push, the door opened on creaking hinges, revealing a stairwell filled with dim light and dripping water. She stuck her hand in and touched the curved wall. The stone was cold and wet. A pool of water glistened on the floor, a cache of rain from that morning's shower caught in a smooth indentation of rock. She skirted it as she stepped into the stairwell. Streams of sunlight broke through the ceiling boards far above her and filtered down, setting the dust motes alight.

Halfway around the first curve, she looked up and, indeed,

something strange caught her eye. Her heart skipped a beat and her breath stopped. An orb hung above her in the air, a metal ball with no visible means of support. She stepped back a stair, planning to turn and run as Erlend must have done, when the curved rod that held the orb came into view.

But what held the rod? she wondered, poised between flight and curiosity.

She continued forward, daring all, yet keeping her hand firmly on the wall to insure a quick escape if needs be.

Slowly, she crept up the stairs, listening for danger and hearing naught beyond the same breeze she'd felt in the solar. She was protected from its windy kiss in the stairwell, but she heard the fluttering of cloth in the chamber above her, and the metal ball dipped and swayed ever so slightly.

As she rounded the curve, more of the rod came into view, along with another and another, each with its own orb, though every orb was a different size. 'Twas just as Erlend had said, a strange demn thing.

Her head peeked over the topmost stair, bringing more of the room into view, and her eyes widened.

"Sweet Jesu," she whispered.

Dain hung his cloak by the hearth and glanced again toward the door to the upper chamber. 'Twas open. A smile curved his mouth. The maid was nothing if not adventurous.

He'd been caught in a rain shower at dusk, a half league from the tunnel, but the journey had been worth the dousing. He'd had news of home.

Laughter floated down the stairs, and his smile broadened. Night had fallen, and he could well imagine what brought the laughter to her lips, the same thing that had sent Erlend cowering into the alchemy chamber. He picked up the package he'd set on the table and palmed a handful of *rihadin* out of a bowl on his *materia medica* shelf, then followed the sound of her laughter.

He mounted the stairs into darkness. Halfway up, he tilted his head back and found stars spinning slowly above him. As he'd thought, she had wasted no time in lighting the orbs. Seven were larger than the rest, representing in ascending order Mercury, Venus,

Earth, the moon, Mars, Jupiter, and Saturn, all mounted on movable bronze rings, one within the other. Numerous smaller orbs, stars, circled and danced around the outside of the planets, their number, if not their arrangement, corresponding to the twelve signs of the zodiac. The orbs themselves were made of thinly pounded copper patinated by the years to a rich verdigris and put together like two hinged bowls, each one connected by a long, slender rod to the cowled central pillar that pierced the rings. The amount of sand in each orb and its placement on the pillar determined the height of its orbit. The pillar itself was encrusted with rock crystal, stones of light chipped away from the vault of heaven, and laden with all the copper shapes cut out of the orbs, a telluric pedestal for the Sun at its core. The whole of the wondrous thing was Nemeton's celestial sphere, the bard's heretical, heliocentric map to the cosmos. It filled the chamber nearly wall to wall and was half again as high as a man at its tallest point.

The idea of the Earth and all her sister planets revolving around the Sun was not new to Dain. Jalal had once taken him to an astrologer in Damascus who had seen such a diagram in an ancient manuscript said to have come from a land that was no more. The East had been full of such missives, though most were not nearly as ancient as their sellers professed. 'Twas not until the Hart, though, that he'd seen any recounting in the West of a Sun-central cosmos. Nor had he foreseen in Damascus how an old man's ramblings would give him the key to a new life as the Mage of Wydehaw, a key in fact as well as theory. In a clever bit of wordplay, Nemeton had incised three rays of the Sun in the keystone of the stone arch around the Druid Door, showing that brightest of celestial orbs at eventide, noon, and morning rise. Three nights into his delicate assault upon the lock, Dain had forsaken the alchemical order of metals—what he'd considered his cleverest idea—and the more obvious Ptolemic order of the cosmos, which had the Earth as its center, and begun manipulating the iron rods in the pattern of heresy. Still, it had not been an easy thing, for each rod had to be moved in a prescribed order within the circular pattern of the lock. That he had opened the door in a sennight had seemed like magic even to him, despite his endless calculations and drawings.

Dain came into the room on silent feet and reached up to touch the first star he came to, designated by its markings as the polestar.

The barest shift in pressure sent the orb circling in the opposite direction, dipping and swaying in a graceful arc around the pillar and the rings. He could not see Ceridwen through the darkness surrounding the spinning lights, but he could hear her on the other side, opening each orb to light the candle within and then setting the sphere adrift.

He worked his way around the circle, changing orbits as he went and dropping in a pinch of *rihadin* here and there. "Fire eggs," Jalal had said when he'd asked for a translation of the word, a word from a language spoken beyond the edge of the known world, a place lost in the frozen deserts that lay along the far reaches of the caravan routes.

Mutterings of consternation met his ears as the newly directed stars floated by her, defying their original course.

A fire burned in the chamber's hearth, warming an iron pot. He set his package on a nearby table and picked up a wooden stirring spoon to taste the cauldron's steaming, savory-scented contents. The soup was hot and flavorful and good for chasing away his chill. He dipped the spoon in again and brought it to his lips, blowing. Ceridwen had spent a busy afternoon, making soup and discoveries. As the broth cooled, the polestar came back from whence he'd sent it. With his gentle touch, the bright orb went spinning off in reverse.

He ate from the pot and waited, and confounded her from his side of the room. She nearly had all the orbs lit. He found a flagon of wine next to the hearth and tipped it to his mouth. 'Twouldn't be long now.

The first fireball sparks showered blue and elicited a startled gasp from her. He grinned. Quickly on the heels of the blue came a shower of yellow and a short squeal. He laughed softly and took another swig of wine. Red followed yellow, and green followed red. Another blue *rihadin* took to flame, but she made no more sounds.

Curious, he walked toward where she'd been, peering through the sparks and circling spheres. When he didn't see her, he kept walking.

"You!" she accused him from behind, nearly stopping his heart. "I knew 'twas you."

He whirled, spilling wine onto his hand and across the front of his tunic. He laughed, his own startled sound.

"You ought to be ashamed." She stood a scant distance from him with her hands on her hips, a warrior's stance, but he thought he detected a smile on her mouth. He tilted his head to put her better into the light and confirmed his suspicion.

"I am ashamed," he assured her, grinning, then lifted his hand to his mouth and sucked off the wine. With his other hand, he offered her the flagon.

She took it, one eyebrow arched to let him know a little wine would not absolve him.

"Want to help?" he asked, holding out the *rihadin.*

She did not reply, only reached out and took three packets from his palm.

"Not too much in each," he warned. "Just a pinch. I'll do the northern orbits."

They worked in opposite directions, her filling the lower spheres and him filling the higher ones. When they met again where they'd begun, the first *rihadin* were sputtering.

"Hurry," he urged her, taking her by the hand and pulling her along. "We have to open the—" A fountain of yellow and green sparks burst into the air from the nearest orb, cutting off his words and their forward progress. They halted suddenly, bumping against each other. He instinctively protected her by holding her face against his shoulder. He could feel her laughing in his arms.

After the first fiery moments passed, she peeked up, grinning. "I put in the green, but I had no yellow."

"And I had yellow, but no green." His own mouth curved into a smile. She had understood as quickly as he.

"I fear we've doubled up on our pinches."

"Aye." His smile broadened.

A shower of red and blue sparks followed by a burst of blue and green confirmed their mistake. He put his mouth close to her ear so she could hear him over the growing din. "We have to open the roof."

She tilted her head back and gave him a quizzical look.

He pointed to a series of pulleys climbing the wall on the north side of the tower. A web of ropes laced through the wheels and led to the horizontal portcullis that comprised the ceiling of the upper chamber.

They closed the distance in a rain of blue and yellow sparks and put their backs into coaxing the oak-plated roof into giving way. It complied with a shudder and a groan and the high-pitched grating of long-unused gears. Moonlight streamed in through the first crack and spread farther down the dark walls with each crank of the wheel, until half the tower was bared to the heavens, and none too soon. One after the other, the "fire eggs" burst into flame, shooting bits and flashes of hot color upward into the night sky.

Outside in the bailey, Father Aric stopped midway to the chapel and fell to his knees. His mouth was agape, his eyes wide as he stared at the top of the Hart Tower. Hellfire was spewing from between the battlements. The lurid colors defied any aspect of holiness and unequivocally indicated the workings of evil power. That damnation should arrive so quickly upon the heels of sin—truly before he'd even gotten himself tucked back into his braies and while the scent of the woman still clung to him—could only mean the worst. The Apocalypse was upon them. The Antichrist had come and—terror of terrors—had chosen Wydehaw as his point of ascension from the bowels of hell. Limb-numbing guilt assailed the priest. All knew the Devil followed naught but paths ripe with the stench of vile sin, and Father Aric feared his was the sin that had brought Satan to their door.

Fire sparks arced and streamed out of the tower, making God knew what demonic signs against the sky. The priest tried to cross himself, but his hands had turned to lead at his sides. He was helpless. Mud churned up by the earlier rain oozed around his knees, sinking him deeper into the cold, wet ground. His body trembled with a palsied fear. His voice could not but croak, "*Gloria Patri, gloria Patri* . . ."

In a protected corner of the rose garden, Vivienne shook out her skirts and smoothed back her hair. The priest had been quick, too quick. A sigh escaped her, then a tear. Perhaps 'twas no more than she deserved.

She sat down on one of the rosary benches, and another sigh left her lips. Her pride had cost her much that she had not been able to replace. Of the five years she'd been wed, she'd spent four scrounging through the depths of humanity to get a man in her bed.

Her birthday would be upon her again soon, and Soren's also. 'Twas time for children to come into their lives, an unlikely occurrence given their current arrangement, and she was far too careful to end up breeding another man's brat. She would not do that, not even for the sorcerer—as if he'd given her even half a chance.

When Lavrans had first come to Wydehaw, she'd thought she was in love with him. There was something appealing about a man who never lied, even if the truth he spoke was often disguised and much less flattering than what she wanted to hear or expected to be told. But 'twas not love she'd felt for him. He was a challenge, a delectable one, true, but not her heart's desire. Foolish girl that she'd been, she'd given her heart to Soren in their first year of marriage, when he'd courted her as a stranger and won her as a lover, showing an appreciation for her wit and no penchant for shyness or sweetness—or virginity—in a bride. He was no warrior, but then she was no maiden in distress. He held Wydehaw through judicious alliances and the willingness to fight if all else failed. They had been a good match, one a mite close for some ecclesiastical tastes, but a good match nonetheless.

A smile flirted with her mouth. In some courts, harboring a *tendre* for one's own husband was considered gauche, yet for Soren, she'd defied fashion, loving him beyond reason, beyond common sense. For the first time in her life, she had been happy and loved in return, secure within the walls of her own home and free to explore any sensual adventure she might imagine. Then Soren had thrown it all away in his lust for a boy.

A bitter sadness replaced her smile. Her defiance had gotten her naught but an endless supply of lonely nights and an occasional crude swiving. Love was such a tangle. She had taken another man in retaliation, and Soren had stood by, angry but silent. She'd taken another, and another, and another, until not even her husband's anger had remained.

Now they both had nothing. Her pride could no longer withstand his indifference, and it seemed his sworn love had not survived her faithlessness.

Tears welled in her eyes. Father Aric had been a mistake: he'd exhorted their sinfulness even in the midst of their joining. Had she been reduced to so little worth, to the taking of hypocritically pious and premature priests? Had she abandoned her faith and her marriage vows only to be abandoned in turn?

The tears fell, making damp tracks over her cheeks and running into the corners of her mouth. Was there no hope of love? No light of truth left to guide her?

She lifted her gaze to the heavens, prepared to beseech the Lord, but the Lord answered before the words could form on her lips. Far above her, floating over the wall between the upper and middle baileys, was a light, a bright yellow light with a blue aureole. She stared, transfixed. The light floated closer, carried upon a gentle night wind, a golden star falling to earth within an azure halo.

Gold and azure, the colors of Soren's standard. There could be no clearer sign. Her heart beat faster as the bit of celestial fire drifted over the rosary wall into her garden. It descended then and delicately extinguished itself on the damp petal of a rose, the flower of love.

Vivienne reached out with a trembling hand.

From the depths of his chamber's embrasure, Soren watched the last of the sorcerer's conflagration. He'd never seen anything like it, the flames, the colors, the sparks floating on the wind. The fool man ought to be brought up on charges for putting the castle in danger. Any one of a dozen or more thatched roofs could have caught fire. None had, of course. Lavrans had the Devil's own luck, whereas he, Soren D'Arbois, Baron of Wydehaw, had none. He looked back at his bed and his thoughts turned brooding.

A strange air of anticipation had come over the castle of late, a strangeness confirmed rather than caused by the Hart's fiery display. Spring was rushing in where winter had been, and the moon was waxing full. The conjunction of the seasonal and the celestial, especially on May Eve, always heightened the effect of both, a truth he'd never been told, but one he'd felt enough times to believe beyond doubt. 'Twas particularly hard on the priests, who seemed to lose their bearings in the midst of so much Nature enforcing Her will.

There would be fires in the hills tomorrow night, he thought, turning his gaze once again to the Hart Tower and the forest that lay past the walls of his keep. Fires not magically conjured, but no less potent than the one the sorcerer had sent to the heavens. Beltaine, as spoken in the old language of the pagan gods, was close upon them, and despite its centuries of Christianity, Wales was still full of pagan gods, none of whom had answered Soren's prayers. But then, his own God had deserted him; he should have expected no better from Nemeton's.

His personal anticipations had come in the form of deep long-ings, for what he was not sure, but he knew for whom—Vivienne, the wife he so easily could have lost yet again to Caradoc. Predictably, his longings had gone unanswered. He was a fool, his appetites beyond even his own understanding.

Dain was besotted with the demoiselle, that much had become apparent with her miraculous recovery within hours of Caradoc's leaving. Soren had gone back to the tower to assure himself that she still lived and would continue to do so, at least until she was out from under his keeping. He'd found Ceridwen ab Arawn quite well, sur-prisingly well, sitting with the sorcerer over their evening meal. Soren had never thought to see such a cozily domestic scene in the Hart. Lavrans had nearly blushed at being caught, a delightful bit of fancy Soren had often dreamed of causing: a sorcerer's blush.

Dain's infatuation made him more human somehow, and, strangely enough, less sexually desirable. The unconquerable had been conquered, the seductive one had been seduced, and by an innocent, no less. At least Ceridwen had been innocent the first night Lavrans had taken her into his tower. Ragnor had sworn to her purity, though Soren would put no coin on the matter at this point in time.

"God's balls," he muttered at the realization. He wasn't going to lose his whole damned demesne over a few drops of missing blood and some torn matter.

Vivienne, he thought. Vivienne would know what to do. Thank the Lord for a practical wife. She would know how to work a virgin's ruse should the demoiselle need one for her wedding night.

He turned away from the window, fully aware of how his thoughts had contrived to bring him what he'd longed for. He had no choice but to call for Vivienne, to divert disaster for them all.

"Soren?" The sound of her voice brought his head up.

He had not heard her enter, not heard so much as a creak of a hinge, but she was there where she had not been for four years, in his chambers, standing opposite his bed. Tears marked her face. In her hand she held a rose.

"*Chérie?*" He strode toward her, concern knitting his brow. His arms opened of their own accord, and she ran into his embrace.

*   *   *

Dain was playing with fire, sitting so close to Ceridwen in the shadowy darkness of the upper chamber, sharing wine, feeling too alive, too good. They'd taken refuge on the floor between the table and the hearth when the *rihadin* had begun to flame, and they continued to sit shoulder to shoulder, knees drawn up, as the last sporadic bursts of color escaped from the orbs. A cloud of smoke had risen from the tower and passed over the face of the moon. Traces of it still lingered, wisps of a soft bluish-gray streaking Luna and obscuring some of her light, but the stars were adamantine, lustrous in their brightness against the night sky.

A grin teased his mouth. He'd explained to Ceri about the spheres and the Sun and the cosmic map, and in her own inestimable way she'd suggested that following such a skewed path could be the source of all his failures in the making of his Stone.

Silently, he offered her the wine. It wasn't part of his plan to fill her with drink, but he'd noticed a general softening of her countenance as they'd passed the flagon back and forth. She took the wine and their fingers touched, hers warm, his warmer still. Latent flashes of *rihadin* color illuminated her face: a band of blue across her eyes, like a Quicken-tree warrior; yellow on her mouth, soft like butter, hot like the Sun. Gazing upon her lips, he could feel the heat and near taste their smooth sweetness.

He had promised himself a kiss, a true kiss, deep in her mouth and in no way chaste.

"I brought you a gift."

"A gift?" She looked over at him, surprised.

He reached up to the table and retrieved the rolled-and-bound package he'd brought with him out of Wroneu. "The trader was known to me, a man named Toranen the Icelander. He came through Havn on his way south and had news of my family."

"Family? In Denmark?"

"*Danmark, ja,*" he said, thickening his accent, his mouth curving into a grin. He untied the rope binding and gave her the package. When she hesitated, he lifted the first fold of cloth and let it fall back over her arm. "*Kæreste?*"

The endearment was no more than a murmur and in Danish, a language she did not speak, yet she lowered her gaze, turning shy on him. "You have already given me so much." On Lady Vivienne he would have called the action coy. On Ceridwen he called it fascinating.

"The gift is yours, Ceri. I would not give it to another."

She nodded once and lifted the next fold of cloth. Inside the coarse wool was the sheepskin Toranen had given him to protect his prize.

"Must be a precious thing," she said.

" 'Tis unique," he agreed. "Like the one to whom it is given."

Compliments and gifts? Ceridwen wondered. Both accompanied by smiles? She hardly knew what to think, other than to be on her guard against herself as well as him. He was her most damned weakness—and her most delightful. They had played like children with his celestial spheres and had surely awakened half the demesne. There would be talk on the morrow of the enchantments wrought in the night. She wondered if all or most of his magic was made up of such simple things, at least the magic that set the castle folk all aflutter and quaking in their boots. The other magic he had in him was subtler, less likely to be noticed, but no less potent, and it was this magic she guarded herself against. 'Twas the magic of allure and promise.

"Your news must have been good," she said, working at the knotted leather cord holding the rolled sheepskin closed. "It has made you generous."

"Aye." Dain laughed at her cynical assessment. "But I would not have passed up this treasure whatever the news."

"And your family? How do they fare?" The first knot came free, leading her to the second.

"My parents live and are well. My youngest brother, Jens, has become secretary to the Bishop of Roskilde. Eric, the oldest of us all, now has three ships trading from the White Sea to the Baltic, and my sister, Magrethe, has married a distant cousin of the king's."

"Richard?" she asked, obviously impressed.

"Valdemar," he replied.

"Oh." She went to work on the second knot until it loosened. When she didn't open the skin, but only held it in her lap, he looked up again and found her watching him, her head tilted to one side.

"I had not thought of you having a family." Her brow was slightly furrowed. "Sister, brothers, a mother and father."

"What did you think? That I was spawned by the Devil himself?"

"Mayhaps." She gave a small lift of her shoulder and brought the flagon to her mouth for a sip.

"Surely I have not been that hard on you."

She finished her drink and eyed him carefully. "Mayhaps by an angel in the midst of falling from grace," she conceded.

"Redeemable?"

"All men are redeemable in the eyes of the Lord, even those tainted by the wickedest of sins." She hesitated again, her next words coming with less confidence. "Is that why you are so far from home?"

Her question took him aback, being too close to the truth, but he recovered quickly enough. He had long since reconciled himself to not returning home. His father would know what he had done, with one look he would know. 'Twas a revelation Dain preferred not to make, not now, not ever.

"I but went to war. It's a fine tradition of second sons." He gestured toward the package, hoping to distract her. When she still didn't open it, he shrugged. "In truth, I was much farther away than Wales. Now, are you going to finish opening your present? I swear 'tis worth the effort."

"I heard you tell the Boar's leech about being on Crusade. Were you with the Lionheart?"

His recovery was slower this time. She was breaching the barrier of his past, a privilege he had allowed no one. The secrets of his life were his alone, yet as he looked upon her in the quiet darkness, the desert years unfolded before him, daring him to reveal their contents to her.

She had asked, had she not? What harm could there be in telling her the barest of facts, about the truce negotiations between Saladin and Richard breaking down in Jaffa?

Richard had ransomed the English nobles among the legates and aides who had fallen afoul of Saladin in the treaty camp, but had left the rest of them to their fates, especially the two young Welsh princes guaranteed to give him trouble back home, Caradoc of Balor and Morgan ab Kynan. Dain had merely been their expendable companion, though the English had good enough reason to rid themselves of Danes. By the time peace had been made in October of 1192 and Richard had sailed for Europe, Dain and Morgan had been four months in the red sands of the Nefud Desert, sold by Saladin as slaves to Jalal. Caradoc had been imprisoned with them in the beginning, but had been bought by another trader, Kalut ad-Din, within weeks of their incarceration. Such was the fate of the youngest captives. The older men had fared much worse.

Yes, Dain almost said to Ceridwen, he'd been with the Lionheart, but the Lionheart had not been with him. Only his strong aversion to confessions of any sort saved him from the folly.

"Aye, I was with King Richard," he finally answered. " 'Twas not an altogether pleasant experience. Are you going to open your present?"

"Have you not been home in all the time since your return from the Holy Land?"

Persistence was one of her strengths and would surely be her downfall, if not his.

"I did not leave the Holy Land near as quickly as the English king," he said obliquely, hoping she would let the matter drop. He should have known better.

"What were you doing?"

He gave a short laugh. "Exploring strange new lands." Very strange lands.

"Wasn't it dangerous to stay after the others left?"

"There is still a Latin kingdom in Palestine, and I was very well protected." Actually, he'd been guarded twenty-four hours a day after his trick with the dagger. The pope couldn't have gotten to him, which was a very good thing for the pontiff.

"What about the—"

"Shhh." He softly hushed her, laying his finger against her lips. "Open your present. It's magic."

Her eyes instantly lit up with a mixture of curiosity and excitement, and he wondered why he had not thought to tell her such before. If naught else, he should have learned by now that magic was the key to her heart.

She tempered her eagerness with care, gently unrolling the sheepskin to reveal the prize within. For a long moment she stared at the gift without touching it. Then she lightly ran one finger down the ivory handle.

"A mirror," she murmured, continuing her exploration by moving her finger up around the circular mount, also made of ivory.

Inside the mount was a round of polished metal covered with glass. " 'Tis beautifully strange."

"Made by a Norse skald Toranen swore to me was from Thule."

"Thule?"

"A place said to lie beyond the farthest known north, a place many men seek, but none has seen."

"Except for the mirror maker," she teased, sending him a side-long glance from beneath her lashes.

"Aye." He grinned. "Except for the mirror maker and mayhaps someday me."

"You would go so far north?"

" 'Twas my destination before Wydehaw caught my eye, to go north and evermore north and let the cold freeze the desert heat from my veins."

"Was it so hot as that?"

"Hotter," he said, telling her more than she knew, but doing it with an ingenuousness that gave none of the truth away, that the heat still crawled through him some nights, burning him.

"What are these holes?" she asked, returning her attention to the mirror. Toward the top of the glass were two almond-shaped holes, side by side.

"Keys to the magic." He turned the mirror over, laying it facedown on the sheepskin, and showed her the runic letters carved around the holes in back. "The runes speak of a god's journey in search of the love in men's souls." He glanced up. "True love, no less, the touchstone of every poet's fancy."

"You don't believe in true love?"

"With all my heart," he assured her, though he let a grin belie the words. "I fear 'tis true love that does not believe in me."

"Posh." She dismissed him with a flick of her wrist. "True love believes in all of us."

"The runes say the gift of immortality, life everlasting, lies within true love."

"Then 'tis the love of God the god was searching for." Her brow crinkled. "That's strange isn't it? A pagan god looking for love from our God."

"Your God," he corrected her.

She gave him a vexed glance. "There is only one God."

"Allahu akbar!" he agreed. "God is great!"

"You speak too many tongues." She took another swallow of wine and gave him the flagon. "Sometimes I think I'm in the Tower of Babel."

At that, he laughed again. "Sometimes I think the same. Here." He handed her the mirror. "Hold it up to my face and tell me what you see."

Ceridwen scooted closer to him while he set the flagon aside and lit a candle to put next to them. If there was love in his soul, she dearly wanted to see it. "Should the mirror be closer to you or to me?"

"To me, so my eyes are in place of yours while the glass reflects your face."

She did as he instructed, bringing the mirror between them, and instantly she felt a breath of wind brush against her left cheek, then her shoulder and arm, spiraling down and reaching toward Dain. The long strands of his hair stirred in the breeze, lifting to caress and twine with her hand where she held the mirror.

The thing was magic, powerful magic. Her attention shifted from the feel of the wind to his eyes, and the sense of profound magic deepened. 'Twas her face she saw, every curve and line, but the eyes were an abyss, rich, dark, fathomless, thick lashed and terribly beautiful.

The runes lied. The god had not searched for true love— though her heart yearned to tell her that she saw some evidence of love looking back at her—but for the way to wisdom without pain. In this the mirror was clear, Dain had not found such a path. The wisdom residing in his eyes had all been wrought by pain. Despair shaded part of the path, degradation another. Fear had been there, and a thousand thousand hurts had lain along the track to wound and scar.

Unable to bear what she saw, she lowered the mirror and averted her gaze. She should not have looked. No one should be laid so bare before another.

"What did you see?" he asked, and she could only shake her head. "Was there so little?"

"No. Too much," she answered.

"And none of it good?"

Her silence condemned him, and she heard him sigh.

"Well," he began, "the mirror does not see all then, for I swear there is some good in me. Not much, but some, and of late, mayhaps even some love."

"Had naught to do with love," she told him, feeling awful.

"No love?"

She shook her head again.

"Then what?"

She would have kept her silence except for knowing he deserved to be told, if for no other reason than to protect himself from another who might try to look inside his soul.

"The knowledge that comes from suffering," she said, still not daring to meet his gaze. "The mirror showed much of this knowledge in you."

"Ah," was all he said, then, "Well, we are friends, are we not?"

"Aye," she said, and in that moment knew it to be true. They had become friends.

"Then you are unlikely to bandy it about."

Her head came up. "Never."

"My secrets are safe with you."

"Forever," she vowed.

"And yours with me." He held up the mirror and smiled in that way of his, making her wonder if he'd been teasing her all along. "Shall I take a peek into your soul, dear Ceridwen?"

'Twas a dismaying thought, knowing the power of the mirror, yet her reluctance was more for his sake than her own.

"I have it on good authority that 'tis not a pretty sight," she warned him. "And though I have learned to live with the darkness lurking in the corners of my soul, I would spare you, my friend."

Dain felt his smile fade. She was serious, and he could well imagine the pious authority that had pronounced her a sinner.

"Dear friend," he said softly, reaching up to caress her chin. "There can be no darkness on your soul that I have not seen even blacker in another, probably my own."

Still she denied him, laying her hand on his when he would have brought the mirror between them. Reluctantly, he settled back against the wall and resigned himself to watching her in the shifting light of candle flame and hearth fire. A breeze was blowing around the tower, swirling up bits of *rihadin* ash. There would be rain before dawn; he could smell it on the wind.

The mirror was no more magic than he, yet she'd seen true. 'Twas Madron's fault for peering around in his mind with her damned Druid's sleep. The witch had stirred things up.

"I did not mean for the gift to make you sad," he said.

" 'Tis not the mirror that saddens me, but that you suffered."

"And now you are suffering. Should we both be sad together?"

She looked up at him, and the candlelight revealed silent tears coursing down her cheeks.

Pure instinct compelled him to move toward her, his back coming off the wall, his arm gathering her close, his other hand cupping her cheek, and everything inside his heart welling up and spilling over like a wave washing over a dam, flowing toward her. "Ceri, do not cry," he murmured. "Do not cry for me."

She paid him no heed, her tears running beneath his fingers and down the center of his palm. He wiped the dampness off her cheek with his thumb and was struck anew by the childlike softness of her skin.

"Hush, *min koerlighed.*" He called her his love, comforting her and kissing her on the brow, indulging himself despite the caution sounding in his head. He kissed her temple and the side of her nose, consoling her, and listened to the cry of caution grow ever fainter. Of their own volition, his lips slid down to the corner of her mouth, seeking contact, and 'twas there that comfort and consolation gave way to desire, in the place where breath and tears pooled in a delicate, wine-scented curve. He paused in the sudden stillness and felt her do the same.

"Dain . . ." His name was the barest of sighs falling from her lips. Her eyes were closed, her mouth partially open, her body warm and alive in his arms.

He could have stopped and taken no more. Verily the thought crossed his mind, yet he turned his mouth more fully onto hers, savoring the taste of her, like nectar and the sea. He bit her gently, so gently, along the fullness of her lower lip and at the corners of her mouth, one side and then the other, and soothed with his tongue, until his message became clear and her instincts responded.

With the opening of her mouth, he did not hesitate. He opened his own mouth wider and slid his tongue down the length of hers. A groan was released from deep in her throat, filling him with the echoes of her pleasure. There was nothing sweet about the sound. It had been born in the surprise of lust and dragged up from the core of her being. She clung to him, and he kissed her, again and again. His mouth roamed at will over the curves of her face, over her cheeks and brow and jaw, returning as often to her lips as she did to his, but he went no farther. He did not dally at her ear or let his teeth graze the side of her neck. He did not fill his palm with her breast, and he licked nothing beyond the inside of her mouth—for a kiss was a kiss and not more.

In the way of such things, the desperation between them weakened its hold, transforming itself into the delight of mutual exploration; a dangerous turn, Dain knew, for he would allow himself far more leeway in the pursuit of delight than he ever would under the influence of desperation. Yet if kept within strict limits, he assured himself, kissing alone could not fail to reach a natural end, and despite the allure of delight and the seductive forays of her mouth, he would find the end of their kiss in time. *In time.*

The moon coursed across midnight in the sky, trailing clouds and stars. Beltaine Eve had begun. All of Nemeton's cosmic map circled over their heads, the zodiacal beasts strung out in slowly swirling chaos: Aldebaran, Eye of the Bull in Taurus, followed by Fomalhaut, the beginning of the Water in Aquarius; Ram passing through Fish in a lazy circumference.

Ceridwen had not known there could be so much gentleness in strength, that one touch upon her mouth could make her whole body soar as if on wings, that the taste of a man would be like honey upon her tongue, making her want more, always more. She could not get close enough, yet she was closer to him than she'd ever been to anyone, her breasts crushed against his chest, her fingers winding through his hair, her mouth everywhere upon his face. The touch, scent, taste, and feel of him conjured a miracle with every breath; his kiss solved a thousand mysteries of life. Man was magic to woman.

Dain knew not how long the whole of it lasted before he lifted his mouth from hers, but he knew 'twas a kiss he would not forget. His body thrummed with the aliveness of it. His mind rejoiced in the pure wonder of it. The kiss had been perfect.

He wanted more. Much more. Not getting it was going to be the price he paid for his indulgence. In her own fashion, Edmee had proved him still a man in his desires. Ceridwen had proved him a man in his needs.

Holding her close, he forced a calming breath into his lungs and looked up at the stars. Vindemiatrix, the bright star of the Virgin, floated by on its rod overhead, dipping low with the breeze and coming alongside the Lion's Heart in Leo. He almost smiled. Fate was truly guided by an ironic hand. His birth under the Red Fire Star put him firmly in Leo, and just as firmly, the virgin was in his heart. Her head rested in the curve of his shoulder, her breath soft and hot on his neck, inviting disaster. The kiss was over, only the fire in his loins remained. He needed to be alone.

"You must go to bed," he said, attempting a light tone. There was no reason for her to know of the new suffering he'd brought on himself. " 'Tis time for sleep."

"I do not want to sleep." She nestled closer, and he immediately began extricating himself from their embrace, rising to his feet.

"To bed with you," he said.

She rose with him, and in the midst of it, took his hand in hers. He wished she had not done so, for even her innocent touch made him yearn. Worse still, she stood too close, her eyes downcast, her clothing brushing against his, her thumb caressing the back of his hand, keeping him from his escape.

She did not speak, but she did not need to speak. What she wanted was very clear.

"I cannot," he said, his voice soft with regret, his fingers wrapping around hers.

"Was the kiss so poor?" She had turned shy on him again. He could see naught but the top of her head shining golden in the yellow light from the fire.

He dared not tell her the truth, and when he said nothing, she withdrew her hand from his and stepped away.

"Mayhaps the Boar will not want me either."

"Ceri . . ." He grasped her arm without thinking, and found himself still with nothing he could say—except the truth. "If I kiss you again, it will not be sleep that whiles away the hours of the night."

"I know, yet I still would ask."

Someday she would surprise the life out of him.

"And I say you do not know." His voice was harsh with frustration. "Your virgin dreams would not last a moment in my bed." One touch from her would have given her what she professed to want, but she had not known enough to put her hand between his legs.

"Virgin dreams are not meant to last."

Truth rang in her words, and too much hope. And wasn't that what he wanted? For her to hope and not give up and finally to push him over the edge of reason with her sweet implorations? He had played the innocent for Jalal, and he knew what a powerful seduction innocence was, especially to a consummate seducer.

The realization gave him immediate pause. A chill ran through his blood. Was he to become like his teacher then? Would that be Jalal's final triumph?

"I cannot," he repeated with conviction, though he still held her arm.

"And I cannot sleep," she told him honestly. "Not like this. You have . . . I want . . ." She stumbled over the words, trying to explain what did not need explaining.

He watched her growing shame and frustration change into anger, and knew himself to be a low bastard. He should not have done such to her. She might be virgin, but she was still human, and she was young. Her emotions were all tangled up with her arousal.

"Do you not know how to please yourself?" he asked, striving for gentleness in the question.

"Please myself?"

"*Masturbari,* Ceri." He spoke the Latin softly. "It will help."

She blushed, proving herself not completely innocent, which only made his body harder. What a pretty picture she would make: her hands, his mouth. His chest tightened with the thought of it.

"I do not want that," she said, jerking her arm free, her voice controlled but trembling. "I wanted you, and you are killing me."

"Then we will die together." He gave her what he could, knowing it was not enough for either of them.

"Bastard," she accused him. "Heartless, heartless bastard."

She gathered her skirts and fled, her slippered feet making nary a sound on the tower stairs. He watched her disappear and heard the door to his solar slam shut with the weight of her anger.

A mere fortnight past, he would have agreed with her, but the words were no longer true. He had a heart. He could tell by the damned stupid breaking of it.

Chapter 17

Dawn had not yet broken the darkness of the night when Ceridwen heard Dain come down from the upper chamber. She had slept fitfully at best, and had known she slept only from the innumerable times she'd awakened. Each time she'd found Numa, her one true friend, loyally by her side.

She hated Wydehaw's mage. He was cruel beyond measure, rivaling the Boar, mayhaps surpassing him. Caradoc only wanted her blood to make his wicked sacrifice and call up his fiendish dragons. With luck, the Boar could be eluded; and if she proved to have no luck, the beast could be faced and fought. But love, she didn't know how to fight love.

Dain had kissed her and taken her heart and filled it with more hurt than she could bear. Her pillow was damp with the tears she'd shed. 'Twas the pain of love squeezing the breath from her lungs in heavy sobs. She didn't want to love him, yet she could find no escape. She'd searched her mind the night long, trying to find respite from the crushing emptiness he'd inflicted on her soul, and she'd found none. She loved the bastard Lavrans and had been forsaken.

Glass crashed somewhere in the room on the other side of the bed curtains. Dain swore, knocked into something, and swore again. She wiped her eyes with the back of her hand, holding herself still, listening. Another crash followed the first, then came the scent of incense.

"Numa!" he hollered. "Elixir! *Kom!*"

Belly to bedsheets, the albino slunk onto the floor and beneath the curtains without giving Ceridwen so much as a backward glance.

A torrent of Danish followed the hound's appearance in the chamber, a diatribe punctuated by heavy, erratically paced footfalls. Dain was crossing the room, his voice too loud for the space enclosed within the curved walls. The dogs began to whimper and whine, sounding so forlorn, their misery sent a shiver up her spine.

Fighting a cowardly impulse to hide, Ceridwen tossed the fur coverlets aside. No good could come from this madness. She would not allow him to hurt Numa in her stead. A loud banging thud brought her to a quick stop, the sheets gripped in her fist, the sable in a pile by her hip. She cocked her head and held her breath.

Could only have been his fist slamming into the Druid Door, she thought. Nothing else in the tower with the solidness of oak had the resonance of iron behind it.

"*Nej!*" he roared, hitting the door again and making her flinch. "*Kvinde, nej!*"

The command reverberated throughout the solar in a strange manner she could not comprehend, as if he spoke from two places at once, and within its dying echoes she heard a new sound—metal sliding and clacking against metal. There was an ominous timbre to the noise, reminding her of the scrape and glide of swordplay or of knives being sharpened. Her hands tightened on the sheets, and she found herself praying he would not come for her.

Dain locked the Druid Door down to the seventh level, shoving home bolts and half chanting, half cursing a litany of luminaries. He called each series of mechanisms by its planetary name, added its earthly counterpart and its element, and a curse torn from his frustration. From within the words he threw his voice to the dogs, bringing them to heel with a dire warning of what would come to pass if they failed in their task.

There was magic here, he swore to himself. He had not come this far only to be denied, not when the sacrifices had become so great. If he could not have Ceridwen, he would have the secrets of the Hart Tower. He would forge the marriage of Sol and Luna and conceive the hermaphroditic corpse from which resurrection became possible, the one spirit with mastery over the Philosopher's Stone. Pure gold could impregnate pure silver, the red stone into the white. The mix of the two, the hermaphrodite, had to die, the corpse in a tomb, and arise again with the blessing of the celestial influence.

"Sweet Jesus," he swore between his teeth. The way of it was written so even in the Bible:

> *Senseless man, that which thou sowest is not quickened unless it die first. And that which thou sowest, thou sowest not the body that shall be: but bare grain, as of wheat, or of some of the rest. But God giveth it a body as he will: and to every seed a proper body.*
>
> *(I Cor. 15:36–8)*

"God giveth it a body as he will." There is only one God, she'd said. He locked down Mercury with a hard twist of his hand and stepped back. Only one God to beseech, yet tonight he would beseech a pantheon of gods for the Quicken-tree, the very same who allowed him access to Nemeton's tower of cosmic mysteries to search for the transforming One. More swiving irony. He would die from it and be damned, if he could not understand it.

"Religion," he whispered as if the word were yet another curse. He reached out and touched the tips of his fingers to the Druid Door. He'd fought for his faith and been consigned to the depths of hell for his fervor. He'd murdered and slain in the name of his God, and his God had forsaken him.

And now this. He curled his fingers into his palm and turned his face toward the eastern window. 'Twas more than the maid eating away at him. The sun of Beltaine Eve had not yet risen into the sky and already he felt the pull of the grove, felt Deri calling to him.

There were seven other festivals of the year, but 'twas Calan Gaef with the magic of death and Beltaine with the magic of blossom that affected him most, this year to his detriment. The whole of it was coming upon him too strongly, the quickening of the earth and his blood, the ripeness of the season and his loins. The Quicken-tree would get more than they had bargained for this night.

He turned away from the door, looking once more toward the eastern window. A dawn wind breached the embrasures, its touch falling lightly upon his cheeks. 'Twould not be long before the horizon ran red with the first streak of day, and there was more work to be done. Yet he took the moment, lifting his face into the fading darkness of the night and letting the wind caress his lips with a sweet kiss from the coming morn.

Ceridwen listened to the silence, and her courage grew. Assuring herself that Dain would not kill her outright, she crept to the side of the bed and opened the curtains a bare slit.

All was quiet. Dain stood in the middle of the solar with a soft wind ruffling the sleeves and hem of his tunic. His hair was wild about him, long and tangled, proof of hands that had run through it over and over again in distraction—or despair. One torch burned bright in a cresset next to the hearth, its flame rippling in the breeze, its light glancing off the heavy, bronze-studded leather belt around Dain's waist.

The gentling wind died down, and the chaos returned. Dain began pacing the breadth of the chamber, his strides uneven, roaming to some unseen will, until a destination seemed to present itself and he was once more on a true course.

"Kvinde, nej!" His hand came down hard on the door leading to the eyrie. The dogs wound themselves around his legs in abject subjugation, sleek white flowing against pitch-black, the two twining bodies lit by flickering torchlight. He issued his command again at each of the embrasures, then one final time over the hatch leading to the alchemy chamber. His voice shifted strangely, from here to there, even when he stayed in one place, making her uneasy, but the dogs responded without hesitation, following him step by step, fawning and cajoling, all but licking his boots in their eagerness to please.

With a sinking heart, she realized he had spoken true. She

should not have put her trust where in the end it must be betrayed; the bitch was his. Totally. There was but one master in the Hart Tower.

From the hatch, he moved to the rows of shelves holding his simples and chose a small earthenware vessel. When he turned to the table, she got her first clear look at his face and drew back with an emotion she could not name, though the force of it raced through her. The chaos of his movements had invaded every aspect of his being. His eyes were fiercely intense, his breath coming short, the very bones of his face etched more strongly beneath his skin. With one broad sweep of his hand, he cleared the table of its contents, sending ampoules, pots, and cruets crashing onto the floor, their once fine forms reduced to thousands of shards and potsherds. Naught was left but the small brazier releasing fragrant fume-terres, the smoke of the earth.

Releasing a ragged moan, he dropped into his great chair, covering his face with one hand while he clutched the small pot within the other. For long moments, the only sound filling the air between them was his breath.

"I know you are awake," he said at last, his voice dark with an edge of bitterness. "I can feel you watching me." She blanched and drew back deeper into the bed. "Hear this, Ceridwen ab Arawn. You will not leave this chamber until dawn breaks the sky again. If you try, the hounds will restrain you, doing whatever they must. Do not count on Numa's loyalty to aid in your escape, for the bitch would as soon tear you limb from limb than go against my will in this."

There was both threat and warning in his words, and the revelation of what he'd done with all his shouting and hitting of doors: He'd sealed the tower. Panic fluttered to life in her breast. She would not be trapped like the animal he had become, awaiting the return of Caradoc and damnation. The time for leaving was upon her.

"I gave my word that I would not try to escape," she said, fighting to control her alarm and bringing all her guile to bear on the falsely spoken promise in hopes of making it appear genuine.

"And your word will be broken," he said with utter conviction.

"I have not yet strayed," she reminded him. "And I have had the chance."

Slowly, he lifted his head, staring through the darkness and the distance with eyes so bright, she trembled. He looked more beast than the Boar. "Your thoughts of love held you here, and I have taken them away. You will try your escape now, but I am warning you: Do not attempt to leave this tower before another full turn of the sun. The hills will be aflame tonight with the fires of Bel, and you will be consumed. I promise you this."

Her face went from the paleness of fear to the red flush of anger. Love? How dare he speak to her of love.

"You have overvalued yourself." She would not be made a fool of twice, no matter how badly he frightened her.

"No, *kæreste*," he said, his gaze unwavering. " 'Tis that I under-valued you. I thought I could not be touched. You have proven me wrong."

If the words had been spoken in any tone other than that of desolation, she might have taken hope, but he had left her none. He sat alone at his table, his form unyielding, his bearing grim, leaving no room for another at his side.

In silence, he broke the seal on the clay pot, then dipped in the middlemost finger of his left hand and pulled it back out. 'Twas covered with a black unguent. Starting on the left side of his face, he put his finger beneath his eye and drew a thick line straight out across his temple to his hairline. With his right middle finger, he did the same to the other eye. The dark potion glittered in the light of fire and candle like a streak of the night sky across his tawny skin.

This was not the banding of the Quicken-tree, Ceridwen thought. It was something else, something much less fair, something baleful.

"What are you doing?" She pulled the curtains aside and slipped to the floor in her bare feet, curiosity overcoming caution. "What is this unguent you use?"

He did not answer, only dipped in his finger again and drew a second line from his right ear across his cheekbone and up and over the bridge of his nose.

She approached him carefully, not knowing how close she dared to get.

"Your courage is ill-placed in this," he told her, and she wondered if she'd ever managed to hide anything from him, or if he'd been reading her mind from the first night.

"So what say you?" She kept her voice soft. "Am I in danger?" She was duly afraid, but strangely and suddenly, far more for him than herself. For herself, she was wary, and curious, so curious.

"Not if you stay in the tower with the hounds to guard you." He finished the line by drawing it across his left cheekbone to his left ear.

"Will you be staying also?"

"No. I go to Rhuddlan's camp." A new line was started below the last, the three of them thick and rich.

She stopped at the table's edge, well away from the broken glass and him. "And what will become of you in Deri?"

A short, harsh laugh answered her question. "The becoming has already begun, *chérie*," he said, trailing the third line across the width of his face with unerring accuracy.

"And is this what you become? This striped, wild thing?" She made a small gesture of helplessness, not understanding what she saw in his face. Something stranger than the alchemical magic they practiced in the lower chamber was happening to him. The shadows, the low uneven light, and the pattern he was painting on his face were conspiring to disguise him. Verily, he seemed to be disappearing before her eyes.

"Wild?" With the reverence of ritual, he touched each of his fingers to the pot in turn, smearing their tips with unguent. "Aye, 'tis something wild I become, wild and fearsome."

He looked down at his hands and slowly turned his palms toward the ceiling. The air stirred, setting the candle flame aflicker and causing the incense smoke to curl around and down upon itself, then rise up again in a winding trail. He lifted his arms, his fingers curved like unsheathed talons, his palms cupped, as if he were pulling something up from the air in front of him.

Ceridwen held herself close, her own hands clasped at her breasts, resisting the need to reach out to him and stop him. In her ignorance, she did nothing, and when his gaze flashed to hers— brightly crazed with an unholy light—she knew 'twas too late. He had gone beyond her.

"You see before you the Demon." The words rolled off his tongue encased in smoke, terrifying her with their proclamation: Evil was here. Smoke flowed from between his teeth and out of his nostrils, circling up in fumed whorls to shield his face and curl through ten-

drils of his hair. He closed his eyes on a breath of uncanny length and power, a deep inhalation of the fragrant grayish-blue haze that filled his chest and pulled a stillness down around them both.

She dared not touch him now. Indeed, she took a step back. He had shown her nothing like this before. 'Twas wondrous, monstrous, dizzily frightening stuff. The heaviest of magic, she was sure, good for the most deadly spell-casting and conjuring.

"What need has Rhuddlan of a demon?" she asked, compelled to the rash question by her own needs. Mayhaps, when the time came, if she had the courage, she could transform herself into one. Heresy in its most despicable form, but what choice did she have? Nothing less than what she saw before her would dissuade the Boar from his wedding bed or frighten him from his damnable course, but that it would do so she had no doubt. Here was a feral being unheedful of the laws of man or God, a demon true, bound only by his own evil intent.

Jesu. Was this how all sinners came into being, forced by circumstance into dealings with a dark manifestation? Falling from grace while clinging to that most divine state?

The barest smile curved the Demon Dain's mouth. Wisps of vapor curled at the corners of his lips and veiled the red-rimmed eyes staring at her from deep in their sockets. "You are fearless, Ceri."

She could have called him liar, despite his gift of sight, for her heart was racing. Yet her only concession to fear was another judicious step back.

"Retreat?" he asked with a mocking lift of one brow.

"Caution only," she replied, though her voice was breathless with fright.

"Then listen, little cautious one." He smiled, and his lashes lowered over his fiery gaze. "Rhuddlan calls up the Sacred Demon of the unknown for his own use, the Demon of despair, for Rhuddlan is as fearless as you." He spoke the words as liturgy, lifting his hands and laying the tips of his fingers upon his cheeks. "Rhuddlan of the Quicken-tree welcomes the true Demon of suffering and sorrow, the one who steals the first sweet breaths of children, the one who cripples and maims youth and the old with no regard to justice, the one who steals souls." With the solemnity of a priest, he dragged his fingers across his face, making four lines on either side to add to the three. "Rhuddlan beseeches the bane of mankind and all beings, the hand of God in destruction. The Demon enters the forest at dawn, the bringer of all divine disasters: the earth cracking open, rivers swelling over their banks and washing the land clean, fires spewing forth from the mountaintops, giant winds swirling down from the sky. The Demon beckons, and the four elements do the Demon's bidding. Earth. Water. Fire. Air. *I am the Demon,"* he said, and his voice echoed upon itself in eldritch tones both eerie and profane.

Aye, she thought, taking in every word and committing it to memory. Here was power to be used, dark power to be feared by all.

"And when the destruction has been wrought, Rhuddlan and all of Quicken-tree will take the Demon and transform him into the Underworld god they need, the god he was before Rome turned him into the Devil." His voice wove a continuing spell of enchantment with its undulating charm, revealing the mystery of what he had become. "Ceraunnos, the Horned One, Lord of the Animals, will come to them on Beltaine as he has for time beyond memory, and there amidst the fires, he will meet Beli, father of the gods and god of the Sun, and Don, Mother Goddess of the Earth and the gods, and of all heroes."

Ceridwen knew the god Ceraunnos, as well as she knew Beli and Don. She'd come across them many times in the manuscripts kept in the library at Usk. Their names ran through the old stories told by her mother. They were worshiped by the Druids, and they consorted with the Light-elves from across the water. Aye, she knew Ceraunnos, for he was spoken of in the red book and she'd seen him once, somewhere, etched into stone with his torc in one hand and a horned serpent in the other, with other serpents by his side, a deity of fertility crowned with a stag's antlers—or so the pagan manuscripts said.

Now she faced the mix of god and demon in its flesh, and she understood the being no better than she had before. God was God. Devil was Devil. One was to be loved, the other abhorred. The lines were clear, the two could not meet, and certainly not within the form of one mere mortal.

"No man can be both god and demon," she told him.

Dain's eyes slowly opened, and a subtly demonic smile lifted a corner of his mouth. "Au contraire, *chérie.* No man can help but be both. Until the ceremony, and even after, you will not be safe in Wroneu. Any man who catches you in the forest on May Eve will take what I have not."

He pushed himself out of his chair, rising with a horrible swift-
ness, and she stumbled back in unabashed retreat. His eyebrow
arched, but he took no more heed, passing by her without comment
on his way to the hearth.

With all his sorcerer's grace, he swung his cloak around his
shoulders and lifted the cowl over his head. She saw nothing more of
his face. If not truly demon and god, he had become what he'd been
the first time she'd seen him: a shadow lost in darkness.

"Remember what I have said, and beware the dogs," he
warned, striding toward the floor hatch. "They will not let you pass
where I have told them you may not go."

Ceridwen watched him descend the alchemy chamber stairs,
pulling the hatch closed behind him. Within moments the bolt slid
home on the underside of the planks, and she knew her fate had been
sealed as surely as the tower.

Yet there was the faintest glimmer of hope, for he had left the
black unguent. 'Twould not be a pale, trembling virgin Caradoc found
when next he breached the walls of Wydehaw.

Shay saw Lavrans first, far below him on the forest floor. The mage
moved with the silent speed of the *tylwyth teg,* his footsteps leaving no
more trace nor making any more sound than the dawn wind soughing
through the trees and billowing his cloak behind him like dark wings
on a bird of prey.

The Quicken-tree youth marked Dain's direction, then signaled
Llynya where she sat on a bough below him, doing her best to entice a
sunbeam into warming the small purple-and-white violet in the palm
of her hand. She was very near success. Shay could see the tiny ray of
light moving along the field maple bough, both advancing and retreating, but growing ever closer to Llynya's outstretched fingers. The
flower still had the freshness of morning dew on it. Night nectar, the
Quicken-tree were apt to call the moisture, for 'twas the cooling of the
night that lured the water out of the air, and morning light that made
it disappear.

He would have let her continue, for there was nothing quite
like sunbeam-warmed violets to break one's fast, but Lavrans was
slipping deeper into the shadows of Wroneu. Shay tried to signal her

again with a gesture, and when that failed to attract her attention, he cupped his hand around his mouth and gave the clear *chir-r-up* call of a lark.

Her immediate reaction was not to look up at him, but to peek down over the side of her bough and, like himself, mark Dain's direction. The flower went in her mouth to be eaten cold.

"Malashm," she said, lapsing into an Elfin tongue. *"Donn Thanieu esa lofar Deri."*

"I agree. He's going to take the Olden Track to the grove."

"He's never done it before." She threw Shay a quizzical glance.

Shay shrugged. "Rhuddlan said he might. The way through the mountains will take him over the high pass of Wyche Elm. The thinner air will help clear his mind."

"Of what?" Llynya's look grew even more confused.

"The maid, sprite. The maid."

"Ah," she said with dawning understanding, then her brow furrowed. "Maybe we should head him off. I don't think Rhuddlan wants his mind clear of the maid."

"No," Shay said. "We'll follow him, nothing more. Deri calls him, but it's up to Lavrans to find his own way."

"As it is for us to find our own way back through the *pryf*'s maze?"

He grinned. "'Tis Beltaine, sprite. Mayhaps I'll find my way with you instead."

Her startled expression didn't bode well for the possibility. Neither did the speed with which she lofted herself off the bough to the ground. "You would have to catch me first!" Her words came back to him from where she'd disappeared in the trees, fast on Lavrans's trail.

From his place higher in the maple, Shay jumped with his arms spread wide, letting his cloak fill with air and slow his descent. One day soon Llynya would grow up.

Dain knelt by the river and slid his hand down into the cool running water. Dawn was rising, sending her golden tendrils of light skimming over the horizon and the land to shatter on the surface of the Llynfi. Just beyond his fingers, trout lay in wait for the morning hatching of insects, their tails swaying languidly between the eddies and the rocks.

Llynya was behind him, smelling of violets. Shay was off to his left, crouched in a low-lying limb of beech, both of them watching and waiting. To any other, they would have been invisible. On any other day, he would not have been aware of them himself.

On this day, though, nothing escaped his awareness. The earth was a living force reaching up through the soles of his feet and twining through the fibers of his body, making pathways for the rivers that were the waters of his body. He spread his fingers, letting the icy cold seep into the tender curves of his hand. After the cold came the liquid element, lapping at his skin and passing through him. He was the river.

The sun broke free of the earth and flooded his senses with light; after the light came the warmth, carried on a gentle breath of air to caress and enfold him. A single sphere burned bright and deep in his chest, shining with a clarity beyond fire, with a luminosity he could scarce conceive. Rhuddlan had called a demon of earth and fire, but would receive a being of water and light.

'Twas Ceri who had done this to him. She had offered herself in love and had not left enough darkness in his soul to conjure up a good demon. She was the *Petra Genitrix,* the Stone Mother, unshakable, unconquerable, she who yields only to time. What need had Rhuddlan of a demon? she'd asked. The need of all men for demons, he should have told her, to illuminate the path to God. It was the simplest possible truth.

Instead, he had sucked the centaury smoke into his mouth and let it escape with his spoken words, using his voice to lure her into fear. Or so he had tried. Brave Ceri had done naught but retreat a single step. What strange matrix comprised her heart and soul, he wondered, that she had no fear? Must be the purest he'd ever beheld.

Caradoc was no match for her.

He brought his hand to his mouth and drank the water cupped in his palm. The day would be long with no food, the hours filled with the singing of many sacred chants. He drank again, replenishing the water he would soon lose as sweat in the cavern to the west of the gorge. The Quicken-tree would have already begun building a pyre next to the warm pool that bubbled up from the floor in the cavern, using for fuel the trees that had died in the past year: yew, oak, beech, hazel, elm, all but the dead rowans, for those would be burned in the Bel-tinne. Stones would be heated in a circle close to the flames and water from the pool poured on the stones. 'Twould be night before he emerged from the dark, steaming womb, purified as Ceraunnos.

The scent of sweet william wafted to him on the breeze. He turned his head and rose, drying his hand on the edge of his cloak. 'Twas time to lead the sprite and Shay into Deri. The Wyche Elm Pass started off to his right, little used and overgrown, with a scree slope on its southernmost flank. He himself had discovered the track only late the previous autumn and had not used it since. The seclusion and beauty of the water trail had always beckoned to him more, but the river-hollowed cave behind the waterfall did not appeal to him this morn. He would rather walk the mountains and fill himself with the smell of gorse and heather, with violets and sweet william and sunlight, and avoid all dark places that smelled too much of rich earth, until he was called by the Quicken-tree.

"Nuuuuma," Ceridwen crooned, leaning forward from where she sat on the floor. "Look, Numa. Look what Ceri has for you." She dangled the monkshood-laced meat in front of the albino's nose. 'Twas a risk, to be sure, but all her other attempts to circumvent the dogs had come to naught. The meat trick was proving no better. Numa was ignoring her. Elixir had growled when she'd offered it to him, a low, deadly sound that had near scared the heart half out of her.

Damn dog. The black hound was Satan himself, aloof, needing no one. Not even Dain touched him, not so much as a scratch behind the ear.

But the bitch liked a good scratch.

"Numa." She smiled, reaching toward the dog's head. Numa's lip curled, and a growl issued from deep in her throat. The sound was not friendly, but neither did it have the menace of Elixir's warning.

Regardless, Ceridwen relented, bringing her hand down to her side. There was no sense in pushing the albino to violence. Dain had told her the dog would tear her limb from limb, and though she doubted that Numa would go so far, a bite was not out of the question. Her memory of Numa's teeth sinking into old Erlend's throat was quite clear.

She sighed and tossed the meat back into the bowl of physick. The day was nearly done, the sun setting far to the west, the forest sinking into night. She had seen no fires yet, but she knew they would be lit. 'Twas May Eve.

Elixir padded by her and stopped at the bowl to give it a sniff. The draught was of her own making. She'd been careful with the monkshood, wanting the dogs only asleep, not dead, though neither was likely unless they ate her concoction. The hunting hound finished his inspection, and his black eyes flicked up and impaled her with what she was sure was a curse.

"Fie," she scolded him. She was already damned. The hound could not hurt her. "Fie," she repeated for good measure, then immediately wished she had not, because he grew so instantly still, 'twas as if he had suddenly, upon her utterance, been turned into stone. Nary a hair nor lash moved on him, nary a whisker twitched. His eyes, no longer malevolent, had hardened into glassy, sightless ice. He was frozen, with only his ears cocked in a manner to imply life.

Had she conjured a spell with her "fie," she wondered, accidentally using a word with powers far and beyond those of the insipid "sezhamey"?

No, she had felt nothing. She would know if magic was working within her, and if "fie" was a charmed word, people would be frozen like statues over half the demesne.

But if not magic, what?

She looked to Numa. The bitch was quiet too, but without Elixir's unnatural control. There was a trembling in the white hound's haunches and hocks. Ceridwen slid her gaze back to Elixir. Would whatever held them hold them long enough for her to grab her pack and break through the locked hatch? Not even breath appeared to move through the black levrier. They were waiting, the both of them, but waiting for what?

Then she heard it, a far distant singing coming from beneath the floor. A single phrase floated in the air, silvery and clear, rising and falling with the melody of wind over water. The voice grew closer and the notes quickened, swirling around each other with an added phrase. No man sang the fantasia, but a woman, making her way up the tunnel leading to the alchemy chamber. 'Twas enchantment pure and simple transfixing the dogs, enchantment rich with memories and emotion. Rhiannon had made similar magic with music, long ago upon the cliffs overlooking the Irish Sea. Her daughter remembered it well. The sweet sound of harp strings came to her often in her sleep, suffusing her deepest dreams.

> *"O Rhayne anna bellammenaseri*
> *Conladrian, Conladrian ges*
> *Be strong! Be strong! Come to me!*
> *Rhayne, Conladrian, come to Quicken-tree!"*

The voice broke into a rhymed song, echoing off the tunnel walls, and the dogs began to whine. Ceridwen gave them a shrewd glance. Rhayne? Conladrian? Dain was not their master after all, but another, a woman of the Quicken-tree. She wondered if he knew.

> *"Abban euil a' ritharmian*
> *Nov galliot As besteri*
> *Be strong! Be strong! Come to me!*
> *Rhayne, Conladrian, come to Quicken-tree!"*

Three more verses, each slightly different from the one be-fore, but all having the same last two lines, brought the woman di-rectly below her. The song trilled off into silence on the other side of the oak planks. Ceridwen scooted away from the hatch and waited. Quickly enough, she heard the bolt slide free.

Only a moment's hesitation stayed her hand before she helped raise the hatch door, her trust being in the dogs to know the difference between friend and foe. To Dain's command, she gave not a thought. He had trapped her inside the tower, and she was being set free.

A small hand showed first on the floor, then a dark head peeked up. Twigs and leaves were stuck this way and that in the woman's ebony braids—or rather, almost-woman.

"Llynya!" Ceridwen cried, reaching for the sprite. The dogs danced around them, no longer whimpering, but yapping. Even Elixir—Conladrian?—had shed his aloofness to jump and prance with Numa.

The sprite's presence brought cheer and hope into the gloom of the Hart. Ceridwen hugged the Quicken-tree girl close, wrapping her arms around the sprite's strong, slender shoulders. Within her embrace, Llynya felt as promising as a sapling, both imps by another name, both bursting with the freshness of life.

"Sweet child, you have come to save me."

"Oh, aye." Llynya grinned and kissed her on one cheek, then the other. "Come to save you true. We'll be off and away into the woods quickety-split, for the day is running short. Hurry now. Let's gather your things."

Ceridwen wasted no time. She had prepared a pack with the Quicken-tree cloth and tied it closed with the ribands from her plaits, filling it with only the barest necessities: the unguent, a gourd of *aqua ardens*, a pouch of *rihadin*, the red book with Mychael's letters, the runic mirror, and Brochan's Great Charm. She'd kept Madron's pouch for her elf shot and wore it as an amulet.

"Can you show me the way to Strata Florida, once we are free of Wydehaw?" she asked Llynya, angling the pack across her back. The blanket roll was held in place by a rope of riband crossing her chest from her left shoulder to her right hip. They would be traveling in Wroneu at night, on May Eve, and she would not lose her precious supplies to either stray branches or quick fingers.

The sprite looked up from where she played with the dogs. "You would go to the hooded men in the mountains?" The hounds licked her face and nipped at her fingers, growling in tones far sweeter than Ceridwen could have imagined coming from either of them.

"To my brother." She sheathed the Damascene in the belt at her waist.

"Brother?" Llynya's eyes widened. Elixir barked, and she shushed him with a strange command, calling him by his Quicken-tree name. *"Behamey, Conladrian. Behamey."*

"My twin, Mychael," Ceridwen said. The dogs played about the sprite more like pups than the menace Dain had set to guard her. They tumbled and rolled, crushing strewing herbs and releasing the orange scent of hyssop into the air.

"Ah." The girl's voice softened. "So there is a brace of you. He must be very beautiful, your brother."

"I last saw him as a child of five and mostly remember his troublesome goodness. He was always good, which made me appear always troublesome." Ceridwen smiled at the memory, then set about adjusting the pack to a higher position on her back, working the cinch she'd contrived on the riband. "From his letters, he seems to have gotten only more thoughtful and in no ways less troublesomely good. He will probably be sainted."

"And this makes you sad?"

Her gaze lifted at Llynya's question. She hadn't meant to reveal her feelings about Mychael—in truth, she was surprised the girl had discerned them—for mixed in with her sadness was a shame she would rather keep hidden.

But the truth would out with the green-eyed maid. " 'Tis not his goodness that makes me sad," she confessed, "but that I must use it to save myself. I am in desperate need of a saint."

"Dain would not suffice?" the sprite asked with naught but the utmost innocence.

"Dain?" Ceridwen's eyebrows arched, and her hands stilled. Did Llynya not know that even now Dain Lavrans stalked her woods as the Demon? He was no saint in any way, shape, form, thought, or deed.

"Aye. Do you not find his goodness also troublesome?" The girl brushed aside a twig that had slipped partway free from her hair to dangle over her eyes. The success of the action was short-lived, with the tiny stick falling back into her face.

"Goodness? What goodness?" Ceridwen exclaimed.

"Why, the goodness that keeps him chaste."

Ceridwen colored. Had she no secrets left anywhere in the whole of Wales?

Llynya worked the twig free and stuck it back in her hair higher up.

"Why not drop it into the rushes and be done with it?" Ceridwen asked, grateful to change the subject.

" 'Tis rowan from the Deri grove. Wearing it helps the other trees recognize me."

Of course. Fanciful child.

Sure that Llynya would have another fanciful answer, Ceridwen didn't bother to ask what blessings the rest of the twigs in her hair granted, or the leaves, arboreal badges that none of the other Quicken-tree seemed to require. Instead, she hurried to provision herself with a cloth sack of bread and cheese.

"What do you think, Ceri?" the sprite asked, rising to her feet. "Are the dogs prepared to leave with me?"

Prepared? "I don't think they like being trapped here any more than I." She gave her honest opinion, while wondering what possible preparations a couple of dogs would need to make.

"So you think they're ready?" Llynya still sounded in need of reassurance. She was petting the dogs and scratching their ears and ingratiating herself with cooing noises. How could the hounds not want to leave with her?

"Are they not yours?" Ceridwen asked, becoming a little perplexed.

"Rhayne? Mine? Oh, no." Llynya laughed. "And Conladrian? They say he belongs to no one, but answers to Rhuddlan out of respect. 'Tis Rhuddlan who calls them home now. I am merely the messenger."

"Then I say they adore the messenger and would follow you to the ends of the earth," Ceridwen said, settling the matter. The quicker they left Wydehaw, the better.

" 'Tis not so far that they must go." Llynya grinned. "Only into the woods, then north in the morning. Come then, let us be off and see if what you say is true."

North. Mychael and Strata Florida lay to the north.

"*O Rhayne, Conladrian ges,*" the sprite began to sing, swinging into an easy march down the stairs. Sure enough, the dogs followed behind. "*Anna bellammenaseri-i-i-i . . .*"

Ceridwen looked once around the Hart, checking to see that she had forgotten nothing, and giving one last glance to where Dain had sat at the table and turned himself from sorcerer to demon. Even as the demon-beast, a part of her had wanted him. His pull on her was beyond venial sin, tempting her into damnation with lures so sweet she knew even now she would abandon her faith for one more kiss.

"Christ save me," she murmured. For the sake of her soul, her escape was coming not a moment too soon.

Chapter 18

In the heart of Wroneu, a half league north of Deri on the southern flank of Wyche Elm Pass, a fern-covered opening on the side of a hill led into the cavern of the Quicken-tree. Deep inside the dark, airy space, where limestone walls gave way to feldspar and quartz, was a grotto, and 'twas from there that Dain felt darkness complete its hold on the land above. The quietness of birds roosting and animals bedding down for the night permeated the rock and spoke to him of the rising moon; the subtle scent of a cooling forest clarified the air. It had been such with him all through the day, with hour after hour of messages from the natural world stealing upon him with the softest of treads. The earth was heavy with spring, and naught could hold back all she had to say and give.

He sat with the men of Quicken-tree in a circle around a dying pyre, chanting in an ancient tongue,

entranced as much by exhaustion and hunger as by the low steadiness
of voices filling the air around him. Trig and Wei, two of the
Liosalfar, were on either side of him. All the men were drinking from
a shared bowl, passing it from one to the other. If 'twas consecrated
wine or magic elixir, Dain had never been able to tell. The scent of
grape was in it, but so were many other things he could not identify.
An unusual sludge of leaves and whatnot had settled into the bottom
of the mazer, and the faraway looks in the men's eyes proved the
libation to be more potent than in years past. For himself, he ab-
stained. He knew too well the destination arrived at by ingesting
sacred potions. Jalal had introduced him to a number of such simples,
though without the accompanying spiritual rites, and few were as
benign as Catholic wafers and wine.

There were plants and herbs that could give a man visions of
the future and help him recall the past, even the far distant past.
There were concoctions that could take a man to an unimagined
heaven and concoctions that could take him to his most horribly imagined hell. Ofttimes they were one and the same, with a little bit of the
ecstasy of heaven granted for an eternity in hell.

The wooden bowl came around again, smelling of bitter fruit
and oddments, and Dain passed it to Trig. The Liosalfar bowman was
older than the other men in the grotto, younger only than Rhuddlan.
His face was hard set among the fair people, his body marked with
woad tattoos and the scars of battle. He lifted the mazer to his mouth
and drank, and for an instant Dain saw the bowman's eyes mist over
and turn a milky green. Though naught else visibly happened to Trig,
Dain classified the occurrence as a warning. None of Jalal's potions
had ever had the power to change the color of a man's eyes.

His gaze fell to his own hands as the ancient words of the
Quicken-tree chant filled him, their rhythm pulsing beneath his skin
like a heartbeat. 'Twas a long night he faced, balanced between one
world and the other.

The chant changed with the leaving of daylight, and with the
change came a new awareness. In the grove south of the cavern, the
women of the tribe were performing their own ceremony. Their
voices reached Dain through the avenues of the earth, the melody of
their song much fairer than the darkly ponderous one echoing
through the grotto; a song so fair, 'twas sure to bring them the bless-

ings of the deities they invoked. The men, for certain, would come to them in the grove, and in the coming together, the nightfire of Beltinne would be lit and the rites of spring begun.

Long before night, while the sun had still been high in the sky, Rhuddlan had called Dain forth as the Demon, and he had done his part, feeding the flames with *rihadin* and roiling up the brightly hued smoke into a swirling tower that had reached farther than it ever had before, past the light of the pyre and into the darkest, highest recesses of the cavern. The Liosalfar had poured water from the grotto's warm pool onto the stones of the fire ring, and the resulting steam had saturated all of them to their skin. Stripped naked, they had then taken up the chant.

Only after the water from their bodies had cleansed them and the songs had been sung into the air, had Dain been prepared by a white-haired woman for his descent to the river running deep in the earth. Old hands curled with age, but soft with their touch, had marked him with woad, beginning with circles in the centers of his palms and drawing serpentine swirls up the underside of his arms to his chest, where the lines curved over each other thrice before separating for the long course down his legs to the soles of his feet. The same trembling fingers had painted his face, banding him like the Quicken-tree with one broad blue stripe across his eyes. A loincloth of the softest deer hide had been hung about his waist.

The crone's last act had been to have him kneel at her feet for the braiding of his hair. Five widths of chestnut strands from above his left ear she'd used to weave the plait, finishing it with tightly bound thread of Quicken-tree cloth.

Now, while he and the others chanted, she did much the same to Rhuddlan, painting him as Belenos, the Sun-God, down the front of his body, but she did not stop there. From the soles of his feet, her aged fingers slid up the backs of his legs and across his buttocks. Singing softly, she continued up and over his hipbones and circled his groin with bold blue strokes. She drew an arrow coming out of the circle up to his left rib cage and painted the sign of the sun above his genitals, marking him as the mate of the Goddess. No leather touched Rhuddlan's body. A cloth of leaves, oak, and the mountain ash, rowan, was brought forth to garb him.

"*Malashm,*" Dain heard her murmur as she knotted the leaf-stalks around the blond man's waist. She spoke a few more words in the ancient language, the melody of them clear to him above the monotone of the chant, and Rhuddlan smiled.

With the surety of his instincts, Dain knew the woman had once been the Goddess for the Quicken-tree leader. Given her age, mayhaps she had been Rhuddlan's first.

Off to his right, Dain sensed a parting of the dark and another person entering the grotto. Elen, a young woman of Moira's family, walked into the circle of men, bearing a golden chalice encrusted with jewels. Chrysolite and jacinth, amber and sapphire gems sparkled along the rim, and below them, a row of amethyst. Dragons were chased into the metal, some with emerald eyes, others with ruby. Topaz and diamond fire rolled out of their sharp-toothed mouths. Their bellies were softly lustrous with pearls.

The woman came directly toward him, and Dain rose to his feet. Elen smiled shyly, and as she gave him the cup, their fingers touched. Dain returned her smile, for she was lovely, far lovelier than he remembered from a fortnight past. Silky brown curls escaped from her crown of braids and caressed cheeks as soft and as prettily blushed as peaches. Her lips were alluring with the red stain of berry juice upon them. Her body was lush beneath her shimmering gray-green dress. Here was a being to grant a man oblivion.

Unbidden by conscious reasoning, he let his hands linger on hers, holding them around the golden cup, making a promise he had not made before. There were no restrictions against his taking a Quicken-tree woman, and the time had come. Tonight he would mate in the forest with the others. Like the earth, his body was heavy with spring, and he had much he wanted to give: the touch of mouth upon mouth, the outer warmth of two bodies pressed close together, the inner warmth of hearts meeting in a place beyond the boundaries of the skin that held them. Tonight he would share these things with the Quicken-tree woman; he would learn of her secrets and give her secrets of his own—for she was here, a part of the grove, and Ceri would always be beyond his reach.

Always.

Elen stepped away from him and melted into the shadows of the grotto, taking her shy smile and her secrets with her. He lifted his hand to stop her from leaving, then let it fall back to his side with a soft curse. He did not normally indulge in futile, sentimental acts. The ceremony was a set piece; he would not see Elen again until they met in the grove—if they met in the grove. He'd left Ceri locked in the tower while the taste of her kiss had still been on his tongue. Centaury smoke had not banished it, neither had the river water.

"Lavrans." Rhuddlan's cool, clear voice broke into his thoughts. He turned to where the man stood on the other side of the flames. " 'Tis time, my friend."

My friend. *I would spare you, my friend,* Ceri had said.

Rhuddlan gestured toward the tunnel leading to the subterranean riverbank, but Dain did not move. He could not have her, yet he dared to want her. The question was, did he dare enough to return to the tower and take her?

She had talked of love.

"Come, Dain," Rhuddlan called to him. "You will find your answers in time. Come. Bring the wine and do what must be done."

To do what must be done. Had that not been his creed? And tonight, with or without Ceri, he must be Ceraunnos for the Quicken-tree. More than the debt he owed, or the promise of future gain, he was compelled by the ritual itself. On Beltaine, he was the Lord of the Animals, and this year the wild creatures of the earth were calling to him more strongly than ever before. They stirred, and he felt it; they breathed, and air flowed into his lungs. They spoke, and 'twas the sound of her name he heard.

"Ceridwen," he whispered. She was everywhere inside him.

Within his hands, the cup warmed, drawing his gaze downward. No leaves marred the purity of the chalice wine. 'Twas translucent, allowing the gold to reflect through the crimson liquid. Beautiful, deadly stuff.

The men began rising about him, and to do what must be done, he moved forward. The stone floor was smooth beneath his feet. The scent coming from the river was fresh and beckoning, until he reached the tunnel entrance. He hesitated there, stilled by a sudden shift in the air and by a silent warning arising from deep in his mind. He tried to trace the warning to a source, and came up with naught but vague fragments of Madron's dream. Frustrated, he looked back at Rhuddlan, and the moment of wariness passed as quickly as that, eased back into the pleasant drone of the chant by the calm verdancy of the Quicken-tree man's eyes.

One step inside the narrow passage and the sweat cooled on his skin. Water churned against the rocks below, the sound reaching him half a league from where the river broke free from its underground bearing and plunged into the gorge above Deri. Candles, fine, tall beeswax tapers, had been lit and placed along the twisting path to the river's edge. Dain followed the lighted curves and turns, avoiding the tunnel's many offshoots that made the tract beyond the cavern a dangerous maze. 'Twas said a Quicken-tree child had been lost in the labyrinth once, never to be heard from again.

Water lapped at his feet where the candles ended. With no further ado, he poured the sacred liquid out of the chalice into the river, and the river quieted and grew placid.

'Twas the one truly mysterious part of the ceremony. He knew many ways to make water in a container bubble and foam, but he knew of no potion to calm the natural flow of free water—except for the Quicken-tree's, and neither Rhuddlan nor Moira would talk of their *gwin draig,* their dragon wine.

But calm the water it did, to a glassy sheen of transcendent beauty that lasted no longer than a breath before it was churned under by the returning waves, washed down the river and out to the sea. The first year, he'd near missed the instant of stillness, so busy had he been devising his next trick. The tail end of it had caught his eye, though, and the second year he'd paid closer attention. He knew of scrying pools, and was sure that was what was created with the offering, but only for someone with much quicker sight than his. The third year, he'd tasted the dragon wine before pouring it into the river, the barest bit of it from the tip of his finger to the tip of his tongue, and he had not regained his senses until dawn. No one had asked him what he'd done, though his insensate state could hardly have been overlooked, and he had not said.

'Twas the last time he'd given in to his weakness and tried to find something like *kif* to ease his mind and soul, to wash him in languor and give him peace without destroying him as the opium had been wont to do.

This night, he watched, nothing more, and with the strangeness of time in a dream, the length of stillness in the water stretched three-, five-, mayhaps sevenfold of that in previous years. He saw nothing, but the stillness was full of anticipation, then once again a sense of warning came upon him. A moment later he knew he was not alone.

'Twas no man with him at the river's edge, and no forest creature. A soft keening came out of the darkness, and with it a breeze,
soft and rich and smelling of deep earth.

Pryf. He knew the truth of it beyond doubt.

The candle flames flickered, tossing shadows against the rocks.
The warm wind wrapped around him, swirling up from his feet to
the top of his head and then slipping away, leaving him alone in the
midst of the quiet. He felt tasted, strangely, seductively so.

Drawn by the scent, he stepped forward into cold water up to
his shins, peering into the darkness and reaching for something. Before he could go farther, a strong hand encircled his arm.

He turned and recognized a face made macabre by the flickering candlelight. "Trig."

The bowman grinned, revealing broad white teeth. "Unless ye
can walk on water like the Christian God, I don't recommend following the *pryf* down the river."

Pryf. The creatures of the red book and the universal salts.
Madron's serpents, and they'd been nearly within his grasp.

"Ye called them fine." Trig was no longer naked, and his eyes
were clear. He was dressed for travel with a heavily quilted jerkin of
silver and green on over his tunic.

"What are they?" He'd smelled them, felt them, heard them,
but he had not seen them.

Trig shrugged. "*Pryf* is *pryf*. Rhuddlan can tell ye more, but for
now, they've all left for Deri, as should we."

Dain cast a glance at the river. Rhuddlan's mysteries ran deep.
He turned to follow the Liosalfar up the tunnel passage and was
disconcerted to see the beeswax tapers burned down to nubs, some of
them already guttering themselves out in the earthen floor. He looked
back at the river once more and saw the waves begin again, the eddies
and the flow, the churning of the waters, and he wondered how long
he'd stood there, transfixed by the stillness with the scent of the unknown *pryf* surrounding him and the warmth of their breath licking
at his skin.

Llynya had taken Elixir and said to wait, and Ceridwen waited,
nested into the curved branches of a hazelnut tree, while Numa stood

guard at its base. She'd watched the moon track its course across the sky; she'd found the polestar and knew which way her path lay. North, ever north. But she dared not move 'til Llynya returned. Wildness reigned in Wroneu. The pulsing beat of drums filled forest and glen, while Dain's warning echoed in her memory and filled her heart with wariness—*Any man who catches you will take what I have not.*

She'd seen men in the forest. She and Llynya had skirted by them, and women too. Fires burned on every hillside, drawing castle folk and cottars alike into the woods. The rivers Wye and Llynfi rushed through the night, carrying voices raised in ancient verse, a beseeching of the earth for her bounty and a siren's song to lure others into the pagan disgrace called May Eve. At Usk, they'd always spent the night in communal prayer. Now Ceridwen knew why. Any but the purest of heart could be tempted by such overt licentiousness, and Abbess Edith had shown no mercy to pregnant nuns and novices. To be with child at Usk Abbey had meant to be expelled, no matter the hardships. Not four years past, one such faithless sister had been left to her own devices outside the convent walls and had been ravaged by wolves. Naught but scraps of her had remained.

Ceridwen shivered. They had heard no wolves this e'en, nor had she the last time she'd been in these woods. Mayhaps there were none in Wroneu.

"*Cerrr-i-dwennn.*"

She started at the sound of her name upon the wind. Below her, Numa came to all fours.

"*Hurry, Cerrr-i-dwennn. Come.*"

She turned toward the voice. 'Twas coming from the northeast and sounded like Llynya. A torch flickered through the trees there, a short distance away, moving in an arc, beckoning.

She eyed the drop to the forest floor and checked to make sure her pack was securely fastened. The ground was not so far after she climbed down another branch or two, and she made an easy leap of it.

'Twas warmer closer to the earth and out of the wind. The moon was high and full, lighting a path through the brambles and thicket, with the torch acting as a beacon, telling her which way to go. Yet she hesitated.

Numa nudged her hand, but she paid the hound no mind. The night had been full of risk. In truth, her whole life had been beset with risk since Morgan's coming, but suddenly she felt as if a threshold loomed before her, and to cross it would mean she would never again be what she was at this moment.

"*Ceriiii.*" The voice called again, and within the shortened rendition of her name, Ceridwen found the reassurance she needed to go forward. None but Llynya and Dain ever called her Ceri. Mychael had called her thus, but that had been so long ago, she oft wondered if he would remember. She feared he would not.

"*Kom,*" she said to Numa, then grimaced. She'd spent far too much time in the sorcerer's company, if she so easily fell into the Danish tongue. 'Twas good she'd left, and if she felt any regret, 'twas only for what never could have been.

She struck out on a course around most of the bracken, expecting to quickly reach the sprite, but such was not to be. No matter how close she came, Llynya and the torch were always a bit farther on. She remembered the first night she'd met Llynya and how the girl had disappeared in a twinkling. The sprite was not moving so fast this e'en, but much to her irritation Ceridwen could not catch up with her.

"Little scalliwag," she murmured to herself. As long as she could see the torch, no harm was done, but she wished the child were not quite so capricious. There were dangers about, and Llynya was not so young as to be overlooked by a man. Truth be told, though, the forest had become quieter.

Much quieter, she realized. She stopped to listen, and Numa halted at her side. No living creature stirred. No wind rustled the leaves. A stillness lay upon the land.

She looked behind her and was surprised by the darkness. 'Twas as if the moon didn't shine to the south. Up ahead, the woods were full of silver light. It streamed down from the sky and poured through the trees.

Behind her, though, the forest disappeared in a black void. No May Eve fires burned on the hillsides. No sounds of song echoed in the air. An uneasy feeling swept through her, starting at the base of her spine. She bunched her skirts up in her hands, preparing to run, but then stopped short. The torch no longer bobbed and weaved a trail up ahead.

It had been there not a moment past.

Not a moment past, she swore.

"Damn you, Llynya, where have you gone?"

A skittery sound made her jerk around. She took a step back, edging away from the darkness. A small gust of wind stirred the night, and shreds of the black void broke away and reached out for her, licking at the toes of her boots.

"Sweet Jesu!" She skipped backward, her heart pounding in fear. The darkness slipped forward again—all on its own, without so much as a breath of wind behind it—and she turned to flee, following the brightest path.

The Beltaine fire crackled and snapped in the middle of Deri, a funeral pyre for all the dead rowans of the year past. Hard sap grew liquid in the blaze and ran down the burning logs in a sizzling trail, the last of it dripping into the bed of white coals at the heart of the flames.

Dain sat cross-legged on a dais covered with the hides of hart and hind, the place of the Horned One. His hands were covered with the furred paws of a bear. In one he held a torc of twisted gold, in the other a staff of rowan carved into an antlered serpent. The sweet strains of lyres and the thrumming of bodhran drums being played by Quicken-tree hands wove a net around the grove, enclosing all within a circle. Elen was there, between the tall roots of the mother oak, swaying to the music, her hair and body garlanded with fresh green leaves. He felt the pull of her promise in his groin.

Rhuddlan held court as Belenos to the west of the oak, beneath a bower of alder trees, their branches entwined overhead, their sturdy trunks standing guard beside the great oak throne from which Rhuddlan oversaw the festivities. The wood of the kingly chair had been rubbed to a deep shine and was carved from one end to the other with the leaves of the plants found growing in Wroneu. It had filials in the shape of pinecones and mighty acorns at its feet. Wild grasses were incised up its legs, and woodland ferns were fanned out across its back.

The chair beside Rhuddlan's, a throne in its own right, was more gracefully built and carved with flowers and bees. A thousand petals each of freshly gathered tansy, cowslip, pasqueflower, daffodil, and celandine wrought into garlands with periwinkle wreathed the

arms and back of the chair, giving it a most welcoming countenance.
But for all its beauty, the flower throne remained empty. No Goddess
yet sat at Rhuddlan's side.

Each year, 'twas the Goddess whose lush sweetness blessed
them all. She was at Her most seductive in the spring, when She
urged the earth and all its plants to flourish, one within the other,
pollen to pistil to make the seed of new life. 'Twas for Her that the
gods came, to be quickened by Her touch, and Dain felt the lack of
Her presence. Though he had not vied with Rhuddlan for Her attention in years past, without Her, the ceremony had an emptiness he
found unsettling. She should have been chosen by now.

Mayhaps 'twould be Llynya. He had not seen her there, and the
sprite was ready to take another step toward womanhood. So was
Shay ready for the sprite. The young Quicken-tree man was walking
the perimeter of the grove, gazing outward into darkness, as if he
would find her in the forest. 'Twas Llynya's favorite hiding place, out
among the wild trees, but night was full fallen, and whether she was
the Goddess or not, she should have been safe in Deri by now. Rhuddlan would not have allowed her to run free on May Eve, when any
man from Wydehaw to Hay-on-Wye might come across her. Knowing Llynya, she was probably going from hut to hut behind Shay's
back, avoiding what would someday be inevitable.

Moira, the Goddess from a year past, stood close to the bower
near a cauldron of honeymead, stirring the iron kettle with a wooden
paddle and pouring cups of brew for the dancers. For dance the
Quicken-tree did, their bare feet in contact with the earth, moving in
a rhythm to match the driving beat of the drums. All of them wore
garlands of leaves, grasses, and flowers draped around their necks,
across their shoulders and chests, and tied around their waists to wor-
ship the vegetation-spirit from whence their lives flowed.

One man, Wei, did not dance, but strode through the others
bearing a drinking horn frothed to the top with Moira's mead. He
brought the horn to Dain, who drank long and deep, quenching his
thirst and his hunger with the rich brew before passing it back to the
Liosalfar. At a signal from Rhuddlan, the drums ceased, their silence
calling Dain forth as the Horned One to lead the dance, to change it
with his presence into something it had not yet been.

He rose to his feet, steadier away from the grotto's heavy influence, and stepped down off the dais, leaving the torc and serpent lying

on the hides. He knew more of his part than Rhuddlan had told him, knew more of their need of him than Rhuddlan had revealed. The Quicken-tree did not eat the flesh of animals. They did not hunt. They did not make sacrifices with the blood of the earth's beasts. Yet like all beings, they had need of the animal-spirit in their lives. On Beltaine, they welcomed that spirit into their midst with one who embodied the quickness of animal life. Dain wore the trappings of the animals and made them sacred with his acceptance of their deaths.

The Quicken-tree separated before him, opening a passage to the bonfire and making room for him to walk through untouched. There was deference in their action, and a wise degree of wariness. He was alien, the other, there for his ability to rouse latent memories of the Animal Master in each of their breasts. For 'twas as animals that they would mate in the grove, with powerful innocence, utterly compelled by the needs of flesh, bone, and sinew to re-create; and through the act of creation, through their own fertility, they would aid the blossoming of spring, most wondrous season.

Dain made his way between them, every step bringing him closer to the richly scented heat of the pyre. He felt it reaching out for him on airy tendrils of rowan smoke, felt it flowing around him and through him, flowing across his face, beneath his feet, through his skin, sliding deep into his veins and heating his blood. The rich, sweet-smelling heat was redolent of a long ago time, and it brought him to the Horned One's mark, across the fire from the throne of Belenos. He stopped, and lifted his arms toward the night sky. Light from the pyre glinted off the claws protruding from the bear paws on his hands. His fingers were stretched out between the ursine blades, reaching for the stars and yearning for the cooling moon. She was beautiful Luna, wet and cold. She moved with Sol and pulled the tides. The oceans changed course at her command. All things female felt the force of her power. She ruled the night and the rain, as her consort ruled the day and the wind, ever in tandem.

Ceraunnos's crown was brought out by the white-haired ones and put upon his head. 'Twas a crudely wrought corona of gold set with a stag's antlers, the metal chased and engraved with creatures that were half man, half beast. A necklace of claws was hung around his neck. The pelt of a wolf was put upon his back and tied to his arms. Feathers of kites, sakers, peregrines, and gyrfalcons were woven into his hair along with the feathers of owls and short-winged hawks, all birds of prey. Bracelets of iron and of long sharp teeth were wrapped in layers around his wrists and his ankles, their soft jangling meant to call the gods with every movement he made, and tonight, even he believed the gods would come.

There was power in the grove this e'en, as there had been power in the cavern. 'Twas more than Ceri changing him. The magic brought by spring out of the darkness of winter had sunk deep, reaching an unseen core both in the earth and in him. He who mocked all could not mock what he felt in Deri on this Beltaine.

When the last feather had been braided into his hair and the last bracelet had been wrapped around his wrist, the bodhran drums began a slow beat, and the Quicken-tree danced once more. Following a serpentine design, they slipped to one side of him or the other, gradually weaving him into the pattern, until he no longer stood alone. 'Twas then he changed their dance by beginning his own. His foot hit the ground in counterpoint to the beat of the drums, sending a wave of sound from iron and teeth through the dancers. To all in the grove, it announced that the Horned One was among them.

In a wave, the Quicken-tree widened their distance from him, flowing outward from the fire, but keeping to their pattern—except for the Liosalfar. The warriors welcomed him by staying close and following the new dance. Dain moved around the fire, forcing the music to a faster tempo by raising his arms higher into the sky, urging the drummers on and on and on, until they matched the ceaseless rhythm of the wind, and the sound of his bracelets was one with the drums, and the sound of the drums was one with his heartbeat. The air became charged with the frenzy of the dance, drawing the others back, closer and closer. A bolt of lightning rent the night, tearing through the darkness with its brilliance. Thunder followed in a rumbling chorus—and beneath his paint and feathers, Dain smiled. Thus it happened every year. Fortuitous coincidence, he'd always thought before, but this year he knew 'twas he who ripped the skies apart with *mellt a tharanau,* thunder and lightning.

Around him, the dancers lifted their voices in answer to the sky as they whirled and stomped the earth. The circle tightened again and again, with new dancers continually coming to the fore. When they were near enough to be touched, he lowered his hands and touched them, letting his fingers and the bear claws run through their garlands and gently scrape against their skin. It took a sorcerer's grace. Beautiful people, ripe with the juice of the earth, he would not have them marked with blood.

Rhuddlan sipped the horn of mead, watching Dain make his magic with the dance. He'd seen the flash of the mage's smile, and he'd smiled to himself. Dain knew what he was about, even if he did not yet understand the deeper significance of the ceremony.

Llynya had arrived with Conladrian, the two of them slipping into Deri under cover of the darkness. Behind them, the trees whispered of another's coming, shooed on by a restless wind and by the trees themselves closing the path behind her—limbs bending toward one another, leaves touching to block out the moon and the stars. Rhuddlan tipped the horn and drained it dry. She would be there soon to sit upon Her throne.

Chapter 19

Ceridwen ran through the woods as if her heart would burst. Lightning arced across the sky, throwing jagged light onto the trail winding through the trees. The wind pushed at her back and went beyond, picking up the leaves in her path and swirling them off to either side, clearing the way in a manner she distrusted—but not as much as she distrusted the darkness following her. When she veered from the path, *it* seemed to push her back, though she conceded that *it* could easily be her own fearful imagination.

Lightning flashed and thunder cracked again, bringing the scent of rain and the promise of another misery to add to the evening. A stitch in her side nearly forced her to stop; she could not run so hard forever, but a quick glance over her shoulder spurred her on to new speed.

Damn, damn, damn. Strange happenings were afoot in Wroneu this eve. She would swear to any who asked that the very trees were closing in behind her, swallowing up the earth as she passed.

Numa loped at her heels, matching her labored strides with ease. The hound was not panicked, and Ceridwen found some reassurance in Numa's steadiness. Elixir had deserted them along with Llynya. Damn dog.

A faint glow, more golden than silver, emanated from the forest up ahead. Soon she heard the sound of *crwth* and bodhran, and mixed in with the music, voices raised in song. Her steps faltered. She dared not halt, for between the darkness and the danger of men, 'twas the darkness that frightened her more; yet she barely dared to go on. Mayhaps she could circle round the group of revelers.

Clamping a hand over the aching cramp below her rib cage, she altered her direction the slightest degree, watching to make sure her feet stayed clear of the shadows. She got no farther than an unseen hawthorn. The shrub's thorns pricked her skin and snagged her gown, forcing her back onto the path.

She swore again, using one of Dain's vile words, and drew the Damascene. There was naught to do but face what came.

Rhuddlan shifted in his chair, turning his face into the wind and smelling the message-scent of the trees. Ceridwen was once again testing the boundaries he'd set, trying to forge her own path. The maid from Usk had a strong will, but not strong enough to negate his need of her, not yet. She would come to the grove, and in Deri she would learn of sex and magic. She would mate with the Horned One to seal a bond.

The sorcerer was ready for such. There was not a man or woman among the Quicken-tree who did not sense Dain's arousal, each of them taking a part of it inside him and herself and nurturing it into a living flame. Like the burning rowans, the flames bespoke of lives past and of life yet to come. Slumbering seeds brought to fruition with warmth and lust, quickened into being on the forest floor.

Rhuddlan smiled and turned back to the dance, where men and women were already pairing off and disappearing into the trees. Another's scent came to him on the wind, sneaking in from behind the throne to tease his nose.

Rhayne.

All was well.

With a lift of his hand, he signaled the Liosalfar to leave the grove. 'Twas time for Ceridwen to be brought home.

Dain saw the bitch first, a white streak of hound cutting across his line of sight, betraying him with her presence. His first instinct was to follow her and bring her to heel. Something stronger made him look instead to the bower from whence she'd come.

For an instant, no more, he felt the circles of life stop their ceaseless wheeling. For an instant, no more, everything around him faded away, 'til naught was left except Her.

The Goddess had been chosen.

She graced the flower throne with a beauty made stark by anger and fear. Her cheek was scratched, her gown torn and ragged at the hem. On either side of her, Liosalfar stood guard, their faces banded with the diagonal stripe of warriors, their bows drawn.

Rhuddlan's betrayal made Numa's look as nothing.

Dain started forward and was stopped by the glint of a knife in Rhuddlan's hands.

"She came armed, Lavrans," the Quicken-tree leader said, smiling, "and nearly cut Trig."

"Then I taught her well." He kept his voice steady despite the confusion surging through him. He had been part of the dance, weaving a spell out of firelight and drumbeats, and though the spell had been shattered, neither his mind nor his body was free of it. He was still the Horned One.

Rhuddlan nodded, lifting the knife. "So 'twas you who gave her the dagger. Tell me, mage, did you also teach the blade what it knows of death?" He ran the pad of his thumb along the knife's edge, incising a thin red line into his skin. "This steel has tasted more blood than most. See how it draws mine into its groove? It fair reeks of carnage."

"You speak of the knife's past."

"And its future, I fear, my friend." Rhuddlan gave him a knowing glance. A fresh wind dropped down from above and swirled through the fire, stirring up the flames and filling itself with rowan smoke before disappearing back into the sky. The eddies of its passing rippled through the grove in the wake of Rhuddlan's prophesy—for the Quicken-tree's words had been no less.

"If we are friends, you will choose another." Dain made his terms clear.

"Because we are friends," Rhuddlan replied, his smile growing cold, "I will let you fight with your own knife."

"No!" Ceridwen lurched to her feet and was pulled back into the chair by one of the men who had caught her in the forest. She now recognized the darkness for what it had been, Rhuddlan's magic. Wood demon, indeed. Dain was not the only sorcerer in the grove.

Rhuddlan gave her a long look, his eyes far too innocent to be those of a satyr, yet she knew why she'd been brought to Deri. Dain had warned her, and she had ignored his warning, trusting instead her own damned instincts and a sprite named Llynya.

She struggled against the strong hands holding her shoulders and gripping her pack, but the men about her were serious in their intent to keep her in the flower-draped chair.

"Hush, child." Rhuddlan's voice was low and oddly reassuring. "Do not squirm so. Nothing will happen here that you do not wish."

"I do not wish to be held," she said between gritted teeth, again trying to jerk free, and again failing.

"So be it." The Quicken-tree man gestured with his hand and the men retreated from around her.

She wasted no time in leaping up and away, running to the end of the arch-roofed bower before realizing she had no safe place to go. The forest was no haven, not with Rhuddlan about. He had charmed her into Deri, and she had no doubts that he could keep her there.

She looked to Dain—and blanched. There was no safety in his dark gaze, only a quiet, seething rage trying to break through an unsettling disorientation. He did not look himself. She took a step back, and he started toward her, dropping his crown into the grass, shedding the clawed gloves from his hands, letting the wolf's cloak fall to the ground. She retreated farther, her gaze darting across the grove, searching for a refuge, yet never truly letting him out of her sight. He was frightening in his beauty, with raptor feathers braided through his hair, his bare torso gleaming in the firelight. His face was banded in woad. Lean, supple muscle corded his arms and legs. He looked fiercer than she remembered from the night of his bath, more feral, even a little mad about the eyes.

Mayhaps he was still the Demon.

Mayhaps the transformation to a god had not worked. Had she not doubted it from the beginning?

Mayhaps Rhuddlan was the safer of the two after all.

She stumbled in indecision as Dain kept coming toward her. A cry lodged in her throat, cut short by Rhuddlan's shout.

"Lavrans!" The Quicken-tree leader rose from his throne and strode down the alley of trees, his voice strong and sure across the grove. "The Goddess may in truth choose to be with Ceraunnos tonight and not this green man, but the choice is hers. So take your blade, friend"—he tossed the Damascene forward with an underhanded throw—"and parry to first blood with me for her favor."

From where she righted herself on the ground, Ceridwen saw Dain pick the dagger out of the air in a move so full of grace, 'twas as if the haft floated into his palm. A muffled groan escaped her. She feared the contest was over before it had begun, and that the Demon would have her in the end.

Dain harbored no such illusions. Rhuddlan would not be easily dissuaded from his folly, but folly it was. The man had erred badly in his taking of Ceridwen ab Arawn. If the earth grew fecund only with the sacrifice of her virginity, then the Quicken-tree were in for a damned lean year. Dain had not saved her from himself to let another have her. He had locked her in the swivin' tower, and he had expected her to stay there.

His jaw clenched, and his hand tightened around the knife. *Son of a bitch.* He was in no mood to parry for a virgin's favors. His blood and his life were demanding what had been denied, overruling every shred of interfering intellect and shame. The heat of the fire burned at his back, its sizzle and crackle the only sounds in the grove, the silence of the drums a potent reminder of where all the dancers had gone.

He watched Rhuddlan walk steadily closer, the full, high moon throwing a dappled shadow upon the bower path. At the end of the alders, the Quicken-tree man reached down and drew a blade from the sheath on his belt. 'Twas a dazzling, gold-encrusted thing, catching the firelight with its crystal haft and throwing diamondlike sparks into the air.

Dain forced himself to loosen his grip on the Damascene, bal-

ancing the dagger and fitting it to the fingers and palm of his left hand
with an ease he'd learned as a boy. The other side of parry was thrust,
and with a well-placed few, he could disarm Rhuddlan and be done
with it. There would be no more blood on his knife.

But such was not his opponent's game. Rhuddlan circled
slowly, looking for an opening, holding his knife lightly, too lightly.
His fingers did not quite close around the clear bluish-white haft. The
dagger was a truly fine piece, a rare glassen treasure, and suddenly
Dain realized it was much more than it seemed. He wasn't sure what
gave him the crucial moment of insight, whether the openness and
size of the grove lessened the dreamstone's power, or if having succumbed once to the dancing lights, he had built up a resistance; but
the warning was enough to save him when Rhuddlan turned the hilt
of his knife more fully toward the fire. Light gathered in the white
heart of the crystal, coalescing to a pulsing brightness for no more
than a blink's worth of time before Dain lunged, forcing Rhuddlan
to close his hand around the crystal and meet his attack.

Twice more they came together, once with the scrape and slide
of metal ringing throughout the grove. Dain took the Quicken-tree's
measure even as his own was being weighed, and 'twas a fair match,
he decided, fairer than he had expected. Rhuddlan was fast enough by
a hairbreadth to elude any thrust he made. Or mayhaps the dreamstone was slowing his own movements, for even with Rhuddlan's
fingers on the haft, flashes of light escaped from the crystal and grew
more brilliant with every parry—blindingly brilliant. Soon he would
not be able to see Rhuddlan's hand. He would have the rest of the
Quicken-tree's body to guide him, but where the man's movements
terminated, where the pain would come from, would be naught but a
ball of light.

'Twas an eventuality he wasn't inclined to wait for, having less
interest in seeing his own blood than in seeing Rhuddlan's. Thus he
changed his attack to a retreat, slowing his movements to draw
Rhuddlan out, baiting the Quicken-tree with an advantage. The risk
was a calculated one. Rhuddlan was a good fighter, highly skilled, but
he was far older, and his age showed in the way he slowed his parries
to match Dain's. Dain didn't hesitate when he saw his opening, rushing in with a high inside feint, then marking Rhuddlan across the ribs
when the Quicken-tree man exposed his torso with his blocking parry.

A shadow seemed to fall over the grove as the light went out of the dreamstone. Rhuddlan immediately fell back, and rather than the curse Dain expected, he smiled. "Well done."

"There is not much blood," Dain said.

"And I am duly grateful." The smile broadened.

Moira hurried forth with a pot of *rasca* and began tending the slight wound. Elen was soon at her side with a cloak of Quicken-tree cloth. She was beautiful still, her hair as shiny and soft-looking, her cheeks as prettily blushed, but the allure was gone. Whatever promise had been between them had been broken along with the spell.

Rhuddlan extended the crystal and gold-hilted dagger. "The Goddess may choose, but the blade must be won. Her name is Ayas, and like your knife, she has a compassionate streak."

That he was offering the dagger was apparent, but Dain did not step forward to take it.

"Come, Lavrans. She is yours. See?" He opened his palm to show the dark crystal. "Already my mastery over her is gone. She is your dreamstone and will cast her light only for you."

"And if I do not wish to conjure a Druid's sleep every time I hold the blade?"

"Then do not ask for one. Dreams come in many forms, mage. You'll find Ayas is much more easily controlled than your Goddess." Rhuddlan grinned and gestured toward Ceridwen. "I do not begrudge you that one."

Madron did, though. Dain had not forgotten the witch's warning.

"In all truth, friend," Rhuddlan went on, "she is yours with my blessing, for the price of another hour's magic."

Dain looked to Ceridwen. She was standing at the far side of the grove next to Ceraunnos's dais, her uneasy stance indicating wariness—justifiable wariness. Madron could not save her now, for he was no longer counting the cost of having her.

"Aye. I will pay your price, Rhuddlan." And Madron's too— damn him to hell.

She had spoken of love. He would see what she knew of the depths of love.

He took the crystal blade and started toward her, sheathing the Damascene in the band of leather that belted the loincloth around his waist.

"Run," he warned her in a whisper too soft for her to hear, yet her eyes widened, and she stepped back. "Run, and do not stop."

Her hands came down to lift her skirts. He would not take her in Deri among the Quicken-tree. She was his in a way Rhuddlan could not understand, his need of her different from the Quicken-tree's for a Goddess.

Run, Ceri. Run as fast as you can, and still you will be mine.

She took off like a doe in flight, darting into the trees on the north side of The Bramble. Dain kept his strides even, letting her gain distance. It did not matter. This night, there would be no escape for the quicksilver maid.

"Sweet Jesus, save me." Ceridwen came to a stop, leaning against one of Wroneu's sturdy oaks. She gulped in air and wrapped her arm around her waist. To her left, the trees were awash in silver light, but there was no sign of the beast stalking her. Brushing the hair back from her face, she looked hesitantly to the east—and swore. He was there, the damned crystal dagger glinting moonlight in his hand, not ten yards distant. He had come no closer, but neither had he allowed her to get any farther away.

She struggled to slow her breathing and prayed she could thus slow the beating of her heart. She had no plan except to go north, ever north into sanctuary.

A sob broke from her throat. He had her knife. She had been doomed from the start. Another sob followed the first, and she rested her forehead against the oak, squeezing her eyes shut while drawing in a shuddering breath. She had naught but herself to save her, naught but— A shift in the air brought her head up.

There! He'd moved.

Moonbeams streamed down through the boughs, marking him with bands of light and shadow, golden light. 'Twas strange. She bent her head back and looked up through the towering branches of the oak to the sky above, and there she beheld an amazing sight. A gilded veil—of what? the very ether itself?—appeared to be falling over the moon in silken folds. All the light in the forest changed to the aureate hues, the silver remaining only as sparkles hanging in the air.

Magic. Beltaine magic.

She looked back to Dain and found him much closer, startlingly close, no more than three yards away. Their gazes met, and her mouth went dry. There was still a hint of madness in his eyes, and behind the madness, desire. 'Twas a palpable thing, reaching for her across the short distance of sweet grass and lavender.

She wet her lips and nervously watched as his gaze tracked the tip of her tongue. A slow, hot ache pulsed to life between her thighs. He had kissed her and made her yearn for more than kisses. Now he stood before her, wild and silent, promising more than she could imagine. What did he know, she wondered, that put such desperate need in his face?

Did she dare hold her ground and find the answer?

He walked closer, stepping forward with a soundless tread, and she grabbed her skirts and fled, proving herself too great a coward.

Dain followed, keeping pace with her, yet indulging her with the illusion of freedom. Her booted feet fell lightly upon the earth, racing through shafts of golden moonlight and night-blooming flowers wet with silver dew.

They ran together, with him subtly guiding her toward their destination. She did not know it yet, but she was already becoming his. The stars were wrapping them together with distant light. The wind was binding them with its soft caress, enveloping them one with the other.

At the first rise of the land, he slipped to her left, forcing her to move to the right, onto the lower path. The trail quickly narrowed and grew darker as the woods thickened on either side. Wyche Elm Pass towered above them, yet they continued to descend. Soon he had no need to guide her, for the earth itself delineated the path. Moisture entered the air, warmer than the breeze. Woodland ferns unfurled their fronds and brushed against her skirts. Mosses grew over the rocks.

He was taking her to a place beyond the cavern of the grotto, where the grass was softer than goosedown, where water bubbled up warm from the ground, and the trees made a nested bower graced by slivers of the moon. Carved from the rock that formed the base of the hills, the glade had only one way in and out—the path they were on, with him closing in behind her.

Dain sensed the moment when she realized she was running into a trap. She hesitated slightly, her pace slowing, but 'twas already too late. What looked like the darkness of night between the trees ahead was the exposed face of the limestone. There was no going past it. When she understood, she whirled to confront him, and he was already so close, her gown swept against his legs.

Rebellion burned brightly in her eyes. Her hair had been tangled by the wind and fell in tumultuous disarray to her waist. Her hands were white-knuckled as they gripped her skirts. She tried to dash by him, but he raised his arm to block her escape, the unintentional threat of Ayas enclosed in his palm. She tried the other side, and he did the same—then he walked forward, pressing her ever backward, gathering her against the rock wall. When she could go no farther, when her body lay up against the stone, he placed a hand on either side of her shoulders, and there they stood, not touching, but close enough for him to feel the shallow, uneven expulsions of her breath and the heat rising off her skin.

Warm, honeyed, female scent. He wanted to fill himself with her.

She did not look at him, but kept her head bowed, her chest rising and falling with the need for more air in her lungs. She had run far. His own breath came hard too, but had naught to do with the run from Deri. Tonight he was the Horned One, and with the stamina of a hart, he could have chased her for leagues without tiring. Catching her, though— Ahh, that made air hard to draw, and thoughts hard to order, and words impossible to speak.

He lowered his face to the crown of her head and rubbed his cheek across her hair, giving himself a small pleasure to keep from devouring the whole. It wasn't enough. It never could have been. A flame curled to life in his groin, and he let his mouth slide lower, holding her pale, tangled curls away from her face so he could nuzzle her with his lips and tongue. He kissed her downcast lashes and her eyebrows, her scratched cheek and her temple, and heard a small sound catch in her throat. He traced every delicate curve of her ear and warmed her skin with his breath, and he felt her tremble. She was musky sweet, like life, and salty with sweat, so lovely and erotic in her acceptance of his touch. She could have pushed him away with a fingertip—he used no force—but she did not. She stood silent and quivering in his embrace, the Goddess to his Horned One, a willing doe in heat. He smelled the scent upon her, that sensual ripeness known to every rutting stag, and it intoxicated him. He opened his mouth on her neck, tasting, and pressed his phallus against the soft curves of her body, giving in to his most heartfelt desire.

"*Jesu,*" she gasped, and he groaned, letting the heat pour into him. She had wanted, she had asked, and now he was giving.

Reaching up, he buried Ayas in the tree limb arching above them, then brought his hand down to cradle her head in his palm. He kissed her hair and shifted nearer to her, closing his body around hers and relieving her of her pack—the beginning of her deshabille. Unbidden by him, the crystal began to glow, bathing them in soft blue light. 'Twas as close to pure magic as he'd seen by the river, a stone working with no trickster to manipulate it, and he wondered what had called forth the dreamy incandescence, whether 'twas the carnal power of the sex he and Ceri were conjuring, or the aching tenderness he felt for the woman in his arms. There was wonder in both, and even more so for having them together.

Aye, a tender carnality was what he felt, that he could take her with all the crude simplicity of an animal and love her with all his man's heart.

One tug freed him from his loincloth; the Damascene clattered unheeded to the ground. Deft fingers made impatient with need unlaced her gown and kirtle and discarded them into a pile on the grass, leaving her in the linen chemise. He bunched that soft cloth into his hands and brought it up around her waist, exposing her skin to the night and the heat of his body.

She grew utterly still beneath his hands, speaking to him in a voice so soft that even though her mouth whispered close to his ear, he could not hear her words through the haze of lust driving him. He held her hips, and her soft, damp curls welcomed his forward thrust, their mere touch more tantalizing than any well-taught flutter of tongue. She was slick and warm, and no doubt sweet.

The vision proved impossible to resist. He bent his head and nuzzled and licked her breasts through their soft linen covering, working his way down to the bareness of her belly, and then lower still. He kissed her deep, his mouth open on her vulva—the hidden secret place between her thighs—exploring every fold and finding her most luscious and sensitive spot to savor with his tongue. Gasping, she pressed herself closer, and excitement surged through him.

Ceridwen fought panic even as she opened for him, her knees

weak, his hands and body her sole support. She was hot, so very hot, and frightened, and desperate to have him close. There was madness in his touch, and she had caught it. The pulse of the earth was beating in her veins, rising through the soles of her feet and urging her on to an unknown end. The trees were alive around them, and the stars above them, their silent energy and light rushing through her. If he was god, then she was goddess receiving the cosmos. She had tried to tell him, repeating to him in a whisper the songs being sung in the forest and the sky, but her words had melted into a sigh of unutterable sensual delight as that part of him called "cock" by the cleric at Usk had slid between her legs, high up against her most private area that not even the cleric had named.

Then his mouth.

Good God, she feared she might die.

But 'twasn't death that overcame her as he plied his tongue ever more quickly, then sucked on her ever so gently. No, 'twasn't death a'tall, but ecstasy—pure and clean and untouched by any thought. The flash of pleasure suspended time, arcing through her like heat lightning before the aftermath rolled through her, rippling like a succession of waves, nurturing places inside herself she had never felt.

She sank to her knees, and he took her in his arms, laying her down in the tall grass and in the same move pushing himself inside her, filling her. The pain was sharp, and quickly over. She wrapped her arms around him and kissed his cheek, his mouth, ran her tongue along the curve of his jaw, tasting salt and man. To have him so close was a gift. He was Dain, the mage of Wydehaw, untouchable, and yet he touched her and made her feel whole. Sweet Jesu, no wonder he had longed for this. Groaning, he partially withdrew, and she murmured a soft protest.

By the light of the crystal and the moon, she saw the flicker of his smile. "Shh, Ceri, shh. I can go nowhere other than deeper inside you."

And he did, slowly sliding back into her, then withdrawing and coming on again, filling her with wondrous pleasure. His smile faded as each thrust built in intensity. Silky hair and feathers fell over his shoulders, drifting back and forth across her breasts with his movements. 'Twas so beautiful to watch him, his muscles flexed and straining, to feel the strength and power of his body striving for release. She caressed his back from shoulder to buttocks and felt the tremors running through him. She held him and whispered gentle urgings, for now she knew what had put the desperation in his face. The pagan magic of Beltaine was incontestable.

Yet 'twas more than the golden moon causing tension to gather all along his body. His breath quickened, and with the knowing ease of a woman, she shifted beneath him, taking him deeper, holding him tighter. His thrusts came faster, then he thrust once more and held, a low groan rising from his throat.

In her mind's eye, she saw his seed spill out of him and into her, the rich, creamy fluid flowing up against the opening of her womb. He was the river; her body was the yielding earth. She followed the life-giving stream deeper, into a sanctuary hidden in a soft, warm cave, the core of her being—and a voice whispered to her in the dark . . . *Kael.*

Madron woke with a start. She had not meant to sleep. She swept a few straying strands of hair off her face and blinked. Time had passed. How much?

She pushed out of the maple chair and walked quickly to the cottage window, where her nimble fingers made swift work of opening the shutters. She bent forward over the sill, looking out and up at the sky. The Eve of Beltaine was over, thank the gods, the ruby wash of morn breaking on the eastern horizon, but daylight alone was no balm for the strange and disagreeable night she'd spent. Something was gravely amiss. The woods were still silent.

The trees had stopped talking to her at dusk—Rhuddlan's doing, without a doubt—and her mind would find no ease until they spoke to her again. 'Twas as nothing for the elf-man to close her out of the forest's scented murmurings. She'd always known his skills far surpassed those of the other Quicken-tree. Truly, she had once believed that the trees spoke only on his command—a smitten girl's fallacy, she'd later learned. The trees acknowledged no earthly lord. Yet the rowans did his bidding; they'd carried Quicken-tree messages to her since the time of Edmee's conception, and always during the fire festivals such as Beltaine, his intent on those nights to lure her back into the fold.

A small drop of morning rain fell through the trees and plopped onto the sill. Madron caught it up with the pad of her finger and brought it to her mouth. There was taste, fresh and dear, but no hint of anything more.

Rhuddlan was keeping something from her.

Chapter 20

Dain held Ceridwen in his arms as dawn breached the night, his body half covering hers. Her gown and kirtle were haphazardly tossed over them for warmth; her chemise was tangled about them both. Silk ribands trailed down the pale, creamy contours of her body, looping onto her breast and coming back up, dipping into the curve of her waist and rising again over her hip like a meandering silver stream. She had drifted into a light sleep—trusting soul. Her faith might redeem him yet. Or mayhaps she had felt it too, his total surrender.

He wanted her again. Her hand was soft on his hip, her fingers delicate in their unconscious caress. He kissed the corner of her mouth, and she stirred, but did not waken. Just as well. He had not been so gentle. There was blood between her thighs and on her belly where his half-aroused penis rested, and blood on him as well. Such was to be expected, and despite the evidence of pain, her desire had been clear. She had wanted him and welcomed him.

The color of the sky changed while he held her, from velvet-black to midnight-blue to a chatoyant pearl-gray, the last sending rich, lustrous light running down through the trees, glazing branches and picking up an edge of gold from the east before reaching the forest floor. Birds began their morning songs with the dawn, *tee-yairing* and *chir-rupping* their calls.

Being careful not to disturb her, he eased out of their grass nest and went to clean himself in the small freshets of hot water flowing from fissures in the stone and gathering in rock basins at the bottom of the limestone wall. They were offshoots from the grotto pool that steamed and bubbled inside the cavern. When he was finished, he wadded together a handful of spongy moss and soaked it in the water, getting it hot and wet.

Back at her side, he cleaned her and pressed the warm moss between her legs and against her mons, knowing the heat would soothe.

Her lashes fluttered open on a sigh and closed on another. "Dain," she murmured.

He lay down beside her and kissed her again, letting his mouth linger on hers and warm her lips. Her response was to tease him with her tongue. He smiled and felt her do the same.

"Are you god or demon this day?" she asked when he raised his head. Her hand came up to trace the blue band painted across his face.

"Only a man." She was beautiful beneath him, her smile not so innocent, her body the loveliest haven, so essentially female. "And you? Goddess or demoness?"

"Whatever you wish . . . for another kiss." Her smile took a sultry turn as she tunneled her fingers through his hair and pulled his head back down. She plundered his mouth, her tongue deliciously sensual, tasting and exploring.

Her blatant seduction tantalized him, going straight to his groin and bringing him fully erect. So she would play the demoness for him? Mayhaps he would teach her how. For now, though, it would not take much to have her again as the angel-woman. 'Twas no more than the length of his cock from where he was to where he wanted to be. Yet he held back, losing himself in her kiss, but taking no more.

"Dain?" She pulled away and looked up at him, her question clear.

" 'Tis too soon after your first time, Ceri." He smoothed her hair back from her brow. The long silvery-gold tresses were spread out around her in every direction, a brilliant, mussed pillow strewn with leaves. "Your body is tender, and I would not hurt you again."

"And what of you?" She glanced down to where they touched.

A grin teased his mouth. There was no shyness in her question. 'Twas as if she, too, realized that what was now between them went beyond the tangent boundaries of skin and bone, beyond the ever-shifting surfaces of emotion. She was his, and he would have no other. He had not known that love, that the act of love with her, would bind him so greatly or grant such a heady sense of freedom.

He brushed his thumb across her cheek and watched her eyes drift closed. Her hand trailed up his ribs and under his arm, before coming across his shoulder. They were tangled together as surely as her clothes, their legs intertwined, strands of her hair intermingled with his and flowed over their chests and arms. His gaze wandered down to her breasts and hips. Every curve enchanted him, so very pale against his darkness, so rounded against his much larger, more angular frame. Her allure was incarnate, needing no conscious effort. She simply was, and he wanted her.

"Lying this close to you, it would take little more than your hand to please me," he told her. Desire was in him, fed by lust into a heavy need, and he would have it assuaged.

"My hand?" Her lashes rose in a leisurely sweep.

"Aye." He interlaced his fingers with hers and brought them to his mouth, pressing his suit. She was willing and curious, and was for her that his loins ached.

Ceridwen watched in fascination as he opened their clasped hands and laved her palm, then her fingers, one by one. His tongue was soft and wet and moved over her hand with the ardency of a hungry cat licking cream; a big cat, like a rampant lion with his mane of wild hair falling over the two of them and snaking across their torsos. His eyebrows were drawn toward each other with the depth of his concentration; his lashes were lowered into dark crescents on blue pagan cheeks.

She had not thought one's hand capable of being seduced, that there was so much sensitivity in her fingers and in the skin between her fingers. He proved her wrong with every caress. She was entranced, and she wanted more. She wanted to touch him, to discover the part of him that had been inside her.

Dain felt the same need—to have her touch him. Thus when her skin was warm and moist, he slipped her hand down his chest and closed it around his phallus. Heat . . . luscious, erotic heat. He groaned, showing her the way of it, the varying rhythms of stimulation and the one that created the most intense pleasure for him. She kissed his face as she stroked him, proving herself adept at divining his desires, the silky pressure of her hand and lips giving him a glimpse of heaven. Even with his guidance, her touch was so very different from his own, delightfully, profoundly different, marking him with a deep rush of feeling, adding an element of tender care where for too long there had been only animal need.

With an ease born of empathy, he moved his hand from around hers and into the triangle of curls between her legs; and he bent his head to her breast, bringing her into the same swirling chaos consuming him. Her nipple was incredibly soft in his mouth, a lure for his tongue, just as her lush folds were a lure for his fingers. She was gratifyingly wet, the moisture he slid into like nectar, no different, for he remembered the wondrous, womanly taste of her vagina. He had thought to never know such again, to never again have the deepest scent of a woman infusing his pores. Then Ceri had come to him.

He moved his mouth up her body, kissing her and whispering to her of the fire running through his blood and of where virgin dreams ended and lover's dreams began. Words created passion in the darkest corridors of the mind, and he wanted her to experience passion in all its shades. To that end, he closed his teeth upon her neck, gently, gently, until he could feel her pulse beating against his tongue and echoing in his throat.

Here was life.

Small sounds of distress and arousal escaped her, revealing the naked needs he had nurtured to fruition. With a move he had anticipated, she had him slipping inside her, guided by her hand. He knew a thousand ways to give and take pleasure without that invasion—but he had not the strength to deny her or himself. He wanted to sink into her, to feel her slick, velvety sheath close around him.

He groaned, holding back from going too far, too soon, but she was whispering his name over and over, and his last good intention went for naught. He began his thrusts, shallow at first, then deeper . . . deliciously deeper.

The pressure built and built inside him, centering his awareness between their legs where they met and came together, so hot and sweet. He felt her impending climax in the inexorable tightening of her body, he saw it in the tautness of her face, and when her low cry came, he was with her. Her intense contractions pulsed through him, along the full length of his shaft, along the full length of his body and down to the bottom of his soul. He bared his teeth, burying himself to the hilt inside her, coming as deeply as he could. He forgot to breathe. There was no thought or sight or sound, only exquisite sensations jerking through him, one after the other into oblivion. There was no dream, only the purest essence of the woman stealing him away.

At the end, he collapsed next to her, wanting nothing more than to never move from her side. Long moments passed as he held her to him and labored to catch his breath.

"So help me God, you are a witch."

"Whose God?" she asked, her own breath shallow with the same latent thrills he felt coursing through his body. "Your God? My God?"

"It matters not." Without withdrawing, he pressed himself closer to her, deeper, wanting to feel her, all of her, and know she was a part of him. "By any God, you are the fairest witch of all."

Far, far above them, in the crowning branches of an oak, Llynya lay stretched out on a limb, peering over its side with her chin in her hands, watching her charges. Not that there was much to see. Dain and Ceridwen had been rolling around in the grass all night, like everyone else in Wroneu Wood, and they were still at it.

With a quietly grumbled complaint, she turned over onto her back to better continue her skywatching. She'd done what she'd been told. She'd followed them to the Mid-Crevasse glade, so named because it was midway between the Great Western Crevasse and . . .

and someplace else she couldn't quite remember at the moment. She'd kept anyone else from stumbling into the glade, weaving a dab of bramble here and there, and she'd left Dain's clothes and cloak in a pile on the path. Wouldn't do for the O Great One's butt to get cold on the long walk back to Deri. Oh, no.

No one seemed concerned about her butt getting cold sitting up in a tree all night.

"Hmmph." She dug a honey-stick out of her pouch and stuck it in her mouth.

The morning star had disappeared with the first flash of the sun, and the other stars had long since been chased into the west, but the moon remained. 'Twas a wondrous thing, the moon, rich in elfin lore and woman's magic, a perfect, white orb hanging in a sky that was turning blue with day. Unlike the sun, which one could not look upon even if she squinted her eyes into teensy-weensy slits, the moon was made for gazing, for long hours of contemplation. Its presence never failed to soothe. Llynya liked nothing better than running through its light at night. Though of late, Rhuddlan had been clipping her wings.

A green finch flittered in to share her leafy perch, a welcome bit of company. Llynya whistled at her, and the bird sang back, hopping closer.

"Hallo, peach," she crooned, putting out her finger. The finch hopped up, and Llynya smiled. *"Malashm."*

She rummaged through her pouch and came up with a seed, which the finch ate, and a bit of thistledown fluff the bird took into her beak.

"Nesting, hmm?"

Spring had been hard-won this year, making the laying with the Goddess of utmost importance. By Llynya's count, Dain had lain with Ceri twice. Rhuddlan would be pleased.

The finch flew off, toward daybreak. There had been a promise of rain in the night that had not come to pass except in a few stray drops. But the changing color of the sky hinted at more moisture yet to be shed, and not long coming by Llynya's reckoning.

Sure enough, within a short passing of time, rain began to fall, swept up from the south by the wind. Llynya closed her eyes and caught a few droplets on her tongue, and was startled to find a warning in the taste. She had smelled nothing, but rain had the quality of intensifying whatever message was in the trees and spreading it over a greater distance, and what she tasted was undeniable. Danger was coming.

She quickly clambered higher into the oak. At the top, she pushed aside smaller limbs and peered through the leaves, looking across the rest of the forest to the downs beyond. Riders were moving on the southern horizon, but she was too far away to see them clearly. She watched the shadowy line wind its way north and west, and tested the rain again. 'Twas worse than danger coming. 'Twas evil. But whose?

Curious, she swung down onto a lower branch, to a place where she could make her way to the next tree. Rhuddlan would have already sent out scouts. If she had been in Deri, she might have been chosen. Shay was among them, no doubt.

"Sticks," she swore, and leaped into the neighboring oak. She landed lightly on a sturdy limb, catching herself with one hand on a higher branch. Thus she left the Mid-Crevasse glade behind, one tree at a time, quite forgetting what she was about.

Ceridwen stood in the gently falling rain, fiddling with her laces. Her fingers were awkward, her eyes downcast. Dain had seen the phenomenon before: The return of clothing brought a return of shyness. He stood close in front of her, tying the leather strings of the loincloth around his waist. When he was finished, he reached out and caressed her breast with the back of his fingers, one brief downward stroke. Her head came up, a blush full-blown on her cheeks.

He teased her with a smile. "Even with your clothes on, I can still see every curve and remember every taste."

Her blush deepened.

"Shall I tell you what you taste like?"

Flustered, she lowered her gaze. "You are without shame."

"Aye," he agreed softly, and bent his head to give her a kiss. "And you are beautiful. Come. The quicker we are away, the better. Madron has put a price upon your virginity I would rather not pay." He reached around her and pulled Ayas out of the overhanging branch.

"Oh?" Her gaze came back up, and her fingers stilled.

" 'Tis not marks or riches she wants, Ceri," he reassured her, "but my soul." She had no reason to doubt him. He would give for her all that he had, and pray she did not suffer too greatly for lack of what he'd lost long ago.

"Then she and Caradoc deal in the same coin."

"And they both shall be denied." He sheathed Ayas in the loincloth and looked around for her pack and the Damascene. What he spied was a neatly folded pile of clothes getting rained on in the middle of the trail. He touched Ceri's arm and pointed to them. "Llynya." A miniature garland of violets crowned the garments.

"The little bugger," she swore, her shyness forgotten. They both looked up into the trees.

"She's gone."

"But she was here."

"Aye, she was here. I wondered where she was hiding all night."

"Llynya was not here all night," she said, her voice tight with irritation. " 'Twas she who freed me from the tower, enchanting the dogs with her song."

"So the hounds did not prove completely worthless," he murmured, his gaze raking the treetops. The sprite was gone, but mayhaps there was another. He got some satisfaction out of knowing what had happened in the Hart. The hounds had never before disobeyed him, but he would not have expected them to ignore the calling of the Quicken-tree.

"They were charmed senseless, as was I," she admitted, clearly not happy with her gullibility. "I thought we were going to Strata Florida, but she led me into Wroneu to be captured by those men."

"Liosalfar," he said. "Quicken-tree warriors." He checked the trees once more, assuring himself they were not being watched. "Come. We should not tarry, for we have both too easily played into Rhuddlan's hand."

"To what end?"

"I don't know. Madron counts him as an ally, but she would not have sanctioned what happened here. Whatever he needs of you, 'tis not that you go to Caradoc as Madron wants. That alone makes me less wary, but we should be to Wydehaw, the better to make our bargain when the time comes."

"Wydehaw?" she questioned. "I have nothing with which to bargain. Despite what I . . . we . . . have done, I must be gone from here."

He brought his hand up to cup her chin. "Because of what we've done, *kæreste,* we shall leave together, but we need supplies and the Cypriot." He brushed his lips across hers. "Caradoc is not due for a sennight, and by her own admission Madron is no tracker." They would need gold for their journey, and food, and they had to get it before Madron could close him out of the tower.

"And Rhuddlan?"

"Rhuddlan's price is my magic, and I will pay, but in my own time." He let his fingers glide across her cheek. The first glistening light of dawn had given way to a watery morning that served to underscore her exhaustion. He had run her to ground and made love to her half the night, and now had her on the march. He could have gone on alone and come back for her, but he dared not leave her unprotected. "There is nothing left for you to fear, Ceri. Last night, before the ceremony, I met your dragons. 'Twas as written in the red book, but without blood. Just as wine is the blood of Christ in the holy sacrament, 'tis wine, not true blood, that calls them."

"Where did you find them?" Her eyes widened with surprise and mayhaps a bit of horror.

"In a grotto north of Deri," he told her. "Neither Rhuddlan nor Trig were frightened of them in any way and called them also by the other name in the book, *pryf.*"

"*Pryf* is not dragon. Of this I'm sure."

"Mayhaps. Mayhaps not. Madron didn't make a distinction between the two. I did not see them. 'Twas too dark, but I could feel them, and they seemed more curious than dangerous."

"My mother told stories of dragons," she said, "and there were pictures of them drawn on the rocks at Carn Merioneth. They had huge teeth."

"If they still do, they did not use them on me." He smiled. "I have seen many strange beasts, creatures called elephants that are bigger than any dragon I ever saw imagined, and the man who owned them used no more than a stick and his voice to order them about. Camels, tigers, wild horses with black and white stripes— They are all out there in the world, Ceri, frightening only to the people who have never seen them, and seeming as mundane as a cow to the people who live with them. I think 'tis the same with the dragons of the red book. A rare and shy creature, not seen by many, can become a dragon in people's minds."

"Aye, they are rare. My mother said there are never more than two, but I don't think they are shy. The abbess at Usk called them and all my mother's stories heresies made up to confound the ignorant and children." A troubled frown marred her brow. "It has been hard to figure out what to believe."

"You are not alone in that, Ceri. We will not be long at Wydehaw," he promised, "and when we leave, I will find a safe place for us to rest."

"Is there such a place?" She sounded doubtful—with good reason. There was only one possible destination, and it was the last place he would have chosen for himself. Not so for Ceri.

"Despite my aversion to piety, I hope to find such a place for you at Strata Florida."

Even in the rain, he saw her face brighten. If nothing else, she would have the comfort of her brother for a while, should he prove to be still alive. After that, they would journey north, far north, past Balor, and Wales, and the Isle itself, across cold water and into the lands of ice and snow, to the place he'd been heading before the Hart had caught him up in its promising mysteries.

The horses half plodded, half trotted through the early morning rain, no happier than Caradoc's men to have been on the march before dawn. Helebore's mount was particularly phlegmatic, falling farther and farther behind. The leech did not mind. They would reach Wydehaw soon enough.

The Cardiff mission had failed. They had found a fair-haired novice newly escaped from Strata Florida, debauched and in his cups, but it had not been the one they sought. Under Caradoc's questioning, delicately administered so as to leave a few marks to be remembered by, the young man had confessed his impure love for Mychael ab Arawn and how he had begged Mychael not to take his vows. Alas, as with much young love, it had all come to naught, for Mychael had disappeared shortly thereafter without leaving a trace.

Helebore had suffered much the same situation as a novice, but he had not taken the coward's way out. When faced with mortal sin, he had contrived to poison the lecher, and thus came by the name Helebore. To this day he remained perfectly chaste, never having even touched himself, not truly, and certainly to no good end.

The other horsemen gave him a wide berth as they passed him by, all except for one who fell in beside him.

"Ifor." He nodded to the man, a porcine archer, dark of brow and beady of eye.

Ifor grunted in acknowledgment, staring straight ahead. Wet, greasy hair straggled down over his face and into his bushy beard. A peculiar stench rose about him, indicative of a vice Helebore preferred to ignore, for his own sanity's sake.

"I missed you last even," he continued. "I thought for sure that you would be hungry by nightfall."

The beady eyes flickered in his direction.

"Mayhaps I should find another to do my bidding?"

"No," Ifor was quick to reply.

"Ah," he sighed. "So you are hungry for another drop of life's immortal elixir?"

Ifor gave a short jerk of his head.

" 'Tis murder I want this time," Helebore warned. "Do not mistake it for anything less. I want the sorcerer's body cold and blood-less, or none of us will be safe. Do you understand?"

Another nod.

"Then give me a bolt that I may touch the tip with poison."

Ifor looked ahead to see that no one was watching, then handed over one of his crossbow bolts. The horses' slow pace was no hin-drance to the poisoning of the steel tip. Helebore kept all manner of simples and physicks in small gourds and ampoules tied to his belt, and by nature, he was a careful man.

When he was finished, he handed the bolt back to Ifor. "A dagger would be more subtle, but Lavrans would have you dead before you'd drawn your blade. Thus, we will be crude and effective. If he fights to keep the woman, kill him then. To protect your lord, you'll tell Caradoc. If there is no fight, stay behind and kill him when we've gone. Either way, after your work is done, I will give you a flagon of the elixir that you may join the ranks of the immortal."

A spark of something came to life in the archer's eyes. Greed, perhaps. Or lust. 'Twas a mystery to Helebore what motivated some-one of such limited mental capacity to long for immortality—not that

Ifor was in any danger of getting it. Helebore would not be so cruel as to condemn the man to eon after eon of a coarse and brutish existence.

A sadist's smile twisted his mouth. Elixir of life, indeed. Poppy juice in wine could transport a man to a netherworld, or, in sufficient quantity with a hint of foxglove, to the underworld, and he feared 'twas to the latter that Ifor would be going. Quick justice for the murderer to follow the mage into an early grave. Caradoc would be enraged. Since seeing his old friend, he'd become quite obsessed with the idea of having Lavrans at Balor.

Helebore's lips curled in distaste. Disgusting, disgusting creatures. Bad enough to yearn for a woman, let alone to yield to one's desires and bring a viper into your nest. Caradoc's foolishness would get him naught but a memory to warm his sick heart.

"Wydehaw!" The cry came from the front of the line, and as a man, the riders kicked their horses into a gallop. The day's deed was upon them.

Chapter 21

"How many days out from Wydehaw are we, do ye figure, Morgan?" Rhys asked, passing a leather jack of ale to Dafydd as they worked at breaking camp in the morning light. A gentle rain had blown up from the south, warmer and sweeter than the spring rains had been thus far.

"Two, if the mountains don't turn to mud." Morgan looked to Owain on his left. The big man grinned. Next to him, Rhodri and Drew let out loud guffaws. The lad's infatuation with Ceridwen ab Arawn had not abated with the passing of a month's time and, in fact, had reached new heights since their coming from Balor a night past. Ceridwen had not yet been delivered to her betrothed, who himself had not been in residence. Gone to Cardiff, the seneschal had told them, while declining to offer them hospitality they would not have accepted.

They had not ridden south to Wydehaw from Dolwyddelan in early April as Morgan had planned, but had been sent farther north by Llywelyn to fight English raiders on the eastern border. The Prince of Gwynedd had not thought the fate of one maid to be of much importance, other than to further indebt Caradoc to him. Holding the reins of power in Wales meant ruling among ever-shifting alliances, and Llywelyn assured Morgan that he did not overestimate Caradoc's loyalty. As to the Boar's unsuitability for marriage, Llywelyn had smiled and told Morgan most men were unsuited to marriage.

Yet Morgan could not dispel a sense of unease. A man on his way to Cardiff would pass within hailing distance of Wydehaw, and though they would have heard about it in the north if the castle had been attacked, such was not the same for the death of a lone Dane living in a tower. Dain had no princely protection in Wales, nor the protection of England's king, and Caradoc had not been pleased by the price Dain had set for the maid.

Morgan had seen for himself how little it took to push Caradoc into a rage. D'Arbois might put up a fight to save his mage, but Soren was no match for the Boar of Balor. Dain was, but not against the Boar and a traveling force of men.

A soft breeze brought new rain against his face. He should not have stayed gone so long. Dain had more wits than most and had survived worse than Caradoc's anger, but neither of those facts lessened Morgan's sense of responsibility, and the farther south they traveled, the surer Morgan was that he should have come quicker. The damned English had taken too long to rout, and though Llywelyn had his loyalty, he would not see harm come to his friend, not without first putting himself in the way of it.

Llynya stood quaking in her boots, no less than a befuddled sapling besieged by a cold wind. Rhuddlan was furious. She'd left her post. She'd left Dain and Ceridwen, and as quickly as that, they'd left the glade and were nowhere to be found.

Too much leaving all way around, to her way of thinking.

The Quicken-tree leader had sent scouts to the south—Shay with them—and was shorthanded in the search for her charges. The last remaining scout, Nia, had been sent to head them off from

Wydehaw, the most logical destination, but Rhuddlan feared she would be too late. Dain moved near as quickly as the *tylwyth teg* in the woods. Llynya had begged to go and been flatly denied. She was not to leave Deri. To make matters worse, the scent of danger and evil had become stronger, permeating the trees in a manner that unsettled all of the Quicken-tree.

Moira had explained that 'twas not so much the smell of imminent danger they sensed as that of impending doom. The trees warned of forces set in motion that must be stopped to avert disaster.

A disaster of her making, Llynya thought, miserable with guilt and fear. She glanced up to find Madron staring at her—or mayhaps glaring better described the witch's fierce gaze—and quickly looked away. Nothing good could be up and about if Madron had hied herself to Deri at dawn.

"Rhuddlan!" Trig dropped out of the trees.

Rhuddlan quickly crossed the grove, and despite her trepidation, Llynya followed close behind.

"Nia spotted Dain and Ceridwen heading into Wydehaw," Trig said. "She was at the last oak in Wroneu and could not reach them, so came quickly back to report to me. Rhuddlan, I fear the horsemen from the south are also to Wydehaw and mayhaps are already inside the castle. They were at full gallop when last seen."

"And who are these horsemen who bring such danger into my woods?"

Trig hesitated, as if his next words were too awful to speak. " 'Tis the same as we found traces of in Merioneth, the evil-smelling one, riding with Caradoc and a force from Balor."

"Then the worst has happened."

"Aye."

Rhuddlan swore and turned to face the grove, raising both of his arms high above his head. *"Khardeen!"* His voice rose in the ancient Quicken-tree war cry. *"Khardeen! Asmen taline! Meshankara mes!"*

Llynya and everyone in Deri reacted, running to collect their weapons and prepare themselves for battle—except for Madron. She stood rooted to the ground, seething. Fool man, Rhuddlan, she thought. He was getting no more than he deserved for tricking her with the maid. She'd come to Deri early that morn and gotten the truth from Rhuddlan's own mouth: Dain and Ceridwen had been mated in the Mid-Crevasse glade. He'd won, and because he'd won, they all would lose.

"Edmee," she called to her daughter, working to keep the sharpness out of her tone. The girl rose from where she'd been sitting with Moira by the mother oak and ran lightly across the grass. Madron took her hand and drew her close. "The Liosalfar are to Wydehaw, and whatever the outcome, Rhuddlan will waste no time in heading north. I must be there, for I dare not leave him alone in this folly he has contrived."

Damn Rhuddlan for ruining her plans and leaving her no choices. 'Twas the last time she would become a pawn in his game. This she swore.

The girl nodded her understanding, though her hand tightened on her mother's.

"Aye, sweeting. You must stay. Aedyth and Moira must also go north, but I would not leave you alone. Naas will go with you to the cottage," she said, naming the oldest of all the Quicken-tree and the one best suited for what Madron needed. Rhuddlan would not begrudge her Naas. Edmee made a small face, half grimace, half resignation. 'Twas true, with her white eyes and constant chewing of *kel,* a sweet grass found only in the far west, Naas was not much company, especially for a young maid, but the Quicken-tree woman had a strength of mind that could befuddle even the cleverest of mortal men, and naught other could bring harm to them. With Naas guarding the cottage, even the Sheriff of Hay-on-Wye would find himself inexplicably lost should he enter the pine forest.

"Naas will listen to the trees for you, and either tell you of my coming, or know when to bring you north," Madron said. Deri was emptying out. The Liosalfar were already gone, in a twinkling as the stories were told, but Rhuddlan would not have allowed her to go with the Liosalfar anyway.

Edmee nodded again, and Madron clasped the girl to her breast, cursing Rhuddlan even as she kissed their daughter farewell.

Once inside the safety of the tunnel, Dain breathed easier. They could have easily been overtaken in the woods. In truth, he'd sensed someone licking at their heels. He wasn't concerned about Rhuddlan hurting them—'twas not the Quicken-tree way—but he would have detained them, and time was in short supply. Too short of supply for him to spend any of it in opening the Druid Door. He'd locked it down to the second level to keep Ceridwen contained, for all the good it had done him. Now the quickest way into the castle proper was from the outside. There was a little used postern in the west wall that would give him access to the small stable where he kept his horse.

"You go on from here," he told Ceri. "The Cypriot is stabled in the upper bailey. 'Tis best if I bring her around on my own and meet you in the tower. The castle folk are used to seeing me come and go at odd times, but your presence would create naught but questions." He squeezed her shoulder. "If you cannot get inside, come back and wait for me here."

"I had nothing with which to lock the trap when I left last evening," she said. "Unless Erlend was knocking about, there should be no trouble."

"Has naught to do with Erlend. Madron may have sealed the tower against us."

Her brows lifted incredulously. "This was the price she asked?"

"Aye."

Dismay replaced her surprise. "Then you have paid too dearly."

"I think not," he said simply, reaching up to caress her face. "There can be no price on the"—he hesitated the merest instant—"pleasure you give me, Ceri. Tonight, when we are safe, we will lay together again and see if you do not feel the same."

Ceridwen knew she would. The mere touch of his hand was enough to send shivers down her body. She had not known what it would mean to lay with him, that the feel and taste of him would make such an indelible impression, that her every thought would be so easily lured back to him. She saw the sky, and the tunnel walls, and the sweet grass growing up through the tumbled rocks at the entrance, but they were as an illusion compared to the rich reality of her lover, the saturated color of his hair and his clothes, the strong form of his body, the artful curves and angles of his face. Even as she blushed at the memories of what they'd done, she wanted to touch and taste him again, to be so close that his breath was hers, to feel her breasts crushed against his chest. There was life in such physical oneness.

"Aye," he whispered, and she smiled shyly.

"Can you read my mind, sorcerer?"

"When you think of us, aye." His lashes lowered, and he brought his mouth down on hers.

She took the kiss and felt the warmth of it seep down to the tips of her fingers and toes. Was not as hungry as his kisses in the glade, which made it seem more of love somehow, if she dared to put the word between them.

"Go now," he said, lifting his head. "There is gold beneath the hearthstone in the upper chamber. Bring it and extra food besides, but if the tower is sealed, come and wait for me here. I shall not be long."

Ceridwen watched him go before turning and making her way up the tunnel. The place no longer seemed as eerie as it had the first time Dain had brought her through. They had used it a number of times in the last fortnight, sometimes bringing their supper to eat in the meadow. She prayed with every step that Madron had not locked him out of his home, but if the witch had, Ceridwen would go to her and play upon old ties and loyalties. She would not have him lose so much for what she had freely given.

At the door to the lower chamber, she paused with her hand on the latch. "Please, sweet God of mine," she whispered, then pressed down. The latch lifted, allowing the door to swing open.

Her smile of relief was short-lived, lasting no longer than her first step into the tower. Three men stared at her from across a worktable strewn with broken glass and spilled containers. Her heart stopped in a moment of surprised terror. She turned to run, but a rough hand grabbed her and swung her into the room, then jerked her arm up behind her back. She gasped in pain. Someone sent up a cry, and more men came clattering down the stairs, bringing chaos into the alchemy chamber. In the midst of them all was a tall, broad-shouldered man with flowing blond hair, a bulwark of power and strength among the lapping waves of guards surrounding him.

"Interesting," he said, casting a glance at the door of shelves that disguised the entrance to the tunnel. He shifted his gaze to her and looked her up and down. "You're wet."

He walked closer, terrifyingly beautiful with his fair hair and strangely colored eyes. Near turquoise they were, but with an iciness in their depths.

"We have not met, *cariad*," he said silkily, extending his hand to touch her cheek. "I am Caradoc." He smiled, and the smile was sinfully seductive. The Boar of Balor was no monster, but an angel.

Then she saw it, the glint of madness behind the ice, the cruel twist lurking in the sensual curve of his smile.

She shrank away from his touch and was brought up short by a quick jerk on her arm. She gasped again.

"Bring the lamp," Caradoc ordered. A man obeyed, coming forward with Dain's rock crystal lamp held high. The light spilled across her face and into her eyes, making it harder for her to see her enemy. "Helebore!" he called, and a cadaverous face appeared over his shoulder.

Sunken eyes, the hairless arch of an eyebrow, dark lines running from the corners of his mouth—here was the embodied demon, the incubus who had touched her with his heavy key. His evil was no trick of unguent, nor was he a fey creature running wild in the woods. Her mouth went dry. Fear unlike any she had known gripped her and made her tremble. He smiled at her, showing sharp, jagged, rotting teeth, and a whimper was torn from her throat. Her knees began to give way. The man behind her twisted her arm, sending an excruciating pain around her forearm and up into her shoulder. She tried to pray, but her mind could not form the words.

The incubus whispered into the Boar's ear, the sound hissing through the air, and the Boar replied with a nod and, "Yes, yes, I see it." His look turned more discerning, and he rubbed his thumb across her lips, an ungentle pressure. The madness in his eyes flickered. "Lavrans has made a deadly error, *cariad,* as have you. Come, Helebore. Let us take our tarnished prize home. I'm sure my friend will follow."

Helebore barely contained his glee. The stupid slut had put the rope around her own neck. The lasciviousness of her deed with Wydehaw's mage was written all over her face and her much kissed mouth. A small croak of a chuckle escaped him. There would be no more talk of virgins and begetting children. She was now his to do with as he pleased, and he pleased to take her blood to make his magic mix. He would distill it down to an irresistible potency and use it to call forth the strange beasts. They would lap at his fingers to get the stuff . . . Mayhaps he would taste it himself.

Mayhaps.

The tiniest shiver trickled down the inside of his body, the littlest convulsion of obscene pleasure. He felt himself flush, his lashes fluttered, and 'twas all he could do not to let his eyes roll up in the back of his head.

No, he told himself, not yet, not yet, if ever again. 'Twas enough that he'd opened the Druid Door. The key—he chuckled to himself, feeling a bit mad—the key to opening the locks had been carved in the keystone of the door's arch. The Sun was the key. Nennius, the cursed whisperer from Ynys Enlli, a black-hearted raven of a priest, had known about the Sun. He'd shown Helebore the heretical placement of the planets in a book. Much of what Helebore had seen in Nennius's books had helped him open the door: *mathematica, mechanica,* and *magica.*

Aye, he'd opened Nemeton's door and proven himself as great as the Brittany bard Nennius had so admired. Pah!

He clasped his hands tightly together, his long nails digging into his skin, and stepped aside to let the others pass. Only Ifor hung behind with him, hiding in the gloom. When all the guards and Ceridwen were gone up the stairs, Helebore turned to his lackey.

"Span your bow and wait for Lavrans here," he ordered. "When he enters the tower, shoot him, and if you would have the elixir of life, bring me his head."

"Said naught about his head before," the archer grumbled.

Helebore bared his teeth and hissed, and watched in satisfaction as the lout stumbled back.

"I did not have a use for it before," he said. "Now I do. Bring it, or die a natural death."

Ifor grunted disagreeably, but he would do it. He didn't want the mess of a head, but neither did he want to die, naturally or otherwise, for he had long ago consigned himself to the depths of hell with his deeds. Depraved, he was, and he knew it, but life everlasting would trick the devil from his due.

The archer watched Helebore leave and allowed himself a smug smile. The leech thought him a fool, but Helebore was the fool. For immortality, he would have killed a hundred men for the medicus and brought him all one hundred of the heads. Heads wasn't the part he liked—which reminded him. He'd seen a wee bowl of meat on the floor in the room above.

He eased himself around the worktable and cocked an ear toward the stairs. All was quiet. They'd gone. Helebore was twice a fool for thinking he would stay in the cold, dark dungeon when there were coals smoldering in the hearth upstairs. He could add a fagot or two to get a blaze and eat his found supper in the warmth and luxury of a fine room.

Ifor hauled himself up the stairs, ruminating on the small feast awaiting him there. He had no trouble finding the bowl, for he'd scooted it under a stool with his foot to keep it safe from other spying eyes. He threw a couple of sticks on the coals and sat down on the stool with the bowl in his hand. His crossbow was spanned and loaded, laid at the ready by his feet. The fire warmed his back as he faced the trapdoor. He'd be too quick by half for any moldy sorcerer to elude. The moment Lavrans poked his head above the last stair, old Ifor would have him.

A bit of gravy was pooled in the bottom of the bowl, and he sopped the meat around to soak it up. The meat was old—he could tell by the smell—and the gravy was sure to help. Old meat was nothing new, and if his supper was a little rancid and bitter, well, 'twas still supper.

He stretched his legs out in front of him and took a good-sized bite. Pretty damn bitter. He chewed thoughtfully despite the taste, eking out his enjoyment where he could. 'Twasn't long before he felt his lips and tongue tingle, then burn. Too much pepper, he thought, taking another big bite. By the time he'd swallowed his second mouthful, his lips were numb, and he couldn't see quite straight. He turned his head this way and that, squinting his eyes and trying to focus on something, anything. Of course, the damned headache that suddenly came upon him didn't help. 'Twas as if someone was trying to chisel his head open with a pike. In the next moment his throat grew tight, then tighter. He dropped the bowl and lurched to his feet, panicked, gasping and wheezing, trying to pull in a breath, but could not. Confusion flooded his mind. He stumbled forward and fell down prone on the hearth.

Scorching heat licked at his face. Sweet God A'mighty, the eternal fires of damnation were upon him. He could see Satan beckoning to him from the heart of the flames.

Christ, Christ, Christ, he prayed and swore, trying with all his heart and mind to move away, to escape the Dark One, to run, but the only movement he managed was involuntary, a twitching that grew and grew until the final death convulsions seized him.

*   *   *

Dain strode up the length of the siege tunnel. Ceri had not been waiting for him, which meant the tower was open. Good. The gold would make their journey easier, and he needed his sword. Damned blade, it made the Damascene look like a butter knife, and he had hoped never to wield again.

The door to the alchemy chamber was ajar, as he would have expected, but all was not right. Too much scent was in the air, of powders and sulfurs and distillations he kept in tightly closed containers. He continued forward toward the dim light, drawing Ayas in one hand and the Damascene in the other. Ceri could have knocked a jar or two over when moving the door, but he feared 'twas not the case. He stopped a few steps away from the opening and listened. All was quiet. Had Rhuddlan sent someone after them who had followed Ceri up the tunnel and kidnapped her?

Without making a sound, he slipped into the shadows of the alchemy chamber. A sense of dread washed through him. The place had been torn apart as if there had been a fight. He quickly searched the room, keeping his dread at bay with cold, calculated fury. Blood would be shed if Ceridwen was hurt.

When he found nothing, he headed for the stairs, holding the knives lightly in his hands, though no sound came from the upper chambers. Even the mice seemed to have deserted the place. At the top of the stairs, he scanned his bedchamber, and his fury turned to something far worse—fear. The Druid Door was open.

"She's gone," a voice said from behind him.

He whirled and stared into the shadows at the far wall. Rhuddlan stepped into the light, and all around the tower, the Liosalfar revealed themselves.

"What do you know of this?" he demanded of the Quickentree leader.

"Only that we are too late. We arrived just ahead of you, Dain. I fear the evil one has her."

Helebore. Dain needed no more explanation. The open Druid Door was enough. He should have killed the man when he'd first laid eyes upon him.

"And Caradoc?"

"He is with them." Rhuddlan gestured, and the Liosalfar continued their search of the chambers. "She is too important to both of them to be killed," he said to Dain. "The danger to her will not come until they reach Balor."

"There is danger besides death." Danger and degradation and despair. His hand tightened reflexively around the Damascene. He would not have her harmed, so help him God, and his actions had put her at great risk, at the mercy of Caradoc's rage.

"Ride with us, if you would have her back."

"Aye," Dain agreed, willing to put her under Rhuddlan's control if it freed her from Caradoc.

"Rhuddlan," one of the men, Bedwyr, called from over by the hearth.

Dain turned and saw what he had found, a dead body behind the table, and beside the body, a loaded crossbow.

"I don't think you were meant to live through the day," Rhuddlan said, walking over and releasing the bolt from the bow. He passed the arrowhead beneath his nose and raised his eyebrows. "Poison."

"And the man?" Dain asked.

Rhuddlan pushed the archer over with the tip of his boot. "Also poison. It seems he used one of your simples for sop. Monkshood from the smell of it."

Dain eyed the dead man dispassionately. "Then the world has lost another fool."

" 'Tis him," Wei said, kneeling by the dead man. "The one who lagged behind the other horsemen to speak with the hairless monk."

"Helebore wears the habit," Dain said, "But he is no monk."

"Given his time with this poor sod, I would guess he is the one who wants you dead." Rhuddlan offered the opinion in a dry voice.

"With good reason." Dain looked back at the Druid Door. "I would as soon kill him as not. Mayhaps before the day is finished." He walked over to the door and began locking it down. He would not leave the tower open to packrats and the castle folk. They would have him stolen blind within a sennight, the length of time he presumed it would take for someone to screw his courage up. And if, perchance, he did not return, he wanted something left for the next "mage" to come along. As for Helebore, he would never have another chance to breech the Hart, not in this lifetime. When the door was secure, Dain strode quickly to the upper chamber to get his gold. He would bargain with the Devil himself to buy her back, if his sword would not suffice.

Rhuddlan watched Dain disappear up the stairs, and his gaze strayed to the cornice over the door, to the letters chiseled there by Nemeton: *Amor . . . lux . . . veritas . . . sic itur ad astra.* Rhuddlan smiled. He hoped his old friend had found such a way.

He turned to Wei and gestured for Shay and Nia. "Take the dead man out into Wroneu. I would not leave him rotting in the Hart. Meet us by the horses."

Wei and the scouts obeyed, taking loops of Quicken-tree cloth from their belts to wrap around the archer's wrists and ankles to better carry him. When they touched the cloth to the dead man's skin, though, wisps of smoke arose, followed by faint sizzling sounds. Shay and Nia both blanched and scrambled back.

Wei quelled their cowardice with a single glance. "Finish the work, if you would be Liosalfar one day."

Rhuddlan watched carefully to see if either of the scouts faltered. Only one vice made Quicken-tree cloth burn. He could tell by Shay's and Nia's faces that they knew what it was, but they finished their work without flinching. Rhuddlan continued looking around the tower room. Dain was far different from Nemeton, filling his chamber with rich tapestries and woodland plants, so many flowers. The Hart had been much starker under the Arch Druid's reign.

"Trig?" he called to his captain.

Trig crossed the chamber from where he and Math had been studying the rushes. "They have not been gone long. Mayhaps they've made it as far as Builth. We still have a chance of catching them."

Rhuddlan nodded and signaled for them all to leave. "Lavrans!" he shouted.

Dain descended the stairs, buckling a heavy belt around his waist. The iron-and-teeth bracelets of the Beltaine ceremony still wrapped his left wrist and forearm. He didn't waste time speaking to Rhuddlan. He knew the need for haste and strode to the chest chained at the foot of his bed. The lock on the chain was old and rusted and gave way under the force of his swift kick. Inside the trunk was the past he'd hoped to forget, but he did not hesitate in opening the lid and throwing it back to reveal the contents. Yet for all his fortitude, the sight of crimson wool gave him pause. Bloodred it was, desert sun red, the hot red of a branding iron glowing in a brazier of coals; and snaking through the wraps and folds of the crimson surcoat were the snow-white stanchions of a Crusader's cross—taken in pride and piety, revered as the promised path to God, and saved as a remembrance of hell.

"Come, Dain. We must be off."

"Aye." He squeezed his hand into a hard fist to keep it from shaking. Then he reached within the folds of cloth and withdrew that which had made his fame in Palestine. Ivory-gripped, its hilt chased in gold and silver, the sword was named for an ancient king of the Danes, Scyld. Rune staves were engraved upon its pommel and guards, an invocation to Odin flowed down onto the blade, and the steel—the steel had been tempered in the cold waters of Havn and hardened in the blood of the Holy Land.

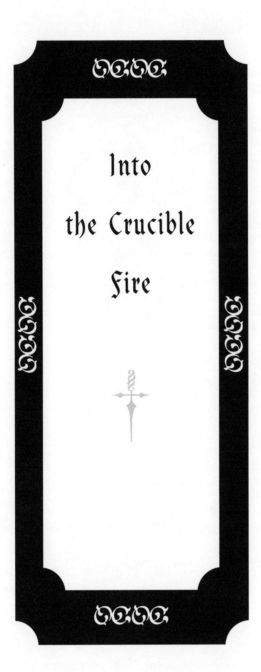

Into
the Crucible
Fire

Chapter 22

Night was falling as Dain and his companions headed deeper into the mountains. They rode through pouring rain, being two days out from Wydehaw and having seen no sign of Caradoc. Even Quicken-tree could not track in a deluge. The road—to give it an undeserved name—was a quagmire that rivaled the sands of Neath. Visibility was nil.

The rain had found them shortly after they had left Wydehaw, while they were still south of Builth, and it had come from the south and east. The fairer weather ahead had only increased Caradoc's lead, though by the previous evening, Trig and Wei had conjectured that the Balor troops must have been overtaken by the downpour and their pace slowed. They had hoped to catch Caradoc at a first night's halt in Rhayader, but when Dain and Rhuddlan had stopped in the village the next morning, they had found not Caradoc, but Morgan and his band journeying south to Wydehaw. Morgan's men were a welcome addition to the company, all good fighters with knowledge of Balor Keep.

Yet as Dain looked around at his companions, he saw not so much a cadre of warriors as a group of bedraggled travelers beset by mud and rain who would have been frozen if not for their cloaks of Quicken-tree cloth, which Rhuddlan and his Liosalfar had generously shared. They were thirteen to the man, and Nia—not enough to storm a castle, but enough to get them all killed.

If they could have caught Caradoc on the road, 'twould have been different. Trig had sighted seventeen riders with the Boar. One was now dead, poisoned in the Hart, and one was Helebore. 'Twould have been a fair enough fight in the open, but not so in Balor. Battling the Boar in his lair was sure death, and thus Dain had decided to go in alone. Fourteen warriors were naught but an invitation to disaster, whereas one man could be invisible, and none knew the way of it better than he.

He drew the Cypriot up beside Owain, Morgan's captain, a shrewd fighting man ungiven to exaggeration either of his own deeds or those of others.

"What do we face in Balor?" he asked.

"Nigh onto a hundred and a half men-at-arms and archers as brutish as their master," Owain answered with a sidelong look. "The keep sits between two baileys. The lower bailey houses the garrison and the gatehouse. There's a barbican with arrowslits aplenty, a portcullis and murder holes. The curtain wall is stone, but inside the wall is mostly timber and earthworks. The upper bailey sits on the cliffs overlooking the sea, and they say it can't be breached."

"They say?"

Owain grinned. "Morgan could get in aright. He scaled the tower at Cardiff with twice as many men guarding it as Caradoc's got."

"What of the keep itself?"

"Simple enough aboveground with the hall on the first floor and storage chambers and such underneath. It's what's below the storage that's cause for worry."

Dain did not press him, but waited for the captain to continue.

"I don't rightly know what it is that lies beneath Balor," Owain said, squinting thoughtfully, "but the passage that leads to the cellar is guarded by no less than four men night and day. 'Tis said Caradoc keeps wild animals down there in a dark dungeon to drive them mad before he fights them in the pit, and I can say I've heard some strange noises comin' up from below, enough so to curdle yer supper. I've seen the pit too, in the southwest tower. Nasty place."

Dain had heard stories of the pit at Balor. 'Twas said to bring Caradoc more gold than his land or his stock. Two bears and a boar were the favored match, a pairing guaranteed to draw even rich English lords from across Offa's Dyke.

"We'd have all been better off just to have left her at Usk," Owain opined aloud. "A nunnery is the only place for Ceridwen ab Arawn. What with her father dead and her brother more devoted to redeemin' his soul than redeemin' his land, there's no one to stand for her."

"I stand for her," Dain said, his voice grim.

Owain looked over at him, his glance sliding briefly to Scyld sheathed at Dain's side. "Aye, and it's going to be a bloody day at Balor then."

"Aye," Dain said.

Ceridwen looked up through the pouring rain at Balor Keep—her new prison, her last prison. Her hands were bound to her palfrey's saddle. Her ankles were bound one to the other by a braided strip of leather running beneath the horse's girth. Caradoc was taking no chance on escape.

The curtain wall of Balor reached across the horizon, surrounding the spit of land once known as Carn Merioneth. Clouds of mist from the Irish Sea rolled up over the cliff edge, stretching into thin wisps that hung about the battlements and clung to the cold, gray stone.

Shudders born half in fear, half from the near-frozen state of her body, wracked her. She would die in that place, and she knew by whose hand. The leech had not taken his eyes from her since he'd loomed over Caradoc's shoulder in the lower chamber of the Hart. Helebore was his name, and he watched her no less intently than a cat eyeing a crippled mouse.

As for her betrothed, he looked at her not. He spoke not a word, and she was sure he would as soon kill her as do either. She was not virgin. He and the leech had read the truth in her face somehow, and the betrayal had made her of no personal worth to him. Her body, though, her blood, was still of prime importance, and he'd given the keeping of both over to Helebore. For the four days of their journey, the leech had hovered over her and about her—without ever touching her—bringing her choice morsels of food and extra cloaks to hold off the rain.

"Lady." The man holding the reins of her palfrey smiled toothlessly and directed her attention to the gatehouse. Gruffudd was his name. "They're raisin' the portcullis."

Ceridwen looked in the direction he pointed, wondering if he did not know what awaited her inside the walls, or if he was as twisted as his master to think the news would cheer her. Indeed, they were raising the portcullis, and a more chilling sight she'd never seen. 'Twas a gaping maw of iron stakes dripping with rainwater, stained with rust.

She had to get her pack back. Her only hope lay within the rough magic she'd learned in the Hart. Dain would come, she knew he would, but there was no one else, and if they were to have a chance, she must be ready to save herself.

Helebore had given the keeping of her pack to Gruffudd, or rather the destruction of it. If 'twas possible, the pale medicus had grown even paler upon first sighting her small roll of baggage while they were still in the Hart. As with all things of her, he had not touched it, but ordered Gruffudd to throw it on the smoldering coals in the hearth. Gruffudd had not, but stolen it instead. She'd seen him tuck it under his hauberk in the confusion of their leaving. He had since moved it beneath his gambeson, allowing her only a rare peak of trailing riband. She had run her mind in circles trying to think of a way to get it back. Her one advantage was that she herself had been given over to Gruffudd's keeping in deference to Helebore's aversion to any physical contact. The leech gave the orders, and big, thieving Gruffudd carried them out.

They entered Balor much as she would have expected, under the pall of a leaden sky. 'Twas not yet night, and a rider had been sent ahead to roust the kitchen into a meal for the returning lord. As they passed under the portcullis, she looked up at the roof of the gatehouse. Murder holes had been cut into the oak.

The keep sat at the upper end of the bailey. A timber scaffold with stairs led to a heavy oak door, and it was at the scaffolding that they stopped. Upon orders, the mesnie dispersed, the men going off in different directions, leaving her unguarded, except for Gruffudd. Ceridwen curled her fists around handfuls of the palfrey's mane and waited with eyes downcast for any chance that might come along. Should Gruffudd drop the reins for an instant, she would try for the gate.

Gruffudd did not relinquish the reins, and every instant that he held them, listening to Caradoc give orders to the garrison commander, pushed her closer to an edge she dared not fall off. She had learned from her dealings with Ragnor that it was better to wait than to waste her strength when there was no chance, but the waiting was hard when the chance was so slim.

Caradoc finished with his commander and turned to Helebore. "Call me when she is ready for your blade." He gave her a brief glance. "I want to watch."

Sweet Christ, she thought, the blood draining from her face. 'Twas all true, the very worst of it. She made to bolt, but Gruffudd reached for her then, just as a stable boy released her ankles, and instead of bolting, she swooned in a dead faint, nearly knocking Gruffudd over. Two men jumped forward to keep them from toppling, and in the melee, she snatched her pack roll from beneath Gruffudd's gambeson and hid it within her cloaks. If he felt the quick slide of cloth down his side, he said naught, being too busy regaining control of the situation and her.

"I got 'er. I got 'er," he said, scowling and shoving the other men-at-arms away.

Ceridwen heard Caradoc swear a vile oath. "I knew she could not withstand the north. I know naught what you can do with such weak blood, leech."

She lay limp in Gruffudd's arms, praying for a miracle.

"Take her above stairs," Caradoc ordered. "We'll revive her before we begin."

Gruffudd grunted his assent and carried her off, his lumbering gait nearly making her ill. She heard a door being opened and fluttered her lashes, hoping to get her bearings. There was not much to see. The hall was dark and cold and unwelcoming.

More stairs followed, a shorter flight, then another door. Gruffudd laid her down on a bed of uncommon softness and comfort, but he did not let her go. Rather he leaned in close, and she felt an ominous change in his breathing. What followed was even more ominous: a low, sibilant hiss sounding from somewhere in the chamber. Her instincts told her it was Helebore, and more than she feared Gruffudd, she feared the medicus, even rape being preferable to evisceration.

Gruffudd started and moved away.

"Leave her, you whoreson," the leech said, "and send me a guard who knows better than to risk his life for his master's betrothed."

Gruffudd retreated farther, but not without grumbling. "It's not to wife or to bed he's takin' her, but to hell."

"As is his right. Leave us."

She heard the guardsman retreat and fought to control her panic. A soft swishing warned her of Helebore's advance.

"Hmmm," he murmured as his peculiar stench assaulted her nostrils. "Hmmm."

She could hear him circling the bed, drawing closer. Beneath her fingers she felt the hard, ovoid shape of Brochan's Great Charm, and she wondered if she dared to use it on him.

With this stone, I impose . . . whether you take it or nay . . . nay, I impose upon thee a wandering, to a land and fro . . . through . . . She went over the spell in her mind, forgetting half of it in her fear, trying to remember Dain's exact inflection. *A land of faerie dreams, that small dwarf . . .*

Helebore came closer, and the spell fled from her mind. Her hand tightened around the charm in a fierce grip, and she realized she was far more likely to throw it at him than enchant him with it.

"Tsk, tsk, tsk," he said for God knew what reason, then with a swish and a soft tread, he left. She heard him lock the door behind him.

Relief flooded through her, making her weak, and suddenly she was fighting back tears.

"Dain." His name was naught but an anguished groan from her lips. She missed him with an ache she could scarce bear. She had fallen in love and given herself to a man, and both love and the man had been lost to her. She closed her eyes against her tears and brought her hand to her face, imagining she could still smell that warm fragrance they had made, the scent that had bound them, and through it

find some strength, some courage to keep her from the madness surrounding her. She had touched him everywhere, gliding her fingers
across his skin, smoothing her palm up the broad length of his back
and over his shoulders. She had tangled her hands in his hair, held
him close and felt safe and truly whole.

She was so very weary. The march had been relentless, with the
rain pounding away at them, day after day. Her nights had been
fraught with wide-eyed fear, lest someone should come for her. Any
sleep she'd gotten had been on the back of the palfrey.

"Dain," she whispered again, and her tears began anew, run-
ning down her cheeks. She was tired, so tired, and cold, and alone.
She closed her eyes, meaning nothing more than to rest for a moment.
One moment was all she asked.

She's here. She's here. She's here, here, here! Snit could hardly contain his
excitement. The lady had come to live in Balor and make it a home, a
very fine place indeed, indeed. *She's here, here, here!*

He rummaged through his cupboard, through this drawer and
that, searching for the fairest treasures of all his great store. Dust and
lint flew up behind him as he tossed things every which way. One fine
ball caught his attention while in the air, and he quickly turned to
capture it in his hand before it could hit the floor.

"Ah, yes," he crooned. It was a prize. Mostly gray, as lint was
apt to be, but this particular little bundle had a red thread running
through it, twisting and curving. Just the thing for a lady.

He set it in a box he'd marked with a "C" for Ceridwen, next
to a smooth piece of driftwood. Actually, he'd made the box for Caradoc the Ingrate, who had proven too true to his name to deserve the
gift. So now it was for the lady, and the ingrate could do without.

He checked a few more nooks and crannies, coming up with
the rare, wee beasty he'd found in March. Women liked soft things, so
he put it in the box. Lastly, he chose the star rock, the one with shards
of the celestial heavens embedded in its hard gray core. Not only
would he welcome her with gifts, he'd make her rich in the bargain.
'Twas important for a person to have a little wealth of his own, and he
knew she came a pauper from the convent, a sweet bride from God's
hands to theirs. He, Snit, could always get by, and any wealth he gave

her, he could easily replace from down in the caves. Dark, wondrous places they were. Not for the faint of heart, especially in the deeper reaches, especially of late.

There was an intruder in the caves.

Snit froze in place and slanted his eyes first to the right, then to the left. A sneaky, elusive intruder well versed in the arts of concealment. Snit had not seen him, but he'd seen sign of him—a thread of white wool, a footprint, and a bit of lost hair, one strand a long silvery gold and the other strands of the deepest, reddest copper. 'Twas a devil-angel for certain.

Devil-angel . . . The words seem to come out of the air, mocking him, or daring him. Snit whirled and pressed his back up against the cupboard.

There was nothing and no one.

He carefully gathered his prizes, watching the room for signs of danger. Sly, sneaky stuff was danger, slipping and sliding out of the dark when one was least suspecting. Danger could crush a person, if he wasn't quick. Snit had learned that in the deep caves.

Gifts safely in hand, he clambered up on top of the cupboard and made a leap for the rafters. Once there, he ran the length of a beam and disappeared into a cubbyhole hollowed out of the rock and earth.

Ceridwen knew not what awakened her, other than mayhaps the slow rise of hairs on the nape of her neck. She had just realized she'd fallen asleep in the same instant she'd realized she was being watched.

She held her breath, listening, but heard no sound other than the rain and the wind beating against the keep. The storm had grown worse. Hearing nothing inside the chamber, she slowly opened her eyes and got such a fright, she sucked the breath she'd held clean down into her toes and nearly choked.

Eye to eye she was with a tiny three-winged bat, a dead bat hardly as big as her thumb, a desiccated abomination of nature. Next to it was a ball of lint and whatnot the size of a quince, and next to that a small piece of driftwood and a box, the four items laid out as neatly as beads on a string, not two handspans from her face.

She inched herself backward on the bed, not knowing what evil

Helebore was conjuring with the odd array. When she reached a bearable distance, she lifted her head and turned her gaze to the rest of the chamber. At first, she saw no one. A low bench sat by the hearth, a pair of chairs with footstools off to one side. A large chest ran the width of the bed at its foot.

Rushes redolent with the scent of hyssop had been spread on the floor, making the room seem better taken care of than the rest of the keep. Her gaze went back to the bench by the hearth, and 'twas then that she saw him, a changeling, hiding between the wood box and the mantel wall. She gasped, and so did he, both of them backing away, her on the bed, and him deeper into the shadows of his narrow hiding place.

His hair was dark and scraggly, reaching to his shoulders, one of which was higher than the other. His eyes shone out at her, two bright spots in an ash-smudged face with a fine small nose and pointed chin. Sackcloth covered him from neck to knee, and naught but rags cross-gartered his thin legs. For shoes, she saw none, only bare, dirty toes peeking out of the rushes.

She had never seen a changeling, but she'd heard about them, wild, cantankerous children. The faeries would come and steal a woman's fair newborn babe and leave one of their own in its place. So said the ladies at Usk. For all of Rhiannon's talk of faeries, she had never told of any who stole children. Quite the contrary. According to Rhiannon, there was no need as faerie children were as lovely as any other.

Yet here was a changeling true, staring out at her from the shadows. She could put no other name to him.

Except mayhaps one, she thought with a growing sense of realization and wonder: *that small dwarf, whose power could steep the king's host in deathlike sleep . . .*

She opened her fist and looked down at the green glass orb in her palm. Brochan's Great Charm. She'd done it. Her heart beat faster, but in excitement, not fear. She'd called the faerie from the Domh-ringr spell, and he could spirit her away and take her to Dain.

She lifted her head to speak—but he was gone, disappeared in a twinkling. All that was left was a rock on the bench, a gray rock flecked with quartz.

No, no, no, she thought, not more charms. She needed no more charms.

"Domh-ringr faerie?" she called softly, hoping to make him reappear. "Little man of the *tylwyth teg*?"

He didn't come forth, and she sighed and looked at the oddments he'd left: dead bat, lint ball, stick, box. The whole of it did not look promising, yet 'twas his, so she took care as she laid each item into the box.

Up above, in the rafters, Snit hugged himself in rapture. She had accepted his gifts. They were off to a fine start, he and she.

Ceridwen closed the box and set it aside. There was hope. She had her pack, and she'd had more success with Brochan's Great Charm than she'd truly expected, though it had come in a surprising manner. For her next magic, she needed more control and even more success. She unrolled the Quicken-tree pack and chose the unguent from its contents. If she were to turn herself into the Demon and not suffer any disastrous results, she must leave nothing to chance. There could be no fearful, misspoken mutterings of the spell, no wavering from her course. She had to be strong and forceful to create a Demon capable of cowing the Boar, and even stronger if she was to bring herself back as Dain had done.

Thus she girded herself with a commitment to strength and touched her finger to the black, earthy mud. Like Dain, she began on the left side of her face, drawing a line beneath her eye and out to her hairline. She did the same on the right side, then dipped her finger in again.

"Rhuddlan calls—" She hesitated, trying to think through it. Magic was so damned complicated, and Rhuddlan had nothing to do with what she wanted, so she began again with her own words and prayed they would prove effective. "Ceridwen ab Arawn calls up the Sacred Demon of the unknown for her own use, the Demon of despair." She closed her eyes, concentrating her will and all her effort into the litany. "Ceridwen welcomes the true Demon of suffering and sorrow, the one who steals the first sweet breaths of children, the one who cripples and maims youth and the old with no regard to justice, the one who steals souls."

"What's this?" a deep, dismayingly familiar voice demanded from behind her.

Her eyes flew open. She turned toward the door, her heart in her throat. 'Twas Caradoc, and behind him, Helebore. She was too late. Simple sleep had been the cost of her life.

"Seize her," the Boar ordered, and guards moved by him into the room.

She scrambled off the bed and kicked out at the first one to come near. He faltered when her foot connected with his shin, but 'twas a hollow victory. The others had her quick enough. She squirmed against their hold, trying to break free, until Caradoc brought her struggles to a halt. It took no more than the touch of his fingers on her chin.

"*Cariad,*" he said, looking upon her with his lovely, mad gaze. He squeezed her jaw, briefly and painfully, then let her go.

He could have crushed the bones in her face, such was his strength. She knew that as certainly as she was standing there. He smeared a finger through the stripe under her eyes and looked down at the black unguent left on his skin.

"What is this foolishness?"

"Dain has bound me with spells," she said, her voice trembling with the faint hope that it may be true. "Any one of you who brings me harm will die a dreadful death."

He looked to his leech, and Helebore shook his head.

"Dain has laid with you, nothing more," Caradoc said, wiping his finger off on her cheek. "For this, he will die a dreadful death, as will you." He stepped closer, blocking her from the leech's view, and bent his head toward her. "I would have kept you alive awhile longer," he whispered, "but Helebore fears the *pryf* will taste the lust in your blood if we leave it too long, and be frightened away instead of coming when he calls them. You chose very unwisely, Ceridwen, to disgrace the Boar of Balor. Remember that as you die under the leech's blade."

"Your leech is the foolish one, if he thinks to call *pryf* with my blood," she said, her teeth gritted, "and even more foolish if he kills me. For I am the daughter of Rhiannon, she who called the dragons in from the deep beyond."

"Dragons?" Caradoc lifted his head and turned a narrowing gaze on Helebore. "You have not spoken of dragons."

"There are no dragons," the medicus said, his lips tightening into a thin, peevish line.

"He knows naught of what he speaks," Ceridwen said. "The dragon nest is empty, but I can bring them back to Carn Merioneth."

"She bargains for her life with lies." Helebore gave her an evil look.

"She is the daughter of Rhiannon, leech, and dragons are much more to my liking than worms, no matter their great size."

"She is a woman and not to be trusted."

"I should trust you in her stead?" Caradoc laughed, a sly, mocking sound. "I think not, Helebore. I have oft wondered what it is you hope to gain with your promise of wealth. I thought 'twas something with the *pryf,* but mayhaps the maid has truly let it slip."

"She knows nothing," Helebore insisted, growing more agitated.

"Then why are your nerves shredding, leech?" Caradoc left her and advanced upon the pale, hairless man. She tried to jerk free again, but was held by too many.

Helebore took a step back, then another as the Boar drew closer. "Dragons are written about in many books, in many lands and languages, but they are myth and fancy, Caradoc, nothing more. No one has ever seen a dragon. No one." He twisted his head to one side and grimaced, showing a mouth full of brown teeth. "Whereas I, Helebore, have seen the *pryf.* I have seen their shiny dark bodies gliding through the deep caves far below the ocean waves that break against Ynys Enlli, and I followed them here. What others have given by their words to dragons, I say belong to *pryf:* gold, jewels, treasures, and more, much more." The leech stopped, his back to a wall, and looked up at the taller man. "The woman lies, Caradoc. Give me her blood, and I will prove it."

The Boar appeared to waver, slanting a glance at her from over his shoulder.

"No!" Ceridwen shouted, pulling and tugging, trying to break free.

"A cup." Caradoc returned his gaze to the leech, decided. "A small cup."

"So little?" Helebore implored.

"Use it to show me what you have seen, and I will let you have more."

" 'Tis not much, but I can make do." Helebore grew smugly

thoughtful and even deigned to smile upon her. "I will have to purify her on the ramparts to cleanse her of her filthy deed."

"Do what you must."

The leech's smile broadened disgustingly. He signaled to the guards holding her. "Take her to the north wall."

Snit watched them all leave the room, his hands clenched into small fists. The Ingrate had gone too far, much too far, showing an ingratitude beyond comprehension. Had Caradoc not seen the fairness of her face? The softness of her hair? The sweetness of the soul shining in her eyes?

The last guard closed the door, and Snit leaped down onto the bed. She had spoken words of mystery and demons, oddly familiar words. They were meant to be friends, he and she. One by one he gathered her things into the middle of her pretty pack cloth. His fingers brushed against it, and a tingling started in their tips, a not unpleasant sensation. Curious, he sat back on his heels and touched it again. Warmth radiated out from the silken warp and weft. Wondrous stuff, this, he thought, picking it up and rubbing it against his cheek.

Sticks! Left a mark, he had. He brushed at the dirt with his hand, but only managed to smear it farther. *Fie!* What a beast he was.

He finished rolling everything up in her pack, hiding the dirty spot as best he could, and tied it with her ribands—except for one he kept for himself, weaving it into his hair. They were friends, were they not? Then he slung the pack over his shoulder and made for the north wall.

Chapter 23

From their vantage point in the hills to the southeast, Dain, Morgan, and Rhuddlan looked upon Balor. Torches had been burning on a section of the north rampart since the rain had diminished to a drizzle. The flames danced against the night sky while flashes of lightning sporadically lit the keep and curtain wall.

"Escalade," Morgan said. "We can scale the west wall. The patrols are always fewest there. There is a path of sorts up the cliffs from the beach, if the tide is out."

"And if the tide is in?" Dain asked without taking his gaze from the castle. 'Twas an ominous-looking place, and Ceri was in there, somewhere.

"Then there is no beach, and we get wet."

"The tide matters not," Rhuddlan said. "I can get you near to the base of the stone wall through the caves."

" 'Tis true," Morgan said. "The caves are directly beneath the bailey and open onto the cliffs, but how are you going to get us into the caves?"

Dain turned to the pair as Rhuddlan gestured to the east. "There is an opening near that copse of hazel on the hillside."

"To the Light Caves?"

"Not directly. We will have to descend into the Canolbarth, the midland caves, and come back up into the Light Caves which open onto the cliff face."

"Canolbarth?" Morgan repeated. "I was in the Light Caves a few times as a child, and there was never any talk of Canolbarth or other caves."

"No one knows the true length or depth of the caverns that begin beneath Carn Merioneth," said Rhuddlan, "but I have traveled many leagues in their darkness and been to the Canolbarth and beyond. As to the openings scattered throughout the hills, no one is left besides Quicken-tree and Druids who know where those openings are hidden."

Dain noticed how Morgan grew still, then the younger man swore under his breath.

Rhuddlan threw a questioning glance at the Welshman.

" 'Tis the talk of Druids Morgan doesn't like," Dain explained. "His God is offended by other religions. What about the Quicken-tree in our plans? Where will they be?"

"We will work from beneath the keep. Morgan's men will also be needed there, if he so agrees."

"Aye," Morgan muttered. "The fewer over the wall, the better." He looked to Dain. " 'Tis a place more pagan than I knew that we go to, friend."

They had made preliminary plans in their camp each night of the march, going over what every man knew of Balor and its defenses. Morgan and Owain were the most familiar with the garrison and the manning of the wall, yet they deferred to Rhuddlan with a naturalness Dain found intriguing. For himself, he would not have chosen any of their plans. The smell of battle, of clashing arms and grunting men coming together in a lust for blood made his stomach churn. If he had to kill to free Ceri, he preferred to kill quickly, silently, and alone.

"You can't bring Ceridwen down the cliffs," Rhuddlan continued, pointing toward Balor. "Our work will be to take and hold the southwest tower, there on the left, and open the passage that lies underneath."

"Under the pit?" Morgan's attention came fully back to them. "You want us to go through the pit to get out of Balor?"

" 'Tis the safest way."

"Safe?" the Welshman begged to differ, his deference waning. "I say we come out through the gatehouse and take our chances with the murder holes, a far safer course than taking on the beasts in the pit."

"It matters not, Morgan," Dain said. "I go over the castle wall alone. Whatever is in the pit will answer to my sword, not yours."

"No," Rhuddlan said. "We must—" He fell silent, as did they all. Though water dripped from the leaves and branches and filled the forest with a soft rushing noise, each had heard the sound that did not fit the pattern. "Llynya," the Quicken-tree man called out after a moment. "Show yourself."

Dain watched as the sprite stepped from behind a tree and into a patch of watery moonlight. Like Rhuddlan, he'd known 'twas her. He'd felt her distant presence on the march from Wydehaw and determined that she was following them. She had become a shadow he could not lose.

Ignoring the girl once she was fully present, Rhuddlan returned his attention to Dain. "Moira and the others are not too far behind, and probably Madron also, but Llynya chose to travel alone, against my orders as she does most everything."

"Why are the women coming?"

"Even more than Deri, this is a Quicken-tree place. They come to fight." Rhuddlan gestured to the sprite. "You will go over the wall with Dain and Morgan. See to it that neither are hurt."

"Aye," Llynya said, though she failed to meet his gaze.

Morgan guffawed, clearly amused.

Dain was not. "She stays with you, Rhuddlan, and Morgan. She has watched my back for too long and in places where I would have preferred to have had my privacy." He directed the last at Llynya, whose only sign of understanding was to lower her head a little more and drag the toe of her boot through the mud.

"Aye, the girl stays," Morgan concurred with Dain, "but you're not leaving without me. So do not waste your effort in trying."

"Nor will you leave without Llynya," Rhuddlan said. "She will help you find the entrance to the southwest passage. I know not what shape it may have taken since the building of Balor over the ruins of Carn Merioneth. There are many false leads in the tunnels and caves. Llynya will guide you through them. Alone, you'll waste precious time and increase the danger to yourself and Ceridwen."

Dain gave the man a questioning look. "Like Madron, you worry much over the maid's safety."

"And yours," Rhuddlan admitted, surprising him.

"To what end?" he asked.

"From you, the promised hour of magic. From Ceridwen, her heritage. Both of you must open a long-closed door, the seal on a weir gate in the deep tunnels, the one trapping the *pryf* in their dark maze."

"They are not trapped, Rhuddlan. They came up the river." Dain had felt them, heard them.

"Their cry will echo for a hundred leagues beneath the ground and wash up against you like a caress," Rhuddlan said. "They are nonetheless trapped and must be freed."

'Twas not so much to ask for what Rhuddlan had given him, Dain thought. Or was it? He didn't doubt his ability to open anything. It had proven to be a rare gift he had, but quick as she was, Ceridwen had shown no such talent.

Then again, she had opened the door to the upper chamber of the Hart. Not a difficult task, to be sure, but beyond many he'd known.

" 'Tis not as complicated as the Druid Door," Rhuddlan continued, "but like Nemeton's it requires a knowing touch. Unlike Nemeton's, it also requires a woman's touch. Someone else is trying to break the seal, and we must be the first. Of this there is no doubt. 'Tis why we came so early out of the west. 'Tis why I came north to Balor before Beltaine."

"And what did you find?" Dain asked.

"Traces of the same evil one who took Ceridwen. His strange scent is all over the caves and in places I thought were safe from intrusion."

"So 'tis Helebore who causes both our troubles."

"Helebore and another who is much more elusive," Rhuddlan said. "Trig found some sign, but not enough to track. Merioneth is a sacred place to the Quicken-tree. I am sworn to protect it and all who dwell there from desecration and destruction."

"You are so sure I can open this door?"

"Aye. I am sure. With Ceridwen's help, you will open it and live to tell the tale."

Ceridwen hung from the ropes that held her arms to a wooden cross planted in the wall-walk behind a northside parapet. The rain had finally stopped, though lightning still flickered and flashed through the sky, and thunder could be heard rumbling across the heavens.

Purification was hell, a very cold, dark, and lonely hell. Only two guards were left with her, neither of them Gruffudd. They talked together between the merlons, distant enough that their voices were naught but noise in cadence. Yet the thunder and the guards did not account for all she heard up on the wall. Another sound came from the east, a strange, intermittent wheezing that could be wind, but which her instincts told her was not. Whatever it was, she prayed it came no closer.

Helebore planned on returning quickly. A short purification, he'd said, should be enough to render her fit for his black magic. Enough, she thought, to render her helpless with cold and fear. After the leech had seen her tied, he'd ordered the other guards to his chambers to bring up an iron cauldron to catch her blood. In case the cup should overspill, he'd said.

She squeezed her eyes shut and jerked against the ropes. They did not loosen. Her heart pounded inside her chest, every beat reminding her that Helebore was going to cut it out of her. He'd promised her as much, with a special knife he called an athame, a witch's blade, after he'd proved her wrong and Caradoc released her fully into his keeping.

Chances were he *would* prove her wrong. What did she know of dragons, other than what she'd read? She had Madron's dream, but dreams could not save her. She jerked and pulled again on the ropes.

Damnation was her destiny. Hell, not heaven, would be her eternal home. She could near feel the fiery flames of that cursed place licking at her through the freezing rain. She would face the Devil already half a demon. The unguent was still on her face, marking her as one of Satan's own. There was no hope, no hope.

She clenched her teeth and tried the ropes yet again. She was damned. There was naught but lightning for her to work with to free herself, and she did not know the way of it. 'Twas her own fault. She'd become so enamored of the other magic Dain had taught her, she'd not asked again for the lightning dance.

Llynya had seen it, had seen him draw fire out of the sky and make it dance to his whim. She would immolate herself, he'd warned, but 'twas a chance she was willing to take, if she could only entice a sliver of the searing heat to escape its bolt and burn through her bonds.

She had no words. Dain was a great believer in speaking words to make good spells. Truthfully, he'd told her that ofttimes the words alone would make the spell without a charm. She had no charm about her either, only the lightning arcing across the night sky and a desperate need.

"Sky fire, sky fire . . . release your power unto me." She improvised, pleading with any words she could think of, straining to infuse them with confidence and meaning. "Break a bolt of lightning from . . . from God's hands and hurl it down through the darkness that it may—"

The great doors of the keep swung open below her. Her breath caught in her throat. A troop of men filed out, two of them carrying a cauldron on a pole. Behind the two, Helebore walked with his head bowed and covered by his cowl. Wisps of fog wound around them all.

"Sky fire, sky fire, release your power unto me," she repeated more strongly, tugging at her bonds.

Torchlight flickered over the slow-moving column as they descended the stairs and crossed the bailey toward the north wall. Helebore stopped once and looked up to where she hung from her cross. The candle the leech held threw macabre shadows upon his face, giving him the ghoulish countenance she feared was his truest nature.

"Sky fire, sky fire." Her voice faltered as he continued to stare, his pale face transfixing her. "Sweet Mary, Mother of God—" Lightning crackled through the darkness, accompanied by a simultaneous crash of thunder. "Aaaah!" The scream was torn from her throat. Pain burned across her wrists and she was free, falling to the stone wall-walk.

For an instant she was suffused with wonder. She'd done it. Then her savior showed himself.

"You," she gasped at the dirty, sharp-angled face looming over her.

"Snit's me name," he said. A small dagger glinted in his hand. "Snit."

"Ho, there!" the guards on the wall yelled, and started for them. One of them held a crossbow at the ready, the other had a sword in hand.

With a flick of blade and flash of steel, Snit pulled a second knife from his belt and shoved the hilt into her hand. "Do yer best."

Her best was to get behind the wooden cross and gird herself for the attack. The little man ran forward to do battle with the guards. He was no higher than their waists, and overmatched by seven stone apiece. At the last moment, he rolled himself into a ball and pitched forward against one of the men's legs. The guard stumbled over him, losing his balance. Snit took quick advantage, jumping back up to his feet and pushing the bigger man over the edge of the wall-walk. The guard's short cry of surprise ended in the bailey turf.

His demise created instant havoc in Helebore's line, sending men scurrying. Ceridwen gave them naught but a glance before the other guard was upon her.

He lunged to the right, reaching for her hair, and she cut him with her blade. He swore, a vicious sound, and lunged again, then Snit was on him, slashing away with his knife. The guard roared and shook free, throwing the little man to the wall-walk. Snit was undaunted, and as Ceridwen threw her weight against the guard, the little man reached up with his knife and severed the tendon in the back of the guard's knee. The man fell with a roar of pain.

"Come," Snit directed her, taking off at a run.

Ceridwen bent and picked up the guard's crossbow, cursing the other one for taking his sword with him over the wall. Then she followed Snit to the east, the two of them racing across the ramparts. At a turn in the wall, she came to a sudden, stunned halt. Another cross had been planted in the stone walk, and a man hung upon it. Or what had once been a man. No human ever looked thus. His skin hung in tatters down the length of his naked body. She stumbled back, away from the gross specter of mutilated flesh and the horrifying stench that consumed him. A single burning torch illuminated the rotting face. Empty eye sockets had become a nesting place for maggots. The wheezing she'd heard was no more than air passing through what little was left of a nose. One ear was missing, and in its place was a bloody mat of wiry red hair.

Ragnor.

Her tormentor.

For all that he'd done to her, she was sickened by his fate.

Behind her, she heard the clattering noise of many men spilling out onto the wall. There was no time to falter. With a quick prayer, she stepped forward, her hand tightening on the knife Snit had given her.

"Go with your God," she murmured, and one neat, deep slice across the side of his neck ended Ragnor's misery.

She stepped back, away from the spurt of blood, then took off after Snit before he disappeared from sight.

Dain eased himself over a crenellation in Balor's wall and was followed by Morgan, Llynya, and a wave of thick fog rolling up from the sea below. The climb had been treacherous, the rock slick with sea spray and rain. The cliff itself had crumbled beneath his fingers too often for comfort. He might not have made it down again with the weight of another on his back. When he found Ceridwen, he would do as Rhuddlan had said and bring her down through the tower.

The last bolt of lightning had struck close with the storm sweeping inland from the sea. If it did not lift, the weather would lodge up against the mountains, and there would be hell to deal with the whole night long.

They each did a weapon check once they'd made the wall. Full quivers hung across each of their backs, daggers were thrust into belts. Llynya's bow was shorter than Morgan's and Dain's, but Rhuddlan had assured Dain that the sprite was a sure and steady shot and an able arm behind the sword she carried.

Men could be seen swarming over a section of the north wall. The torches there were still burning brightly, untouched by the heavy mist sneaking in from the coast. *Nebelmer,* it was called, a sea of cloud.

Dain looked behind him, and indeed 'twas a sea, white-and-gray waves peaking and churning one against the other, piling higher and obscuring everything in their path. The hazy stuff slipped between the merlons and drifted down to the wall-walk, pooling in milky swirls around their feet. The ocean was naught but sound and a vast emptiness filled with the cloud.

"Much more o' this, and we'll be fighting blind," Morgan said.

"It will not hinder me," Llynya said. "I can see my way clear no matter how thick it gets."

"You can see through this?" Morgan sifted his hand through the fog pouring over the wall. His fingers disappeared in the white mist.

"Mayhaps 'smell' is the truer word." She turned her head to the east. "And I smell something horrifyingly awful over there." She pointed, and Dain followed the direction of her hand.

"Is it Helebore?" he asked.

"Aye. He is there, but I smell worse than the evil one."

"Stay behind me," he ordered, "and if needs be, go over the wall. There are arrowslits in each merlon for you to cling to on the outside."

"Rhuddlan did not send me to be a burr on the castle curtain."

"Rhuddlan sent you to find our way beneath the pit. Until we reach it, stay behind me."

The three of them struck out for the north wall, passing no patrols since the men-at-arms were running ahead of them, converging near a northside parapet. By torchlight, Dain could see them milling around the wall-walk and crenellation, as if they searched for something gone astray. The three of them drew closer and the noise of the search could be heard: men shouting, the metallic jingling of mail hauberks, the stomping of feet.

"Cretinous whoresons! I will have the ballocks cut from all of you!" someone screamed above the din. Helebore, by the sibilant, whining sound of it. "One lice-ridden slut outfoxes you to the man and escapes my grasp! Who will give me blood in her place? Who?"

Dain looked to Morgan, and their eyes met above the swirling mist. The dark-haired Welshman grinned.

"She is the damnedest thing to hold on to." Morgan's grin broadened.

The relief Dain felt held him in his place. She was free. But where?

"Llynya. Return to Rhuddlan." He turned to the sprite. "Tell him Ceridwen has escaped and will be looking for a way out of Balor. Have him post scouts."

"I'm not to leave you."

"We are all of us here for one reason, to save Ceridwen. Now go, and when you have delivered your message, return to the southwest tower to await Morgan and me." His tone warned her he would brook no disobedience in this.

She nodded, and as quickly as that was gone the way they'd come.

"What now, Dain?" Morgan asked.

"We search for your cousin from inside the walls. You take the garrison and the lower bailey. I'll take the keep and the upper bailey. If you find her, rendezvous in the southwest tower. If not, go over the wall and come up through the caves with your men and the Quickentree."

"About the pit," Morgan said, and Dain wondered if going to the feared place was beyond the Welshman's ability.

"Aye?"

"It's a maze in itself. I've heard Caradoc runs men through it sometimes and that none has been known to survive. There are traps, dangers besides the wild boars he keeps. If you end up there, keep your wits about you."

"You have never known me to lack for wits, ab Kynan." He felt another wave of relief. 'Twasn't the pit itself worrying Morgan.

"Nor for courage," the younger man admitted. "But your penchant for self-preservation tends to weaken in the face of another's need." He hesitated, lowering his gaze. " 'Twasn't the beatings you took for me that I regret, for in truth, with my leg half open at the time, I was in no shape to take them myself." His voice grew softer, less sure. "Nor was it the buggery that I worried about so much, though I swear I do not know how you bore—"

"I would not speak of this," Dain said, his manner harsh to dissuade his friend from his course.

"Nor I, except for the peril we face," Morgan said, doggedly continuing. " 'Twas the other I never forgave myself for, Dain, what

Jalal did to you with the *kif* and his conjuring arts. I remember one new moon eve near the beginning of our second year in the desert. You and Jalal were sitting around a small gold brazier you'd carried out to the dunes, putting bits of something into the flames and singing words that could have been naught but from the Devil. Demons danced on the sands that night and howled through the camp, and this is what I fear, Dain, that 'tis too soon for you to die. Until you make your peace with God, your soul might still be damned by those darker desert deeds. Deeds that I did naught to stop."

Dain remembered the night. His mind had been swimming in a sea of wine and smoke, and Jalal had taken him out into the dunes, not to call demons, but to speak to him of soothing things and courtesans; and if they'd sung, no doubt the song had been bawdy rather than diabolical. Mayhaps they'd put a pinch or two of *rihadin* in the brazier. But Morgan was right about one thing, that night had been a beginning between him and Jalal. From thence forward, the master had no longer come to his tent as a man, but only as a teacher of potions and spells and magic and stars; and by the end of the second year, no more men had come to his tent at all. Jalal had found his truer worth. Another year had seen Dain able to buy his freedom and Morgan's, for by then he'd learned some things to teach his master.

" 'Twas the wind you heard howling through the camp that night," he said to Morgan, "and as you could not have stopped the wind, no more could you have stopped me from taking my path. You have no fault in all of this, and no debt."

"And your peace with God?" Morgan asked, clearly not yet willing to concede.

Dain smiled. "It is proving to be hard-won, but I do not plan on dying this night."

"Then to better your odds, if the chance should come for a boar fight, I ask that you stay behind me."

Dain clapped him on the shoulder, accepting the note of command in his friend's voice. "If we meet in the pit, I'll let you have first go at the beast."

"Aye, and good hunting then."

"Good hunting."

Dain waited for the Welshman to disappear down the wall-walk, before turning to his own task. He would search the upper bailey and the keep, but first he would kill Helebore. That one's existence threatened Ceridwen more than any other's. With the leech dead, there would be only Caradoc lusting for her death.

The fog was thickening and rising about him, spilling over the wall-walk and blanketing the castle green. Helebore was still to the northeast of him, ranting about his lost prize. A clear shot would be hard to come by with all the other people about, and more than two would give away his position. He checked the area, noting the timbered roof of the stable against the wall to the north and the location of the scaffolding that accessed the ramparts. There was no better place than where he was. He reached for his bow and nocked an arrow into the string—then stopped before he had the bow half drawn. The men on the wall were shouting and pointing down into the bailey. He followed the direction of their attention and felt his heart slow to a ponderous, heavy beat. 'Twas Ceridwen, running through the moonshadows and the fog, following a raggedy child, the both of them racing toward the keep. One of the faster guards was already clattering down the stairs, his sword drawn, heading to cut them off. Dain drew the bow taut, adjusted his aim, and skewered the man through his unmailed shoulder and out through his chest. He fell off the stairs into a crumpled heap in the mud.

Moving quickly, Dain jumped to the stable roof and notched another arrow. The next man down the stairs suffered the same fate as the first, though shot through the neck. Dain didn't wait for the third, but lofted himself off the stable to the ground and took off at a dead run. More men were pouring off the walls. He dropped the bow and drew the Damascene and his sword. Meeting the leading phalanx of three men, he took one out with the first arc of his blade. He blocked a strike with Scyld and lunged beneath the crossed swords to cut the second man under his arm. The third nicked him on the shoulder and received a clean slice across his face for his effort. Blood spilled down the man's cheeks and nose like a mask.

Breathing heavily, Dain turned and met the fourth man to come down the wall. The fifth was upon him before he could recover. Sword blade clanged against sword blade. Others were close behind, covering him from all sides. The last thing he saw before he went down was Ceridwen disappearing around a corner of the keep.

Chapter 24

Ceridwen sat alone in an area hollowed out of the rock somewhere below the keep. 'Twas barely big enough to hold her and Snit's strange cache of booty. The light from the candle he'd left her revealed an assortment of broken pots and half-unraveled baskets, each holding its share of whatnot and "this and that." String was a popular item, and smooth, shiny rocks. Most welcome was the return of her pack. He'd pulled it out from behind the largest basket upon their arrival and unrolled it to show her everything was still there: *rihadin,* unguent, red book, the mirror, the desiccated baby bat, everything except the one Quickentree riband she'd seen braided through his hair. She'd said nothing about that. 'Twas a small price to pay for freedom, even a precarious freedom.

She'd come with him through a tiny door on the side of the keep and ended up in a narrow tunnel that had led them there. Given the regular size of the guards, she wasn't surprised that none had been able to follow. She'd heard them behind her, shouting and running, heard the clash of swords. The sound of their pursuit had put wings on her feet.

She still had the knife Snit had given her and the crossbow, though she had only two bolts and the most rudimentary knowledge of how to work it. Snit had gone to get food, hot pottage to warm her bones, but that had been ages ago, and naught but a tippet of wax remained of the taper. She kept her hands over the flame, taking the heat in through her fingers and imagining it flowing up her arms and into her chest, stealing the icy chill away. She didn't know what to expect next, but had posted herself by the tunnel shaft they'd come down, having decided to make her way back up toward the bailey if Snit had not returned by the time the candle guttered itself in melted wax. She figured 'twas close to dawn, so any further attempt at escape would have to wait until evening fell again, though by then she would probably be crippled from being cramped and frozen in the small tunnel all day.

The candle flame moved with an unseen breeze, and she quickly cupped her hands around it. The flame steadied, much to her relief. Her odd ally was short in words as well as stature, giving her no clues as to why he'd rescued her. That he was familiar with Balor was beyond a doubt, and she hoped to use his knowledge to devise a way out. That he was the Domh-ringr faerie, called by her with Brochan's Charm, was not beyond a doubt. In truth, the more she thought about it, the less likely it seemed. He was from Balor, not the spirit world. Yet, when she'd needed magic most, he'd seemed to be magical, and despite all, there was a hint of something fey about him.

She looked toward the far tunnel, the faint scent of barley frumenty bringing her head up. Snit was returning, and he had food, hot food. He came out of the darkened shaft, bowl in hand, muttering to himself about trouble, trouble, trouble.

"What trouble?" she asked, taking the bowl from him when he offered it. She immediately scooped the food into her mouth, sucking it off her fingers as there was no spoon.

"Master trouble," he said, "and me master's master trouble. Helebore and Caradoc have another below, one like you, not like the one above ye killed." Piercing green eyes, thickly lashed yet older than the face that held them, shifted in her direction. He was more than a boy, yet not so. His skin was smooth, if dirty, without lines, but the crookedness of his body appeared painful and gave him an aged look. "Ye did kill him, didn't ye?"

"Aye," she admitted around a mouthful of warm barley.

"Ye shouldn't have. He was meant to suffer. Caradoc wanted him punished for hurting you."

"And now 'tis Caradoc who wants to hurt me, unless I can get out of Balor. Do you know the way?"

"There's a thousand ways in and a thousand ways out, and nary a one o' them without risk," he told her, emphasizing his words with a narrowed gaze. "People get crushed, ye see, ifs they take a misstep."

"Crushed by what?" She scooped up another dollop of frumenty and stuck her fingers in her mouth. She would escape, and she would find Dain and Mychael, and they would all leave this place called Wales.

"Crushed by hot walls moving in the deep dark," the man-boy said mysteriously. He tossed his hair over one shoulder and carefully leaned across the candle, stroking a finger down the bat's soft body. Next, he touched his finger in the unguent.

She didn't like the sounds of his answer. None of the walls in the caves she remembered had ever moved and crushed, nor had they been hot. "Do we have to go through the deep dark to get out? Is there no way through the bailey?"

"Ach." He dismissed the idea with a wave of his hand, sitting back down on his side of the flame. "Caradoc has the mesnie scouring the bailey for you, and the keep too, but they'll not find you in Snit's hidey-hole. He tried to send small boys down the tunnels with knives, but I sent them all packing." He sniffed the unguent, then smeared it across his cheeks in a pattern to match hers. "Helebore says to smoke you out with the screams of the other one, but me master's master is too shy to mark the sorcerer with the leech's hot irons. Strange, it is. Caradoc's never been shy before to brand."

Ceridwen had not heard a word past "sorcerer." Dear God, Dain had come for her and been captured. She set her bowl of pottage aside. "Does the sorcerer have a name?"

"Helebore calls him Cursed Lavrans. Caradoc does naught but sit and stare at him, and brood." Snit drew his eyebrows close together and tucked his chin into his chest, giving a fair imitation of a striped and brooding Boar of Balor.

"We must save him, Snit, as you saved me." She tried to keep the panic out of her voice. "Take me to him, and I will show you the colors of fire."

Snit cocked his head. "What colors?"

"Gold, red, blue," she said, working quickly to roll her treasures back up in her pack. "Mayhaps I even have some green."

"Green fire to save a sorcerer?"

"Aye, I think it will work." She tied the pack and threw it over her shoulder. "Can we take him with us into the deep dark?"

"He's big." Snit sounded unsure, voicing her concern. She'd barely squeezed herself through his small passageway. "But the tunnels below Helebore's chambers are bigger than the ones above, and in the deep dark, the size is ever shifting, yet always big enough to hold a man, unless the walls decide to crush him and grind his bones to dust inside his skin. A man thus rendered does not need much room."

"No," she agreed, horrified. "No, of course not."

Before she'd even finished her sentence, the man-boy was disappearing down a dark shaft, leaving her to scramble behind and hope he was indeed taking her to Dain.

The way was long, seeming more so in the dark, and twice she thought she'd lost him, his sole source of guidance being a humming noise he made.

"Hmmm, hmm, hmm." The sound bounced off the cold stone walls curving around them, growing softer whenever he made a turn. 'Twas her clue to listen closely so as not to wander in the wrong direction.

Finally, a lightening of the gloom and the barest hint of warmth told her they were nearing a chamber. Voices echoed up the shaft, one a mumbling, muttering thing, incomprehensible, the other low and deep.

"That we have come to this is surprising," the low, deep voice said, and she knew 'twas Caradoc, his silent brooding past. He paused, and his voice took on an undercurrent of anger. "That we have come to this over your fucking my betrothed bride will be the death of you, old friend."

Only silence greeted the pronouncement.

She tried to rush ahead, but Snit blocked her way and waved her back, forcing her to a crawl as the end of the tunnel came into view. The light was brighter there, flickering from a fire she could smell and hear.

"The irons are, Boar, ready and hot, so very hot." 'Twas unmistakably Helebore, with too much eagerness jumbling his words. "Soon enough the maid will come running out of Snit's rat holes, the ungrateful wretch. If Lavrans screams for her, she will come, and we must have her. Must."

"Have you no eye for beauty at all, leech?" Caradoc sounded mildly disgusted by Helebore's lack of appreciation. "For here is beauty." A chair scraped across the floor, and Ceridwen feared she heard a pained gasp. "Look upon it, medicus, and remember that once you saw Jalal al-Kamam's famed Swan, the *bedžhaa,* known throughout the desert for the pleasure he could inflict. And the pain, eh, Lavrans?" The chair scraped again, and Caradoc's words grew softly menacing. " 'Twas said you could give a man pain so exquisite he could see the angels coming for him, and pleasure so dark 'twas like falling into the abyss of hell."

Strange, awful words—they made her heart race in fear. She and Snit stopped at the edge of the tunnel, high up on the wall, and looked down into the cavernous chamber. 'Twas all she could do to hold back a cry. Caradoc had his fist wound through Dain's hair, holding his head back at a painful angle with a knife to his throat. Blood ran down the side of Dain's face. His arms were tied to the chair.

Helebore stood to one side, impatient, sour-faced, his gauntleted hand holding a branding iron in a nest of red-hot coals. The place smelled like Dain's alchemy chamber, sulfurous, with glass and earthenware containers stacked on tables and shelves. She recognized an athanor and the still. As far as she could see, there was no one in the room besides the bald leech, the Boar of Balor, and the man she would free.

"Do you remember the desert prison at Jaffa, Lavrans? The screams of men, the agonizing heat, and the bitter cold?" Caradoc leaned close, drawing the knife ever so carefully across Dain's neck, leaving a thin red line in its wake. Ceridwen could not take her eyes from it. "I thought nothing could be worse, that I had truly reached the depths of depravity, fighting with old men for rotten dates." He chuckled. "So young back then, so stupidly young."

Dain seemed made of stone, or death. His eyes were closed, and not even breath seemed to move his body.

"I was proved wrong about depravity," Caradoc went on, "as

were you, I fear. Do you remember marking a man thus? With the bare tip of a watered steel blade? The trick of the pleasure, they told me, is to do it without drawing blood." The knife wavered, and Ceridwen saw Dain's fingers tighten into a white-knuckled grip around the chair arms.

He lived.

"I never did manage it without the blood," Caradoc said. "I would cut them, no matter how carefully I wielded the knife, without breathing, without hardly moving it, trying so desperately to keep the edge and tip on the bare surface of the skin. Yet I always cut, and they would curse me and beat me and tell me of Jalal al-Kamam's Swan from the far north. Ahh, they would sigh, silky chestnut hair like a woman's, soft brown eyes like a camel's, and the touch—Praise Allah!—the touch of a king's mage." Caradoc stopped and lowered his gaze down Dain's body in a wickedly debauched visual caress that made Ceridwen's stomach roll. "They say Jalal awaits you still." He stroked Dain's face with the blade, without leaving a mark. "Do you remember the first time your master sold you to a man?"

Dain did not speak, and Caradoc started a new cut on his neck below the last.

"Nor I. They had a drink the first time, sweet like ambrosia, more potent than wine, a simple mixed to steal a man's mind. They were generous in the beginning, not so later." He hesitated with the blade. "Surely you remember the ambrosia? Its sickly sweet scent, how they burned it to fill your nose and mouth with smoke when 'twasn't in the wine. A person could kill for another taste of such heaven, eh, Lavrans?"

Ceridwen bit her lip and began easing the crossbow around into her lap, being careful not to scrape it against the tunnel walls.

"What say you, Lavrans?" Caradoc inquired softly, tightening his hand in Dain's hair and pulling his prisoner's head back an extra degree. "What of the worst comes upon you in the night and makes you sweat? Which nightmare haunts you more than the others?"

Still Dain said nothing. The Boar swore, and in a lightning-quick move, the knife went up and down, cutting Dain on the face and slicing through the bonds holding his right arm to the chair. Two cuts, one bloody, the other rash.

Caradoc shoved his face into his captive's, holding Dain's free hand in a fierce grip. "I heard the whispers that you'd been sold the same as me," he hissed, "and I wondered—is Lavrans holding out, is he stronger, braver, more of a man than I turned out to be?" He turned Dain's hand into the light and traced a shallow path with his knife, making a red line to cover the white scar already there. "Not in the end, it seems. For what besides utter weakness could have brought you to this, *bedźhaa*?"

Ceridwen knew what the scar meant. *Dear God.* How had she not seen it before? The mirror had spoken true; there was boundless pain in his wisdom, and he had seen the darkness on men's souls. A desolate novice had once damned herself to everlasting hell by cutting such a line upon her wrist. That Dain had faced such desperation for the strange deeds Caradoc talked about tore at her heart.

"Did you gag in your dreams and wake to the same foul stench as I?" Caradoc demanded. "Did you?"

"I did not dream." Dain's first words were spoken with dead calm, and she prayed 'twas true; that he had not dreamed. She was not so naive that she didn't understand what Caradoc was talking about. The images made her hands shake and her face flush. A pain pressed deep in her chest, a hurtful, dark pain.

With the bow free, she gestured to Snit to help her span it. 'Twas more difficult than she'd imagined, taking their combined strength. There would be time for only one shot.

She heard Caradoc speak again. "Tell me you were no better than I, and I will let you live."

"Like Ragnor and your father? I think not."

"Father?" Caradoc snorted in disgust. "Gwrnach tithed me to Saladin, and I tithed him to hell. 'Twas a fair trade for father and son. As for Ragnor, the chit put a blade to his throat and he no longer lives to give me pleasure. Mayhaps you should take his place." There was a menacing pause, then a guttural sound that could have come only from Dain. Ceridwen swiped at a tear with her knuckles. "Aye, Dain, think on it. I could cut you for a sennight, before you would need the support of a wooden cross."

The bow was finally loaded. Snit laid in the bolt along the groove, and she raised the whole of it to her cheek to peer down the sight. There was no room for error, yet her hands still shook. Dain was bleeding from a new cut.

Snit looked once to the pair below and back to the bow. Then, with a confidence she found encouraging, he changed the angle of the crossbow stock, pushing it a few degrees away from himself and the ceiling. At his nod, she pulled the trigger, and Caradoc went down screaming, shot through the thigh. She looked to Snit, and he shrugged. Dain leaped up and used his right hand to swing the chair around, smashing it into the wall and breaking himself free.

By the time Helebore snapped out of his stupor, she had tossed *rihadin* and *aqua ardens* into his coals. The instantaneous flash of flame and burst of color sent him diving for the floor.

"Dain!" she yelled. His head came up. After he sighted her, he reached for his knives and a sword that had lain by the chair. Then he climbed to the top of the table and jumped up to catch a beam. Guards were shouting and pounding on the door, their noise adding to the confusion of fire bursts and screams.

Dain reached the opening of the tunnel, breathless and bleeding, and as the guards broke through the door, she and Snit grabbed him by his gambeson and pulled him into the shaft.

Morgan slipped along the inside passage of the southwest tower, his jaw set, his mood dangerous. He had done naught but chase his tail this night. The walls on either side of him were timbered and led him down toward the pit. He'd searched the lower and upper baileys and the garrison and had found no one and nothing, but given the happenings earlier in the night, he had not gone over the wall. If there was to be more trouble, it would take place in the southwest tower, and if Dain and Ceridwen were together, Dain would bring her there. As it was, they both seemed to have disappeared off the face of the earth.

The tower was strangely empty, with most of the castle guards scurrying around the baileys and swarming over the keep. Even at that, they were a loose-fingered bunch. There had been the sound of battle around midnight, the clash of swords unmistakable in the air. He'd raced back along the wall only to find himself too late. Dain had been taken and the maid lost, so shouted the captain deriding Balor's mesnie.

Where Dain had been taken had been easy to deduce. Balor was no great castle. Breaching the keep had also been relatively easy, with only one man killed in the process. Getting to Helebore's damned dungeon and finding himself again too late, because hell had already broken loose and Dain was gone, had not been easy. He'd been quick enough to be part of the group breaking down the door, and anonymous enough in the dead man's helmet and hauberk. He had been quick enough to hear a woman's cry and to see Dain disappear—of all the damned things—into a tunnel hole near the ceiling of the damned smelly room.

But so help him God, no matter how hard he'd tried, he had not been able to squeeze himself through the same hole. Being no bigger than Dain, he didn't know how his friend had done it.

The sound of approaching footsteps had him drawing his dagger. Dawn's light filtered down into the hall through the cracks in the timbering, enough to see and be seen, but he was in no mood to hide and possibly too eager to fight. Each man of Balor killed now was one fewer to face later.

The footsteps faded down a different corridor, giving the man another day of life, and Morgan continued on toward the pit and the ironclad door that sealed it. Beyond the maze of the pit he would search for the passage that led to the caves below. Mayhaps Dain and Ceridwen would show up there from their sojourn through the guts of Balor's keep.

As he neared the door, he tilted his head to one side to listen. He had been to the pit only when Caradoc was taking wagers and fighting animals. Be they boars, bears, dogs, cocks, or a combination thereof, men were always stationed at the door during the spectacles to confiscate weapons in an effort to keep the bloodletting in the pit itself and out of the gallery. Whether there would be guards at dawn, he did not know.

Someone coughed up ahead beyond where he could see, and he cursed to himself. His luck was holding at bad. At least one man guarded the door.

Wisdom dictated that he proceed with caution, but he gave wisdom not a pittance of consideration. Tossing his dagger into his right hand, he drew his sword with his left. He was going through the damn door, no matter how many blocked the way. His strides were long despite his limp, and as he rounded the last corner, a quick glance proved the odds not in his favor.

There were three guards.

He did not hesitate, but clasped his two hands together, melding dagger hilt to sword grip, and swung a mighty blow at the first man, hitting him on the side of the head and knocking him senseless into the wall. The man slid down the timbers, blood running from beneath his helmet, yet even as Morgan raised his sword to block the second man's blade, he lunged in with his dagger and cut the first man's throat. There would be no dealing with the same guard twice.

The third man flanked him, and near hacked Morgan's arm off with his initial attack. Morgan countered with a quick cut up the man's forearm as part of his defensive parry. He met blow after blow, pressing his attack on two fronts with his sword and dodging in close to wound any unprotected flesh with his dagger. The lack of maneuvering room threatened him more than either of the mediocre swordsmen, but it was a true enough threat with the two of them bearing down on him. He blocked a thrust and ducked beneath another while the scrape of metal against metal rang in his ears. Then, of a sudden, the third man slammed back against the timbers, impaled by an arrow. The remaining guard was dispatched by another even as he gawked at his comrade.

Morgan let his sword arm fall, but kept his dagger up. That had been close. The swivin' flight of the second arrow had brushed his cheek, he'd swear it. Breathing heavily, sweat running down under his stolen hauberk, he looked down the hall for his rescuer—or his next opponent.

'Twas Llynya who stepped into the dusty stream of sunlight.

"*Malashm,*" she said, looking unkempt and yet wildly pretty by the light of day.

Surprised, he lowered his dagger. Her hair was dark, as he would have guessed, but from what he'd seen of her in the night, he would not have guessed her so lovely, her eyes so green, or her mouth so lush. "Good shot," he said, wiping the sweat off his brow. "Both of them."

"Ceridwen?" she asked.

He shook his head, still catching his breath. "Might have heard her voice. Couldn't tell for sure."

"Dain?"

"Alive. Last saw him diving into a tunnel on his way out of Helebore's dungeon."

"Aye, the place is riddled with holes snaking through the

ground." She walked over to the first dead man and rolled him onto his back. Quickly efficient, she patted him down for keys. When they weren't on his belt, she went to the next man.

Morgan watched, very aware of the shortness of her skirts and the graceful length of her legs as she bent over each guard. Her clothes moved with the fluidity of water. The twigs and leaves in her hair gave her a woodland nymphish look he had not noticed in their haste to scale Balor. But now, with the heat of battle flowing through him and dawn's light revealing her face, he wondered if she knew how perfect the moment was for a kiss.

She looked up then, and he had his answer. The sprite had no notion of the fetching picture she made, or of the path his thoughts had taken. Yet such innocence could be transformed with even a chaste kiss and a caress. He knew the way of it well enough.

"And you, Morgan ab Kynan," she said. "How do you fare?"

He grinned. There would be no kissing of dark-haired maids this morn. "I am but warmed and ready for the next foe," he assured her.

"Then let's hope the third man has the key." She gestured to the body at his feet.

He dropped to one knee and searched the guard. "There are none."

"Sticks!" she swore, though 'twas her tone rather than the word that let him know she was cursing. *Sticks?* He'd said worse as a babe.

He rose to his feet and gave the lock a thoughtful look, then reached into her hair for one of her sturdier twigs. "Oak?"

"Aye." She nodded, and a silky loop of curls tumbled down the side of her face.

Morgan near swore himself then, to counteract the sudden lurch he felt in his heart. He forced his attention back to the necessary deed, and with the tip of his dagger and the stick, contrived to release the lock.

"Stay light on your feet," he warned her, opening the door a bare crack and peering inside. "The pit is known for traps and wild boars, either of which could kill you in a heartbeat." He looked over his shoulder at her. "Mayhaps you should stay here. I'll come back for you, if the way is clear."

She gave him a look that plainly said she was not staying anywhere, and pushed by him. "You have not seen light on your feet, until you have traveled with me, ab Kynan. As for boars, I know their tricks better than the sows that dropped them."

There was naught for Morgan to do but follow her into the pit and pray she told the truth.

Dain pulled Ceridwen to a stop as soon as they reached a place where he could stand.

"Wait," he said, leaning his back against the wall, one hand gripping hers tightly, the other arm wrapped around her waist.

"Snit," she called ahead to her strange companion. He'd caught a glimpse of the boy before they'd dragged him into the tunnel, if boy he was. "Can you get some water?"

"Aye."

'Twas dark, yet Dain knew when Snit was gone. He felt on his belt for the cool crystal grip of Ayas and pulled the knife free, squeezing it in his palm. Blue light emanated from the crystal as he had hoped. Rhuddlan's magic was strong.

"Have you been hurt?" he asked, holding the dagger out far enough for the light to reach her face.

"Aye," she said, a pained catch in her voice.

A deep chill washed through the center of his body, his fear realized. He closed his eyes in defeat and dropped his head. Utter fool that he was, on the long ride to Balor he had succumbed to desperation and prayed to her God to keep her safe, and her God, the same who had abandoned him in Palestine, had refused him again.

"But only for the pain you have suffered, Dain," she said. He felt her hand on his cheek, the caress of her thumb. "Caradoc did not touch me with so much as a look. 'Twas you he tortured with his knife."

His eyes opened. "He did not rape you?"

She shook her head, and relief sapped the last of his strength. Still holding her hand, he slid down the wall, until they were both sitting on the earth and stone floor of the tunnel.

"Ragnor?" he asked. "Did you kill him?"

"Aye. I slit his throat," she said without a tremor.

" 'Twas a blessing, no doubt."

"No doubt." She was quiet for a moment, then said, "When Snit returns, I'll wash the blood from your face. Do the cuts pain you?"

A short laugh came up from his throat. "His intent was not to cause me pain, but to give me pleasure, the lying bastard, as if I had acquired a taste for his sickness. Like me, he is far better with a knife than he would wish. Any cuts he gives are apurpose and caused by no lack of skill." He adjusted his position and winced. She and that Snit of hers had near squeezed the life out of him, dragging him through the tunnel. "Caradoc could shave the down off a babe's buttocks and leave less than a blush to mark the blade's passing."

"I don't understand," she said in a softly confused voice.

He should have expected no less, but it was not easy to hear the question in her words. Still, he would not lie to her. "And I do, and mayhaps that is what you don't understand."

"Mayhaps," she admitted.

A sigh that was half groan escaped him as he reached into a pouch on his belt. She must have heard the worst of Caradoc's soliloquy and apparently wasn't going to have the grace to lie to him either. He brought out a Quicken-tree cake and broke it in half.

"Rhuddlan swears by seedcake for all that ails a person." He gave her a portion, then watched until she took a bite. "You heard Caradoc speak of a man, Jalal al-Kamam?"

Her gaze lifted and met his, the blue of her eyes enhanced by the light of Ayas, and for a moment he feared he would falter.

"Jalal trades in people, traveling the desert with his caravan of slaves to be bought or sold, for pleasure or pain, to whomever has gold enough to buy." He forced his gaze not to waver from hers. "I ended my Crusade as one of those slaves, some said the best he ever had. As *bedźhaa* I was sold many times to many people, until my worth as a magician proved more to Jalal than my worth as a whore."

Her lashes swept downward, and the hand he'd held she withdrew into her lap.

That hurt. He released another sigh. "I cannot be other than what I am, Ceri, and I cannot change what I once was—though God knows I try," he added in a disgusted mutter.

"I would have you no other way, except for the pain you have suffered." Her voice was a whisper, barely audible. She reached out and tentatively touched the bleeding scar on his wrist.

"Ah. That was only foolishness," he assured her with a small lie. "Nothing more. I was no child when Jalal chose me from out of Saladin's prison, and I, too, was given a choice." He slipped his hand around hers. "He was both savior and destroyer, and I often did not know where the one began and the other left off. He taught me the magic you like so well, Ceri, and much more besides the lowest paths of pleasure. Without Jalal, I could not have opened the Druid Door and would not have been in Wydehaw to save you."

"A steep price to pay for the saving of an unknown maid."

"But I know you now . . . and I have known you." His thumb caressed the back of her hand, adding an intimate meaning to his words.

Tears spilled from beneath her lashes, and when he bent to kiss them from her cheeks, she moved so that their mouths met.

"You are mine, Dain Lavrans," she whispered against his lips. "All that you once were, and all that you are, are both a part of me, will always be a part of me."

He kissed her then, unable to resist what she offered, even as he vowed to hide the worst of it from her with at least as much success as he hid it from himself. Caradoc with his talk of knives. Christ, even the buggery had been worse than the knives. If a man wanted to be cut, Dain had not suffered any qualms in doing it. If a man wanted to be tantalized with razor-sharp daggers scraped along his skin, he'd been happy to comply, and unlike Caradoc, careful enough not to draw blood unless Jalal had been paid for blood.

But the ambrosia. When demons crawled out of his mind in the night and slid beneath his skin to make him shiver and shake, they smelled and tasted of opium-laced *kif*. The fiendish stuff had stolen more of his soul than buggery had ever stolen of his manhood.

"If yer through, I haves the water." Snit, sounding none too happy, had returned.

Dain lifted his mouth from Ceridwen's. They were far from safe. Truly, he would not feel so until he had taken her north.

They both drank, and Dain offered Snit a piece of Quickentree cake, which improved the boy's mood.

" 'Sgood." Eyes as green as summer leaves watched Dain from above a black stripe of paint. The pair of them were marked as demons, though Dain doubted if they could conjure up a thimbleful of evil between them. A dirty *fif* braid hung down the left side of the boy's face. Dain said nothing, but wondered if Rhuddlan knew he'd lost one of his own. Despite the deformity of his body, Snit was undeniably Quicken-tree, and young enough to still have dark hair.

"I s'pose yer looking for a way out too," Snit said.

Dain shook his head. "A way in, to the pit, and beyond the pit to the Light Caves."

"The pit?" Snit wrinkled up his fine nose. " 'Tis a rank place, the pit, and good for naught but teasing the boars that run there."

"Loose?"

"Not all, but one pretty much 'as his way with the place, a big, nasty boar, name of Old Groaner. Caradoc's made a fortune off of that one, he 'as."

"Can you take us there?"

"Aye, if yer sure that's where ye want to go." Snit looked doubtful.

Dain was not. "I'm sure."

"Llynya!" Morgan yelled. Light, he needed more friggin' light. He'd lost her. She was as quick as she'd said, too damn quick.

The awful noise that had sent her running came again, a low, pained, and brutish groan echoing back and forth through the maze. It ended in a deep, rasping squeal that tore through the air and made the hair rise on the nape of his neck.

"Shit," he swore. 'Twas a boar. Mayhaps one left from the last match. A wounded boar someone had not finished off.

This far in, the pit smelled of blood spore and offal. Debris and bones were thick upon the floor. She'd get herself lost for sure. No one could smell their way through such a stench, and the light offered by the few smoking torches along the walls did little to illuminate the maze. He kicked aside a rotting carcass.

"Llynya!" He strode forward, sword at the ready, wishing he had a spear. Meeting a wounded boar with no more than the length of a sword between them would be a quick death.

He swore again, determined to find her. They had traversed most of the maze with her unerringly leading the way. Why she had spooked with the boar's groaning, he did not know. One instant she'd been next to him, and in the next, she'd been gone. Disappeared in a twinkling.

"Llynya, damn you! Answer me!" he bellowed, demanding a reply. If he drew the boar, so much the better, for he'd formed a sudden, inexplicable attachment to the sprite and would not have her harmed.

A softly sung song came to him then, winding its way through the maze on a melody of lilting notes. Could only be she. He followed the sound, and as he came closer to the source, noted the strange words of the verse:

"Fai quall a'lomarian, es sholei par es cant . . ."

A tremor of fear trickled through her voice. A blue light shone up ahead, around a bend in the walls, and he broke into a run.

"Pwr wa ladth . . . Pwr wa ladth . . . Pwr wa ladth . . ."

Her song became a nervous chant or a pleading.

Morgan skidded to a halt at the turn. 'Twas Llynya, aright, cornered by the boar in a dead end of the maze, holding him off with the wrong end of her dagger, which was doing the most peculiar thing. It was glowing.

Magic. He swore and crossed himself. Just his luck to fall for a pagan maid who wielded magic with the grip of her blade. She had the beast transfixed with the crystal light and her song.

Something was going wrong, though, for the rangy old boar was tossing his head, slicing at the air with his tusks, and stepping closer, his cloven hooves stamping up small puffs of dust. Her voice faltered.

Morgan did not hesitate, but moved in with his sword held high and brought it crashing down in a mighty blow, slashing into the beast's neck with the force of every muscle in his body. The cut was deep, severing the animal's spinal cord and dropping him paralyzed to the floor. The boar's eyes rolled back at him as blood gushed from the wound.

" 'Twas my duty . . . Rhuddlan told me . . . protect you," Llynya babbled breathlessly. Morgan put his boot to the animal's flanks and shoved the beast off his blade. "I thought to bait the boar, to keep you safe . . . I thought I could—"

With his sword free, he took two strides to her, gripped her chin, and silenced her with a kiss. She grew utterly still, and when he moved his mouth over hers, her lips parted, so soft and lush, for him to take his taste.

When the kiss was over, he raised his head and gazed into her eyes. "Sweet," he said, and would have said more, for all he'd felt, but words eluded him. She was sweet, aright, like nectar before honey, and warm, with her heat spreading out to wrap around him like a velvet cloak. Her eyes were the green of forest leaves and shallow seas, filled with stars, beckoning, beckoning. He bent his head to touch his mouth to hers once more.

"Morgan!" The call came from behind. He looked over his shoulder and swore for the kiss he would not have. 'Twas Dain, and Ceridwen, safe.

He turned back to Llynya. "When Balor is behind us, I will come for you," he promised. At her nod, he let her go and stepped aside.

Chapter 25

Llynya led them out of the maze and into a honeycomb of cave-ins and debris that marked what had once been the path to the Light Caves from Carn Merioneth. Rhuddlan had been right, Dain thought, the destruction had obscured any clearly marked passage, leaving only rubble to be picked through and narrow cracks to be squeezed through and even narrower ledges to be traversed above seemingly bottomless chasms. Without the sprite guiding them from above and the Quicken-tree working from below, they never would have found their way. Snit had not come with them, but had disappeared within moments of leading him and Ceridwen through the pit and to Morgan and Llynya.

Long after Llynya had brought them out of the pit, they'd glimpsed another blue light shining in bits and pieces through the dark up ahead. " 'Tis Bedwyr," she'd said, and been proven right when they'd finally spoken with the Quicken-tree man through a pile of rocks and broken beams blocking the tunnel. He'd helped each of them through with a warning to be careful, for the other side was naught but a rock slide into a yawning chasm, revealing to Dain for the first time the true breadth and depth of the caverns. The path they'd taken the night before with Rhuddlan, through the winding shafts of the Canolbarth, had not shown so much.

As they neared the Light Caves, they were hailed by others of the Quicken-tree, Liosalfar scouting the farthest reaches of the caverns, each carrying a dreamstone crystal blade. Trig was among the five to reach them.

"You've done well," he said to the sprite, then gave orders for one of the other men to backtrack Llynya's path with Bedwyr and guard the trail. Two others of the Liosalfar he directed with a gesture and a raised voice. "You know where you are needed. Go, and tell Rhuddlan all are safe."

The blue lights converged in a line down the rocky slope, flickering with each curve in the trail, until they disappeared into the abyss of darkness.

To the remaining man he gave a piece of material he pulled out of a pouch on his belt. 'Twas white cloth, finely spun wool, patched together and sewn with a shimmery thread of the Quicken-tree gray and green. "Give this to Aedyth and see what she can make of it. Tell her we found it near the Crwyn Track." The man left, and Trig turned to them. "We will await Rhuddlan at the scrying pool so there will be no delay in the ceremony."

"So soon?" Llynya asked, casting a glance in Morgan's direction before returning her attention to Trig. "They are tired and have been through much. I thought there would be time for all to rest."

"They can rest after the ceremony, if Caradoc is not already upon us. He will not lose Ceridwen without a fight. Nor will the monk."

"But Dain has been hurt."

Trig lifted his dagger for light to see by and swore under his breath.

"It looks worse than it is," Dain assured him.

"It looks like butchery." The Quicken-tree man's voice was grim.

"Caradoc calls it artistry. Do not worry overmuch, Trig. I still have the strength for Rhuddlan's hour of magic, though the ceremony part of his door-opening ritual might need to be expunged. I do not relish another 'purification' so soon after the last."

"There is no time for purification," Trig said. "Rhuddlan and the others have already been engaged beneath the keep, and though they have beaten back Balor's men, the victory is far from complete."

"What of my men?" Morgan interjected.

"They are with Rhuddlan, preparing what defense we can on the perimeter. When Caradoc comes again, we will be warned."

"Any of the mesnie who saw me or Llynya are dead," Morgan told the Liosalfar captain with a look to the sprite.

"And no one followed us," Dain said. "We came underground from the keep to the tower, through bore shafts barely large enough to hold a man."

"The place has more holes than a pauper's boot," Trig said, disgusted. "It didn't used to be such. The monk had a tunnel into the caverns we missed a fortnight past. We thought we'd sealed the caves from his tampering and had only the original passage to find when next we came."

" 'Twas one of your lads, Trig," Dain said, "who showed us the way. A lost boy, I think."

"Snit is his name," Ceridwen added.

"I know of no Snit," Trig said, "but there are enough of us here for anyone to find. If he knows his way about the holes, he won't be lost long. Come. There is no time to waste."

The Liosalfar led the way down the rocky slope into the Light Caves. In places they used stairs carved into the stone floor and worn smooth by the years, remnants of the cavern's history. Other times 'twas a cautious picking across scree and rubble. The deeper they went, the wetter the walls became, suffused with the briny smell of the ocean. A breeze came in along with the sea spray, carrying the warmth of sunshine into the cold dark.

Beside him, Ceridwen stopped. "Wait," she said, turning her face into the warm wind. "I know this place." Excitement edged her voice. "Come, Dain." She reached for his hand.

Following the drifting scent of sea and air, she led him from the main shaft. For all his worry of time, Trig said naught against the delay, and Dain saw the captain stretch his arm out in a gesture warning the others to wait.

The path widened, the walls on either side belling and rising to new heights. The air became fresher and warmer, and the light bright enough that Dain sheathed Ayas in his belt.

"Aye," she murmured. "Here 'tis." She reached out and touched a sinuous black line snaking along the wall. "As a child, I had to stand on tiptoe to reach them." Another line curved down from the ceiling to join the first, and she smiled. "My mother said she had to do the same when she was a little girl, stand on tiptoe to touch the dragons, the sea dragons."

"They do not look so fierce, Ceri," he said, watching her, waiting for what would come. She had been a child here.

"No," she agreed, trailing her fingertips along the single lines, spreading her hands as the lines parted and the paintings became more intricate. "They do not look so fierce . . . yet."

He moved with her farther into the light. The misty rays of the sun rimmed her face and streaked across the demon marks on her cheeks. Her hair was wild about her, uncombed and unbound, falling to her waist. Her gown was dirty, the hem caked with mud. She looked the perfect hell angel, and the love he felt for her hurt, leaving him completely unmanned.

A grin tugged at his mouth. He should have known 'twould take a woman to finally do the deed.

"See?" she said, casting him a quick smile. "Here are their claws, and the wings that make them fly under the waves. The scales start back there, like great fish. They have whiskers and golden cat's eyes." She moved her hand over a broad curve crowned with a long, scalloped fin. "This one is Ddrei Glas. She's pale green to match the sea foam by moonlight. And this one . . ." Her hand moved higher to the bigger creature whose tail wrapped around the smaller one's body. "This one is Ddrei Goch. He's red to match the first break of dawn across the water."

"Fangs as big as boar's tusks." He traced one long tooth of many, his fingers sliding along the blackened groove. The rock was warm, warmer than he would have thought possible for a cave wall on a cold cliff above an ocean. He flattened his hand, touching more of the stone, and with sudden insight knew exactly what he was feeling—a trace of magic. The vitality of it was unmistakable.

His desert master would have been pleased.

"Fierce," she said, looking up at him.

"Aye, Ceri. Fierce." He removed his hand and reached out to tuck a wayward strand of hair behind her ear. Mayhaps there was room for forgiveness in his heart. Not every day in the desert had been dark. Jalal had shown him wonders beyond most men's imaginations: towering cities, ancient and abandoned, lost in the sands; maps to all the stars in the heavens, and to all the lands and waters of the earth; the way of magic itself.

"Come," she said. "There's more." She took his hand and walked with him to the mouth of the cave. The outcrop was of rough limestone set high on the cliffs above the westward ocean. Sea thrift hugged the rocky nooks and crannies, showing pink in the late morning sun. "This was my mother's place, where she would come to play her harp. The Dragon's Mouth. We could hear her, Mychael and I, while in our bed. 'Twas she who saved us that night, the night Gwrnach—" She stopped, a catch in her voice, and released his hand. After a moment, she continued, but did not renew their contact. Her hands were clasped at her waist, holding only each other. "She was playing, you see, and the music woke me. I was ever into trouble as a child, long before I was imprisoned in the abbey at Usk, and that night I made Mychael come with me on my grand adventure. I got us both lost in the Canolbarth."

A hastily wiped tear smeared the demon unguent on her cheek. He was tempted to offer his sleeve, but did not. His love could not save her this pain.

"Mayhaps we should have died in our bed and been gone with the rest of Carn Merioneth," she said.

"When it is time to die, you will die, Ceridwen. Not before."

A gust of wind rushed up the cliffs and curved around the natural bowl where they stood, ruffling her hair and gown.

" 'Twas so long ago," she said shakily, turning and looking at him. "Seems as though it happened to another."

He held her gaze, and when she came to him, he took her in his arms and kissed her. The trembling of her body subsided in the warmth of his embrace. The salt taste of her tears vanished on his tongue. He slid his hand up the side of her face and into her hair as he deepened the kiss. There was sweetness to be had in her, enough for a lifetime, and fierceness too, for she had survived Gwrnach's destruction, and she had killed Ragnor.

He did not release her when the kiss was over, but held her close, letting her rest against him as they looked out over the Irish Sea.

"Shall we be married?" she asked.

"Aye, we shall be married."

"And have children?"

"When you like, and when you don't like, you will be glad to have married a mage who knows the way of such things."

She was quiet for a moment, then asked, "Are you truly a sorcerer?"

He laughed that she had finally begun to doubt what he had so heartily denied. "Mayhaps," he admitted. "I have a small—"

"Gift of sight," she finished for him, laughing against his chest.

He leaned down and nipped her ear. "Wench. Aye, we will be married and have children. I will take you north and carve a palace for you out of ice, and every night I will melt it with my love."

She tightened her hold on him, then lifted her face to speak, her pale blue eyes warm with the golden light of the sun. "Do these things, Dain Lavrans, and I will ask for nothing more."

He brushed her cheek with his fingers before lowering his mouth to hers for another kiss. Waves crashed on the rocks below, sending sea spray up into the air as he held her. Such was the blessing she gave: to kiss and be kissed, and to be filled with the succor of her love.

Trig was showing only the slightest impatience when they rejoined the others.

"The Dragon's Mouth," he said, nodding in the direction from whence they'd come. "There's power there, and sanctuary, if it's needed."

"Aye," Dain said, meeting the Liosalfar's gaze. He'd recognized Rhiannon's place for all that it was.

The journey continued through the Light Caves to a great cavern on the edge of the Canolbarth. Dain remembered the place; Rhuddlan had brought them through it on their way to scale the cliffs of Balor. Torches now burned throughout the immense cave, lighting the high, dark reaches and casting halos in the clouds of warm vapor rising off a deep pool in its center—a scrying pool, Rhuddlan had said. Numa and Elixir came running to meet them, exuberant in their greeting, while others of the Quicken-tree prepared for the battle to come. Besides the Quicken-tree, there were strangers not from Deri. Ebiurrane, Rhuddlan called them, brought from the north by their leader Llyr.

Moira was there, ready with *rasca* and her healing touch. She cleansed him with water from the pool, which made him doubt its holiness, since she washed his blood back into the water each time she wetted the cloth.

"Will take more than that," a familiar voice said from behind him.

"Hush, child," Moira said.

"Madron." He greeted the newcomer without turning, holding still for Moira's ministrations. Elixir had not left his side.

A lavender skirt swirled into his line of vision. "In this place I am Moriath, daughter of Nemeton, and you are a fool who should have taken my advice rather than the maid, and saved yourself much trouble." She came full circle and sat in front of him on a smooth, flat rock.

"My trouble is naught but scratches," he said. She looked as lovely as ever, her auburn hair rolled, not braided, beneath her coif, her green eyes clear.

"Fool, fool, and twice a fool, your trouble has yet begun," she said, but not unkindly. "I have always liked you, Dain. Mayhaps too much. For you opened the Druid Door and provided some wit in my days, but this, what you have done, will cost you dear."

"Ceridwen is mine," he said, lifting his gaze to where the maid sat across the cavern with Elen and Aedyth, eating small cakes and drinking warm honeymead. She still had her crossbow, and he'd returned the Damascene to her. The women had cleaned her face and were braiding her hair while waiting for Rhuddlan. Numa lay at her feet in a fine show of canine loyalty. "Caradoc no longer wants her as a bride, and Rhuddlan wants only that we open a door. Then we go north."

"There are doors and there are doors, dear mage of Wydehaw," she said, "and I fear Rhuddlan's will test your mettle to the breaking point."

"My breaking point was reached long ago, Madron, and I am still here."

"But are you whole?"

His gaze strayed back to Ceridwen. "Nearly."

"Nearly will not be enough. Rhuddlan bound you to her for his own purposes, Dain, not yours," she warned him, and mayhaps would have told him more but for Rhuddlan's coming.

The Quicken-tree leader strode out of the dark reaches into the light, flanked on either side by Liosalfar and calling to all within hearing distance to begin the ceremony. Before he even reached the pool, the beat of bodhrans filled the air, and the Quicken-tree began circling around.

Ceridwen joined the others converging at the center of the cave, accompanied by Elen and Aedyth, with Numa staying close by her side. Like the Dragon's Mouth, the cavern of the scrying pool was a familiar place to her, a rock womb of the earth redolent with child-hood memories of feasts and dances and of being lulled to sleep by chants sung in many parts. During those times, her mother had held sway over the waters. This day, 'twould be herself, Ceridwen, who ruled—so she'd been told by the white-haired one, Aedyth, who had cleaned her face of the demon unguent and rubbed a warm salve into her hands, all the while gently singing, *"Domnu, Domnu, Domnu a matria patro leandra, eso a prifarym, Domnu."*

Ceridwen remembered Domnu, She who had the Earth as Her womb. Rhiannon had sung of the Goddess, and so had another on a long night in Wroneu. But she had no memory of how to rule the waters of the scrying pool. Since Aedyth had told her what she must do—yet had not continued on to tell her how, seeming to expect her to know—she had searched her mind for the way of it and had found naught. Nor would Dain's magic help her. Brochan's Great Charm had no place in the rituals of Merioneth. The knowledge she needed came from mother to daughter, down through the matriarchal line of an ancient Magus Druid Priestess, Arianrod. So the red book said with a brevity she wished it had accorded to dragons and blood. Though the book recalled such a lineage for her, she had been a child when Rhiannon had died. If her mother had given her the knowledge, she had long ago forgotten it.

'Twas then she noticed the woman in lavender sitting next to Dain. Her steps faltered, and the woman turned her head, capturing her gaze.

"Moriath," she whispered, and knew it to be true. Here was the crone unmasked, the diaphanous dream-giver, fair-skinned with eyes as green as the trees in high summer.

"Ah, Ceridwen," Moriath called, brushing down her skirts as she rose from beside the pool. "Come and let me see you." There was affection in the words, and an underlying command of such subtle strength that Ceridwen was unsure about ignoring it—for all that Dain had told her the witch was no friend.

Yet ignore it she did, choosing to hold her ground where she stood.

A faint smile played across Moriath's mouth as she measured the distance between them. "For certes you are a child no more."

"Have you tidings of my brother?" Ceridwen asked.

"No," the older woman said. "Not for many months, but then my concern has always been with you, as you are Rhiannon's daughter. 'Tis why I stayed so close to Usk, to watch over you."

Aye, Ceridwen thought, and there was that damn daughter thing again.

"Yet you would have had me wed Caradoc." 'Twas an accusation Ceridwen made, not a question she asked.

"I thought it best for all, to ensure the sanctuary of Carn Merioneth. I would have been here to see that no harm befell you." Moriath spoke without so much as a hint of apology, enduring Ceridwen's inquisition with galling grace.

"You did not tell me who you were that night in Wroneu, in your cottage. Why?"

"But I did, Ceri," the witch chided, her smile softening. With a small movement of her hand, she called Numa forth. The hound responded without hesitation, padding forward to circle around the witch twice with nuzzles and sweet growls.

Ceridwen accepted the refutation and Numa's desertion with her own good grace, for in her heart she had to admit the truth in Moriath's words: Deep in the dream, the crone had shown herself as the maid from her childhood, the trusted nurse who had found her and Mychael and protected and cared for them until she had left them with the nuns and monks.

"That Ragnor captured you was not meant to happen," Moriath continued, absently directing the hound back to Ceridwen's side with another slight gesture. "Nor that you were taken to

Wydehaw and put under Dain's care. These things created trouble and discord where there would have been none, if you had come to Carn Merioneth and taken your rightful place."

Ceridwen glanced at Dain. "In this you are wrong, Moriath. That I was given to Dain is the only thing to have saved me. We are but here now to open a door for Rhuddlan, then we go north, together. Carn Merioneth is a memory. 'Tis Balor, with all its wickedness, that rules above."

Moriath's answering smile held a hint of sadness, but no offense. "There is more than a door, little one. Open it, and you will see." She came forward and touched Ceridwen's face, a light caress of fingertips, the gentlest gesture of affection. "I gave you a dream in my cottage. Use it, and mayhaps you can save the man you love."

"Enough, Moriath," Rhuddlan cautioned. "I will not see harm done to either of them, as well you know."

"Nor to yourself," the witch said, her smile fading. "Yet even now you bleed from the battle your course has brought down upon us. I would not have had men with their killing swords in the caves again."

Moira stepped between the two, the solemnity of her demeanor and her sloe-eyed glances admonishing them both. In her hands she held a chalice chased with jeweled dragons, its golden cup full to the brim. " 'Tis time for words to end and the ceremony to begin. They must drink."

Dain looked at the transparent, incarnadine potion and thought not. Not for himself, and certainly not for Ceridwen. "I have drunk your *gwin draig,* Moira, and can guarantee we will accomplish nothing this day if I drink it again."

"The second drink is not like the first," she said. " 'Tis more like wine and less like the dragon." A smile touched her mouth and brought a rosy glow to her cheeks, proof that her chastisement over delay had naught to do with him—truly, never did a woman look more the sweet mother—but Dain was not reassured.

"You must drink," Rhuddlan said. "As must Ceridwen, if we are to free the *pryf* from the caves below the Canolbarth, a place difficult to reach in body, and a door even more difficult to breech, for 'tis a weir gate made of the ethers of the earth and the tides that locks the *pryf* in their bore hole. Far better to journey there through the scrying pool and use its power for the work."

"Ethers," Dain repeated, not liking this turn of things. Ethers were a tricky affair at best, and journeying through scrying pools even more so, if not impossible. Jalal had alluded to such journeys of the spirit, but had shown no inclination to make them himself, or to teach others how. "You, more than most, Rhuddlan, must know the limits of my magic."

"Your magic, if you choose to call it such, will suffice," Rhuddlan said. "The dragon wine will ease the way of it in your mind."

Dain shifted his gaze to Moriath, his jaw suddenly tight. The witch knew. "I have had my mind eased before, Rhuddlan, and still pay the price for the pleasure of oblivion. I will not drink."

Rhuddlan acquiesced. "I cannot force you. 'Tis not our way. But if you will consent to being cut, your blood can forge a path through the pool."

Blood. Worse and worse.

Dain swore to himself. Ceri had shown him dragons, and now Rhuddlan wanted blood. The significance was not lost on him. Damn Moriath and Rhuddlan both.

"And if I do not consent?" he asked.

"You will," Rhuddlan said. "We made a bargain, both sides of which will be kept or broken. I gave you the maid, Lavrans. Give me my hour of magic."

Blood, dragons, and magic, his salvation and his plague, the swivin' mystery of his life.

And the bargain. Did him no good to remember he had made his promise in the heat of lust. That he had been snared by that far-flung net again, even for Ceridwen, was salt in the wound. He looked around the cavern. Trig had called the Dragon's Mouth sanctuary, but Dain feared 'twould not be so for him and Ceri. A hundred Quicken-tree and Ebiurrane lined the ledges of the Canolbarth, and no less than fifteen Liosalfar encircled the pool. There would be no escape.

"You may have your magic, Rhuddlan, for all that it is worth." He pushed up his sleeve and offered the man his arm. He would allow no one to take Ceridwen away from him. They would survive Rhuddlan's hour of magic and then be gone.

Rhuddlan was quick to accept, drawing his dagger and making a fast, clean cut from Dain's elbow to his wrist. Blood immediately welled up from the wound, enough to prove the cut beyond a scratch. Ceridwen gasped as Dain flinched.

"If you go as deep on Ceridwen," he said between gritted teeth, "I will come for you, Quicken-tree man."

"Ceridwen will drink," Moriath said hastily. "No, Dain, do not look so," she added when he turned on her. "*Gwin draig* is in her blood, already a part of her, and will not harm her. The wine will only help her see her way clear."

"And my blood?" he asked, watching it drip off his hand into the pool.

"Your blood will mix with the wine she pours into the water and bind you more completely to her so that, supposedly"—she cast a glance at Rhuddlan—"if you followed her, you could help her or protect her."

"Protect her from what?" he demanded. *"Pryf?"*

"No. She needs no protection from *pryf.* But Rhuddlan fears Ceridwen's nature may not yield enough to complete the journey or the task at hand—whereas you, Dain, know the way of yielding well, whether it be in strength or in weakness. This is what Rhuddlan uses of you, the same skill that kept you from being destroyed in the place where the wind blows hot off the sea and all the mountains are made of sand."

A fair enough description of Akabah and the Nefud Desert. "So you did poke and stir around in my mind that night in your cottage."

"I touched you, aye, and saw the things you have done." Her gaze fell away from him for a moment, and so help him, a blush stained her cheeks.

"Do not judge me, Moriath," he cautioned her.

"I do not. I swear." Her eyes lifted to his. "But no matter your nature or your strength, Dain, 'tis your weakness that endangers you. Believe me, *in remotissimo angulo terrae* is not a destination for you to seek. Let her go, mage, and do not follow."

The remotest corner of the earth, he translated. Latin, like so much in Nemeton's tower. The witch was as learned as her father, but sorely mistaken in her advice.

"Untold suffering awaits you there," she warned him further. "Mayhaps death."

"And mayhaps the power Moriath would keep for herself," Rhuddlan interrupted. "She fears you would take her father's place here as you have in the Hart and in Deri."

"Is that why you gave me the dream?" he asked, turning to Moriath. "To keep me from this remote corner, where you say I must not go?"

"I didn't give you the dream," she told him. "I but looked, and it was there."

An ill-omened sign, he thought, for such a dream to lie unbidden in the depths of a man's mind.

"Can Ceridwen yield and still be strong enough to return?" he asked, knowing that despite all their talk of yielding, 'twas strength Ceri would need if Moriath proved to be right and he met his death in the deep caves—for he would follow her to hell and back if needs be. Mayhaps he was stronger than the witch allowed. For certes, even with a look into his past, she could not have seen all that it had taken to survive.

"She is Rhiannon's daughter," Moriath said with a return of confidence. "Born and bred to make many such journeys in her life's time." She paused, and her voice took on a less sure tone. "Listen not to Rhuddlan, Dain, for my fear is real. You are not Druid, and it has always been a Druid who has forged a union with the priestess through the wine. Nemeton and Rhiannon were the weir amidst the chaos for many years, and before that, 'twas Nemeton and Teleri, Ceridwen's grandmother."

Ceridwen had been listening in silence and liking none of what she heard. Her part in the ceremony had been ordained by her birth. That the Quicken-tree had used Dain's blood much as Caradoc would have used hers was an abomination. That Dain would be put in danger, she would not allow.

"Moriath is right, Dain," she said, stepping forward and taking the chalice from Moira. "You will not come. Rhuddlan will drink with me." She cast a cold glance at the Quicken-tree man. "Let his be the nature that yields, if yielding it takes." 'Twas no request she made, but an order, and before anyone could stop her, she lifted the gold cup to her lips for a long swallow.

When she was finished, she gave the cup to Rhuddlan. Pale gray eyes rimmed in green shone at her over the golden chalice. "You are strong, as I thought," he said. "Let us hope you also know the way of yielding, if yielding it takes, and prove me wrong in the other." He took his drink.

"That is unlikely," Moriath said with exasperated churlishness, "if we are all run through by Caradoc and do not survive the day. Sweet maid, Rhuddlan has it all his way. It mattered not if he drank. He goes when and where he might in the caves, doing whatever he wishes, excepting for opening the weir gate he made the night Carn Merioneth fell. For that he needs you, and you have drunk, as well you should have, but there is no escape for Dain, unless he devises it himself and chooses not to follow you. Moira herself started his blood in the pool. Rhuddlan has but thickened the mix. The two of you are bound, and for that we have a war beneath the keep."

"Watch the water, Ceridwen," Rhuddlan commanded, draining the chalice into the pool. He looked to Moriath. "You shall have your chance. If she can see her way to the weir gate, I will not interfere. If she cannot, I will drag both her and Dain there myself and put them to the task."

"She will see."

Ceridwen looked to Dain and prayed that she would see, and that she would finish her task before anything could go amiss and he tried to follow. Moira was already sealing his wound with *rasca,* which gave her heart. His pain would soon be gone.

"You are not needed here, Dain. I do know the way of this." She spoke the lie confidently, her gaze steady, and he smiled in that way of his.

"You are *alkemelych,* Ceri, the small magical one. More than any other, my faith is in you."

She had not fooled him.

The sound of the drums grew louder as she lowered her gaze to the pool and prayed for guidance, though who she prayed to was a mystery. She could no longer put a name to God.

Wisps of vapor rolled and curled across the dark water like storm clouds brewing far out to sea, *nebelmer.* She felt nothing of the wine, until . . . until the pool beneath the steaming mist quieted itself and she not only saw the quietness, but sensed it slipping inside her.

Daughter of Rhiannon . . . The words slid into her veins along with the dragon wine, soothing her, showing her the way. *Daughter of Teleri, daughter of Mair, Nessa, Esyllt, daughter of Heledd and Celemon from the line of Arianrod.*

Her vision of Arianrod was clear. She rose from the stillness of the pool with a river as her hair and eyes the deep blue calm of the ocean, she whose essence was as one with the waters of the earth. There was power in water, sweet elixir of life.

Beloved daughter of Don, called Danu, Dana of the light, Domnu of darkness who has the earth as her womb.

A chant rose and fell around her in a lilting, hypnotic rhythm, a hundred voices singing. *"Dommmm-nu, Dommmm-nu, Do-amm-nu. A matria patro leandra, eso a prifarym, Domnu."* Stone Mother, lead us to the deep cave of *pryf.*

Aye, she knew where the heart of the earth lay, *in remotissimo angulo terrae,* and she knew she must go there. She bent down and dipped her fingers into the pool, and the water became a part of her, lapping at her skin and sinking through her pores. She had fought this place, this moment, this responsibility, and all of her fighting had been misspent, for there was nothing to fear. 'Twas her duty and her right to open the weir gate and all doors that came before her. Her mother had done it, and her mother's mother, opened doors and seen through gateways farther into the distance than any horizon could hold. The Light Caves and the Canolbarth were her ancient home. 'Twas where she belonged, Ceridwen of the Cauldron, blessed chalice.

And yet she would not stay, for north was where her future lay—north, with Dain.

"Domnu, Domnu, Domnu," she sang, rising to her feet and letting the water flow back into the pool, taking her essence with it.

The vaporous steam slowly stretched into ethereal strands and rose into the darkness, released from the water one by one and in pairs. Without the misty veil, the depths of the pool became visible, and 'twas in those depths that Ceridwen saw the abyss.

She reached out with her hand, thinking how easily she'd found the place where she must go.

In a crystal cavern far beneath the Canolbarth, a man strode along the length of a gaping chasm in the floor. He had to keep his head low to miss the ceiling, and hold his quiver in front of him to keep it from being ripped to shreds by the sharp, jagged walls. His unstrung bow he held by his side, his hand wrapped around the leather grip, which was finished at each end with strips of white wool bound with grayish-green thread. A length of rope was looped across his chest.

The shattered damson stones on either side of the chasm picked up light from the blue crystal he carried and cast their amethystine glow before him, into a tunnel of darkness. Two months past, the floor had been unbroken. He'd watched the crack begin, and grow, and zigzag its way across the cavern; and he'd felt the final giving way of the crystal as it had been torn apart by the twisting and turning of the giant wyrms trapped in the bowels of the earth below. Change was the way of all things, but he sensed doom at the breaking of the damson shaft. He'd tried everything he knew to free the *pryf* and guessed at half of what he hadn't known, taking chances whose risks went far beyond life and death, and still the weir gate defied him.

He reached the end of the low place and slipped into a larger darkness lit only by his crystal. Behind him the damson continued to glow. Without slowing his gait, he slung the quiver over his shoulder. Men were fighting above the Canolbarth, and though the fight was not his, his instincts were running rampant with the need for him to be there.

Chapter 26

Ceridwen put her hand into the rising mist. At her feet, the scrying pool was glass smooth, yet the steam continued to thicken and swirl about her like a cloud, bringing the vapor up into the air. 'Twas warm and growing warmer, and smelled of salt. She stared down into the clear depths of the water, entranced. The sealed weir gate floated there, in the abyss, colored the deepest green, a perfect circle set into the huge bore hole, round and pulsing, a shimmering thing.

"She's taking too long."

'Twas Rhuddlan's voice, but he was wrong. No more than a minute had passed since she'd felt the stillness of the wine.

" 'Tis her first time, elf-man. Patience."

Around her the song to Domnu swelled and receded, the chant sung with a resonance and depth that made her tremble inside, and above and below and beyond the song were the bodhran drums and the sound of a word . . . a word of power and grace. She had felt it upon her lips in Moriath's dream, while she'd searched for the way into the *pryf* nest, into the dragon nest. Now she heard it for the first time—*Ma-rahm, ma-ma-rahm.*

She looked to Dain through the wisps of vapor. "Ma-rahm," she told him, smiling. "Not sezhamey."

He reached for her hand, but she denied him with a shake of her head.

"Do not follow where I go. There is no need." She was Rhiannon's daughter.

The deepening fog spiraled up around her, round and round, with her body as the axis of its orbit, warming her skin and heating her soul, until with an artful sweep of her arm, she parted the veil of white and was at the weir gate.

Aye, she thought, her smile broadening, she knew the way of this. 'Twas in her blood, through and through.

She stood on the threshold of the gate and looked upward to its farthest reaches; seven times her height it was, solid, though with the fluid look of melted glass. The shimmery emerald-green door filled the bore hole, with naught else to be seen except for the rim of rough-hewn rock encaging it.

'Twas a thing of heat. Warmth radiated from it like the rays of the sun. Rich, verdurous light pulsed and streaked away from its outer edges, crackling and resounding in the heights and depths of the vaporous clouds billowing about her. Where the green light faded, heliotrope began, in eight spokes of slowly circling brilliance. She watched the lights flicker and shine and suffuse the mist with color, and thought with awe that Rhuddlan had made this marvelous, extraordinary thing with naught but ethers and the magic of the *tylwyth teg,* for she had heard Moriath call him elf-man.

Filled with wonder, and commanded by a presence she instinctively knew to be Rhuddlan—aye, and she could almost love him, for he was faerie—she lifted her hand to the seal. Ancient markings covered its surface, line after line of mystery flowing down its face in the ridges and curves of bas-relief. She pressed her palm to the shimmering plane, and the annals began sliding beneath her hand, revealing their secrets of dragon keepers, and time watchers, and eon upon eon of Quicken-tree history: a time when Liosalfar and Dockalfar had been one and their place had been Yr Is-ddwfn; tales of the Wars of

Enchantment and of the *tylwyth teg*'s coming to man; a record of the time of trees. The emerald surface spoke of beginnings long lost to the most ancient memory: of the Sun and the stars and the vault of the heavens, of the Moon, and of the Earth, great orb of celestial dust . . . *vessel of matter and thought, of the eternal mystery and miracle of life, death* . . . circling, ever circling and being coiled round and warmed by a great serpent devouring its own tail . . . *held in the grip of wisdom, lightning of the cosmos, sword of the gods, One is All—Ouroboros* . . . The flood of deep knowledge poured into her, pulsed through her in a blaze of searing light, and she pulled her hand back with a pained cry.

Looking down at the flesh of her palm, she saw that she'd been burned with a symbol she'd never before seen. It glowed on that tender space in graceful curves, and the hurt caused her to cry the tears of Arianrod. The drops of salt water splashed into her hand, healing the mark and relieving her suffering.

Moriath had been wrong. She could not open the weir alone. Woman and man together made the bond that ruled the elf-man's gate, one into the other. There was no harm for Dain in this journey through the scrying pool.

Wiping the tears from her cheeks, she reached for him, calling his name in silence, and his hand came through the mists to take hers, the iron-and-teeth bracelets of Ceraunnos still banding his wrist. There was no hesitation in his action, no doubt in his touch, only sureness. Where their hands clasped, pale ivory light surrounded them with a soft glow . . . *Amor, lux, veritas,* such is the way to the stars.

But they need not go so far, not this day.

She tightened her fingers around his, looking past the pagan bracelets and into the fog. He was naught but a dark shape half-hidden within the swirling rising mists. She called to him again, and one by one the layers between them dissipated, until she could see the charm marks on his gambeson and his hair rippling like a veil in the wind of the abyss. Wisps of fog clung to him as the final mist lifted, crowning him in gossamer and trailing down the length of his body in wind-driven tatters.

"Dain." She spoke his name, and he took her in his arms.

Strength was his magic, his body the shield and haven she needed to do what must be done—to yield, and yield yet more, with all of her being, to soften and release her mind so the ethers of the weir gate could come into her and be consumed by the fire of the sun in the Mother Goddess's heart, and thus the *pryf* would be free and the way opened to Yr Is-ddwfn.

"You have come where Moriath has warned you not to tread," she said, her cheek resting against the softness of his Quicken-tree cloak, "but I swear all will be well."

"Aye." He drew her nearer with an easy flex of his arms, bowing his head closer to hers, and his breath came warm and soft in her ear. "In the hours we have watched and waited, I feared only that you would not need me, Ceri, not that you would call for me."

Hours, she thought, not the mere moments she'd felt. "Then have not even that fear, sorcerer"—she looked up at him—"for this door Rhuddlan has set us to cannot be breached without you. 'Tis why he bound us."

At that, he smiled. "The one thing I have learned in this place is that we were bound long before Beltaine, Ceri. Mayhaps even before the night Ragnor brought you to Wydehaw."

She understood. Standing before the weir gate, she felt a familiarity with him that went far beyond the time she'd known him. One short season of spring could not hold all the love of him that ran through her heart, for 'twas even more than she had for the lost Merioneth. When the time came to go north, she would be by his side; her love for Dain Lavrans would set the course of the rest of her days. She raised her mouth to his and gave him a kiss of peace, the sweetest blessing she could bestow, before turning to face the door.

Dain kept one arm around her waist, holding her close and regarding the strange place she had brought him. Jalal had never known such, nor such a woman. In these things he had surpassed his desert master.

But not Rhuddlan, elf-man, Moriath had said, and he knew it to be true. Not the elves of imagination, fanciful creatures, but a man-child of nature, *tylwyth teg*. 'Twas Rhuddlan, even more than the maid, who had forced him to the weir, waiting all these years, it seemed, for only the right bait to bring him to heel—Ceridwen ab Arawn.

The gate was nothing to fear, Rhuddlan had said as they had watched Ceridwen glide through the mist toward the weir gate. Journeying to it through the waters kept them from the gate's dangers, of which there were many, as Moriath had warned, but what was merely seen could not harm, Rhuddlan had assured him, and what was felt would be mitigated by the scrying pool. Dain had turned to the Quicken-tree man where they both stood by the edge of the steaming water. He'd held Rhuddlan's translucently gray gaze, and he'd known the other man had not told all. There was danger for him somewhere in this place. He sensed it strongly enough that he would have turned away rather than walk into the thick of it, if not for Ceridwen.

Aye, the elf-man had chosen well the lodestone with which to draw him in. He had glimpsed the weir through the vapors while watching Ceridwen, yet still felt awe standing before it. As he'd waited by the pool, the heat of it had emanated from the water and warmed the great cavern. Heat from the past, Rhuddlan had told him, for the weir was a thing of the past, and the past was hot. Dain trailed his hand through the mist and watched the fine strands of it leave his fingers and twist into tiny green, white, and heliotrope whorls.

This was true magic, this place out of time where Nemeton had stood. The bard's marks were upon the emerald surface of the gate. Not all of them, not the Latin or Arabic, nor the runes Dain had found amongst all the other writings in the Hart, but only the most mysterious signs, the ones he'd never deciphered. The key to ultimate transformation? he wondered. Or that which would seal his doom?

"Ma-rahm, maa-aa-rahm, la shadana may-am," the Quicken-tree chanted, drawing power into their voices from deep in their bodies, then filling the cavern with that power. "Ma-rahm, ma-ma-rahm."

"Now we begin," he heard Rhuddlan say with satisfaction.

Ma-rahm, Ceridwen thought, and began to sing, matching her voice to the wild ones as her mother had done before her. The word had no simple translation, but she knew that in the way the song to Domnu had led her to the womb of the earth, ma-rahm allowed entrance, as a blossoming bud allowed entrance into the heart of the flower. 'Twas all the same, an opening and a release, the bringing of one into the other.

Dain heard Ceridwen's voice and the echo of it off the weir. He felt the resonance of it caress his skin and set up a counter vibration inside the vortex. On the other side of the mists, the Quicken-tree chant grew stronger, the words sung into the air where they were captured by the swirling edge of the abyss and pulled down inside with him and Ceri.

He knew the use of sound and voice—was a master himself in the skill—but he had heard naught like this, a hundred voices in concert to work magic.

"*Ma-rahm, ma-rahm,*" they sang, and the drums answered with a quickening of their rhythm. A faint color change washed over the bright green surface of the weir, leaving an opalescence in its wake.

This was the way then.

"Take heed, Dain," he heard Moriath warn him. "You can go farther than you can come back."

Mayhaps. But his journey was yet young. He joined his voice with Ceri's, and when she laid her hand once again upon the gate, he laid his beside it.

The gate was warm and silky to the touch.

A hand came down on his shoulder, Rhuddlan's, and Dain felt the elf-man's strength flowing into him, along with a pressure to hold him where he stood. Rhuddlan would have this thing done, he thought, yet no force was needed to hold him at the door. The thing had its own allure, a lush mix of history, ritual, and arcana sliding beneath his hand and being made known to him through the skin of his palm—wondrous trick. Woven through it all was a rich vein of the ageless mysteries of mankind.

Moriath's warning came back to him, for no matter the cost, he feared he would follow that seductive thread to its core. Thus he cautioned himself to let reason be his guide, then he spread his hand wider on the door and glided it slowly, warily, across the green surface. To die for knowledge would be self-defeating at best. He would follow the vein for a moment, no more.

And so the moments passed, one after the other, each more intriguing than the one before, as he learned secrets of time and space and here and there; a map of death showing a progression of states and colors, most interesting and not what he'd imagined; and a flicker of life beneath his hand where he held Ceridwen about the waist— genesis. He looked to her and found her deep in concentration, her eyes closed, her face lifted, the light of the weir dancing over it; a woman looking inward and seeing all. She knew, beautiful woman, radiant within his embrace. The gate could be opened; he learned that. The seal, an ether concoction of earth and seawater, could be broken—if a man would but wean himself from the luxury of the door's touch.

He continued the slide of his hand, soaking it all in, thinking not to deprive himself just yet. He was strong, and here was all he'd ever sought: the keys to transformation, redemption, salvation, even immortality—he was sure—and all of them within his reach. He pressed his hand flatter against the gate, wanting more, and it suddenly gave way, leaving nary a hairbreadth between him and the surface. An instant of fear was quickly ameliorated by a pleasurable heaviness filling his body, a sensation worth the risk and proving the wisdom of his action, for he would have more. Sweet ease. The heaviness caressed him from the inside out in deepening shades of oblivion, sinking him into a life so rich, he wondered if he was nearing the place where death began.

He removed his arm from around Ceridwen, letting her go. She need not follow him here. In fact, 'twas best if he went alone. He knew this country . . . too well.

Another hand reached for him then, much less gentle than the one on his shoulder, and smaller, but no less strong. It cupped his chin and pulled his head up to meet a set of fiery green eyes.

"Fool man," Moriath said, her voice as fierce as her grip on his jaw. "You are at this too long. Follow not that path in your mind—cursed thing from out of the desert. In this place, it can only lead you to a strange death. Fight for what you would have, Dain, before your weakness destroys you."

She released him, and he looked back at the weir gate. It would consume him if he did not break away. Already his hand was sunk into it nearly full across the backs of his fingers, yet the desire to go even deeper was greater than his will to fight, more a need than a temptation, a desperate need. Aye, he knew the way of yielding to pleasure and a thousand ways of surrendering to solace. 'Twas his mortal weakness, as Moriath had said. A strange death, she'd promised him, and long ago she'd told him Nemeton had died here. Had it been thus that the mage had met his demise? In desperate longing?

The question no sooner formed in his mind than it was answered with blood, a red wash of it beneath his hand, obscuring the emerald surface of the gate. *The Beirdd Braint of the Quicken-tree, Nemeton, did not die in search of pleasure or knowledge, but in battle with a blade through his heart, killed by Gwrnach the Destroyer; and behind the Druid, raped and gutted by a golden-haired youth, son of the Destroyer, the lady Rhiannon died in a pool of her own blood.*

Dain jerked his hand away and stumbled back, freed by the truth and the horror and the blood. Always blood. An uncontrollable trembling seized him along with a flash of pain so sharp, it made him cry out and sent him to his knees. He slid his arm around his middle, a vain attempt to contain his body's yearning to return to the insidious bliss of the door. He'd felt such before, which only made it worse, for he'd succumbed again.

Save me.

Grim-faced, he looked down at the red stain covering his palm. Revulsion churned to life in his belly, and he fought the urge to lose the contents of his stomach. Damned, blessed sight. He would have died there, if not for his damned gift of sight. More than words had been upon the gate. A vision had been there: he'd seen the Druid's death and heard Rhiannon's last scream, her voice like Ceridwen's, her hair the same, her body, her face—'twas all of the daughter.

Save me.

He held himself tighter and tried to draw a deep breath into his lungs, vaguely aware of the tears tracking down his face. He had thought it Ceridwen lying there, raped and cut down by Caradoc's blade, the life within her flowing onto the cold stone like wine from a broken cup. The shock and horror of it had overridden every other instinct in his body.

Moriath could not have known, for no matter the gains to be had, the witch would not have sanctioned a betrothal between Ceridwen and her mother's murderer.

He lifted his head to look at Ceridwen. She was still entranced, still working her magic upon the gate. *Christ, Ceraunnos save me.* He'd thought he'd lost her.

Ceridwen knew of Dain's pain, had felt it as it had washed through the weir. She had heard his cry and could feel his tears as if they ran down her own cheeks. He was a part of her, as was the gate and the creatures and the place beyond. She had put her hand upon the emerald surface again and felt not heat, but oneness. The warmth of the whole had lain up against her like the softest coverlet, molding itself to her, to every part of her body, and through its touch, expanding her existence beyond the boundaries of her skin. Then she'd brought the whole of it inside herself.

Her lips were curved by their own accord in a smile. Pure light radiated from the center of her being, the bright core pulsing. The Mother Goddess heart.

Rhuddlan removed his hand from Dain's shoulder, knowing there was no more to be done. Nemeton's and Rhiannon's deaths had initiated the weir's existence. The vision that relived those moments had been the key to unlocking the ether's hold—that fateful wash of life's blood brought forth by Lavrans's gift. And Ceridwen had proven him somewhat wrong. She was quite capable of bringing about and containing the gate's destruction. The dismantling had already begun, with one opening where Dain's hand had been and another where the gate symbol had burned hot in the maid's palm.

He shifted his gaze to Ceridwen, and for her sake was grateful she was no more than she was, surefooted in the mists, a good tracker, and, in the end, strong enough to yield herself to the heart of the Mother Goddess. Without the gift of deep sight, though, she would be useless in the gateway of time; yet the lack had spared her from seeing her mother die. He wished another could have been spared.

He did not need to see Moriath's tears to know she was crying. That one always saw too much. She was her father's daughter and would have claimed a place as Magus Druid Priestess at the scrying pool, except for Rhuddlan himself denying her. She had been bound to him as the Beltaine goddess in her seventeenth year, and he would not see her bound to another for any reason, with or without the magic of sex. She was a weakness he would not renounce, and in the end, his patience would outlast her stubbornness.

For certes she'd saved the mage. Lavrans suffered from a strange malady beyond Rhuddlan's experience, but Moriath had recognized it and known enough to intervene.

A fresh wash of opalescence cascaded through the weir gate, causing it to lighten and thin, and he felt a familiar restlessness begin deep in the earth. Rhuddlan smiled. 'Twouldn't be long now.

Dain reached for Ceridwen as the first tremor hit, pulling her close and bracing himself against the stone surrounding the gate. Her eyes opened with a slow sweep of lashes, and though the ground shook beneath their feet, she appeared profoundly calm.

"It's time to leave," he said, swiping the back of his hand across his eyes. He felt sick, shaken, but was still of a piece. The gate was ripping in places, starting to shred and tear, and the holes they'd made were growing larger. Their work was done. He made to turn back to the mists and was stopped by her hand taking hold of his.

"Wait," she said. "I would see."

He had no time to ask her what it was she would see, for they came then, up from out of the abyss with furious speed, streaking across the other side of the weir as dark shadows, making the earth tremble in their wake.

Pryf.

Larger than he had thought.

Much larger.

The size of castle towers, but alive, serpentine worms of the highest order.

Their keening cry resounded against the back of the weir, and where the seal was broken, a hot, gushing wind poured through, smelling of rich earth. The first worm rolled into a turn behind the gate, its body sliding across the emerald surface, twisting in a tight curve and heading back down into the bore hole. The second worm was bigger, its sheer bulk causing a collision with the weir. The force of the crash knocked both him and Ceridwen over as the ground lurched underneath them. The seal bulged out with a stretching, tearing sound, nearly touching Ceridwen where she'd fallen.

The thing would not hold under another onslaught, yet another would come, for through the gaping emerald holes, he could see tens and hundreds of the giant creatures, their bodies slickly black with a deep green cast, a clew of *pryf—prifarym,* the Quicken-tree had sung—twisting and spiraling up and down the whole interminable length of the abyss. *Born of the froth of a thousand serpents tangled in a frenzy beneath the stones of Domh-ringr.*

The Doom Rings of Judgment. Dain looked at the rim of rock encircling the weir and again into the wormhole, to the chaos at its core, and knew he dared not be judged here.

A bolt of purple light crackled in the center of the clew, and a single *pryf* broke free to make its run.

"Now, Ceri!" he yelled above the growing rush of wind and cries, tightening his hold on her. "We must leave now!"

Aye, he was right, she thought. The *prifarym* would break through soon, some to slide into the deep caves of the Canolbarth, others—the pale, silvery-gold ones farther down than she would ever see—to continue their swirling patrol of the abyss . . . *infinite chasm from whence came the world.*

And a few, like the one heading straight for them, the undulations of its young body propelling it up the shaft, to make their way out to the open sea.

Dain swore, scrambling to his feet and dragging her up with him. She cast one last glance at the giant creature closing in on the weir—its featureless face into the wind, the single-mindedness of its purpose like a shield before it—then with a sweep of her arm, she parted the mists and turned into the opening with Dain at her side, bringing them both back to the cavern of the scrying pool.

Moriath was there, reaching for her as the steamy clouds sank back into the pool.

"You have done well, little one," the older woman whispered, and gave her a serenely pleased smile.

Rhuddlan echoed the sentiment with his cool, gray gaze and a slight nod that implied both gratitude and dismissal.

Exhausted—and aye, she could feel Dain trembling at her side—they were taken to a part of the cave far from the pool and made to rest on soft piles of rugs, where Aedyth and Moira tended to them and brought them honeymead and seedcakes to refresh their spirits and bodies.

Chapter 27

Caradoc stormed into Balor's keep, the pain in his leg and his limping gait adding to his rage. His captain, Dyfn, flanked him on his left, keeping a goodly distance between himself and his master's sword, but by the gods, even at a distance, Caradoc could cut him down before the man could dodge. The only thing that stayed his hand was the battle they faced.

The first sortie had been lost. The pit guards had been found dead, one of them with his throat cut and two others pin-stuck with black-feathered arrows. Dyfn had taken thirty men into the boar's maze to rout Dain and his companions, but all they'd found was Old Groaner with his head cut off and tracks heading into a wall of rubble. 'Twas beyond the rubble that the true depth of their dilemma had become clear. The friggin' caves, deserted for all these years, were overrun by an army the likes of which Caradoc had not seen since he'd fought by his father's side for

Carn Merioneth, an invisible army made up of men hiding in the dark, their presence marked by flashes of cold steel and strange blue light. "The wild ones," his father had called them, and as they'd been defeated before, Caradoc swore he would defeat them again.

He stepped up onto the dais at the end of the hall, then reached down with both hands to lift his injured leg. The little bitch had nearly castrated him with her bolt, and for that she would pay.

"Bring me the hairless leech," he gritted from between his teeth, limping to his great chair. Dain Lavrans had chosen his side badly in this fight. Years ago, Gwrnach had allowed the survivors of the battle for Merioneth to escape. Caradoc was not so softhearted as his father. He would lead the full force of Balor into the caves and crush every living soul who dared to trespass beneath his keep— except for one, Ceridwen ab Arawn. He would kill her separately, with Helebore at his side to catch her blood.

With the ending of the ceremony, those of the Quicken-tree who could fight had gone into the tunnels of the Light Caves with the Liosalfar to help man the defenses. Scouts had reported a marshaling of the forces in Balor after Rhuddlan's first rout, and another attack was expected.

For himself, Dain had decided to make for the surface. He'd gotten what he'd come for; Rhuddlan could fight his own battles.

"Moira is sending over seedcakes for our journey," Ceridwen said, coming up beside him where he knelt by their supply packs. The dogs were with her and began sniffing around, seeing what was what. "And two thick rugs for our pallet, a pot of *rasca,* four gourds of something she called catkin dew—though it's hard to imagine collecting dew off catkins—and seven ells, a small fortune, in Quicken-tree cloth. She said Rhuddlan got far more than his hour of magic."

" 'Tis true," he said, tying down a strap with a quick jerk. He could not be gone soon enough. Unlike the Quicken-tree, who were contentedly overjoyed at the prospect of winning back Carn Merioneth in mortal combat, he had no desire to fight again. Lady Rhiannon deserved avenging; he felt that need down to his core. But just as surely as he felt it, he knew another would come to do the deed. A remnant of the weir sight, mayhaps, or his own gift, it did not matter. Caradoc's death was not to be his.

And the worms. The *pryf*. Was he the only one concerned that the creatures were free and making their way into the Canolbarth and could soon be at the great cavern itself? Rhuddlan had assured him that 'twas not the season for the *pryf* to rise above the midland caves, but given the speed Dain had seen, he feared the *pryf* would rise whether the season be right or nay.

The Quicken-tree leader had promised them a guide, a Liosalfar well versed in the ways of worms and skilled in their handling. Dain had scoffed. The creatures he'd seen were far too large to be handled by even a skilled man. They made elephants look no more than rats, and he'd thought to never see anything bigger than an elephant, not on land.

"And Moriath gives you these," Ceridwen said, holding out a pair of leather pouches.

He glanced at them before continuing with the packing of their supplies.

"Don't you want them?"

"No." God only knew what was inside.

"But you don't even know what they are."

His point exactly. The witch had seen him on his knees, the worst of his needs stripped bare. He wanted no gift from her.

"This one is from Edmee." The larger of the two pouches dangled into his line of sight, extended from Ceri's fingers.

His hands stilled in mid-tie, and his gaze lifted to her face.

She was looking down at him with a challenging tilt to her head, her brows arched in curiosity. He had not forgotten that she'd seen Edmee on her knees, with her sweet needs bared. Nor, it seemed, had she forgotten.

He rose to his feet and took the pouch. He did not hesitate in opening it, but shook the contents directly into his hand. There were six linen packets, each one small though not all the same size, and each one embroidered with fine green thread worked into the leaves of a plant: valerian, chamomile, dill, hawthorn, balm, mistletoe.

A reluctant grin tugged at the corner of his mouth. "She's a practical girl."

"A pharmacopoeia?"

"A receipt for headaches. We had talked of adding hawthorn and balm to the infusion. The mistletoe is her own touch. She must fear that you are going to be hard on me." He glanced at Ceridwen. "A bit of prescience, mayhaps?"

"She but cares for you"—Ceridwen's brows arched a fraction higher—"in her own way."

"In her own way," he agreed, his grin broadening, "though not as much as it may have appeared."

"It appeared to be a substantial amount."

He could not argue the point. Neither was the time right for explaining it, though he tried.

"When Edmee chooses to love, she will give of herself far more completely than she ever gave to me, Ceri."

"Then I wish her love," she said, her smile growing mischievous as she offered him the other pouch. "This is Moriath's gift. Dare you open it?"

Moriath. Madron. She had saved his life. He had watched her father die.

"You," he said, coward that he was. He nodded at the pouch she held, while he repacked Edmee's herbals.

She did as he asked, loosening the drawstring and pouring what was inside out into her hand. "It's a rock," she said, nonplussed.

A rock? He looked over at the small stone in her palm and felt his heartbeat quicken. No mere rock, this. 'Twas red, as all the writings had said the Philosopher's Stone would be, but not the red of cinnabar. Its color was clearer, yet 'twas no crystal like ruby or garnet. There was a transparency to it, though, for below the surface he could see crackling striations of a deep saffron color.

"Or glass," she said upon closer inspection. "Mayhaps it's another charm like Brochan's."

"No Ceri. 'Tis Nemeton's Stone." The bard had known the secret. Dain reached for the long-sought magisterium medicine, worker of wonders, healer of souls, and took it in his hand. No bolt of lightning struck him down, no sudden realization came to him. 'Twas not heavy nor light, not hot nor cold, but moderation itself. Yet he knew the gift for what it was.

He looked up, searching the cavern for Moriath and finding her by the pool speaking with Aedyth. She turned when his gaze fell upon her, and for an instant they were back at the weir gate, with her eyes shining green and fierce, full of power and knowledge beyond his ken, her hair flaming in auburn tendrils about her face. 'Twas what had saved him, her fierceness, and with the look she took due credit for his life.

Pretty thing, she thought, and he heard. She lowered her gaze to the Stone in his hand, then looked back up at him. *Use it as you may, or use it nay, mage. It matters not.*

He closed his fingers around the Stone, holding it dear, and a smile crossed her mouth. With that, she turned away.

Quicken-tree and Ebiurrane laughed nearby, their lilting voices sounding like clear water tumbling over rocks and down hillsides.

"Elves," Ceridwen said, looking to where the fair, wild folk sat around their fire, sharpening their daggers and filling their quivers.

"Aye. Elves." But not Moriath. His glance strayed back to the witch. She was as human as he, mayhaps more so.

He and Ceri had just finished capping their last water gourd when a commotion from above drew their attention and sent a hush rippling through the cavern. Dain's first thought was that *pryf* had been sighted, and he made to grab Ceri and run—he would not face those beasts unleashed, Quicken-tree or no Quicken-tree—but 'twasn't a cry of *pryf* that echoed off the cave walls. 'Twas a cry of Balor.

He swore. The Quicken-tree line had not held. Those who had been in the Light Caves came pouring out of the upper tunnels. Dain drew his sword and told Ceridwen to ready her Damascene.

"Cut quick—"

"And deep," she finished for him.

"And stay here," he ordered, then looked to the hounds and gestured for them to do the same.

The Quicken-tree were taking up arms and rushing to their comrades' aid, some to archers' positions high up on the walls. Dain knew his height and weight would better serve on the floor of the cavern. The foreign elves were not as tall as Rhuddlan's Quicken-tree, and the Deri elves had not his weight. Morgan and his band had realized the same, for even the youngest, Rhys, was bigger than the wild ones. The Welshmen fanned out, adding their strength all along the line.

Hand-to-hand combat resounded throughout the great cave, the clash and scrape of metal mixing with the cries of men. With the influx of fresh fighters, the Quicken-tree rallied long enough to halt Balor's crushing advance.

"To the Canolbarth! To the Canolbarth!" The command went out, and Dain immediately understood. Within the dark, winding shafts, the advantage of Balor's numbers could be overcome.

He finished his last Balor guard with a quick cut above the man's hauberk and raced back to Ceridwen.

Rhuddlan was with her, giving orders. "Go with Llynya. If she can get you out to the mountains, she will. If not, she will fight by your side."

It would be fight, Dain thought, wiping the sweat from his face.

"What of the Liosalfar guide?" he asked.

"The Liosalfar are soldiers first. I need every one to fight in the Canolbarth, enough to lure Caradoc into the maze, and enough to trap him from behind."

A good plan for the Quicken-tree, Dain thought; mayhaps not so good for him and Ceri. He looked at the sprite making her way toward them through the confusion of the retreat. Morgan was at her side. The Welsh prince was always an asset in battle, but Llynya was no Liosalfar, and Dain doubted if she knew a damned thing about handling *pryf.*

"Where is she, leech?" Caradoc demanded, holding Helebore by his throat next to a bubbling, steaming pool in the torchlit cavern they had won. Throbbing pains shot from his wounded thigh up into his groin even as a fresh stream of blood ran down. The whole lot of the enemy had bolted into the tunnels honeycombing the far end of the cave like rats down a hole. But which one held Ceridwen ab Arawn?

The leech gurgled a reply, scratching at the Boar's ever-tightening hands.

Caradoc released him with a curse and a command. "Speak up, man."

"The middle caves," Helebore rasped. "I have been there, and if you had but let me have her blood, I could find her."

"And without her blood, you cannot?" When next he had the chit, he'd gut her himself to get her blood.

"Aye. I can."

"Then show me the way." He turned to his captain. "I'll take eight men down the hole of the leech's choosing. Take the rest into the other shafts and fight to the end of it. Slaughter all of those who dared to trespass in my domain."

Dyfn nodded and lifted his sword for Balor's men to follow.

Caradoc turned back to the medicus. "Find the maid, Helebore, or find your grave."

What had begun as a mass exodus of Quicken-tree quickly deteriorated into small bands of refugees making their escape through the maze. The Canolbarth was a true labyrinth, full of twists and turns, with levels both up and down linked one to the other by smaller holes bored through the rock. Where it all led was a mystery Dain did not like.

He and Morgan had started out by following Ceridwen and the sprite, the better to protect them, but the first Balormen they'd come up against had been ahead of them, proving the capricious nature of the Canolbarth. Llynya had dispatched the scout with an alacritous blade, surprising Dain and allaying any doubts he'd had about her fighting ability. He and Morgan had made short work of the others. As for Ceridwen, he would have given her one of the Balor swords, but he knew from the times he'd held her that she had not the kind of muscle Llynya exhibited, convents being far less strenuous places to grow up than forests. She could never wield a sword with killing force and was better off with the Damascene. None of their pursuers would attack her outright anyway. Caradoc wanted her taken alive.

When they continued they arrayed themselves with Llynya leading, then Morgan, Ceridwen, and Dain, with the dogs bringing up the rear. The light from his and Llynya's dreamstone blades cast a bluish glow before them as they worked themselves deeper, through dry caves and galleries, and ofttimes through pools of water and narrow passages slick with mud. Other lights flickered at each tunnel juncture, and both up and down the smaller holes, and where the walls had worn through, proving them not alone. All of Quicken-tree was in the maze, all of Balor was behind them, and in between the two were the Liosalfar, picking off the garrison one by one, leading Caradoc's men into ambush and the natural traps of the Canolbarth.

Twice Llynya warned them of sinkholes, and more than twice, the sounds of running feet were interrupted by the clash of swords and men's death cries. For themselves, they met no other of the enemy, with Llynya leading them at a light run down every chamber and shaft she chose.

After what seemed like hours, a gradual widening of the passage they were following warned Dain of a broader chamber up ahead. Still, he was unprepared for the sheer immensity of the cavern they entered—and he called it cavern only because they were deep in the earth and reason dictated that no matter how large, the place had to have enclosed dimensions. It had to have ends.

"Abyss," Morgan said. They had all halted at the edge of the tunnel, stopped in their tracks by the vast sheet of darkness before them.

"Nay," Ceridwen whispered. "The abyss is not so dark."

Nothing could be seen—the dreamstone light was swallowed up a mere arm's length from their faces—but the emptiness could be felt. Heavy. Overwhelming.

"We must go on," Llynya said, unhooking her last full gourd from her pack. She sipped and passed the gourd to Morgan, who took a drink and grimaced. She grinned.

"What is it?" he asked, giving the gourd to Ceri.

"Catkins. It's good for journeying. Here." She ate a bite of seedcake, then passed the rest around. "We can get fresh water below. Others will be coming soon, and it won't be so dark."

Llynya spoke true, Ceridwen soon saw, for lights began appearing all across the face of the cavern wall. Blue specks of life heralding other bands of Quicken-tree and the Welshmen with them.

She watched more and more lights appear as from out of nowhere and hang in the darkness, showing where other passages ended. Blue shadows moved within each stationary glow, as if everyone had decided to rest and drink before making their descent.

"Look," Llynya said, a note of excitement in her voice, and Ceridwen turned back toward the cavern.

Her breath caught in her throat, for 'twas pure majesty she saw where there had been only darkness. Pillars of stone hundreds of feet tall rose in front of them, and huge rock icicles hung down from a ceiling they could not see, their tips catching the dreamstone light. Other rock formations jutted up from the floor, some as big as cottages, their gnarled, globular shapes reminding her of sand castles washed over by waves, and of much-burned candles whose wax had dripped and run and hardened, then warmed and dripped again.

A flow of stone covered one whole side of the cave, its opalescent surface like a gigantic frozen waterfall; and scattered throughout, showing in places on the floor and in long, irregular patches on the walls, were multifaceted sections of heliotrope quartz. They soaked up the dreamstone light and reflected it throughout the cavern, transforming the vast darkness into a fantasy realm.

"Rhuddlan holds court here," Llynya said. "See the thrones in the water off to the left, the place surrounded by the Sentinel rocks?"

"Rhuddlan is king?" Ceridwen asked, confused. She looked to where the sprite pointed and saw a still pool studded with candlelike formations. The water reflected the amethystine light and made the dais holding the massive chairs appear to float above the rest of the cave floor. A broad section around the pool was filled with pillars, some appearing no higher than a man, others twice that.

"He's king on this side of the mountain," Llynya answered, taking another bite of cake.

Before Ceridwen could ask who was king on the other side of the mountain, or, indeed, which mountain she meant, or king of what, the sprite took off. In fact, all of the Quicken-tree had begun to move.

Being lower than the others, they were among the first to reach the floor, and looking back, Ceridwen beheld another amazing sight. A magical web of luminescence crisscrossed the cavern face along the Quicken-tree trails, each piece of quartz holding the glow of dreamstone light long after the blade had passed, reflecting both blue and purple against the velvety black background of solid stone.

'Twas a wonder all its own.

'Twas a perfect dragon's lair, Dain thought. From a man who had believed in nothing, he'd been reduced to believing in everything, especially the impossible, it seemed. He looked from the web of light to the rest of the riches-filled cavern. Amethyst was abundant, some of it appearing to be of a quality fit for royalty. Rhuddlan's throne and the one next to it were carved of black marble variegated in a lush dark green that showed nowhere else in the cavern, though a vein of white marble ran through the cave, and there were chunks of ruby in the white. A man with a hammer or a good knife might be tempted to chisel himself a bit of gemstone. Dain hoped Morgan's men would have more sense.

"Once we're through the Hall of Lanbarrdein," Llynya said, "we can try for the surface by doubling back through some smaller tunnels that run up behind the walls." She led her charges across the cavern floor, hoping to reassure them when she herself needed assurance. All well and good for Rhuddlan to send her to Wydehaw to get the quicksilver woman for the O Great One's pleasure, but the end of that night had seen Ceridwen captured and near killed. Llynya had not forgiven herself yet for the damned curiosity and, aye, the yearning for a bit of adventure that had led her astray. She would not fail the maid again, but every time she'd tried to take one of the Canolbarth paths leading to the surface, she had been outflanked by Balormen. It had been only with great skill that she'd managed to avoid them all but once.

Despite what she'd just said, on the other side of the hall her options dwindled considerably, especially if the *pryf* were already present and clogging up the few tunnels that might yet get them into the mountains of Eryri. She had been given her orders, and she was willing to turn and fight if it came to that, but there was still a chance to see Ceridwen free of the battle.

A clear stream poured out of an opening high on the south wall of Lanbarrdein and wound a course east until it disappeared again beneath the rock. They stopped to refill their water gourds, as did others of the Quicken-tree. She searched the faces of those lined up until she found a Liosalfar from Deri. 'Twas Math.

The white-haired ones and the youngest of the Quicken-tree were finding places of refuge in the huge cavern, needing time to rest from the trek through the maze. Anyone of fighting age was either still in the Canolbarth or heading back there, except for the bowmen taking up positions on the high ledges of the hall. If Balormen escaped the trap in the maze, they would face yet one more deadly threat.

"Math, *malashm*," she hailed the Deri man as she made her way through the water runners that were coming and going in their efforts to resupply the men and women fighting.

"Llynya." He lifted a hand in greeting. A bloody bandage was wrapped around his forearm.

"You need to see Aedyth," she said when she reached him, gesturing to his wound.

"Aye, but not yet. Rhuddlan is bearing down on the Balormen from behind. If we can but hold this end, we'll have them."

"And if not?"

He finished a long draw off his water gourd before answering. "Then we'll fight in the hall, and if needs be we'll take Caradoc and all of Balor down into the deep dark and let the old worm crush them into dust." 'Twas Math's first battle, and the excitement of it showed in the bright green of his eyes. He was the youngest of the Liosalfar from Deri, barely older than Llynya herself.

"I would still try to get Ceridwen away to the mountains," she said. " 'Tis what Rhuddlan bade me do."

"Aye," he agreed. "The greater part of the battle is coming through the southern Canolbarth. If you take the passages behind the flow stone, you can stay out of the midst of it, but I would caution you to steer clear of the *pryf* nest. The *prifarym* have not been there in many years and no doubt that will be the first place they head."

"Thanks."

"Malashm." He nodded. "Good luck."

"Malashm." She turned to leave and was surprised to find Morgan standing close behind her. A blush instantly colored her cheeks. Strange man, she thought, to have held her so. His mouth had been warm on hers, and sweet in a way she had not expected of a kiss.

"So we go on?" he asked.

"Aye." She had scarce been able to look at him or keep her eyes off him since he'd kissed her, a disconcerting phenomenon, especially with him so close to her in the maze, but she hazarded a glance now.

He smiled at her, a quick curve of his mouth, and she wondered if he was the sort who could read minds. Her blush deepened as she looked away.

"I have heard you called both prince and thief this day," she said, staring at her boots.

"Aye, and I am both."

Good, she thought, for there was something she would know. She caught his eye for an instant, before retreating back to watching her boots.

"Rhys says you once stole an English earl from his tower bedchamber in the dead of night, though he had a hundred men-at-arms guarding his Cardiff keep, and that you spirited him away to the forest and held him there until he returned the land he'd taken from a Welsh chieftain." She dared to look up.

" 'Tis an old story, and I still collect a cash rent from two furlongs on the estate," he admitted with a slight shrug. His black tunic was torn in places, as was the long-sleeved white shirt beneath. Mud caked his boots up to his knees. He was two days unshaven, yet he still had the look of sunshine in his eyes. Blue sunshine, as clear as a mountain stream.

"Rhys says you nipped half a year's rents from a bailiff over by Hay-on-Wye and gave it all back to the tenants," she continued.

"Not all," he assured her, his tone implying he'd kept more than he'd given, though Rhys had told her different.

"Rhys says—"

"I didn't realize you had spent so much time talking with Rhys today," he interrupted her. "Mayhaps I need to give the boy more work."

Undaunted, she took up where she'd left off, anxious to get the important thing said before she lost her nerve. "Rhys says you can lift the yellow off a buttercup and return it to the sky, and I . . . and I—" She faltered just a bit. "I would know the trick of it, if you would teach me."

It was the most forward thing she'd ever done, deliberately asked a man to spend time with her—and then there was the trick itself. Sticks! If she could lift the yellow from a buttercup, she could learn to lift lavender from violets and green from grass. She could make rainbows at her whim, turn raindrops into colored gems. The possibilities were endless, utterly endless.

Morgan was both charmed and perplexed, thinking she couldn't possibly have taken Rhys's comment literally. The yellow off a buttercup? Why, who but God Himself could do such a thing? Yet he had only to look at the artless expectation shining in her eyes to know she thought it true. Wondrous creature, she was beyond any expectation he'd ever had. She believed in the impossible. And why not? She was the one who made light from the haft of her knife. She was the one who held boars at bay with a song.

"In truth, I have never tried," he finally said, brushing the tips of his fingers across her soft, soft cheek. "Mayhaps when we reach the mountains, we can work the magic together."

At her nod, he would have taken her in his arms and kissed her for the rest of his life, except someone called to her. She looked away, and with a pass of his hand, he stole a leaf from her hair.

She never knew.

"I must see Math before we go," she said, turning back to him. "I will only be gone a moment. Wait for me."

Aye, he would wait, he thought, sliding the leaf inside his shirt, next to his skin. He wondered if Dain had been as easily seduced by magic. As to his friend's damnation, he felt surely that it had been lifted by what he'd seen at the bubbling pool in the other great cave. Elves, Madron had said, and mayhaps that explained her feyness and that of her daughter, the mute and beautiful Edmee. In this place, anything seemed possible.

As she'd promised, Llynya was not long, and soon the four of them and the hounds were making their way up a winding trail cut into the face of the cavern's east wall. Halfway up, the sprite chose a passage, and they all followed, one after the other, leaving the damson beauty of Lanbarrdein behind and stepping into darkness.

"Find your grave. Find your grave," Helebore muttered well under his breath. He'd show Caradoc a grave, aright, and it wouldn't be the leech's.

All of Balor was being massacred in the tunnels. Sharp arrows came out of the dark and impaled guardsmen. Sharp knives did the same, then disappeared, leaving naught but blood and death behind. They'd tried retreating and had been cut off time and again.

He and Caradoc were hurrying through yet another narrow, muddy shaft. Blue lights flashed here and there about them—danger in every one, they'd learned—while their own torches did naught but cast weak glows and fill the damnable passages with smoke. They'd lost four men of their original eight, but had taken on six more who in their stupidity thought they would be safer with their lord. Fools all. They were lost, lost, lost. The blind leading the blind.

He did not tell the Boar that. Oh, no. As far as Caradoc knew, he was hot on the maid's trail, running her down, closing in. Another man might have laughed to have so deceived his master, but Helebore knew better, just as he knew exactly where his own grave lay—

beneath his feet the instant he stopped, if he didn't have the woman in hand.

Yet he did stop, quite suddenly, his head jerking around, his senses alert. There! He closed his eyes and inhaled deeply through his nose. A ragged smile of suppressed glee broke across his face. *Yes. Yes. Yes.* For all his transgressions, God had not forsaken him, though God might regret His benevolence once Helebore was at His side with the reins of time in his hand.

He inhaled again and found the scent true. 'Twas Ceridwen. Unlike before, there was not much between them now, and without all those other bodies messing up the air, he would know her smell anywhere, a sickly womanish thing, but with a disturbing edge of purity about it for all her fornicating with Lavrans.

He opened his eyes, trying to find from whence the scent came. There was naught but solid rock on either side of them. He scuttled backward in the tunnel and lost the scent. He inched forward, through it once more, and lost it four steps away. Curious.

"Give me your torch," he ordered the Boar, and felt a moment's triumph when the light was put into his outstretched hand.

He dragged the flame this way and that over the walls, sniffing first one and then the other. The scent was stronger on the wall to his left where a fine crack parted the stone. He ran his fingers along it and, lo and behold, discovered that the crack was an illusion. Two walls shared a common footing, but were set farther and farther apart the higher one went. Though it was no more than a handspan wide at his head, by lifting the torch he could see the opening grew large enough to hold a man—and 'twas on the air from the hole that he smelled Ceridwen ab Arawn.

"You, there." He pointed to one of the foot soldiers. "Give me a leg up."

Disgusting turn of events, to have to be touched. Yet he endured and was soon following the scent that would give him immortality.

Beyond Lanbarrdein, the tunnels were riddled with cave-ins where the earth had fallen and roundabouts that did naught but circle in upon themselves. Ceridwen was beginning to fear they would wander in the darkness until none could take another step, and they'd never again see the light of day.

"*Behamey!*" Llynya abruptly commanded. Elixir and Numa froze. The order elicited the same response in Dain, Morgan, and herself. Without knowing the word, they all understood to be silent, they all understood the unease they heard in Llynya's voice. The sprite closed her eyes for a moment, turning her face toward a narrow shaft on their left, then slid a grim look to Dain. "Helebore," she said. "The man has a good nose. He's in these tunnels and following us."

"How many are with him?" Dain asked.

"More than one or two others," she answered. "Beyond that I cannot tell."

"Caradoc?" Ceridwen asked.

The sprite shook her head. "The Boar smells like any other man. 'Tis only the evil one who stands out with his profane vice."

"I would have this bur off my back, Lavrans," Morgan said. "Let us stand and fight."

Dain considered it, for he, too, was weary of retreat, but they were three swords only, and the better choice was still escape to the mountains.

"Not while we yet have a chance." He turned to Llynya.

"Aye," she agreed.

Thus they continued on with Llynya taking greater care in the shafts she chose to follow, checking each one for sign or scent of Helebore, all the while trying to weave them a path to the surface.

"Sticks," she grumbled some time later as she halted. Once again, the shaft they were in had dead-ended.

Dain swore. If it wasn't some cave-in blocking their way, it was the smell of the medicus. He turned to retrace their steps, wondering how in the hell they were ever going to get out of there, when Ceridwen gasped behind him. "Jesu!"

He whirled, drawing Scyld, expecting that Helebore was upon them, but such was not the case. The ring of the blade echoed up and down the shaft while all else in the tunnel remained still—Ceri and the hounds motionless at his side, Morgan and Llynya standing one next to the other, their backs stiff with tension. He looked over Llynya's head to the space in front of her and saw nothing beyond the blocked tunnel, until a black sheen of movement, reflecting blue in the light of the dreamstone blades, rippled across the whole end of the passage.

"*Christe.*" Ceridwen took a step back.

Walls did not move, Dain told himself.

As if to belie him, a second gleaming ripple coursed its way across the shaft like silk rippling in the wind, and a hushed sound filled the air.

Walls did not make any sound.

A keening cry, mournful and melodious, followed the ripple, and Dain knew. *Pryf.* The thing moved once more, picking up speed, and the smooth hush grew louder.

Llynya swore, a tangle of words having to do with leading them right into the middle of the *prifarym* nesting ground.

Upon hearing her, Dain's curse put the sprite's to shame. There was no scrying pool this time, no mists in which to escape. He watched her exchange a glance with Morgan, and the two of them began backing away, taking no more than three steps before turning to run. Dain grabbed Ceridwen and did the same.

Now they were in it up to their necks, trapped in the deep earth between the leech and the worms.

Worms. The swivin' leech had given him worms.

Caradoc stood in front of the blocked passage, his fists clenched at his sides, his breath coming hard, and watched the ribbed skin of the greenish-black creature roll by. It filled the whole opening of the shaft, more like a moving wall than a beast.

Giant worms. Huge beyond belief, yet the maid had promised him dragons.

"I see no riches, Helebore," he bellowed above the eerie sound of *pryf* skin rubbing along rock and earth. His voice was too loud for the enclosed space, causing his cowering men to cower even more, but he did not care. Let them wet themselves in fear of him. He needed a release for the pain festering in his leg, for the rage and frustration threatening to burst his heart. He shifted his gaze to yell again at the failed monk and found Helebore crouched in the shadows by the worm's belly. The leech bowed his head to bring his mouth closer to the beast's wet body—and with a flick of his tongue, tasted it.

One of the guardsmen retched somewhere in the dark.

Caradoc was sorely tempted to kill the medicus—one quick cut to the back of the neck, one neat severing of skin, bone, and gullet—for a little blood was a sure and certain balm for pain and rage, but he needed the deranged bastard. His mesnie had been massacred. Each one in the prime of his life, each one sworn to him, and they were all gone. Balor was being overrun by those fleet-footed whoresons they'd found waiting for them in the caves. Rhuddlan, their leader had been called. Caradoc would not forget that. Where Dain had gotten the wild ones, all dressed in shifting green with strong arms and quicker bows, he did not know, but he would see them in hell before he cried surrender.

Hell.

His own strangled cry near choked him. He had lost everything. Everything! He had murdered and maimed and butchered to make his way in the world, carving out a place that was his and his alone, and it had all been taken away by one sniveling bitch. He drew a shuddering breath, lifting his chin to let the air flow down his throat. He needed the maid, and he needed the leech to find her. Through Ceridwen, he would regain it all and be more powerful than ever before. He swore it on Christ's blood, and had he not fought and near died for his Savior?

"A cup ye *sss*said," Helebore hissed, his dark eyes rolling back.

Completely deranged, Caradoc thought through the haze of his anger, taking in the drool and worm slime running from the corner of the leech's mouth.

"A *ssss*mall cup of her blood." Helebore cackled, and the whites of his eyes showed briefly. "And if I'd got it, I could even now turn the *pryf* to my will. Come." He rose to his feet, licking his lips. "She was here, and not long ago."

The end was near. Dain could hear it in the waves crashing on an unseen shore up ahead in the dark. He smelled it in the salt spray filling the air and his lungs as he ran. He felt it in the sand beneath his boots. There was an ocean at the center of the earth as his dream had foretold, and beyond the ocean, his death lay waiting. Stumbling into the *pryf* nest had been their undoing, for the worms had hounded them unmercifully, cutting them out of some tunnels and opening up others—their tapered tails retracting into blunted bodies—leaving them but one passage to follow, the one that would wash them out onto the ocean's shore.

Damn Madron, for 'twas as the witch that she'd shown him his life's end. Yet as Moriath, a fierce weir goddess of the Quicken-tree, the same woman had given him the Philosopher's Stone. He touched the pouch hanging from his belt. He would soon see whose magic was stronger.

Ceridwen raced beside him, the dogs were at his heels, and ahead of them Morgan and Llynya sped through the passage, for they were not alone. Helebore had followed them into the same trap and was being herded toward the sea with them. 'Twas a damnable turn of events that the *pryf* he and Ceridwen had freed were the catalyst of their demise. The Balormen were close, so close they could hear their running footfalls. So close Llynya was choking on the leech's stench.

Too damn close.

A crossbow bolt came zinging out of the darkness behind him and embedded itself in the tunnel wall. Dirt flew. Chips of rock scattered into the air. Ceri let out a short cry, telling him she'd been cut by the sharp flakes of stone. The second bolt near impaled him, and he felt more than saw Elixir turn. Numa moved up to Ceridwen's side with a long, easy lope. A man's agonized cry sounded Elixir's dark victory, and in moments, the levrier was back guarding his flank.

As on Lanbarrdein, the tunnel ended high on the cliff face, a piece of information relayed to them by Llynya, along with an order to jump when they reached the ledge. The beach, she swore, would not be too far below. Following her own command, the sprite did not hesitate, but ran right off the edge, her dreamstone blade held high. For an instant she hung in the air, backlit by a faint damson glow coming off the opposing cliff face, a violet-hued headland jutting into an abyss of darkness. The scent of salt was strong, as was the sound of waves washing up and breaking on the shore somewhere below. Llynya spread her arms wide, and her cloak floated about her like butterfly wings. She was *sidhe,* faerie, purest grace flying through the air. Morgan had the sense to hesitate, but not for long. He skidded to a short stop, giving Llynya just enough time to land on the beach and show him how far down it was before he leaped. Dain took not even that much time, but grabbed Ceridwen's hand and lofted them both out into space.

They'd no sooner landed than a shout came from above.

"Lavrans!" 'Twas Caradoc. "Give me the ab Arawn woman and you may yet go free."

Dain shoved Ayas deep into the sand, extinguishing the blade's light. Llynya had done the same with her knife, but the damson crystals encrusted on the sea cliffs had already picked up enough of the dreamstone luminescence to cast a faint glow.

"We are eleven to your four," Caradoc warned him. "And two of your band are but women. Sacrifice her for the good of all, Dain, or I will kill you every one."

Llynya had the Boar's answer for him before Dain could speak, releasing an arrow from her bow and killing her first man. Morgan got another, shooting from the sprite's side.

"Dain!" Llynya yelled, and when he looked, she pointed to a cliff rising up out of the long crescent-shaped beach. "Take her!"

He shifted his gaze and saw what she meant. A cave opening showed black against the amethystine rock wall. *And so death begins.*

He had not time to dwell on the consequences of his actions, he just acted, shoving Ayas into his belt and closing his hand even tighter around Ceridwen's as they scrambled to their feet and took off at a run.

Ceridwen looked back once, and saw Caradoc and his men jumping down onto the beach, firing on Morgan and Llynya, who were running full out across the sand for the nearest sea cliff cave. She feared they would not make it, for other Balormen were sprinting along a path in the cliff face, racing to intercept them.

As Caradoc's men landed on the beach, they met Elixir and Numa, their canine hearts primed with blood lust for the fight. They worked as a team to bring their first man down, a small one who had his neck snapped with a shake of Elixir's head. Numa's teeth were still in him when she was cut on the haunch. Growling deep in her throat, she turned, fangs bared to meet her new foe and his blade. 'Twas Caradoc, and he proved quicker than the bitch, blinding the dog in her right eye with a slash from his dagger even as he gutted her on his sword.

Ceridwen cried out as if she herself had been impaled, her first thought to run to the dying animal. Dain would have none of it and dragged her into the nearest dark hole.

*   *   *

"Khardeen!" Llynya let out her war cry. She'd slung her bow to the ground and was meeting the enemy with two hands on her sword. She and Morgan had been cut off from their escape and were fighting hand-to-hand with three of Balor's best. Morgan was fast with a blade, thank the gods, but even at that, Llynya feared they'd met their end. He'd been cut twice in the thick of it, and she felt blood running down her own arm. Numa was dead. Elixir grappled with a man on the beach, and Ceridwen and Dain had slipped into a hole. May the gods light their path and the old worm be with them, she prayed, for Caradoc, the evil monk, and two others were after the pair.

She swung her sword in a high arc at the man she fought, leaving herself open—her first and probably her last mistake, she realized. He lunged, and she rallied to block the blow.

She knew instantly she would not be quick enough, but with his sword a handspan from her head, the man dropped the weapon and did naught but stare at her, speechless from the arrow lodged in his throat, the only unprotected place on his helmeted and mailed body.

Trembling, but still on guard, she dragged a breath into her lungs and watched him drown in his own blood. On her second breath, she joined Morgan's fight, evening the odds. The Balorman she chose lasted for no more than a blow before falling to another well-placed arrow. She jerked her head around to see how Dain fared. Only it wasn't Dain shooting from the cliffs, but a stranger.

He was dressed all in white, with a bright copper streak running through his golden hair, a pure flame against the glowing violet wall, and he was drawing his bow for another shot.

Morgan's last opponent went down with a strangled cry.

"We have a savior," she said to him between breaths.

"Then let him save Dain and Ceridwen as well. Come." Morgan turned and ran toward the caves.

Llynya looked once more to the man high on the sea cliff before she followed Morgan.

There was power here. No trace of magic, but the raw essence. Dain felt it immediately upon entering the cave, and the feeling increased with each step as they ran deeper into its depths. The darkness quickly gave way to a luminescence that radiated from the rock itself—an occurrence he no longer found strange. The walls were bored smooth, almost silky in their evenness, and colored in shifting shades of heliotrope and green. Running was difficult because of the perfect circular curve of wall, floor, and ceiling, yet they dared not slow their pace.

Well into the cave, a gaping passage cut across the tunnel they were in, its dark, crudely bored walls a stark contrast to the smooth, lucent rock surrounding them, and its size much larger than what they'd seen in the *pryf* nest. Looking down the passage, he could see where it intersected with another green-and-heliotrope tunnel. A quick glance the opposite way showed yet another tunnel, all of them angling in toward something, like spokes in a wheel angling toward a hub, and all of them cut through by the rough-walled passage looming on either side of them.

He had a bad feeling about the gigantic tunnel and wondered if it was possible that a *pryf*—so much larger than he'd expected—could truly get that big.

He didn't have to wonder for long.

A slow, deep rumbling announced the creature's arrival, a tremor of sound that shook the earth around them. He and Ceridwen stumbled forward, bracing themselves where they could. A clattering of mail and a poorly aimed crossbow bolt careening off the walls proved they were not alone.

Dain looked over his shoulder and saw the band of four after them. The first was the crossbowman, struggling to reload and maintain his balance in the intersection of the great shaft. No keening cry came to warn him of his fate, but a basso profundo hum. Dain saw him turn toward the opening, saw the look of horror that washed over the man's face in the instant before he was swept on by the gargantuan worm barreling through the shaft. No sleek-skinned *pryf* this, but a gnarly, ragged beast, scarred and marked as if by a thousand millenniums spent in the nethermost reaches of the earth. *In remotissimo angulo terrae.*

They were there, the remotest corner, with the weir gate lying just ahead. He looked to Ceridwen and saw the dawning realization in her eyes.

An awful scream echoed through the tunnels, and they both turned back to the worm. Scraping and crunching noises came next.

With little effort, Dain could imagine the pulverizing action of being dragged and rolled between the ancient *pryf* and the walls, how such action would grind a man's bones to dust inside his skin.

" 'Tis just the one man," he said, avoiding her gaze as he caught his breath. "The others were not taken, but are still a danger to us. I might could kill them all without you coming to harm, but I fear that one or the other would find a way to take what they have long wanted—your blood." He glanced over at her. She carried his babe and had felt the life of it the same as he had. She would know he was right in what he had to say. "I might well die here, Ceri, but I would rather not leave Caradoc with power like Rhuddlan's, nor Helebore, not in this place. Leave me now and my chances improve for the fight. They cannot outflank me in this narrow shaft as mayhaps they can at the weir." None would get by him. "Rhuddlan will come for you."

"Aye," she agreed, her expression grim, resolute, "but I have not the strength for leaving you to face them alone." She pulled the Damascene, and he knew this time the quicksilver maid would not make her escape.

"You should run for your life," he said angrily. Did she not know it?

"As should you." She would not be moved, and time was running out. The *pryf* was near through, with the tapering of its tail leaving a breach of light at the top of the tunnel.

"Then we go on together."

The passage narrowed before emptying onto the ledge of a large domed cavern filled with the power Dain had felt pulling him onward. A bolt of lightning crackled in the center of the cavern, shooting up out of the earth through an immense hole that consumed most of the cave floor.

The weir gate. Shreds of the emerald seal fluttered around the rough-hewn rock that rimmed the hole, and down the length of the hole, the sides writhed with *prifarym*. Another flash of lightning lit the darkness from below, sparkling bluish-white and purple, and leaping across the chasm from rock rim to rock rim. The reflection of it off the dome above filled the cavern with jacinth light of murky dark blue.

'Twas as they remembered, a yawning abyss, a trap, yet at their feet rather than placed before them as it had been through the scrying pool. And it was bigger, much bigger.

Dain immediately felt the lure of the abyss reaching out for him on soft tendrils of rich, sweet breath, the promise it held, as if his weakness were the weir's greatest desire. Damned swiving place. It *would* be the death of him. But before the abyss took him, he was feeding it Caradoc and Helebore, piece by bloody piece if needs be.

Off to his right, a wavering circle of heliotrope-and-green light revealed another passageway like the one they'd come through. There were others, barely discernible in the strange blue glow that filled the cavern. A much darker, more ragged opening between two of the smooth shafts close to them proved that the ancient *pryf* ruled in the inner circle as well as the outer. They had come to the end. Domhringr or nay, his future, if he had one, would be decided here.

Another sweet-earth breath blew up at his back, tickling his skin, eager to please. A muffled curse of despairing frustration was torn from him. He would not survive this. He would not. He had given too much of his soul to Jalal's dark ambrosia. Morgan had suspected as much; Moriath had known he was not whole.

And she'd given him the Stone.

He tightened his hold on Scyld with one hand and reached for the pouch with the other. Fingers trembling, he dug the Stone out and grasped it in his fist—and felt nothing.

Still, he did not let go.

"Lavrans!" the Boar called, advancing upon them from out of the passageway with his sword drawn, his gait slowed by a pained limp. Helebore's cadaverous face showed behind the Boar, and he, too, had a sword at the ready. "I will have her, Dain!"

"You'll have death first." He lifted Scyld, and 'twas the dream come true: the wormhole at his feet, the gleaming edge of his blade, and the hopeless hope to save a woman with his courage and his steel.

Caradoc grabbed the lone guardsman left at his side, shoving him forward with a simple command: "Kill the mage, if you can. Die hard, if you can't."

"Boar!" The cry came from Morgan who was in the shaft with Llynya at his side.

*   *   *

Helebore whirled at the sound of the unexpected voice, then did his
best to escape the dark-haired fury bearing down on him. Of the two
they'd left on the beach, 'twas the woman who singled him out, the
very thought of which made him recoil in horror. He'd taken a sword
from the man who had fallen to the dogs, and now used it to hold her
off as best he could, retreating step by step, meeting her blows as she
beat away at him, but unable to make a strike of his own.

She was relentless, her blade clanging against his from first one
side, then the other, as she forced him back onto the rim of the abyss.
More of the heavenly *pryf* scent was filling the cavern, richer than
before. He wanted to shout the truth of it at Caradoc and thereby
wring from the Boar his overdue accolades. That the man treated him
as no more than a leech had long been a thorn in Helebore's side. But
no more. He'd found the maid, as he'd said he would; he'd found the
pryf as promised, and had the both of them together. A quick cut, a
taste of blood, and the world was his, if not in this age, then the next,
or the next, for time was the treasure. While fools dabbled in doubling
gold, and Caradoc looked for riches and lands to rule, Helebore, the
leech, had discerned the essence of it all. Time.

The woman cut him, a neat slice across the top of his arm, and
he fell to his knees, shocked by the pain. He was not a base brawler to
be treated so. Behind him, the leathery, scarred creature who had
taken the crossbowman moved out into the inner circle. Its faceless
head slowly slid by him, so close and silent, and curved back into the
next hole. Lovely, beautiful thing. *Pryf.* He'd first seen the word on a
shaft beneath Ynys Enlli.

Dragons, ach. He did not need dragons. He had worms, beasts
of mythical proportions to bore him a path to the center of the cosmos.

She cut him again, the bitch, and sent him reeling. He flung a
hand out and caught himself on the dark hide of the *pryf.* Cool and
solid it was, a fair support. Blood ran from the side of his face.

He lifted his sword and made an ineffectual stab at the maid.
What a demon she was, hacking away at him. The *pryf* moved again,
the great thing, and Helebore found himself moving along with it, his
fingers curled tightly into a deep scar on the creature's side.

Her blade sank into his thigh, and the agony was beyond any
he had ever known. "Christ's blood," he swore, and struggled to free
himself, but the *pryf* seemed to have taken hold of him. The worm

bulged and heaved, dragging him along the floor. Seeing him move along must have frightened the woman, for she backed away, finally subdued into retreat.

A demonic sneer twisted his lips. His victory would be complete. A mighty heave of the worm near pushed him over the edge of the hole, causing him a moment's panic, but his hand held, saving him from the abyss. He laughed aloud, riding his wave of glory and the undulations of the worm, until he realized with an odd sense of detachment that he was going to be dragged into the tunnels and crushed between the worm and the wall.

Llynya stumbled back, her sword arm throbbing and hanging limp at her side, and though her hand still gripped the haft of the blade, the point scraped the stone floor.

Gulping great breaths of air, she watched the monk. The old worm had him now, and not an instant past the evil one had understood exactly what that meant. His fleeting look of triumph had turned to stark, raving fear.

"Help me! Don't let—Aaauuugggh . . ." He squirmed and rolled, trying to free himself. "Bitch, filthy, whoring bitch." She had wanted him dead, had been willing to fight to the death to see it so. Such rage as he engendered was a new and awful feeling for her. It left her trembling and hurting with a strange, all-encompassing pain. "You will burn, slut. Burn! Please, help me, cut the *pryf,* cut me, please, don't—"

His screams started then, as the old worm dragged him behind the wall, and she turned away. Holding her side against a cramp, she looked for Morgan through the shadowy blue light, and when she found him, she began to run.

Morgan felt his strength ebbing with every blow he blocked. His boots were slick with his own blood, making each step treacherous. His shirt and tunic were soaked along the right side with more blood, and his chausses too. Caradoc fared little better, but the Boar had the advantage of two stone more in weight and an extra ten years of living with a blade in his hand.

It would be enough this time.

Caradoc landed a bone-cracking blow to his ribs, and Morgan stumbled on the rim of the abyss. He clenched his teeth against the white-hot pain. *Christ have mercy, Christ have mercy,* the litany began. He shook his head to clear his sight, and was hit again, this time with a cutting edge. His mouth filled with blood, and the next blow sent him flying.

Off in the distance, through the jacinth light, a pair of green eyes met his, eyes set in a dark angel's face. *Llynya . . .* He reached for her as he fell.

Dain put a boot on the dead guardsman and yanked Scyld out of the man's chest. He had died hard as ordered by his lord. A quick look toward the source of the screams filling the air proved Helebore to be doing the same. Only one other battle still sounded in the cavern, and when Dain saw it, his heart stopped for one agonizing, awful moment.

"Morgan," he whispered, starting forward. "Morgan! *Morrr-gannn!*"

Llynya, too, screamed, but she was too late, too late. With a beautiful, dying grace, his body arcing out over the abyss, the Thief of Cardiff fell into the weir. A blinding flash of blue-white lightning welcomed him, crackling and sizzling up from out of the wormhole to dance upon the dome even as a dark cloud of mist and thunder rolled up to suck him in.

Llynya faltered, her gaze fixed in horror on the skittering bolt of heat and light that marked Morgan's passing. Her sword fell to her side, her breath came in pained, shocked gasps. She stood for an eternity, trembling, but unable to move, until a great wave of sadness washed over her and sank her to her knees.

He was gone.

Morgan was falling, falling, falling as in the worst of dreams, endlessly. Fear had locked up his mind to where he couldn't even think, and he didn't have so much as his sword to hold on to. The blade had been left on the rim. He could see it hanging half off the rock, glinting in the bright flash of lightning. He had heard Dain call his name, and Llynya too.

But now he was alone. So alone. And cold.

The warm wind of his falling had suddenly turned cold, incredibly cold. He felt a frigid numbness start at the base of his spine and work its way up and spread out like cracks in the ice on a lake, covering his back and curving round his ribs, reaching out into his arms and legs and up his neck. He was freezing solid, from the outside in, and quickly.

Amazingly, the realization brought no new sense of terror. In truth, it came more as a blessing. The icy numbness was soothing away all the pains he'd gotten in the fight with . . . with . . . He had forgotten who, but there had been a fight, and he'd been hurt, but he didn't hurt anymore, and that was a blessing from the cold.

He was no longer afraid; the cold had frozen his fear out of him. In truth, he could no longer remember what it was that had frightened him. There was nothing to be afraid of, nothing at all.

His fingers grew numb, then his toes, and he felt the iciness slip completely up over his head and come down onto his brow and cheeks and chin. In truth, the only parts of him that weren't freezing were his breath and a patch of skin on the left side of his chest.

Ahhh, he remembered. The leaf. He had put it there, beneath his shirt. He even remembered the one from whom he'd stolen it—Llynya, the sprite. A smile curved his cold lips and brought the warmth of the summer forests down into the center of his heart.

Veritas. He was the Thief of Cardiff. And he was on his way to the stars.

Dain broke into a run, filled with all the berserk fury of his ancestors. Morgan was gone, sentenced to God knew what fate. Strange death, Moriath had said, and Dain wanted to scream his rage. Of them all, Morgan least deserved death, least deserved strangeness in any form.

Caradoc stood at the weir, sweat running down his face, his chest heaving with the exertion of murder, yet he turned to meet his enemy. Their swords rang out with a clash. The force of Dain's attack sent the bigger man reeling, and Dain used his advantage to beat at the bastard, striking blow after blow, sparing nothing, driving Caradoc along the edge of the weir, working with each swing of his blade to feed the Boar a length of steel.

'Tis too soon for you to die, Dain, Morgan had said, *for you are damned,* and it was all true. He was damned to have seen Morgan die. He would be twice damned if he did not see Caradoc do the same.

Blood, the Boar wanted. He would give him blood. Dain would drown him in it.

Caradoc's limp was in his left leg, and Dain cut him there, once at the ankle, once at the knee, a deep cut meant to sever tendons, crippling him. The Boar fell into a heap on the rim, and Dain readied his killing strike, but such was not to be, for the tide of battle shifted inexplicably, or mayhaps not so. Dain found no purchase on the rock with his next step, only air fluttering with the green shreds of the seal. He lost his balance, and Scyld left his hand in a whirling rotation of the blade around the haft that carried it out over the center of the wormhole before it fell. When Dain felt himself begin to follow, he lunged for the Boar and dragged his foe down over the edge with him.

In the abyss, there was chaos, a raging storm swirling through the vortex, both hot and cold. Here was Rhuddlan's journey through time without the ameliorating presence of the chant. Dain was pummeled and pressed by the wind, ripped at by forces that had no name—and he had lost Nemeton's Stone, dropped it in his killing fury.

He could hear the sound of his own rough breathing and that of Caradoc's below him as the Boar scrabbled for a hold on Dain's boot. They had not fallen cleanly into the hole, but slid down the side of it. Dain's fingers were dug into the earth and rock, his toes pressed into a hollow above a protrusion of stone, while not an arm's length away, the *prifarym* slid in a spiral dance around the circumference of the dark cylinder, creating thunder and tremors that threatened to shake him from his perch. But he clung, and kicked at Caradoc, who was trying to drag him down.

"Lavrans! Dain!" Caradoc pleaded, and within the dark space, the Boar's voice ebbed and flowed like storm-tossed tides. "Dain!" Caradoc screamed, and Dain looked.

Terror defined the Boar's face, etching white sparks in the frigid greenish-blue of his eyes, incising deep lines on each side of his face from nose to mouth. Terror ran along the strands of his hair, turning each one into a writhing, fiery flame. He was hell personified in rage, fury, lust, and desire.

Above, another called to him, her voice broken with fear. Dain looked up, and 'twas as if he lay on the bottom of a river with the flow of water making a thin, fluid barrier between them. She was reaching for him when a lightning bolt crackled in the depths below, sending a white flash of light streaking upward. He saw the bright outriders of luminescence stream by him and pass through her body, and he heard her soul-wrenching cry as she fell back from the rim.

    . . . *kissed by the worm in his mother's womb.*

Second and third bolts rose from the thunder of the first, roiling up from below with great heat before encasing him. No stars burned as brightly, nor as completely. The light passed through him with a purity that seared his soul, shooting from the soles of his feet through the top of his head like an unleashed ray of the sun, catching him in the life stream and transforming the basest elements of his existence. He could not move, or breathe, or speak, but was held in the chasm from whence came the world, transfixed by a power no weakness could survive.

This, then, was life and death together, one into the other.

Chapter 28

Ceridwen lay as if in a dream. Colored lights flashed off the dome and swirled around the perimeter of the cavern; white light streamed from the weir, while vaporous fog poured out of the abyss and snaked across the ledge. The cool mists swept over her in waves where she'd fallen on the rim, dampening her face and chilling her body. Everything was quiet except for the low rumble of thunder emanating from the hole. No more screams and death cries reverberated off the walls, no more swords clashed. The battle was done, and all had lost.

Llynya sat in a crumpled heap not too far distant, utterly still, her head bowed, her knees splayed, the only sign of life being the white-knuckled grip she maintained on her sword. Behind her, Elixir dragged the body of Numa through the low-lying fog. Sweet bitch, Ceridwen thought. There was naught she could do for the hound. Light had pierced through her when she'd reached for Dain—how long ago had it been?—and left her feeling not completely of this world, but caught somehow betwixt and between.

She shifted her gaze to the weir gate. He was still there, caught in the light. She knew it.

By sheer force of will, she made her hand slide across the rim and claim Morgan's sword. 'Twas stained with Caradoc's blood, which made her love it all the more. She needed to get back into the luminous stream, and the sword was going with her, for if Dain was alive, so Caradoc might be. Beneath the hilt of the blade was another treasure—Nemeton's Stone. She claimed it too, dragging it close and slipping it into her pouch with the elf shot. Mayhaps it would yet prove its worth, for she did not believe Moriath had given Dain a worthless thing. Charms, the mage had taught her, were delicate baubles, useful only in their predestined niche. Verily, the trick itself was to find the niche. Thus she would hold to Nemeton's Stone.

The sound of rapid footfalls drew her head around and quickened her heartbeat, giving her a welcome surge of life. Had a Balorman survived? she wondered. She struggled to her knees, gritting her teeth, and used Morgan's sword to leverage herself to her feet. Time was of the essence. The truth of that was everywhere around her, yet time was so elusive, slipping through her fingers more easily than water.

Before her, the lightning had coalesced into a solid sheet of brightness. She reached her hand out to touch it, and was stopped by the calling of her name.

"Ceri! No!"

Fifteen years had changed the timbre of the voice, but not the quality of it. Stunned, she turned and saw him, a man running out of the mists, dressed all in white.

"Mychael." The name fell from her lips in a hoarse whisper. Pale blue eyes met hers across the length of the cavern. His hair was to his shoulders, a rich mélange of golds and silvers with the addition of a strange copper stripe down the right side. His nose and mouth were near replicas of her own, only not so softly defined. His chin and jaw had naught to do with her, for both were purely man.

The fog rolled up on either side of him as he ran, opening a path to the weir, and his gaze shifted from her to the hole.

"How many are in?" he asked when he stopped at the rim. Though he had the look of an angel, she could tell by his labored breathing that he was merely a mortal, one who had run far.

"Two," she answered, "but there is only one that I want back."

He glanced up. "Then pray, *gefell,* that I choose correctly, for I cannot enter the same live wormhole twice, and neither can you."

He'd called her twin.

Kneeling, he shrugged off a length of rope looped across his chest and began threading it through an intricately incised groove in the rock, one of many she had not noticed before. When he reached the edge of the weir, he threw the rest of the rope off into the hole and reached down with his hand. The briefest smile of satisfaction crossed his mouth.

"What is it?" she asked.

"The temperature is stable. 'Tis neither hot nor cold, meaning they haven't slipped into the past or the future, but should still be here, somewhere." The light skittered across the white wool of his tunic, picking out threads and making them shimmer blue and purple against the cloth.

The past and the future, Ceridwen thought. The flow of time.

A sudden fear seized her. 'Twas what Dain had long sought, the mastery of time. She could not hold him against that, yet she could not let him go.

She fell to her knees and grabbed Mychael before he slipped over the edge. "Bring him back to me," she ordered, her face close to his, her fingers tightening on his shoulder. "As you are my brother, bring him back to me."

The Boar was no longer with him. Dain knew that the same as he knew that he, too, would not last much longer. The light that held him was also drawing him down. Strange stuff. Bliss and terror both had a place in the luminescence. He watched them play across his emotions as if from a distance. Whatever he was—and a thousand thousand ideas on that score had come to mind—he was at his core something beyond the extremes of feeling, something beyond the con-flagration of life and death raging around and through him, some-thing beyond the visible movement of time.

Yet, if given a choice, he would choose life, sweetest blessing, the catalyst and nurturing medium of change, and he would choose the time of the quicksilver maid. Aye, he knew this with all his heart: He would choose life and Ceridwen.

. . . and from within the most brilliant flux came that which he had thought beyond his grasp, salvation. A golden arm, garbed in white, reached down into the abyss and took his hand.

Rhuddlan and Moira knelt by the trail of blood in the sand. They had found others, but this one was too dark to pass by, speaking as it did of death.

"Rhayne," Moira told him, looking up, her green eyes growing sad.

Dead men lay all around, but they were of Balor and not of the Quicken-tree company. The Ebiurrane elves were dragging them out to sea, letting Mor Sarff have their bodies to feed the fishes and return them to salt water.

Trig called from the headland caves, having found the trail through the heavy mists pouring out of all the openings. The presence of so much turmoil could not bode well for what had taken place at the weir.

"Come," Rhuddlan said to Moira, touching her lightly. "You will be needed."

Inside the shaft were other signs of carnage. A Balorman had been crushed, and they could hear another one being ground up even as they entered the cavern. The old worm had roused himself mightily to come up from the deep dark.

"Math, find Conladrian," Rhuddlan ordered, though he feared the hound had chosen a path from whence he would not return.

"Rhuddlan!" 'Twas Shay calling, and when they reached him, they found him with Llynya, holding her close and looking far more frightened than he had at any time during the battle.

Rhuddlan dropped to her side and gently took her face in his hands. His palms grew wet with her tears. "Llynya?" He spoke her name softly, but received no response.

"What happened here?" Trig demanded, running up, his tone far gruffer than he would normally take with his leader. Rhuddlan understood. For all her wildness, the little one was expected to become Liosalfar. Aye, and mayhaps she already had.

He smoothed his thumbs across her cheeks, watching her intently. There was life and warmth behind the closed veil of her lashes. "She has fought herself beyond exhaustion; that is all." He rose to his feet and called for Wei. "Help Shay take her back to the Light Caves and give her to Aedyth."

Wei laid his hand upon her cheek, and slanted him and Trig a questioning look.

Rhuddlan nodded, and Trig grew grim, reaching down to feel Llynya's brow for himself. There was more wrong with the sprite than exhaustion. She had suddenly grown older. Rhuddlan had felt the sadness on her heart, but did not want to frighten Shay any more than he was, for all knew sadness could crush a person as thoroughly as the old worm could.

Wei took her in his arms and started off at an easy lope toward one of the shafts with Shay at his heels.

The rest of them ran forward through the jacinth-hued cavern, fog washing up against them to their knees and higher, the vaporous tendrils winding through the air and obscuring their view. Yet they all knew where they were needed, for nothing could hide the wall of light streaming up from the weir.

There were three on the rim when they reached it.

Dain groaned and rolled over onto his back, and for an instant thought he was seeing double. Two identical faces loomed over him, both fair, though only one was crying; both golden-haired, though only one had an odd streak of auburn running through the tresses.

"Ceri?" he asked, and the sweet face wet with tears bent down and began smothering him in kisses. He let himself sink into the warm, healing pleasure of having her pressed against him, showering him with love. 'Twas so easy to take it all and for once not wonder about the nature of the God who had answered his prayer, but merely accept that it had been done.

Others gathered around—Quicken-tree, he could tell by the sound of their voices and the green scent of them—and the need for leaving became clear.

Moira knelt by their sides and spoke to them both, and when their mouths parted from their kiss, she gave them each another on their cheeks.

"The tide is coming in," she said. "We must hurry. Can you walk?"

"Aye," Dain said, but Ceri shook her head.

"Do not worry," Moira said at Dain's stricken look. "She is but with child, and what she has done this day would have exhausted even the strongest. Indeed, it has."

"Llynya?" Ceri asked, her voice soft with concern, even as Dain wondered how Moira knew about their child.

"Llynya has killed many times since this battle began," Moira said. "Each death takes something from us no matter how worthy we deem the cause. Wei and Shay have already started for the Light Caves with her. Tomorrow I will take her to the forests. 'Tis from the trees that Llynya will regain her strength and find her peace again."

"Morgan?" Dain asked, and Moira shook her head, confirming what he'd already known. That hurt would take time to heal. "What of the battle itself?"

Moira responded by handing Ceri one of a pair of small gourds she had worked off her pack. The other she gave to him. "Drink it, every drop." When they started, she answered his question. "Balor is no more, and all of its men are dead. 'Tis Carn Merioneth above, and you are its lady, Ceridwen."

His love looked to him before speaking. "Do you fancy yourself lord of a castle keep?"

He knew his answer without having to dwell on it. "'Tis a wondrous strange place you have here, Lady of Merioneth, and what you offer is most men's dream, but in truth, I would take you north and be lord of no one."

"Then 'tis north we go, Moira," she said to the Quicken-tree woman, "and rather than a Lady Ceridwen, you will have a Lord Mychael, for I think 'tis my brother Rhuddlan needed all along." She slanted her gaze up at the Quicken-tree leader and her brother, and the other two followed her lead.

"You have been in the wormhole?" Rhuddlan was asking, looking at Mychael with a keen interest that was being returned in equal measure, with an added degree of wariness and mayhaps a hint of threat.

"Aye, many times," Mychael answered, and Ceridwen thought how strong and beautiful her brother had become. His hair was peculiar, and not just because of the streak. He'd been tonsured as a monk, and though most of his hair fell to his shoulders, there was a good bit on top that had grown out only partway. Regardless of length, though, the stripe was consistent.

Rhuddlan smiled, a bare curve of mouth. "And you have survived them all, thus far. We have much to talk about."

"If you are Rhuddlan of the Quicken-tree or Llyr of the Ebiurrane," was Mychael's measured reply.

Rhuddlan's smile broadened. "Not many know Llyr of the Ebiurrane, but I am Rhuddlan."

The tension flowed out of her twin, and though he did not smile, he removed his hand from the dagger shoved into his belt. "Aye, then Rhuddlan." He nodded. "We do have much to talk about."

"But not here," Rhuddlan said. "Bedwyr, Nia, take the lady before we are washed out on the tide with Balor's dead."

The journey through the *pryf* nesting grounds was much smoother with Liosalfar leading the way and clearing the tunnels as they wished. Despite their great size and what Ceridwen had perceived as a general intractability, the worms responded to commands from the Quicken-tree warriors, though the voice they used was unlike any she had ever heard. 'Twas a deep, resonant, multitoned thing that seemed to come from deeper in their throats than normal sound. Mayhaps it came from someplace even deeper still, for it set up a vibration she felt strongest in an unnameable area in the center of her torso. They stopped in Lanbarrdein to refresh themselves before making the great climb up the wall to the Canolbarth, and from there the trek to the Light Caves was grim.

Most of Balor had died in the midland caves, and though the bodies were proof of their great victory, none of the Quicken-tree or the Ebiurrane took pleasure in the deaths. Through every passageway and gallery, the *tylwyth teg* sang a song meant to ease the passing of souls, and to hear those fair voices raised in a mournful dirge was near more than Ceridwen could bear. There had been too much loss, and 'twas not all Balor. Amongst the piles of hauberked and mailed bodies were those of elves clad in shimmery cloth.

By the time they reached the Light Caves, dusk was falling over the Irish Sea. From the Dragon's Mouth, Ceridwen watched the sun slip below the western horizon. Behind her a fire burned brightly, casting shadows on Ddrei Goch and Ddrei Glas, and beside her was Dain, sitting with her on a pile of soft rugs, holding her hand in his.

"We can stay if you wish, Ceri," he said. "You must be thinking of it."

"Aye," she admitted, "but I believe I spoke more truth than I knew at the weir. Look." She directed his attention to the group talking farther back in the caves. 'Twas Mychael and Rhuddlan and half the Liosalfar, speaking of the keep and the castle wall, and of the wild boar reported loose in the caves, and speaking also of things she did not understand, of what was beyond the deep dark and the damson shafts being torn asunder there.

"I have wondered, Dain. In the abyss . . . What happened to you?"

He grew thoughtful for a while. "Words can bare describe it, Ceri," he finally said.

"I felt the light go through me."

"I felt it too, a flood of light, and I know not if it came from God or another, or from nothing at all except the earth and what it is. Either way, 'twas a glimpse of something beyond what I knew before. I know I had to give up a measure of my cynic's heart to get out."

She smiled and kissed his face. "Aye, and I'll miss that I'm sure."

"Mayhaps I can no longer play the demon," he said, giving her an ingenuous look from beneath his lashes. At her crestfallen expression, he laughed. "Aye, and you *would* miss that, wouldn't you, Ceri."

Her blush was sweet, and he laughed again, pulling her into his lap for a kiss that had naught to do with demons and much to do with mouths and the sharing of breath, one into the other, with the feel of her in his arms and the even greater softness she promised.

"So you will go north with me?" he asked when she lifted her head.

"Aye," she whispered, her eyes languid. "We will build a palace out of ice, and every night melt it with our love."

"Rhuddlan has arranged for us to travel with the Ebiurrane."

"Good," she said, and snuggled closer.

"We will leave in a sennight. Does that give you enough time with your brother?"

"Enough," she murmured against his neck.

Breath by breath, limb by limb, she slowly drifted into slumber. He held her and lazily stroked her back, watching the last shades of sunlight fade from the peaks of the waves until all was night over the open sea. Out above the northern horizon, a single star flashed in the new dark sky and fell toward the water in a glittering arc of celestial dust. 'Twas the sign of a child to be born, his child by the quicksilver maid. He cupped her face in his palm and placed a kiss upon her mouth. There was life in love, and as he gave, so would he drink it from her lips.

Gently, so as not to wake her, he laid them both down on the deep-piled rugs of softly woven Quicken-tree cloth, magical stuff, and drew her close to sleep and dream with her, safe in the Dragon's Mouth.

Epilogue

Outside the castle walls, on a wooded slope overlooking Balor and the Irish Sea, Mychael sat high up in an old oak tree spread with age. He was skimming the pages of the red book Ceri had given him two days earlier, before she and Lavrans had left on their journey north. 'Twas from Usk, she'd said, the Latin in it being the prophesies of Nemeton that Moriath had written down.

He remembered Nemeton, a large man with a flowing red beard and a single iron-gray stripe running through his hair. Mychael had his own such anomaly now, copper running through blond, the mark he had gotten for venturing into the wormholes.

As for the rest of the red book, the strange languages filling some of the other pages, Ceridwen had not known what they said or who had written them. Neither did he, but he'd seen fragments of the odd scripts before, seen characters from them carved into the rock in the deep dark. Aye, the red book was a treasure.

The Latin in the book spoke much of dragons, as he'd hoped, and of maiden's blood, which did him no good. He was no maiden, nor was he likely to have access to one. He was a man of God and had not abandoned the life of Strata Florida, despite the strange turn he had taken by coming north. In truth, the longer he had been in the caves, the more he'd come to fear the holy sanctuary of the monastery might be his only salvation when his task beneath Merioneth was done.

A grim smile crossed his lips. He had once considered restlessness the bane of his monkish existence. Then he had been called by a vision, one of power and grace and frightening beauty, and of pagan things to be done, sure to damn his soul—and he had been unable to resist.

Three days of hard travel had brought him to the cliffs overlooking the Irish Sea. From there he had followed an overgrown trail and his instincts into the heart of the caves, and he had remembered a long-ago night and grown afraid, thinking of Ceri. Mayhaps he would have left then, run back breathless and penitent to his monastery, except for the keening cry that had risen out of the dark and touched him like a caress. 'Twas that which had lured him onward, the yearning in the cry, the hint of desperation and of things coming undone.

Thus he'd found the *pryf* trapped in the maze behind the weir gate and the old worm moving through the deep dark on a course of his own making. He'd found the great crystal cavern with its floating thrones; he'd found signs of those who ruled it all, and he'd found the gemstone that warmed to a man's touch and burned bright.

He turned another page of the book and his hand fell upon familiar likenesses. Ddrei Goch and Ddrei Glas swirled and writhed across one of the pieces of parchment that was far older than those written on in Moriath's hand. He smoothed his fingertips over the curved lines and felt the power of the ancient creatures reach for him from across the ages. This was what had called him from Strata Florida, the dragons he had yet to find.

He'd seen their nest and the words carved into the rock that bespoke of dragon care and dragon need. He'd touched those words and remembered all the tales his mother had told, beautiful Rhiannon with her angel's voice and the mother's love he had learned to live without. But he'd found no dragons other than the ones calling to him from inside his heart.

"Ddrei Goch," he whispered, tracing a golden eye and the beast's long, whiskered snout, a fierce creature with an incarnadine hide. "Ddrei Glas." His touch turned tender. She was glass green, of air and water, pale and silvery, fierce and so essentially female, so other than himself that she fascinated him.

A movement in the glade below caught his eye and drew his attention from the book. Leaning forward, he swept aside a veil of leaves better to see. A girl was walking alone through the woods. He remembered her from the weir of the *pryf*'s dark maze. She'd fought well, but had lost her friend, and the sadness of the loss still clung to her. He saw it in the unnatural heaviness of her movements, as if every step were a burden she scarce could bear, and her face was drawn, her eyes downcast. Llynya was her name.

He watched her bend low over a patch of yellow flowers at the base of a hazel tree. She picked one and brought it to her lips. 'Twas a buttercup.

Eyes closed, she blew into the bright lemon-colored petals, setting them all aflutter. Delicate pistil and stamens trembled within the sweet draft of her breath, tangling together, and for an instant . . . a twinkling, no more . . . the aureate hue appeared to lift off the flower and grace the air with its light golden tones, as if the girl had blown the color from the petals themselves.

A fanciful musing, he thought, yet he still gave the girl a closer look, and 'twas then that he saw the tears upon her cheeks. Her sadness ran deep, but in time he knew she would find comfort in memories and a lessening of her grief, just as he would find the dragons, for all things came to pass in time.

Glossary

anthanor—an alchemist's stove

aqua ardens—"water that burns," alcohol

athame—a small ritual knife

bedźhaa—Arabic word for "swan"

Beirdd Braint—"privileged bard," the second class of the Druidic Order

Beltaine—Celtic festival falling on May Eve and May 1

Calan Gaef—Celtic festival falling on October 31 and November 1

Canolbarth—the midland caves beneath Carn Merioneth; ceremonies are held in the largest cavern by the scrying pool

cariad—love, lover

crwth—musical instrument, a bowed lyre

Cymry—Welsh name for themselves

Ddrei Goch, Ddrei Glas—the dragons of Carn Merioneth

Ebiurrane—northern band of the wild folk

gwin draig—dragon wine

hadyn draig—dragon seed

kif—hasheesh

Liosalfar—Quicken-tree soldiers

penteulu—leader of a great Welsh prince's war-band

pryf—dragon larvae, worm

pudre ruge—a red powder used in the healing of wounds

Quicken-tree—southern band of the wild folk

rasca—Quicken-tree medicinal ointment

rihadin—small combustible packets of resin that ignite in various colors

tylwyth teg—Welsh fairies